Man Gone Down

Michael Thomas

W F HOWES LTD

This large print edition published in 2010 by
W F Howes Ltd
Unit 4, Rearsby Business Park, Gaddesby Lane,
Rearsby, Leicester LE7 4YH

1 3 5 7 9 10 8 6 4 2

First published in the United Kingdom in 2009
by Atlantic Books

ISBN 978 1 40745 168 8

Typeset by Palimpsest Book Production Limited,
Grangemouth, Stirlingshire
Printed and bound in Great Britain
by MPG Books Ltd, Bodmin, Cornwall

For Michaele—
My wife, my love, my life: the one. Everything
is for you

We proclaim love our salvation . . .
—Marvin Gaye

PART I

THE LOSER

If you came at night like a broken king.
—T. S. Eliot, 'Little Gidding' I

CHAPTER 1

I know I'm not doing well. I have an emotional relationship with a fish – Thomas Strawberry. My oldest son, C, named him, and that name was given weight because a six-year-old voiced it as though he'd had an epiphany: *He looks like a strawberry.* The three adults in the room had nodded in agreement.

'I only gave you one,' his godfather, Jack, the marine biologist, told him. 'If you have more than one, they kill each other.' Jack laughed. He doesn't have kids. He doesn't know that one's not supposed to speak of death in front of them and cackle. One speaks of death in hushed, sober tones – the way one speaks of alcoholism, race, or secret bubble gum a younger sibling can't have. Jack figured it out on some level from the way both C and X looked at him blankly and then stared into the small aquarium, perhaps envisioning a battle royal between a bowlful of savage little fish, or the empty space left behind. We left the boys in their bedroom and took the baby with us. *'They don't live very long,'* he whispered to us. *'About six weeks.'* That was C's

3

birthday in February. It's August, and he's not dead.

He's with me on the desk, next to my stack of books and legal pads. I left my laptop at my mother-in-law's for C to use. She'd raised an eyebrow as I started to the door. Allegedly, my magnum opus was on that hard drive – the book that would launch my career and provide me with the financial independence she desired. *'I write better if the first draft is longhand.'* She hadn't believed me. It had been a Christmas gift from Claire. I remember opening it and being genuinely surprised. All three children had stopped to see what was in the box.

'Merry Christmas, honey,' she'd cooed in my ear. She then took me by the chin and gently turned my face to meet hers. *'This is your year.'* She kissed me – too long – and the children, in unison, looked away. The computer was sleek and gray and brimming with the potential to organize my thoughts, my work, my time. It would help extract that last portion of whatever it was that I was working on and buff it with the requisite polish to make it salable. *'This is our year.'* Her eyes looked glazed, as though she had been intoxicated by the machine's power, the early hour, and the spirit of the season. It had been bought, I was sure, with her mother's money. And I knew Edith had never believed me to have any literary talent, but she'd wanted to make her daughter feel supported and loved – although she probably

had expected it to end like this. C had seemed happy when I left, though, sitting on the floor with his legs stretched under the coffee table, the glow from the screen washing out his copper skin.

'Bye, C.'

'By-ye.' He'd made it two syllables. He hadn't looked up.

Marco walks up the stairs and stops outside his kid's study, where I'm working. He knocks on the door. I don't know whether to be thankful or annoyed, but the door's open and it's his house. I try to be as friendly as I can.

'Yo!'

'Yo! What's up?' He walks in. I turn halfway and throw him a wave. He comes to the desk and looks down at the stack of legal pads.

'Damn, you're cranking it out, man.'

'I'm writing for my life.' He laughs. I don't. I wonder if he notices.

'Is it a novel?'

I can't explain to him that three pads are one novel and seven are another, but what I'm working on is a short story. I can't tell him that each hour I have what I believe to be an epiphany, and I must begin again – thinking about my life.

'Want to eat something?'

'No thanks, man, I have to finish this part.'

I turn around on the stool. I'm being rude. He's moved back to the doorway, leaning. His tie's loose. He holds his leather bag in one hand and a fresh beer in the other. He's dark haired, olive skinned, and long nosed. He's five-ten and in weekend racquetball shape. He stands there, framed by a clear, solid maple jamb. Next to him is more millwork – a solid maple bookcase, wonderfully spare, with books and photos and his son's trophies. There's a picture of his boy with C. They were on the same peewee soccer team. They're grinning, holding trophies in front of what I believe to be my leg. Marco clinks his wedding band on the bottle. I stare at him. I've forgotten what we were talking about. I hope he'll pick me up.

'Want me to bring you something back?'

'No, man. Thanks, I'm good.'

I'm broke, but I can't tell him this because while his family's away on Long Island for the summer, I'm sleeping in his kid's bed and he earns daily what I, at my best, earn in a month, because he has a beautiful home, because in spite of all this, I like him. I believe he's a decent man.

'All right, man.' He goes to take a sip, then stops. He's probably learned of my drinking problem through the neighborhood gossip channels, but he's never confirmed any of it with me.

'Call me on the cell if you change your mind.'

He leaves. In the margins, I tally our monthly costs. '*We need to make $140,000 a year,*' Claire told me last week. I compute that I'll have to teach twenty-two freshman comp sections a semester as well as pick up full-time work as a carpenter. Thomas Strawberry swims across his bowl to face me.

'I fed you,' I say to him as though he's my dog. He floats, puckering his fish lips. Thomas, at one time, had the whole family copying his pucker face, but the boys got tired of it. The little one, my girl, kept doing it – the fish, the only animal she'd recognize. *'What does the cow say?'* I'd ask. *'What does the cat say?'* She'd stare at me, blankly, giving me the deadeye that only children can give – a glimpse of her indecipherable consciousness. *'What does the fish say?'* She'd pucker, the same way as when I'd ask her for a kiss – the fish face and a forehead to the cheekbone.

I packed my wife and kids into my mother-in-law's enormous Mercedes Benz at 7:45 p.m. on Friday, June 26. It was essential for both Claire and her mother to leave Brooklyn by eight with the kids fed and washed and ready for sleep for the three-and-a-half-hour drive to Massachusetts. Claire, I suppose, had learned the trick of planning long drives around sleeping schedules from her mother. Road trips required careful planning and the exact execution of those plans. I'd have to park in the bus stop on Atlantic Avenue in front of our building then run the bags, toys, books, and snacks down the stairs, trying to beat the thieves and meter maids. Then I'd signal for Claire to bring the kids down, and we'd strap them into their seats, equipping them with juice and crackers and their special toys. Then, in her mind, she'd make one last sweep of the house, while I'd calculate the cost of purchasing whatever toiletries I knew I'd left behind.

After the last bathroom check and the last seatbelt check, we'd be off. We'd sing. We'd tell stories. We'd play I Spy. Then one kid would drop off and we'd shush the other two until Jersey or Connecticut and continue to shush until the last one dropped. There's something about children sleeping in cars, perhaps something felt by parents, and perhaps only by the parents of multiple children – their heads tilted, their mouths open, eyes closed. The stillness and the quiet that had vanished from your life returns, but you must be quiet – respect their stillness, their silence. You must also make the most of it. It's when you speak about important things that you don't want them to hear: money, time, death – we'd almost whisper. We'd honor their breath, their silence, knowing that their faces would be changed each time they awoke, one nap older, that less easily lulled to sleep. Before we had children, we joked, we played music loud, we talked about a future with children. *'What do you think they'll be like?'* she'd ask. But I knew I could never voice the image in my head and make it real for her – our child: my broad head, her sharp nose, blond afro, and freckles – the cacophony phenotype alone caused. I would shake my head. She'd smile and whine, *'What?'* playfully, as though I was flirting with or

8

teasing her, but in actuality, I was reeling from the picture of the imagined face, the noise inside her dichotomized mind, and the ache of his broken mongrel heart.

X was already beginning to fade when Edith turned on the engine. The sun was setting over the East River. The corrugated metal warehouses, the giant dinosaur-like cranes, and the silver chassis of the car were swept with a mix of rosy light and shadow. I used to drink on a hill in a park outside of Boston with my best friend, Gavin. He'd gotten too drunk at too many high school parties and he wasn't welcome at them anymore, so we drank by ourselves outside. We'd say nothing and watch the sun set. And when the light was gone from the sky, one of us would try to articulate whatever was troubling us that day.

'Okay, honey.' Claire was buckling up. 'We're all in.' Edith tried to smile at me and mouthed, *'Bye.'* She took a hand off the wheel and gave a short wave. I closed C's door and looked in at him to wave good-bye, but he was watching the dome light slowly fade from halogen white through orange to umber – soft and warm enough through its transitions to temporarily calm the brassiness of Edith's hair. I saw him say, *'Cool'* as it dulled, suspended on the ceiling, ember-like. Perhaps it reminded him of a fire he'd once seen in its dying stages, or a sunset. I watched him until it went off, and there was more light outside the car than in and he was partially obscured by my reflection.

C said something to his grandmother and his window lowered. He unbuckled himself and got up on his knees. Edith put the car in gear.

'Sit down and buckle up, hon.' C didn't acknowledge her and stuck his hand out the window.

'Say good-bye to your dad.'

'Bye, Daddy.'

There was something about *daddy* versus *dad*. Something that made it seem as though it was the last good-bye he'd say to me as a little boy. X's eyes were closed. My girl yawned, shook her head, searched for and then found her bottle in her lap. C was still waving. Edith rolled up all the windows. Claire turned to tell him to sit, and they pulled away.

Thomas Strawberry's bowl looks cloudy. There's bright green algae growing on the sides, leftover food and what I imagine to be fish poop on the bottom – charcoal-green balls that list back and forth, betraying an underwater current. Cleaning his bowl is always difficult for me because the risk of killing him seems so high. I don't know how much trauma a little fish can handle. So I hold off cleaning until his habitat resembles something like a bayou backwater – more suitable for a catfish than for Thomas. He has bright orange markings and elaborate fins. He looks flimsy – effete. I can't imagine him fighting anything, especially one of his own.

I tap the glass and remember aquarium visits and classroom fish tanks. There was always a sign or a person in charge warning not to touch the glass. Thomas swims over to me, and while he examines my fingertip, I sneak the net in behind him. I scoop him out of the water. He wriggles and then goes limp. He does this every time, and every time I think I've killed him. I let him out into his temporary lodgings. He darts out of the net, back to life, and swims around the much smaller confines of the cereal bowl. I clean his bowl in the bathroom sink and refill it with the tepid water I believe he likes. I go back to the desk. He's stopped circling. I slowly pour him back in. I wonder if his stillness in the net is because of shock or if he's playing possum. The latter of the two ideas suggests the possibility of a fishy consciousness. Since school begins for the boys in two weeks and I haven't found an apartment, a job, or paid tuition, I let it go.

I wonder if I'm too damaged. Baldwin somewhere once wrote about someone who had '*a wound that he would never recover from,*' but I don't remember where. He also wrote about a missing member that was lost but still aching. Maybe something inside of me was no longer intact. Perhaps something had been cut off or broken down – collateral damage of the diaspora. Marco seems to be intact. Perhaps he was damaged, too. Perhaps whatever he'd had was completely lost, or never there. I wonder if I'm too damaged. Thomas Strawberry puckers at me. I tap the glass. He swims away.

I had a girlfriend in high school named Sally, and one day I told her everything. How at the age of six I'd been treed by an angry mob of adults who hadn't liked the idea of Boston busing. They threw rocks up at me, yelling, *'Nigger go home!'* And how the policeman who rescued me called me *'Sammy.'* How I'd been sodomized in the bathroom of the Brighton Boys Club when I was seven, and how later that year, my mother, divorced and broke, began telling me that she should've flushed me down the toilet when she'd had the chance. I told Sally that from the day we met, I'd been writing poems about it all, for her, which I then gave to her. She held the book of words like it was a cold brick, with a glassy film, not tears, forming in front of her eyes. I fear, perhaps, that I'm too damaged. In the margins of the yellow pad I write down titles for the story – unholy trinities: *Drunk, Black, and Stupid. Black, Broke, and Stupid. Drunk, Black, and Blue.* The last seems the best – the most melodic, the least concrete. Whether or not it was a mystery remained to be seen.

The phone rings. It's Claire.

'Happy almost birthday.'

'Thanks.'

It's been three weeks since I've seen my family. Three weeks of over-the-phone progress reports.

We've used up all the platitudes we know. Neither of us can stand it.

'Are you coming?'

'Yeah.'

'How?'

It's a setup. She knows I can't afford the fare.

'Do you have something lined up for tomorrow?'

'Yeah,' I answer. As of now it's a lie, but it's nine. I have till Labor Day to come up with several thousand dollars for a new apartment and long overdue bills, plus an extra fifty for the bus. It's unlikely, but not unreasonable.

'Did you get the security check from Marta?' she asks, excited for a moment that someone owes us money.

'No.'

'Fuck.' She breathes. Claire's never been convincing when she curses. She sighs purposefully into the receiver. 'Do you have a plan?'

'I'll make a plan.'

'Will you let me know?'

'I'll let you know.'

'I dropped my mother at the airport this morning.'

'It's her house. I like your mother.' It's a lie, but I've never, in the twelve years we've been together, shown any evidence of my contempt.

'I think C wants a Ronaldo shirt.' She stops. 'Not the club team. He wants a Brazil one.' Silence again. 'Is that possible?'

'I'll try.' More silence. 'How's your nose?'

'It's fine.' She sighs. She waits. I can tell she's crunching numbers in her head. She turns her voice up to sound excited. 'We'd all love to see you,' then turns it back down – soft, caring, to pad the directive. 'Make a plan.'

CHAPTER 2

The last time I saw them was late July at Edith's. The boys and I were in the kitchen. X was naked and broad-jumping tiles, trying to clear at least three at once. C had stopped stirring his potion, put down his makeshift magic wand and was pumping up a soccer ball. I was sipping coffee, watching them. We were listening to the Beatles. C was mouthing the words. X was singing aloud while in the air. As he jumped, he alternated between the lyrics and dinosaur names: Thump. 'Dilophosaurus.' Jump. *'She's got a ticket to ride . . .'* Thump. 'Parasaurolophus.' His muscles flexed and elongated – too much mass and too well defined for a boy, even a man-boy, especially one with such a tiny, lispy voice. He vaulted up onto the round table. It rocked. I braced it. He stood up and flashed a toothy smile.

'Sorry, Daddy.'

X looks exactly like me. Not me at three years old, me as a man. He has a man's body and a man's head, square jawed, no fat or softness. He has everything except the stubble, scars, and age lines. X looks exactly like me except he's white.

15

He has bright blue-gray eyes that at times fade to green. They're the only part of him that at times looks young, wild, and unfocused, looking at you but spinning everywhere. In the summer he's blond and bronze-colored. He looks like a tan elf on steroids. It would seem fitting to tie a sword to his waist and strap a shield on his back.

X could pass. It was too soon to tell about his sister, but it was obvious that C could not. I sometimes see the arcs of each boy's life based solely on the reactions from strangers, friends, and family – the reaction to their colors. They've already assigned my boys qualities: C is quiet and moody. X is eccentric. X, who from the age of two has believed he is a carnivorous dinosaur, who leaps, claws, and bites, who speaks to no one outside his immediate family, who regards interlopers with a cool, reptilian smirk, is charming. His blue eyes somehow signify a grace and virtue and respect that needn't be earned – privilege – something that his brother will never possess, even if he puts down the paintbrush, the soccer ball, and smiles at people in the same impish way. But they are my boys. They both call me Daddy in the same soft way; C with his husky snarl, X with his baby lisp. What will it take to make them not brothers?

X was poised on the table as though he was waiting in ambush. C had finished pumping and was testing the ball against one of the four-by-four wooden mullions for the picture window that looked out on the back lawn. Claire came in, holding the girl, and turned the music down.

'Honey, get down, please.' X remained poised, unlistening, as though acknowledging that his mother would ruin his chance of making a successful kill.

'He's a raptor,' said his brother without looking up.

'Get down.' She didn't wait. She put down the girl, who shrieked in protest, grabbed X, who squawked like a bird, and put him down on the floor. He bolted as soon as his feet touched the ground and disappeared around the corner, growling as he ran.

'They'll be here soon,' said Claire. 'Can everyone be ready?'

'Who'll be here?' mumbled C. His rasp made him sound like a junior bluesman.

'The Whites.' His shot missed the post and smacked into the glass. Claire inhaled sharply.

'Put that ball outside.'

C looked at me. I pointed to the door. He ran out.

'No,' Claire called after him. 'Just the ball.' The girl screeched and pulled on her mother's legs, begging to be picked up. Claire obliged, then looked to me.

'"*Look what the new world hath wrought.*"' I said.

She looked at the table, the ring from my coffee cup, the slop in the bowl C had been mixing, and the gooey, discarded wand.

I shrugged my shoulders. 'To fight evil?'

'Just go get him and get dressed. I'll deal with the other two.'

I put my cup down and stood up at attention. 'The Whites are coming. The Whites are coming!' When we moved out of Boston to the near suburbs, my cousins had helped. I'd ridden in the back of their pickup with Frankie, who had just gotten out of Concord Correctional. We'd sat on a couch speeding through the new town, following the trail of white flight with Frankie shouting, *'The niggers are coming! The niggers are coming!'*

I snapped off a salute. My girl, happy to be in her mother's arms, giggled. I blew her a kiss. She reciprocated. I saluted again. The Whites were some long-lost Brahmin family friends of Edith's. As a girl Claire had been paired with the daughter. They were of Boston and Newport but had gone west some time ago. They were coming to stay for the week. I was to go back to Brooklyn the next day and continue my search for a place to work and live. 'The Whites are coming.' Claire wasn't amused. She rolled her eyes like a teenager, flipped me the bird, and headed for the bedroom.

I went outside. It was cool for July and gray, no good for the beach. We'd be stuck entertaining them in the house all day. C was under the branches of a ring of cedars. He was working on step-overs, foxing imaginary defenders in his homemade Ronaldo shirt. We'd made it the summer before – yellow dye, stenciled, green indelible marker. I'd done the letters, he'd done the number nine. It was a bit off center and tilted because we'd aligned the form a bit a-whack. It hadn't been a problem at first because the shirt had been so baggy that you couldn't detect the error, but he'd grown so much over the year, and filled it out, that it looked somewhat ridiculous.

He passed the ball to me. I trapped it and looked up. He was standing about ten yards away, arms spread, palms turned up, and mouth agape.

'Hello.'

'The Whites are coming.'

'So.'

'So you need to change.'

'Why?'

'Because your mother said so.'

'I haven't even gotten to do anything.'

'What is it that you need to do?'

He scrunched up his face, making his big eyes slits. Then he raised one eyebrow, signaling that it was a stupid question. And with a voice like mine but two octaves higher said, *'Pass the ball.'* Slowly, as though he was speaking to a child. *'Pass the ball.'* As if he were flipping some lesson back at me. *'Pass the ball.'* Then he smiled, crooked and wide mouthed like his mother. He softened his voice – *'Pass, Dad.'*

Almost everyone – friends, family, strangers – has at some time tried to place the origins of my children's body parts – this person's nose, that one's legs. C is a split between Claire and me, so

19

in a sense, he looks like no one – a compromise between the two lines. He has light brown skin, which in the summer turns copper. He has long wavy hair, which is a blend. Hers is laser straight. I have curls. C's hair is red-brown, which makes one realize that Claire and I have the same color hair. *'Look what the new world hath wrought.'* A boy who looks like neither mommy nor daddy but has a face all his own. No schema or box for him to fit in.

'Dad, pass.' I led him with the ball toward the trees, which served as goalposts. He struck it, one time, *'Goooaaaal!'* He ran in a slight arc away from the trees with his right index finger in the air as his hero would've. *'Goal! Ronaldo! Gooooaaaal!'* He blew a kiss to the imaginary crowd.

Claire knocked on the window. I turned. She was holding the naked girl in one arm. The other arm was extended, just as C's had been. X came sprinting into the kitchen and leapt at her, legs and arms extended, toes and fingers spread like raptor claws. He crashed into his mother's hip and wrapped his limbs around her waist all at once. She stumbled from the impact, then regained her balance. She peeled him off her waist and barked something at him. He stood looking up at her, his eyes melting down at the corners, his lip quivering, ready to cry. She bent down to his level, kissed him on his forehead, and said something that made him smile. He roared, spun, and bounded off. Her shoulders sagged. She turned back to me, shot a thumb over her shoulder, and mouthed, 'Get ready!' She sat on the floor and laid the girl down on her back.

C was still celebrating his goal – or perhaps a new one I'd missed. He was on his knees, appealing to the gray July morning sky.

'Yo!' I yelled to him, breaking his trance. 'Inside.'

'In a minute.'

'Cecil, now!' He snapped his head around and stood up like a little soldier. C had been named Cecil, but when he was four, he asked us to call him C. He, in some ways, had always been an easy child. As a toddler you could trust him to be alone in a room. We could give him markers and paper, and he would take care of himself. He was difficult, though, in that he's always been such a private boy who so rarely asks for anything that we've always given him what he wants. *I want you to call me C.* Cecil had been Claire's father's and grandfather's name, but she swallowed her disappointment and coughed out an okay. I'd shrugged my shoulders. It had been a given that our first child would be named after them.

I thought, when he was born, that his eyes would be closed. I didn't know if he'd be sleeping or screaming, but that his eyes would be closed. They weren't. They were big, almond shaped, and copper – almost like mine. He stared at me. I gave him a knuckle and he gummed it – still staring. He saw everything about me: the chicken pox scar on my forehead, the keloid scar beside it, the absent-minded boozy cigarette burn my father had given me on my stomach. Insults and epithets that had been thrown like bricks out of car windows or spat like poison darts from junior high locker rows. Words and threats, which at the time they'd been uttered, hadn't seemed to cause me any injury because they'd not been strong enough or because they'd simply missed. But holding him, the long skinny boy with the shock of dark hair and the dusky newborn skin, I realized that I had been hit by all of them and that they still hurt. My boy was silent, but I shushed him anyway – long and soft – and I promised him that I would never let them do to him what had been done to me. He would be safe with me.

Claire was still on the floor wrestling the girl into a diaper. She turned just in time to see X leave his feet. His forehead smashed into her nose, flattening it, sending her down. C shot past me and ran into the house, past the accident scene and around the corner. The girl sat up and X, unsure of what it was that he'd done, smiled nervously. He looked down at his mother, who was lying motionless on the floor, staring blankly at the ceiling. Then her eyes closed. Then the blood came. It ran from her nostrils as though something inside her head had suddenly burst. Claire has a very long mouth and what she calls a bird lip. The top and bottom come together in the middle in a point, slightly off center – crooked – creating a deep valley between her mouth and her long, Anglican nose. So the blood flowed down her cheeks, over and into her ears, into her hair, down the sides of her neck, and onto the white granite floor.

C came running back in with the first aid kit and a washcloth. He opened it, got out the rubbing alcohol, and soaked the washcloth. He stood above his mother, looking at her stained face, the stained floor, contemplating where to begin. He knelt beside her and started wiping her cheeks. The smell of the alcohol brought her back, and she pushed his hand from her face. C backed away. She raised her arm into the air and began waving, as though she was offering up her surrender.

I came inside. I took the kit from C, dampened a gauze pad with saline, and began to clean her up. She still hadn't said anything, but she began weeping. Our children stood around us in silence.

'It's going to be okay,' I told them. 'It looks a lot worse than it is.' X began to cry. C tried to hug him, but he wriggled loose and started backing out of the kitchen.

'It's okay, buddy.' He stopped crying, wanting to believe me. 'It's not your fault.' I activated the chemical ice pack and gently placed it on her nose.

'Don't leave me,' she whispered. Her lips barely moved. I wondered, if it hadn't yet lapsed, if our insurance covered reconstructive surgery. Her chest started heaving.

'Hey, guys. Take your sister in the back and put

on a video.' They wouldn't budge. 'C,' I pointed in the direction of the TV room. 'Go on.' Claire was about to burst. 'Go.'

They left and Claire let out a low, wounded moan, stopped, took a quick breath and moaned again. Then she let out a high whine that was the same pitch as the noise from something electrical somewhere in the house. *My wife is white*, I thought, as though I hadn't considered it before. Her blood contrasted against the granite as it did on her face. *I married a white woman.* She stopped her whine, looked at me, and tried to manage a smile.

'Look what the new world hath wrought.'

Her face went blank; then she stared at me as though she hadn't heard what I said, or hadn't believed what I said. I should've said something soothing to make her nose stop throbbing or to halt the darkening purple rings that were forming under her eyes. I shifted the ice pack. Her nose was already twice its normal size. She closed her eyes. I slid my arms under her neck and knees and lifted.

'No.'

'No what?'

'Leave me.'

'I'm going to put you to bed.'

'Leave me.'

'I'm not going to leave you.'

Although she'd been through three cesarean sections, Claire can't take much pain. She was still crying, but only tears and the occasional snuffle. Her nose was clogged with blood. She wasn't going to be able to get up. Claire has always been athletic. She has muscular legs and injury-free joints. It seemed ridiculous that I should need to carry her – my brown arm wrapped around her white legs – I knew there was a lynch mob forming somewhere. I laid her down on the bed. She turned on her side away from me. There was little light in the room. The air was as cool and gray inside as it was out. I left her alone.

C was waiting for me outside the door. He was shirtless, trying to ready himself to face the Whites.

'Dad, is Mom gonna be okay?'

'She'll be fine.' He didn't believe me. He tried another tack.

'Is it broken?'

'Yeah.'

'Is that bad?'

'She'll be fine.' I patted his head and left my hand there. C has never been an openly affectionate boy, but he does like to be touched. I'd forgotten that until he rolled his eyes up and, against his wishes, smiled. I steered him by his head into the bathroom and began to prepare for a shower and shave.

'Have I ever broken my nose?' he asked, fiddling with the shaving cream.

'No.'

'Have you ever broken your nose?'

'Yes.'

He put the can down, stroked the imaginary whiskers on his chin, and looked at my face. I have a thick beard – red and brown and blond and gray. It makes no sense. The rest of my body is hairless. I could see him trying to connect the hair, the scars, the nose.

'Did you cry?'

'No.'

'Really?'

'Really.'

'Did you break your nose more than once?'

'Yeah.'

'And you never cried?'

'Never.'

'What happened?' I had taken off my shirt and shorts, and he was scanning what he could see of my body, an athlete's body, not like the bodies of other men my age he'd seen on the beach. He looked at my underwear, perhaps wondering why I'd stopped at them.

He grinned. 'You're naked.'

'No, I'm not,' I said sternly.

He tried mimicking my tone. 'Yes, you are.'

'What are these?' I gestured to my boxers.

'The emperor has no clothes,' he sang.

'I'm not the emperor.'

C stopped grinning, sensing he shouldn't take it any further.

'What happened?'

'When?'

'When you broke your nose.'

'What do you mean?'

'How did you break your nose all those times?'

'Sports and stuff.'

'What stuff?'

'Sports.'

He squinted at me and curled his lips in. He fingered the shaving cream can again. His face went blank, as it always seemed to when he questioned and got no answer. I hid things from him. I always had. Perhaps I was a coward. C already seemed to know what was going to happen to him. Just as I had been watching him, he'd been watching me, making the calculations, extrapolating, charting the map of the territory that lay between us – little brown boy to big brown man.

He was already sick of it. He was sick of his extended family. He was sick of his private-school mates. He seemed world weary before the age of seven. His little friends had already made it clear to him that he was brown like poop or brown like dirt and that his father was ugly because he was brown. He was only four the first time he'd heard it and he kept silent as long as he could, but his mother had found him alone weeping. He'd begged us not to say anything to his teachers or the other children's parents – they were his friends, he'd said. Claire wanted blood spilt. There were meetings and protests and petitions and apologies. People had gotten angry at the kids who'd ganged up on the little brown boy. One mother had dragged her wailing son to me, demanding

27

that he apologize, and seemed perplexed when I noogied his head and told him it was okay. Other parents were even more perplexed when I refused to sign the petitions that would broaden the curriculum. Claire had been surprised.

'Why don't you want to sign?'

'What good would it do?'

'What do you mean?'

'No institutional legislation can change the hearts of bigots and chickenshits.'

Bigots and chickenshits, my boy was surrounded by them, and no one would come clean and say it, not even me. They would all betray him at some point, some because they actually were the sons and daughters of bigots and would become so themselves, some because they would never stand by his side – unswervable. Which little chicken-shit would stand up for him when they chanted, *'Brown like poop, brown like dirt'*? They would all be afraid to be his friend. Even at this age they knew what it was to go down with him – my little brown boy.

The Whites were coming. I had to be ready.

'Get ready,' I said. I sent my little brown boy out and took a shower.

As soon as I finished, C knocked on the door. It was as if he'd been waiting right outside.

'Yeah?'

'Can I come in?'

'No.'

'Why?'

28

'Wait.'

Noah had appeared naked before his son Ham, and Ham's line was cursed forever. I didn't want to start that mess again. I dressed quickly. I opened the door. My three children stood there: the brown boy, the white boy, and the girl of indeterminate race. They wore the confused look of children who'd just finished watching TV.

'She's got a poop,' C said, pointing at his sister's bottom, holding his nose.

'Yeah, poop,' said X.

'No poopoo,' said the girl. I scooped her up and smelled, then I peeked into her diaper.

'No poop.'

I got them dressed and presentable and lined up near the front door. I could hear Claire in the bathroom, fiddling with her mother's makeup. She seldom wore anything besides lipstick. We heard the car pull onto the gravel driveway. C leaned toward the kitchen.

'Let's go.'

'Wait until you've said hello.' Claire emerged from the bathroom. It looked as though the kids had shoved a golf ball up her nose and then set upon her sinus area with dark magic markers. Her children looked at her in horror, as though their mother had been replaced by some well-mannered pug.

C pulled on my arm. *'Please.'* He sounded desperate. He was looking at the door as though something evil was about to enter. The screen door whined and the knob turned and he bolted to the back. Edith walked in, saw her daughter, and gasped. She remembered she had company with her and turned to welcome them in.

The Whites were here: the grandmother, the daughter, the grandchildren, and the son-in-law. Edith held him by the wrist, squeezing it as though to reassure him. I don't think Edith had ever touched me, other than by mistake – both reaching for the marmalade jar, both pulling back. Edith is still very beautiful. I think she's a natural blonde. She has blue eyes, not lasers like X's, but firm, giving strength to her diminutive self. Her skin is beach worn, permanently tanned from walks in the wind and sand. High cheekboned, long nosed, as if she was trying to assume the face of some long dead Peqout or Wampanoag. *Massachusetts.* I thought about the word, like a name, *Massasoit,* as though I was he, welcoming a visiting tribe from the south, the Narragansett.

The prelude to the introduction was taking too long. I offered my hand to my alleged peer. I'm six-three and have the hands of someone a foot taller. They are hard and marked by the miscues of a decade and a half of absentminded carpentry. His hand disappeared in mine, but he didn't flinch. He did his best to meet me.

'Good to see you.' He let go, stepped back. The two women had joined Edith, staring at Claire's nose.

'Hello,' said Claire to the elder, trying to break

the spell. They stopped staring, but they couldn't move. Claire hugged both of them, kissing the sides of their faces as well.

'It's been so long,' she said to the younger. Claire is truly beautiful – in visage, in tone, in manner. She's always had the ability, at least in the world she's from, to make everything seem all right, to make people feel that things are in their proper place and all is well. It wasn't working. As she held the younger's hand, the elder surveyed the wreckage of miscegenation: the battered Brahmin jewel, the afro blonde in her arms, the brown man. What was there to say other than hello and good-bye? The elder looked from Edith to Claire to the girl to me. Her eyes darted faster and faster. For a moment I wanted to explain, begin the narrative simply because I believed I could and I knew she couldn't: *Milton Brown of Georgia raped the slave girl Minette. That boy-child escaped and was taken in by the Cherokee peoples on their forced march to Oklahoma.*

Claire knelt to address the children – two boys, perhaps three and five. They were both hiding behind their mother's legs. The younger bent down and pushed her sons in front of her. They couldn't look at Claire. They buried their faces into their mother's skirt.

'And who is this?' asked the younger, looking at X. 'Oh, my goodness – those eyes!' She gasped, forgetting herself, forgetting her children. It was as if X really was reptilian and she'd fallen under

31

his hypnotic spell. The White children, against their better judgment, turned as well. They looked as though they'd been bled, particularly next to X, who seemed ready to jump, howl, or sprint. He stared back at them, not with the fear and wonder with which they regarded him, but in an equally inappropriate way, as though he was a boy looking at cupcakes, or a carnivore looking at flesh – child-eyed, man-jawed. If there was to be a battle, it was obvious who would be left when everything shook down. The new world regarded the old world. The old world clung to its mother's legs.

The younger tried to snap out of it. 'You're such a big boy.'

'I'm not a boy,' said X in his lisp-growl. 'I'm a Tyrannosaurus rex.'

'Oh my,' she said, summoning courage for her and her brood. The other Whites tittered nervously. The elder joined in.

'You must be Michael.'

X kept staring at the children as though they were tasty meat bits.

'I'm not Michael! I'm X!'

The younger pressed on.

'These are my boys, James and George.' The smaller of the two leaned his head forward and smiled.

'Hi.'

The Whites and Edith smiled, and then cooed in unison, *'Oh.'*

Edith leaned into X. 'Michael, can you say hello?'

'I'm not Michael. I'm X.'

'Hello,' said the older child.

The bastard half-breed son of Milton and Minette was a schizophrenic. He married a Cherokee woman and they had two children. He disappeared, and she and her children were considered outcasts on the reservation. One day she left with them and headed east.

'I'm brown,' said X.

'No, you're not,' said the older child. 'You're white.'

'I'm brown!' he growled. 'I'm the tyrant lizard king!' He snorted at them. The boys took a step back. X widened his nostrils and sniffed at them in an exaggerated way. He opened his eyes wide so that they were almost circles and smiled, coolly, making sure to show his teeth. He leaned forward and sniffed again.

She met the traveling preacher-salesman Gabriel Lloyd, settled in central Virginia, and had one child with him. Then she and Lloyd died.

'I eat you.'

As she tells it, once an acquaintance of Claire's who knew nothing of me had asked her upon seeing C for the first time, 'How *did* you get such a brown baby?' Claire had shot back, 'Brown *man*.' I went outside to find C. Like his younger brother, he can smell fear. It makes X attack. The same fear causes C to withdraw – to keep his distance.

He was standing in the middle of the yard with his back to the window and his ball under one arm.

'Yo, C-dawg.' He turned and saw me, smiled weakly, walked over and took me by the hand. We turned toward the kitchen. The adults had entered and Edith and Claire were handing out drinks. My boy, big-eyed, vulnerable, brown, looked in at the white people. They looked out at him. The White boys ran into the room. The older one was crying. His father scooped him up and shushed him. The younger hid behind his mother. X came in, arms bent, mouth open. He was stomping instead of sprinting. He roared at everyone and stomped out.

'Do you have to go?'

'Yeah.'

He let go of my hand.

'He's definitely a T. rex now.' C turned and punted the ball across the yard into a patch of hostas. He watched it for a while as though he expected the plants to protest. He turned back to me, squinting his eyes, I thought, to keep from crying.

CHAPTER 3

In the midst of the ocean
there grows a green tree
and I will be true
to the girl who loves me
for I'll eat when I'm hungry
and drink when I'm dry
and if nobody kills me
I'll live 'til I die.

Claire's grandfather wanted to sing that song at our wedding, but he'd stopped taking his Thorazine the week leading up to it and 'flipped his gizzard.' So he'd sat quietly next to his nurse, cane between his legs, freshly dosed, staring into the void above the wedding party.

My father tried to assume the role of patriarch. In the clearing, between the woods and the sea, under the big tent, he'd stepped up on the bandstand. Hopped up on draft beer and with ill-fitting dentures, he'd taken the microphone. 'May you and your love be *evah-gween*.' He'd been unable to roll the *r*'s. The drink and the teeth had undermined his once perfect diction. He raised his glass to tepid cheers.

Ray Charles is singing 'America the Beautiful.' It's a bad idea to put on music while trying to make a plan. It may be that I need to stop listening altogether. Dylan makes me feel alienated and old; hip-hop, militant. Otis Redding is too gritty and makes me think about dying young. Robert Johnson makes me feel like catching the next thing smoking and Satan. Marley makes me feel like Jesus. I thought for some reason that listening to Ray in the background would be good, or at least better than the others. He's not. I'm confused. I never know what he's singing about in his prelude. It makes no sense. A blind, black, R & B junkie gone country, singing an also-ran anthem – dragging it back through the tunnel of his experience, coloring it with his growl, his rough falsetto. The gospel organ pulse, the backing voices, not from Nashville, not from Harlem, Mississippi, or Chicago – they float somewhere in the mix, evoking pearly gates and elevators going to the mall's upper mezzanine, *'America, America . . .'* It falls apart. I remember back in my school when people used to co-opt philosophy. They'd say that they were going to *deconstruct* something. I thought, one can't do that; one can only watch it happen. Only in America could someone try to make the musings of a whacked-out Frenchman utile. Anyway, the song falls apart. Perhaps even that's incorrect; I hear it for its many parts. It's not like a bad song, which disappears. In this, the multiplicity sings. *'America . . .'* Democracy's din made dulcet via the scratchy bark of a native son. *'God shed his grace on thee . . .'* Things fall apart, coalesce, then fall apart again. Like at the beach – fish schools, light rays. It's like being a drunk teen again, waiting for Gavin in the freight yard under the turnpike. The whistle blows. I see him appear from behind a car, bottle held aloft in the sunset. Things fall apart, come together, and sometimes I feel fortunate to bear witness. The timpanis boom. *'Amen . . .'* I have to hear that song again.

I don't. I turn it off. I go into the kiddie bedroom, turn the light off, and lie down in the kiddie bed. I need to make a plan, which means I need to make a list of the things I need to do. I need to get our security deposit back from our old landlady. I need to call the English Departments I'm still welcome in to see if there are any classes to be had. I need to call more contractors and foremen I know to see if there's any construction work. I need to call the boys' school to see if I can pay their tuition in installments. I need an installment. I try to make a complete list of things in my head. It doesn't work. I open my eyes and try to picture it in the darkness. Claire has always been good at making lists – to do lists, grocery lists, gift lists, wish lists, packing lists. They have dashes and arrows to coordinate disparate tasks and do the work of synthesis – laundry to pasta, pasta to rent check, rent check to a flower or animal doodle in the margin, depicting perhaps the world that exists beyond the documented tasks or between them: of fish minds and baby talk and sibling-to-sibling, child-to-parent metalanguage or microcode; the green tree that grows in the middle of the ocean; the space in which the song exists.

From downstairs Marco's clock chimes out the half hour. Outside, around the corner, the busted church bell sounds its metal gag. I'll be thirty-five at midnight. The phone rings. It's Gavin.

'Mush, what's up?' His speaking voice, accent, and tone are always in flux. It's never contingent on whom he's speaking to, but on what it is that he's saying. Now he uses a thick Boston accent. Not the bizarre Kennedy-speak that movie stars believe is real outside that family. *R*s don't exist and only the *o* and *u* vowel sounds are extended: *Loser* becomes *loo-sah*. It's a speak that sounds like it needs a six-pack or two to make it flow, to make it sing. He sounds happy, full of coffee, still inside, yet to be struck by the day.

'S'up?'

'Nothin', mush.'

'All right.'

'Happy birthday, mush. I'm a couple of days late.'

'You're a couple of hours early.'

'Sorry.' He switches to another speaking voice, closer perhaps, to what his must be – a smoker's voice, in which you can hear both Harvard and Cavan County, Ireland. Gavin spent much of his adolescence with his father in jazz bars and can sound like the combination of a stoned horn player and a Jesuit priest.

'It's all right.' I've been told that my accent's too neutral for me to be from Boston.

'You don't sound so good, man.'

I almost tell him why – more out of resentment than camaraderie. He owes me at least four hundred dollars: a credit card payment, or a couple of weeks of groceries.

'I'm fine.'

'What's the matter, white man gettin' you down?'

'You're the white man.'

'No, baby, I'm the Black Irish.'

'No. I'm the Black Irish.'

'Whatever, man. You drinking?'

'No.'

I had three friends in high school: Shaky – née Donovan – Brian, and Gavin. Brian had to become a Buddhist monk to sober up, went missing for a decade in the Burmese jungle, disrobed, became a stockbroker, and died in the Twin Towers attack. Shaky, who in high school and college had been named Shake because of basketball prowess, had moved with Gavin and me to the East Village, where he had a schizophrenic break. He was now roaming the streets of Lower Manhattan and south Brooklyn. Privately, between Gavin and myself, his name had evolved to Shaky. Gavin fluctuated between poems, paintings, and biannual death-defying benders, losing apartments, jobs, and potential girlfriends along the way.

When I moved out of the place I shared with him and in with Claire, he'd come to visit and use her mugs for his tobacco spit. We'd drink pots of coffee and cackle about institutions and heebie-jeebies and never ever succeeding. Gavin never dated much. Never *settled down*. He rarely had a telephone and was reachable only when he wanted to be. *'He checked out,'* Claire once said in such a way as if to be asking me if I'd done the same. She liked him, perhaps even loved him, but she was scared of him and he felt this. By the time C was a toddler she'd unconsciously pushed Gavin out of our lives – to the point where I didn't even think about him in her presence. But after a while, when Claire could see that I'd had enough of the gentrifying neighborhood and private-school mixers, she tracked him down and invited him to a party at our place. He'd had a good five years clean and had managed to start over again in Boston and get himself a Harvard degree. 'He's too smart and cute to be single,' she'd said, looking at a commencement photo. When he returned to New York, she'd thought it would be a good idea for us to escort him back into the mainstream.

It was this past spring and he looked well – tall, dark haired, blue eyed, strangely russet skinned,

40

as though some of his many freckles had leaked; the Black Irish. He'd made the transition, despite a good decade of delirium tremens and shelters, from handsome boy to handsome man. His lined face and graying hair made him look rugged and weary, but his freckles and eyes still flashed innocent. He'd just had a poem rejected by some literary rag, but on arriving, he seemed fine. We sat around the table. My girl was in my lap playing with my food. There were three other couples besides us, a single writer friend of Claire's, and Gavin. The woman, his alleged date, asked him what kind of poems he wrote.

'Sonnets.'

'Sonnets?'

'Petrarchan sonnets.'

She giggled. 'How quaint.'

'Quaint, hmm.'

He emptied his water glass, refilled it with wine, and swallowed it in one gulp. Claire looked at me, concerned. He drank another glass, excused himself, and stood to leave. I caught him in the hallway.

'Where are you going with this?' I asked.

'Down, I suppose.'

Three days later he showed up, beat up and already detoxing. Claire used to try to swap stories with us, about drunken uncles and acquaintances that had hit it too hard. She's never seen me drunk. I never had a fall as an adult. I never suffered Gavin's blood pressure spikes, seizures, or bat-winged dive bombers – only some lost years, insomnia, and psychosomatic heart failure. But she watched Gavin convulse on her couch while her babies played in the next room. She realized that the stories we told had actually happened to us and not to someone we used to know. The damage was real and lasting. And more stories were just an ignorant dinner comment away.

'How are you, Gav?' I ask. It sounds empty.

'I'm all right. I guess. My bell's still a'ringing a bit.' He pauses for me to ask where he's calling from, how the last jag went down, but I don't. He covers for me. 'You bustin' out for the weekend, or are you staying around?'

'I'm supposed to go.'

'So you're going to be away Friday?'

'I suppose.'

'Kids making you a cake?'

'Yeah. Probably.'

'Hey, man?'

'Yeah.'

'Your kids start giving you Old Spice yet?'

'No.'

'What's going to happen?'

'C's going to count to thirty-five, and even though he knows the answer, will then ask me how old I'll be when he's thirty-five.'

He snorts a laugh. 'Children – a paradox.' He shifts to Mid-Atlantic speak, the accent of one who hailed from an island between high-born

42

Boston and London. 'I have no wife. I have no children.'

'Yes.'

'I'm calling from a pay phone in a detox.'

'Yes.'

'I went on a twelve-week drunk because a girl didn't like my poems.'

I should say something to him – that I'll come visit with a carton of cigarettes, or pick him up, like I always used to – but Claire's list opens up in my head like a computer file and I stay silent.

'Mush.' He switches back. 'Do something. Get your head out of your ass. Go get a coffee.' More silence. 'Happy birthday.'

I go downstairs. It's dark. Out of respect for my host I leave the lights off. I go into the kitchen. It's posh and industrial, clad in stainless steel, maple, and absolute black granite. I open the over-sized refrigerator. There's a Diet Coke and a doggie bag. Butter. Marco is a good bachelor. The house seems far too big for the three of them. I close the door and wonder if it's better to have an empty large refrigerator or a full one. There's a white ceramic bowl on the center island full of change. I pick through it, taking the nickels and dimes, leaving the quarters, as though big-change larceny would be too great a crime.

There's a big window in the back of the house. It's double height. It rises up through a void in the ceiling above. The mullions are aluminum,

43

glazed with large panes of tempered glass. The curtain-wall spans the width of the building with one centered glass door. It's a structure unto itself. Like everything else in the house, it's unadorned. It looks out on the backyard, which isn't much, gravel, an unused sandbox, two soccer goals, and the neighbors' tall cedar fences on all three sides. There's no ocean, river, woods, or great lawn to look upon – functionless modernism. It may well have been a mirror – two stories tall, twenty-five feet wide – the giant mirror of Brooklyn. People could come from far and wee to look at themselves in it. *I could run the whole thing for you, Marco. I'll only take 20 percent. It'll pay off whatever it cost you to put it in within the first year.* I realize I don't know how much it cost, how much the whole house cost to buy and renovate and furnish. I don't have any way to price the glass, the metal, the labor, the markup. Marco had asked me my opinion on the quality of the work overall, the natural maple doorjambs and stairs and cabinetry – not with any bravado – he just wanted to know if he'd been treated fairly. I never told him anything. Perhaps he's still waiting, though it did seem strange, the master negotiator, asking me for reassurance. What could I say to him now? I've stolen his change and watched his building fall.

I take the money and go out. I have a twenty in my pocket, too, but I don't want to break it – not on coffee. Breaking it begins its slow decline to nothing.

I've forgotten that people go out, even on week-nights. Smith Street, which used to be made up of bodegas and check-cashing stores, looks more like SoHo. It's lined with bars and bar hoppers, restaurants and diners. Many of them are the same age I was when I got sober. There was a time when people spoke Farsi and Spanish on the streets and in the shops, but now there's white people mostly, all speaking English, tipsy and emboldened with magazine-like style. They peer into the windows of the closed knickknack emporiums that have replaced the religious artifact stores and social clubs.

It's hot but not muggy. I walk north with the traffic, trying to stay curbside so as to avoid getting trapped by meandering groups and hand-holding couples. I hop the curb and walk in the gutter to get around the outpouring from a shop. There's a party going on or breaking up. Inside there are paintings hanging on the wasabi green walls. There are small halogen track lights on the ceiling. Their beams wash out the paintings. Nobody's looking at the work.

'Hey!'

I can tell whoever is calling is calling for me. It's a woman's voice – full of wine and cigarettes. A bus approaches. I have to step up on the sidewalk toward the voice. She's standing in front of me.

'Hey,' she says again in a cutesy, little girl way. Her hair's in pigtails. Her face is as hot as the lights. 'I know you.'

Her name is Judy or Janet or something close to that. Her daughter was once in a tumbling class with X.

'Hello,' I answer. I'm a foot taller than she is. I can't help but look down at her. She looks up at me, still smiling.

'Jeez, I never realized you were so tall. Now I know where that boy of yours gets it.'

'Actually,' I say, looking over her into the crowd of partygoers – I don't recognize anyone – 'I was a small kid. I grew after high school.' She's still smiling, but her face has lost some of the heat it held. She doesn't seem to care about the info.

'Whose show?'

She looks surprised. She touches her chest lightly with both hands. The bus rolls behind me, hot with diesel funk. My first job in New York was as a bike messenger. I once watched a guy skid on an oil slick and go down on Madison Avenue in front of the M1. It ran over his head – popped it open. Everyone watching threw up. She leans against the bus stop sign, flattening a breast against it.

'It's mine,' she says.

I look over her into the glare of the makeshift gallery. It looks as if a flashbulb got stuck in midshot. I think it will hurt my head if I go into all that light.

'Come on. I'll give you a personal tour.' She turns, expecting me to follow, which I do. She doesn't seem at all concerned with the light. Perhaps I have nothing to worry about, or perhaps she's become inured over time. The crowd parts for her, some smile and check me out. Now I recognize some of them, from the gym, from the coffee shop. They range in age from twenty-five to forty. Most of them appear to be single or dating. I can tell they're all childless; they're too wrapped up in what it is they believe Jane or Judy and I appear to be doing. I'm sure some of them will query her as to *what is going on* as soon as I leave.

Claire was still a dancer when we started dating. She'd had a show at the Joyce and a party afterward at her apartment. When I arrived, she was busy introducing Edith to her friends. The loft was full of admirers – new and old. There were prep school and college mates, other dancers, East Village divas both male and female. I watched Claire take Edith around. Her mother, as always, was unruffled by the chaos of new faces and personalities – gay boys and bi-girls and art freaks and the loud pumping disco on the stereo. Cigarettes and magnums of cheap Chilean wine. Edith was in full support of her daughter. Then she saw me. Perhaps Claire had described me to her mother and Edith was trying to determine if I was me. She looked at me too long. Claire noticed her mother's attention had shifted and looked to where she was looking. She smiled and made sure that Edith saw it. The dancers she'd been talking to looked as well. There was a nudge, a whisper, then Claire led Edith by the waist over to me. I met

47

them in the middle of the room. Claire took each of us by the forearm and placed her mother's hand in mine. She made it clear to everyone there that she was mine and that our budding romance was mine to fuck up.

Judy or Jane offers me a glass of wine, then a bottle of beer, and seems somewhat taken aback when I refuse, as though the drinks are inextricably linked to the paintings, and by extension to her. They're all headless nudes of women except one, which has her face and an enormous erect white penis. She's slumping, sexily, I suppose, in a Louis XIV chaise.

'What do you think?'

'Do you like Freud?'

'Freud.' She laughs sharply, perhaps to hide her offense. She looks up at me, raises an eyebrow, and shakes her head. 'Freud?'

'Lucien.'

'I know.'

'I'm sorry. I like them.' She looks deeply into the representation of her face. The nose is crooked and one eye socket is smaller than the other, which on her real face is true, but not to the extent that she's depicted it. In the painting, she's made a slight asymmetry much more pronounced, as though her defect is an expression, as though winking would make the bone rather than the flesh atop it contort. She's made a mess of her skin tone, which is medium to dark brown. But she's shaded her painting with peach and pink and gray – layer upon layer of paint, like theory upon theory to solve a problem. What is the problem? She's a sloppy theorist who can't paint? The penis is perfect.

'I'm ignorant,' I say. 'I'm not very good at articulating my responses to art.'

'Bullshit. You don't like them. It's cool.' She smiles a fake smile and squints her eyes. I wait for her skull to morph. It doesn't.

'Show's over. Let's get wasted.'

We walk south, deeper into the neighborhood. She sets the pace, walking easily through the crowds. People smile at her. She smiles back. They smile at us, as if there is an us. Sometimes people smile when I'm with Claire. I wonder if liberal white people smile at each other, pass out happy approval of each other's mates – *I approve. You may pass.*

She stops outside of what I remember to have been a sheet-metal fabricator's place. It's now a bar. In place of the steel roll-down door is a glass-paneled one. It's halfway up – as though it got stuck when they opened for the day.

'I've never been here before, but I hear it's kind of cute.'

She gestures for me to go in first, but I extend my arm as if to say, 'No, after you.' She shakes her head. 'You're funny.' The music is loud – some girl band. There's a round bar in the center and large Eames-like common tables throughout the room. Along the walls are banquettes with bullet-shaped tables. All the surfaces are clad in periwinkle Formica. Except for the bartender, waiter, and ten or so scattered patrons it's empty.

There are large television monitors up in each corner and four more above the bar. All of them are playing videos. On one a troop of astronaut dancing girls are in outer space. It takes a moment for me to realize that they're all the same out-of-sync video and a bit more time to figure out that the music booming out of the many speakers is linked with only one of the monitors, the one above the bar, facing the door. There's about a second delay between each monitor. They must have spent about three weeks' take on this A/V system. They're not going to make it. Somewhere an old tin-knocker is laughing. The cat-suited astro-girls do a kick-ball-change in the intense gravity and poisonous atmosphere of Saturn. It's amazing that they haven't suffered any casualties on this unique mission to the stars.

She chooses a banquette. It's blue-painted plywood with orange vinyl cushions. The back isn't sloped, so it's uncomfortable to sit in unless I slouch. The waiter comes over, bored stupid by the lack of business. He's skinny and young and his posture is terrible.

'Stoli martini – dirty.'

'May I please have a Coke? Thank you.'

He calculates his potential tip from us and

decides it's not worth straightening up or smiling. She looks at me.

'That's all you want?'

'Yes, thanks.'

'I'm buying.'

'That's fine, thank you.' He trudges back to the bar, far too heavily for his slight build.

'Do you not drink?'

'I do not drink.'

She slouches and squeezes her pigtails. She's quite lovely, but she's tiny, as though she's another species. She can't weigh much more than a hundred pounds. One martini will probably stupefy her.

'How's Claire?'

'She's well. Thanks.'

She shakes her head, closing her eyes as she does. 'You're so – formal?' She laughs and drums the table. I can see why she's prone to smiling. Her teeth are straight and white and beautiful against her dark lips.

'Where is she?'

'She's at her mother's.' She stares at me, toothy and amused. Perhaps I'm still too formal.

'Oh.' She closes her eyes. 'At the beach for the summer.'

'Where are your people?'

'Upstate. Greg took Toby up to see Nana and Grandpa.'

'Are they coming to see your show?'

'Oh, no,' She scoffs, losing the teeth. The waiter

comes with the drinks. The astro-kids are doing backflips. He sets them on the table.

'Should I start a tab?' He asks rhetorically.

'Yes,' she says, surprising both the waiter and me. She starts on her martini, then stops. She raises her glass.

'Sorry. Here's to family.'

I hold mine up as well. 'Cheers.' We drink. I can feel the cool tingle of her vodka on my lips, the warmth on the roof of my mouth, the olive's dull fruitiness, the point of the spirits on my tongue, and the incongruity of the heat and ice in my throat.

'I got this show – whatever – on a total lark. Someone else backed out.' She looks at me as though I should say something, about either the show or her family. I don't. I wonder if the waiter's spiked my drink.

'So how's that crazy boy of yours? What's he calling himself now?'

'X.'

She spits out her drink. 'I'm sorry.' She dabs at the spittle with her napkin. 'That's hilarious.' She sighs and gives me her teeth again. 'What does Claire think of that?'

'She calls him X.'

'What's that about?' She doesn't wait for an answer. I imagine she already has one. I first saw her on the street, pregnant, one hand resting on her tummy, with her man, waiting for the light to change. I was alone and she was anxious and he kept his head down, the way many white men do when they're with a black woman and they encounter a black man – as though I cared. I would see them later, walking around with their stroller. She would smile at me when she was alone. She brought her girl to the same kiddie gym classes and the same kiddie art classes that Claire brought X to, although she never talked to Claire, never even acknowledged her until I showed up one day. And then there were inquiries and invitations – she let Claire pass on my ticket.

She looks off dreamily to the monitor above my head. She smiles. A few seconds later I see why: One of the astro-girls has grown to enormous size. She throws a spinning crescent kick to the side of a space monster's head, which sends him into orbit – all while singing. She bends down and rips the top off a space cage, where I assume the space monster has incarcerated her pals.

'School starts soon?'

'Yes.'

'How do they like it?'

'Cecil loves it. I suppose his brother will, too.'

'Is it worth it?'

'What do you mean?'

'The tuition. The homogeny?'

A new video has started. Three brown women of varying shades and hair texture are in leather thong bikinis dancing on what looks to be a panzer tank. They're out of step because they're moving to the beat of the previous song. Finally, their beat kicks in. They're still out of sync, but it's a little better. They start shaking it.

'Even if we could afford it, I don't know if I would do it – you know?'

'X likes to be naked.' I look down from the video. 'They'll let him be naked. All day.'

She shakes her head. 'What about your other son?'

'He's doing fine.'

She's ready for another drink and signals the waiter. Her arm is unusually long for her body, but she extends it gracefully – the dark skin complemented by her sleeveless pink top. Her shoulders are the same size as her breasts. She senses me looking at her. I look back up at the monitor. A college-age white kid with heavy sideburns and a Brooklyn Dodgers cap gestures spastically at the camera. In the background the girls are still shaking it. The video cuts to a close-up of one of them. She's stunning. My butt gets warm. I look down. Judy or Jane has had prior knowledge of the flesh parade and has been watching me watch. She's smiling again, extra toothy, as though she's discovered some great secret about me: I'm a man.

'She's pretty hot, huh?'

I shrug my shoulders. She's not entirely right, anyway. I'm a man, yes, but my thoughts shift from her and the dancing ladies to junior high English – Ms Rizzo's class. She's only twenty-four. She calls me to the board, rolling the chalk in one hand, her other on her jutted-out hip. I'm in my seat, stiff and immovable in my wide-wale corduroys. Ms Rizzo has just said 'diphthong' and let her tongue peek out through her perfect teeth and stay there. I know she has peppermint breath and her perfume smells like citrus water. The other boys are in heaven. I'm in hell. I try to think of ugly girls and bland literature. *'It nods and curtsies and recovers . . .'* The heat from my ass moves its way up my body and settles in my neck and cheeks.

'Sure you don't want a real drink now?' she asks. Her first, on top of the wine before, has gotten to her. She has boozy confidence. It enables her to slouch, speak in low tones, and stare.

'I'm sure.'

'A bohemian who doesn't drink – what's that?'

'Why am I a bohemian?'

'Well, you sure ain't a lawyer. I know them. I've got one.'

I wonder if she leaves her paintings out to torture him, the assistant DA. I only shared selected paragraphs with Claire, complete with contextual introductions, and I always read them to her. I picture her husband in the coffee shop, beaky, dark bearded, and thin, ashamed when seeing me, shocked when I say hello. I see her paintings hanging in their house, her sketches and doodles beside the telephone and on the fridge along with their son's. I wonder how he exhales in the galleries of her depicted flesh.

The video is ending. The panzer drives off

into the sunset with the dancers. Now a blonde tart on a jet ski zips along the coast of the Riviera. She's wearing a Stetson hat and wielding a boomerang.

'Oh, that bitch is so dry,' she hisses. My mother used to call white girls tarts and hussies. If I were in the video, and if she were drunk, I'd walk the jet-ski tart home. Jane or Judy closes her eyes and leans back. She opens her mouth in the shape of a small circle and exhales. Black girls, as I remember being told, were fast. She will have to be walked home, too.

'That was harder than I thought.'

'What was?'

'Finishing the work for that show.' She leans forward, exhaling heavily. She puts her elbows on the table and her head in her hands. Her radii and ulnae are mantislike, longer than her humeri. No bone in her arm can be thicker than a chopstick. With all the soft, bright colors on and around her she almost looks like a child except her face is showing signs of age. She has two deep creases running alongside her nose and another across her forehead. Her age and her fatigue against the creamsicle backdrop make her look out of place, and because of this, I imagine her to be lonely. She smiles at me again, broadly, and her eyelids droop.

I had always put girls to sleep. It was a gift. Whenever I was broke and hungry, I would go to a bar or a party, meet a girl, and listen to her talk about her parents, her job, her last or current boyfriend, about her dissatisfaction with her life, and her theories on how life could be different. I'd listen and that alone would be enough – a great enough act of heroism – to be invited home with them, where I would then talk about pretty much anything until they couldn't listen anymore. They'd drift off. In the morning I'd make breakfast and they'd look at me strangely, no longer a hero, just a symbol of their great dissatisfaction. I'd leave them wherever it was they believed themselves stranded – hero-less – two eggs and a slice of toast short. They all fell asleep. All except Claire. I'd lain beside her, hand in the air, not touching her. I talked and talked until she told me to put my hand down on her hip. I did.

'How's writing going?'
 'Fine.'
 'What are you working on?'
 'A book.'
 'Who's your agent?'
 'I don't have one now.'
She finds the energy to raise her eyebrows. My last agent had told me that I needed to do some serious editing, that it didn't seem *urban* enough, but that mostly, somewhere in the philosophy, I'd lost the story and, therefore, the emotional core. It had reminded me of what William Lloyd Garrison said to Frederick Douglass, that Douglass should tell the story and leave the

philosophy to him. Which would mean, if Garrison was correct, then there was nothing beyond the simple narrative – no context. Or that everyone understood the context, that the context was available for all to decipher and that they all had the scope and the willingness to do so. Perhaps it was me. Perhaps I had only disconnected thoughts and anecdotes flaring up in me like bouts of gastritis. *'By the rivers of Babylon . . .'* Perhaps I have no narrative. Perhaps I have no song.

'Tell me a story.'

'Why?'

'You're a storyteller.'

'About what?'

'You're a storyteller.'

She smiles – too sexually for her to be interested in art or arcs. She seems to have a great deal invested in my story, as though if it was good enough she could get naked for me without guilt or reservation. That was what a good narrative was supposed to do, be naked and make naked.

The tart's boomerang flies at the camera and the screen goes white. There's an aerial shot of a dusty road. Someone strikes a chord on an acoustic guitar. The camera moves and pushes in on a crossroads tableau. The camera levels out, parallel with the ground. Someone's sitting on a tree stump. It's a white kid wearing a porkpie hat. He's strumming an old Cherry Sunburst jumbo. It's too big for him. He plays awkwardly on the clichéd Rubenesque form. He looks like he's trying to choke a chicken-necked fat girl with one hand and caress her with the other.

A pedal steel slides in, but it sounds more Hawaii than Mississippi. In the music track he's already singing, but in the video I'm watching the camera pan across a field and into the sky. Now he's singing, walking along a railroad line. The following frames are filled by sorrowful images: black and white faces; toothless, broken men; hardened women; and filthy children. A drum program marks the beat. If the sound and image were in sync, it would tap out his cadence in the gravel along the tracks. He opens his mouth and sings. His voice is somewhere between tenor and baritone and sounds like he's in some adolescent purgatory bemoaning his stasis.

'White boy blues.' She shakes her head. 'Greg likes this shit. Do you?'

'I haven't heard this.'

'But do you like it?' She's fully alert now.

'I had this friend in high school . . .'

'Yeah?'

'Well, I went to school just west of Boston – Newton.'

'I knew you came from money.'

'No, I wasn't wealthy. Sometime before then Massachusetts passed legislation that made it mandatory for all cities and towns to have public housing.'

'Suburban projects? Ridiculous.'

'Well, kind of. Anyway, my mother got on the waiting list and moved us in.'

'Single mom?'

'Yeah.'

'She must be something.'

'Yes, well, she's dead. Anyway, Gavin and me are seniors and we're at a party. Do you know Boston?'

'A little bit.'

'Do you know Commonwealth Avenue?'

'No.'

'It runs west out of downtown. Anyway, Gavin and I are at a party at one of the mansions, in the side yard, sitting up high on the crossbar of a swing set. We are beer-less and broke. He's got a black eye, a quick jab from his old man earlier. He's been telling me about the marathon. How at this point, near where we were sitting, on the other side of the hedge in '72, the pack had caught his dad. He finished as the fifth American and missed qualifying for Munich.'

I look up. She's still awake – involved even.

'"*Heartbreak Hill. Oh, well.*" He kind of sings it with a quavering voice. He wipes his nose with his hand. His right pupil is red with hemorrhaged blood. His sinus looks swollen. Inside the big house our classmates are talking about their college choices. Some are celebrating; others have already begun the process of burnishing the reputation of their safety school. My ex-girlfriend Sally is inside as well. I can see her.'

'She white?'

'Yeah. I can see her in the window – moon face, freckles, and blue pie-eyes – a concoction of German Berger and hardscrabble Irish. I can see her, the sensible part of her acquiescing to the moment's demands. Gavin points at her. *"That's your true love. Hah."* He elbows me. *"I'm kidding, man. I'd love her, too."* Gavin always wore an old corduroy coat as his top layer. He opens it, reaches into the torn lining and produces two tall boys. He's like, *"After a hard day's work."* He hands me a can. I give him a cigarette. He's like, *"Symbiosis. Good show."* So we open the beers and toast.

'To oblivion.'

'Godspeed.'

'We hear someone on the back porch. *"Quick,"* he says. *"No evidence."* We chug the beers and throw the empty cans into the bushes. Two girls we don't know walk toward us. They stop, confer with each other, then continue. They're cute, but they look awkward, ridiculous, you know, like girls who haven't had sex trying to be sexy in front of boys who refuse to recognize their libidos. I light our cigarettes. They're there under us. *"Hey,"* says one. *"Do you have anymore?"* So I toss the pack down and the lighter. "I thought you guys were athletes," says the other. And she's really pretty, you know, like some wood nymph. But she's got a whiny voice and she watches her friend light up with all her teen disdain. I take a deep drag and exhale a thick formless cloud.'

'How do they know?'

'How do they know what?'

'Who you are.'

'Everybody knew who we were.'

She's stunned by the perceived arrogance.

'It's not like that,' I say. 'We were pretty good athletes. We did pretty well in school. You know, the poor kids usually mowed the rich kids' lawns. It wasn't that we were popular. We just stood out in groups like that.'

She laughs. She seems to have only one, but it serves as many. It's context dependent, but she won't give the context. I can't tell if the laugh is born of amusement, irony, condescension. It's a yip-laugh, a hyena laugh – but cut short. I look up. The blues-boy is leading a mule down a dusty road. He approaches a chain gang.

'Then what?' She beckons with both hands.

'So the smoker crosses her arms and holds the cigarette poised for another drag between her rigid index and middle fingers. *"You know,"* says Gavin, pointing over the hedges into the street, *"my dad ran this marathon smoking two packs a day."*

' *"Yeah,"* whines whiny in a sanctimonious tone, *"but did he finish?"* They snicker at him. Girls were always snickering at him after he said something.'

'Oh, they probably loved you. And you probably loved it.'

'No. No, we didn't. We were just having some drinks and talking – like we always did.'

Suddenly, I'm angry. And I'm angrier still that

she's made me angry – made me anything. And then I want to talk more, but I stop. I can't tell if she's even interested in the story, let alone anything more. She smiles again, this time wide and close-mouthed. Then her lips part slightly. She must have had braces and caps and regular cleanings. She takes the olive out of her glass, pulls it off the stick, and pops it into her mouth.

Still chewing, she says, 'You stopped.'

I remember times in my life when I stopped talking. A camp counselor had found me in a stall in the boy's room, fetal and battered. I'd managed to pull my briefs up, and I remember the look on his face when he realized they were soaked with my blood – a bug-eyed gasping fish – *'What happened? What happened?'* he'd finally gagged out, knowing on some level full well what had. I couldn't answer him. I couldn't answer the guidance counselors in junior and senior high who were convinced (but asked anyway) that my drinking and my silence could be traced to the fact that I was a troubled adolescent – *but why?* They never asked, *'What happened?'* Claire had wanted to know, too, the first time she was naked in front of me and I couldn't touch her. I wanted to. I remember that. I wanted to tell her what had happened, but I didn't know what to say, where to start. I opened my mouth and only a dry rasp, a death rattle, came. She wrapped me in a blanket and whispered over and over, 'It's okay. I'm here.'

And then I finally did speak. *'You must have*

something to say.' She coaxed my voice out into the light of her and hers, and then the people beyond. And I sat in classrooms and workshops and when I wanted to stop talking again, I couldn't. It was like the inverse of what I had done as a boy – I spat out hoping to glue everything back together that seemed to have fallen apart.

'You're funny,' she says. 'You just get lost. I like that.' She reaches for my hand, stops, and rubs the Formica. 'I'll stop butting in. I really like it.'

'So Gavin points eastward, to Boston and an imagined finish line. *"He set the American record – twice."* He finishes his smoke, throws it hard at the ground, and cocks his head to one side. *"Look it up."*

'They look up to me to get confirmation, but I look out to Commonwealth Avenue – Heartbreak Hill – following its meandering twist downtown. It has a grass-lined median running down the center. The houses are enormous. *"What are you guys doing next year?"* Gavin thumbs my shoulder. *"He's going Crimson."* They both crane their necks as though it will help them process the information. Gavin shakes his head and mumbles to me, *"Gotta walk around armed with documents these days – fucking junior cynics."* Then he points at them, *"This is the last American hero, ladies, the only true noble left. He's good to his ma – good to my ma, too."* They act like he hadn't said anything. They just ask, *"What about you?"* He doesn't answer. He pulls out another stolen beer. *"Where'd you get* that?" they ask, and he snaps, *"What are you, pigs?"* They turn to each other. Some unspoken code sends them away. *"Fuck,"* whispers Gavin. He hands me two beers. He guzzles his and breaks out a pint of rum, which he begins drinking like a beer. *"I should make a map of where I hid the stash before I get too wasted."* He looks around the yard. Then back out to the avenue, like he's already forgotten that idea. *"Maybe we should take a few and git?"* I say.

'He considers this for a second. *"Nah."* He traces his swollen cheek with a fingertip. *"Fuck 'em."* He passes me the rum. I drink and hand it back. "We gotta make this quick and messy." He gives me a snort, then takes it back. *"Fuck,"* he says again, but more like a bark. He sings, *"What's a boy to do? What's a boy to do?"* The back door opens again. We hear boys' voices. Angry. Moblike. I thumb back at the boys who are approaching us. I tell him that the jig's up. He smirks. *"C'mon, man."* He finishes the pint and smirks again. He throws the bottle into the hedges.

'*"Where'd you get the drinks, Gav?"* He opens another beer. Most of the party has emptied out into the yard. We're surrounded by angry boys. They look up at both of us, but they yell at Gavin. *"Where's the beer?"* He doesn't answer. He sips at his new tall boy. *"Asshole!"* one from behind shouts. They have us outnumbered thirty to two, but they're tentative. Gavin finishes the beer and drops the empty in their midst. *"Look, Gav,"* one tries to appear reasonable. *"Just give the beer back."* Gavin touches his chest and whimpers in mock distress. He raises his voice an octave. *"Gentlemen. Are you accusing me of stealing?"* He pulls out another beer. A roar goes up in the crowd. They pull him down from behind. He lands on his back. Everyone goes silent. They back off, scared of their violence. In classes we've taken with them, they've read Emerson and Thoreau. Some of their parents have told me stories about marching with King, campaigning for Bobby Kennedy, going to jail. The children of the latest enlightenment watch as Gavin comes to.'

'*"You shouldn't have taken the beer."* Some nod in agreement. Gavin stands slowly. He holds his hand up to me to assure me he's okay. One kid tries to implicate me. Asking, *"What were you doing?"* They all ponder the question, but they don't press it. They knew better than to attack a black kid, not because of what might happen to me, but what would happen to them. And they haven't completely reconciled the gap between black man myth and reality.

'Gavin fakes a punch and the whole mob flinches. He laughs. He looks at me and gestures at them with his thumb. He winks. They're angry again. But suddenly he's gone – pushing his way through the crowd. They grab him. Thirty boys hoist him over their heads. He's still laughing as they take him inside. I break through the hedges and make my way to the sloping front lawn.

They're gonna kill him for stealing their beer. They've got him on the porch. His coat's gone. They throw him down ten stairs and he rolls into the gutter. I run down the lawn. I see him, skinny, freckled, semi-conscious on Heartbreak Hill. I see the arc that's brought him to that moment: the boat that brought his grandfather from Cavan, the docks where he welded and riveted the hulls of the great mercantile ships. I see his father, a young man, running up the hill and Gavin, a young boy, watching him fail. Then today, his father's fist in his freckled face. Gavin has always been my best friend. The mob descends the stairs.

'I try to get him up and he pukes on himself. I turn to face the mob, ten feet above me on the mansion's porch. The children of doctors and lawyers, liberal WASPs and Jews, well-educated teens preparing to go to Harvard and Stanford. They want to kill the poor Irish boy because he stole their beer. Gavin is my best friend. We rescue each other from our screaming harridan single moms. We steal liquor together and hide in parks, looking at the stars, sharing stories and drink. I square up and raise my fists. *"Move!"* someone yells. *"Don't be a fucking loser!"* I don't move. Sally's on the porch, too. I look up at her – try to catch her eyes. I do. She rolls them and looks off across the street far above my head. Gavin stirs behind me. He spits. 'Dude.' I stay in my stance. *"What?"* I don't look, but I can tell he's trying to get up. *"Run, dude. You're gonna lose.*" I hear him go down again. *"You're going to lose terribly.*'"

The waiter drops off the check. I take it, and before he can leave I put down my twenty.

'Change?'

'No thanks.'

'Thank you.'

'Thank you,' she says. 'We should really get together when everyone is back.' I nod while sliding to the edge of the banquette. 'Here.' She pushes a card across the table. I pick it up. It's heavy stock – linen. In pale blue it says:

Delilah Trent-Usher
Fine Artist

Delilah. I think I only think it. But I suppose, at least, my lips move. She reaches for my arm, smiling, as though she can barely contain a laugh. One eye *is* much larger than the other when she opens them wide like this.

'You're not finished.'

'With what?'

'What happened?' I don't say anything. 'Thirty against one. Your lone friend down and out – what happened?'

The waiter counts his few tips at the bar while yapping at the bartender, who's washing something in a low sink. On the monitor, migrant farmers and sharecroppers are on parade. Porkpie's leading them, strumming hard, singing, 'Yeah, yeah.'

'The cops came.'

'They broke it up?'

'I kicked the car. They took us in.'

She smiles. She shakes her head, slowly, sucks her teeth, like some sex and maternal hybrid.

'So you were a bad boy, huh.'

Gavin's mom had told me earlier that year not to bring him home drunk anymore. Even the cops had heckled him. *Your buddy stinks, Sammy.* I wonder where Gavin is now – where he'd been calling from.

She knocks on the table. 'Are you there?'

'No. We weren't bad.'

She pats the table as if to say, 'Sure.' She's figured me out again. She picks up the swizzle stick. Her hand looks like a pincer. She holds the stirrer as though she's about to tack me to the seat back. The singer walks off a porch full of damaged people and heads back to the cross-roads. His voice howls. Something sounds wrong. He hits the note, and it seems to be a lament, but it's a lament without sorrow.

'I'm getting tired,' she says.

Outside the traffic on Smith Street is thinner.

'Well, I guess I'll be seeing you.'

'I'll walk you home.'

'Thank you.' She does a mock curtsy. 'Such a gentleman.' She winks. Perhaps her way of inviting me to do ungentlemanly things to her. She stretches her tiny two-martini body and rubs her back against the wall of the old factory.

We walk deeper into Brooklyn, down under the Ninth Street EL, under the BQE, where phantomlike shapes push shopping carts filled with debris or hide in the shadows of the steel and concrete columns, toward the old warehouses that line the waterfront. She's quiet. Perhaps it's the booze. Perhaps she's taking in the shapes and shadows along the way, giving them sharper form, animating them with purpose – a future sketch or painting. Perhaps she has nothing to say. We turn west before the projects and into the bright light of the Battery Tunnel. The opening wriggles in the wave of heat and exhaust.

Brooklyn is not the Brooklyn I imagined while in Boston, or Manhattan, or even Brooklyn. I've seen the supertankers coming in and out of the harbor through the Verrazano Straits, but I don't remember them ever docking. I've seen the cranes from Atlantic Avenue, idle, and followed their line south, here, to Red Hook, where the dead warehouses sit. And then somehow without machines or hands, the containers get lined up in the shipyards. It's as if the ports are still thriving and the longshoremen are busy with their hooks. A ship a quarter mile long passes an island with a scraggly sapling, its roots thirsty in the sand or bare upon granite piles.

Her street is cobbled. It's like a residential oasis in a desert of dead trade. The oaks and birches are thick with leaves. An air conditioner hums and rattles somewhere behind them. An older man sits on his stoop. She stops in front of a narrow town-house.

'This is it.'

She starts to the stoop and turns. She closes her eyes and tilts back her head – waiting for a summer breeze. It doesn't come. She waves. 'Bye.' She comes back to me. She wants a kiss goodnight. I bend for her and give her my cheek. She rubs her cheek against mine and says bye again, too loudly in my ear. I step back. She ascends the stairs, finds her keys, unlocks the door, and disappears.

There are ghosts on the street tonight. There's a giant moon in the eastern sky, low and orange. It throws light on the asphalt, light and shadows of tree leaves and telephone wires. My father ran out on us when he was the age I am now, but he didn't have the heart to just go. First he went to the couch, then to the Ramada, and only after a decade of coming in and out of my life did he finally allow himself to completely disappear. Then he returned – again – for my wedding and stood with me and the minister and Gavin behind what was left of an old farmhouse, the stone founda-tion wall. I hadn't seen him in six years and in that time he'd lost his hair, his teeth, and I thought any claim to me as a son.

I gave Claire my mother's ring, a white gold band with the world's smallest diamond. And her face fell like I'd just broken her heart, but then the smile came – long, trembling. I remember being quiet, staying quiet, waiting for her to speak, but she didn't. She kept looking from her ringed finger to me – back and forth.

She wore ivory. It took place at Edith's in a clearing, just before the rosehips and the dunes. It was five thirty and an August storm was rolling north up the coast. I could hear thunder booming from Rhode Island. Edith gave her daughter away. Claire's veil whipped about her head in the wind. Above us seabirds squawked and flew inland as the clouds rolled out – charcoal and billowy. I looked out at the congregation, my family on one side, hers on the other. We read our vows and we kissed and the clouds burst. After the rain, a double rainbow appeared with one foot in the little guery pond and the other out in Buzzards Bay. In the receiving line people commented – as though their observations were original – on the auspicious beginnings of our union. We shook hands with people. We hugged people. And Claire seemed to be truly happy – raindrops or tears on the end of her swooping nose, unblinking green eyes. Her cheeks were like two suns at magic hour – what the day was fading into. Double rainbows: double rosy suns. Her grandfather was the only one who shot straight.

'I think I gave you silver.'

'Thank you, sir.'

'Twelve or sixteen settings. You'll see soon enough.'

'Thank you, grandpa.'

'You know, he'd said, taking in her cheeks or the rainbows behind. It's going to be an awfully rough road to hoe.'

Claire read when he died. 'Little Gidding' – the fifth movement. She'd announced in the pulpit of the old barn church, and the congregation had smiled and nodded in approval, 'What we call the beginning is often the end / And to make an end is to make a beginning. / The end is where we start from . . .' She read it with lock-jawed precision. I had typed it out for her the night before on bond paper and left it sitting beside her coffee and grapefruit that morning. 'Every poem an epitaph. And any action / Is a step to the block, to the fire, down the sea's throat / Or to an illegible stone: and this is where we start.' When we sang 'Jerusalem,' I couldn't help but think we were each the last of our lines.

Smith Street is empty except for the ghosts and the moon and one woman who walks toward me unaware, phone to her ear, talking loudly. She's buzzed and mocking someone on the other end about her choice in men. Ten feet away she finally sees me. She readjusts the phone. She smiles. 'Hey,' she says, as though we know each other. 'Nothing,' she says into the phone. 'Just someone outside here. I'm walking home.'

A car passes and Marley floats from the open windows – *'No, woman, no cry'* – more ghosts. I scroll through things in my head. Memories.

Images out of sync with song. 'We die with the dying: / See, they depart, and we go with them. / We are born with the dead: / See, they return, and bring us with them.' My father, not dead, but toothless and struggling for language. Struggling, perhaps, even for the force, the feeling, the idea, that drives the word. When her grandfather lay in bed in the ICU dying so far from England, so far from anything that was familiar to him, the last thing he saw was my face. His breaths were slowing. He looked at me. He closed his eyes and clutched the gurney rail as though summoning the strength to battle the guardians of memory. He sang: 'In the middle of the ocean there grows a green tree . . .' He cried one tear – spare and poignant and easy to miss. He inhaled sharply – a whooshing vortex sound marking his emersion into history – drawing him in as though his words went first, then thought, then memory. The ninety-year stoic, how had he managed to hold on to even that much – weeping – lost nobility or nobility revealed? He died without exhaling.

I remember my mother, not dying, but always – her fear. I remember how lost her up-south drawl sounded. I remember her slaps, ice cubes and liquor, her stories: the orphaned children in Virginia – the half- and quarter-breeds – the unrecognizable human mélange: the line of Ham; the line of Brown. I was the one who'd given Claire the poem, because she didn't know what to say.

The moment of the rose and the moment of the
yew-tree
Are of equal duration. A people without history
Is not redeemed from time, for history is a pattern
Of timeless moments.

And so in blessings, and so in song, and so in bottles and beatings. And so in absence and death, they pass themselves on to me, like they were torches ablaze but now seemingly without heat, without light – perhaps only a history of fire – a symbol of that which was once warm and bright and useful. My mother, ashes in the urn waiting to be spread.

And all shall be well and
All manner of thing shall be well...

I think that I would like to leave this world with a song and a tear – that I would've held just enough in reserve to still have one of each, that there will be someone there to listen and watch and they in turn will whisper their secret affections – but there's no way to be noble anymore. Perhaps there never was. *'I will be true to the girl who loves me...'* There are echoes of ditties unsung, therefore promises unmade. The green tree. The yew tree. The grassy hills of England. The tarmac of Brooklyn. A concession of love, a casualty of failure, disappearing down the maw of a vacant avenue, reft of language, left with memory. A phantom who leaves no legacy, only haunting, marring who you loved and who once loved you, chilling those you are near. I shudder on the avenue. What if nothing lies beneath my spasm, my stomach's descent? What if there are no ghosts in Brooklyn, and my love's cheeks are unspeakable and all gone?

> *When the tongues of flame are in-folded*
> *Into the crowned knot of fire*
> *And the fire and the rose are one.*

The big broken clock hiccups the hour. There's really no choice in the matter.
I will run.

CHAPTER 4

My father had always been a lousy listener; then he started going deaf – just after his first heart attack. It had been mild enough that he'd been able to call a cab to take him to the emergency room. And during his convalescence he'd been torn between dismissing the gravity of his condition and milking it for every drop of sympathy he could get.

He's always been an odd man. He's never seemed to possess any discernible rage, only a kind of jazzy melancholy – lighter than the blues. Not daunting or dark: good lounge conversation – his troubles, his travels. And he was good in a lounge conversation – even toned, soft yet resonant, aloof, but not cold – with lots of high-end diction and low-end beer. I've always thought of him as Bing Crosby's public persona on half a Percodan – *boo-biddy-doo* – breezing through life. Or Nat King Cole, just a little bit high. And it was because he was so smooth that almost everyone forgave him almost everything: the failed business ventures, the lost jobs, his potbelly and skinny legs, his balding and his absence. *He was gone*. It seemed ridiculous for anyone, his family, my mother, me, to attempt to retrieve him for punishment or salvation.

I don't believe he ever considered himself gone. I shouldn't be too hard on him. I try never to be. He was lying in bed in the ICU of the Boston VA.

'How are you doing?'

'You know, your grandfather had his first heart attack at forty-one. That's a lot younger than me.'

'Yeah. How are you doing?'

'He lived another thirty years. You never met him.'

'I know.'

'He was the first pharmacist of his kind to practice in the city. Kenmore Drug. You know, he came up from the Carolinas with nothing. I don't think he was even a teen.'

'Yeah.'

'They let him practice in the basement. He swept up upstairs.'

My father had torn up his knee as a high school halfback. He used to say that it cost him his free ride to Harvard but kept him out of Korea. When I was small, we'd play on the sidewalk in front of the old house. He'd call a play, break the huddle with a soft clap, and limp up to the ball, surveying the imagined defense. He'd hike it to himself and hand it off to me. After my run he'd watch me, a bit dreamily, jog back to him. *You really can hit the hole,* he'd say, taking the big ball back.

78

He must have sensed me regarding his scar, ashes, and bumpy, hairless follicles because he pulled at the hem of his johnny. It wasn't long enough to cover, so I looked away.

'I'd go meet him at the store. The girl at the counter would give me a hard candy then send me down. He'd be gathering the filled prescriptions to bring upstairs. Your grandfather was very exacting.'

He scratched his stubble. His face, pockmarked from ingrown hairs, rasped like a zydeco washboard.

'He hit me once.'

He sucked on his loose teeth.

'We were just sitting down to dinner. I couldn't have been much older than eight.'

He extended his right index finger into the air above his chest and pushed at something he saw.

'The doorbell rang. My father got up to answer it. From where I sat I could see that a policeman was at the door. My father called for me. There was another man on the porch, too. The man looked at me, turned to the policeman, and shook his head. My father told me to go sit down. I did. When he finished, he came in, sat, and said grace. I was just about to pick up my fork when all of a sudden I was on the floor. My cheek was numb. He was staring at me – cold. *'Get up,'* he said, really quiet. I got back in my chair. We ate dinner like nothing happened.'

He inhaled thinly.

'I haven't had a cigarette in three days.'

'That's good. You shouldn't smoke.'

'What?'

'Nothing.'

He pushed at the doorbell again and heard it ring in his head. I'd never seen a picture of my grandfather, but it had been said that he looked nothing like my old man. He never said much about his people at all except that they were *hard people . . . mean people . . .'* That they used to own a town but were swindled out of it and had to move to northern Florida. The only one in his family he ever really loved was his maternal grandmother. She was the daughter of a medicine man. He only saw her once. My mother would roll her eyes or leave the room when he talked about her or how he thought that his father, who one day disappeared, was alive somewhere in the swamps.

'When the war came, they let him practice upstairs.'

'Then he got sick?'

'What?'

'Nothing.'

'How are you – you keeping your chin up?'

Marco's just taken out the trash. He's on the stoop wearing a T-shirt, baggy shorts, and flip-flops. He sees me and waves. When I get closer, he points at my coffee.

'Staying up tonight?'

'Just a prop.'

He thumbs at the doorway. 'Sox are on replay.'

Inside, the foyer lights are on low – halogen, recessed. They make the hall seem to curve where the walls meet the floor and ceiling – and it lengthens – a tube of soft light rimmed by shadow.

'Come on. Take a break.'

I sip the coffee. It's weak and bitter. I haven't watched a game all summer; perhaps out of self-punishment, perhaps because the game is no longer the game of my childhood, or perhaps it is and I'm no longer a boy. Somehow baseball lost its charm. I found it hard to root for corporate-sponsored mercenaries. From boy to man my feelings have turned from awe to envy to spite.

My father took me to Fenway. He'd watched the Braves as a boy. He'd seen Ruth's last at bats. Then the Braves left and he became a Sox fan. He told me about the old park and the tradition: Young, Foxx, Doerr, Pesky, Williams, and what Yaz was like as a rookie. *'He won the triple crown the year you were born – what a year.'* He'd tell me stories – the curse, the Impossible Dream team – in that baritone crooner, Lucky Strike voice. Finally, one day he put me on his shoulders and walked us along the Charles to Kenmore Square, up Brookline Avenue, the bridge over the Mass Pike. We looked down at the cars speeding inbound and out. And then up to Lansdowne Street and the Monster with the net above. I got dizzy looking up at it in the vendor yells and smells. It seemed as though he knew, so we didn't go in right away. He put me down among the legs and cart wheels and then disappeared up into the bodies and heads. When he returned, he handed me a sausage in a bun, flicking the peppers and onions off for me as he knelt. I ate it as we walked around the ballpark, east, behind the right-field bleachers, and then down the line toward home. I haven't taken C yet. He hasn't shown much interest – the Brooklyn boy. It was all I could do to keep Yankee paraphernalia out of the house – banners, hats, balls with imprints, bobble-head dolls, goodie bags from birthday parties. Once we burned a hat on the roof of our building and then tuned into the game on the radio. He fell asleep in his chair, the game he'd never played, the grandfather he barely knew, the field he'd never seen; all abstractions to him.

'Come on. They haven't tanked yet,' Marco says while repositioning a garbage can. They haven't, but they will. They always do in a manner so predictable that I can't see it coming – the implosion. It's late night. They'll show a compressed version of the earlier live broadcast. I've heard some compare baseball to opera. Some have said that the Red Sox's story is tragic. This replay then – only the highlight innings – is like a dark cantata.

I follow him inside, into the great windowed room. The television is on already. His laptop is open on the glass coffee table. He drops heavily

82

onto the couch and waits for me to sit. He slides some stapled pages to me.

'What do you think of this?'

'What is it?'

'A legal document. What do you think of the writing?'

The first paragraph has three comma splices and one subject-verb disagreement.

'It's a mess, right? It gets worse.'

I slide it back to him.

'They all graduated at the top of their classes from top schools, made law review. They can't write for shit.' He pats the sheets. 'But what burns me is they think they can. This was handed to me as a finished document. Now I have to stay up all night to correct the work of someone who sticks it to me every chance he gets that I didn't go to Harvard.'

'*The Red Sox take the field.*'

'Fuckin' bums. Come on, you fucks . . . Oh,' he slides me a note, 'someone called. He left a time and an address.'

'Thanks.'

'Meeting?'

'Yeah.'

He jumps up from the couch quickly, as though he's forgotten something. He calls from the kitchen.

'Want anything?'

'I'm good.'

'How's the picture?' he asks, coming back with

a bowl full of ice cream – chocolate with choco-late sauce. I shrug, not knowing what he means. 'Satellite. I don't know. I've heard good things and bad things.'

I gesture at the television. 'It looks fine.'

I don't recognize the pitcher. He's skinny, adolescent looking.

'Oh no, the youth movement. The downward spiral has begun.' He turns up the volume.

'The Sox are still playing for a postseason bid.'

It's twilight at the park, so it seems to me that Boston's in a different time zone, perhaps even a different place in time. There are long shadows in left field cast by the green monster and the light towers atop it. The players run to their respective positions. I've always thought there was something anti-American about baseball: the definite defen-sive positions, the batting order, the lack of fluidity between offense and defense. It seems anachro-nistic, old-world – its rituals, its built-in stasis – and can turn all who watch and honor it into anachronisms dreaming of golden ages. And each fan or group of fans has a golden age – before the live ball era, before the Negroes, before tele-vision, before free agents, before steroids. No, I have forgotten. Baseball is American – as America has aged from a country of dreamers into a country of rememberers. It is better then, to live in memory and not be made to reconcile how the then is rejected by the now. The grass is emerald, the infield dirt raw umber. The first pitch is a ball.

Marco slaps a pillow.

'That stringbean can't throw ninety-five. The gun's fixed.' He takes a spoonful of sweets. 'How hard did Koufax throw? Carlton? You're telling me that he brings it like them? Who is this guy?'

'He's not Koufax.'

'Damn right. Every lefty who shows up and can throw a little hard they try to sell you as Koufax.'

'Well, he's not Koufax. *He's* probably not even *him.*'

'Outside. Ball two. Another fastball.'

'Six back with twenty-five to play. Is there a chance?'

'No.'

'No?'

'No.'

'You think if they make a few deals this summer?'

'No.'

'No never, or just no this year?'

'Ball four. He lost him. Lead-off walk'll make a manager lose his hair.'

'It doesn't matter. I quit.'

'Quit?'

'Yes.'

'Shut up. Stop it. Come on.'

'No more.'

'Why?'

'Exactly.'

Marco shakes his head and eats more ice cream.

'Want popcorn or a soda or something?'

'No thanks.'

The first baseman is having a friendly chat with the guy who's just walked. The runner takes off his batting gloves, hands them to the first-base coach, and puts on his sliding gloves. Both he and the first baseman are serious now. I almost say something about it, but I don't. I've killed the game for me, but there's no need to kill it for him.

I turn to Marco.

'Is your dad a fan?'

'Bit of a jam the young southpaw finds himself in here. Two on, nobody out.'

'Not so much. I think he's always appreciated the sport, the competition, but baseball's hard to get to know late in life.'

'Would like a double-play ball here.'

'But he's not a ground ball pitcher. Everything he's throwing seems to be hard and up in the zone. I'm sure he'll take a pop-up or a strikeout.'

'He was in his early thirties when he came here. I went to games with my friends and their families. What about you?'

'My father did this to me.' He laughs and nods as though he knows what I mean, although we both know he doesn't. 'I started out as an A's fan. I was little, and there was something about those guys – the green and gold uniforms, white cleats, the mustaches. Reggie, Campy, Rudi, Vida Blue, Blue Moon, Catfish. But, you know, you go to Fenway. You watch Yaz swinging a bat on deck . . .'

'Fastball. Got the corner. Strike one.'

'Nice pitch.'

'Painted the corner.'

'You guys had box seats?'

'The first time we did. He'd always try to get them if he could. You know, to be close enough to hear the sizzle and pop of the pitches.'

'El Tiante!'

'Yeah, Tiant. I met him in a supermarket once. He was smoking a cigar.'

'Good old days, man.'

'I suppose.'

'He's got good stuff. Big-league stuff.'

Marco skims the last of the melted cream and sauce from his bowl while shaking his head.

'Bullshit.'

'Curve ball. Pulled the string. Strike two.'

'Yeah, he was sitting dead-red on a fastball and he got Uncle Charlie.'

'What's your dad doing now?'

'Drinking beers. Watching games.'

'Is he retired?'

'Steps off the mound.'

'You could say that.'

'He's just trying to slow things down a bit.'

'Yours?'

'No. He won't. He thinks he's still broke.'

'Still welding?'

'Still a steel man. Butchered another finger last month.'

'Fuck.'

'They managed to save it.'

'Looks in. Doesn't like it. Shakes him off.'

'How many has he lost?'

'Two.'

'How?'

'He got a W-28 dropped on them – his left pinkie and ring finger.'

'That's a lot of steel.'

'Fuck yeah.'

'Now he's ready.'

'What happened?'

'I did it.'

'That's a ball.'

Marco looks at the screen as though it will conjure the image, the memory for us both. It doesn't. He looks into the empty bowl, spins it on the coffee table, and looks in again. He frowns. Whatever's in there is a disappointment, as well.

'It was summer. I was twelve. I was working for him. We were hoisting the beam into place, but I hadn't secured the chain properly. His fingers got caught between the steel and concrete. And at the hospital – his English wasn't so great, neither was mine – they told him it wasn't worth sending him to Mass General, so they amputated. We both must have been in shock. It was over before we knew what to do.'

'Three straight balls.'

'What did he say afterward?'

'Nothing.'

'Never?'

'Never. He's never mentioned it.'

'How's your guilt?'

He pats the brief. 'I mastered English and became a lawyer.' He flings the paper off the table. It tries to do a loop on the way down but runs out of time and lands splayed open on the sisal. 'What's a steelworker need fingers for anyway?' He leans back. 'A wop one anyway.'

'He can't lose him here – the A.L. RBI leader's on deck.'

Marco looks back into the bowl – ashamed. 'Sorry.'

'Hey, man. It's all right. What would Romulus say?'

He snorts a laugh. 'Just call me Lucan. Fuck.'

The screen has gone blank. A message appears in the bottom lefthand corner: 'Searching for satellite signal. Please stand by.'

'Fuck. I forgot to tighten the nuts. The dish probably moved.'

'I'll do it.'

'No. Sit. Stay.'

'I need to go upstairs. I want to change. I'm going to run.'

Marco starts to get up. He doesn't like for me to do things, as though helping out around the house is beneath me. In his head he calculates which will be worse, stopping me or letting me go. He concedes.

'I left the wrench and compass up there. Take my cell phone. I'll tell you what's happening.'

Thomas Strawberry is at the bottom of the bowl – still alive, fishily breathing, in fish sleep or a fish torpor. The room is too warm for him. I think it promotes algae growth, and makes him lazy. The overhead light must be like a sun to him. It must be confusing to be forever directed to, for whatever reason, a false point of origin, but I can't tell Thomas anything. He arrived one wintry afternoon in a baggie, and now he lives on a desk. He'd been the last thing I moved from the old place. Marta had put on a sad face for me when I gave her the keys. She'd given Thomas a little pout, as well. He used to swim more at the old place. Perhaps the trip here stunned him, aged him, or stunted him. No. He was well into his gravy years before I walked with him down Court Street in the early evening. People had briefcases and shopping bags and strollers. I carried a fishbowl. And I thought I did well to keep the water still. Maybe he'd been a magic fish and I'd not realized it – that he came with instructions that I hadn't followed or a pact that I'd unknowingly broken. Thomas is dying. I can tell. I lost his magic for him. I tap the bowl. He doesn't notice.

I start changing to go run, but I get caught up while sitting on the floor changing my shoes. I kind of silently spit-curse my helplessness. It comes out as a hiss. I yawn, deeply, as though I'd forgotten for a while about breathing. And then I kind of drift for a moment, wondering if there's anything to be done for the fish, wondering if I'll sleep tonight, how long, caffeine and anxiety considered, I can stay awake.

★   ★   ★

90

'This is my son,' my father had said to the doctor with a sudden shot of energy. His loose teeth had rattled in his mouth from the sudden rush of breath.

'Nice to meet you.'

'He's an artist,' he said with a wink to her and a thumb to me.

'Do you paint?'

'No.' She seemed startled by my terseness next to her chatty patient. He tried to do some damage control.

'No. He's a poet and he's a musician.'

She picked up his chart and studied it. 'What instrument do you play?'

'He plays guitar and piano and saxophone – and a few others, right? Never could make up his mind.'

'That's impressive. Do you play around here?'

'He just moved to New York.'

'Well, good luck.' She rehung the chart. 'I'll be back later.' She went to the door. 'Nice to meet you,' she said without turning.

My father watched her go and continued to look out the door as though he could see her in the hallway and then the elevator.

'She's something, huh?'

Marco is waiting. I have to go through his bedroom to get to the roof. Even though the lights are on, I pause in the doorway as though he and his wife are sleeping inside. It's a big room with a master bath hidden behind a wall of paneling.

91

Marco's left it open. They have a tiled shower, a separate bathtub, and two sinks. On the south wall there's more glass and a cedar deck beyond. There's a concrete planter built into it. It leaks. You can follow the water stains all the way down the east wall to the cellar.

I slide along the wall to the walk-in closet. I've always wondered how many suits one needs to have if one has a job. My father had two – both brown – both, though I hadn't known it at the time, polyester. I remember smelling him in them – his smoke, his rotting-gums breath. He'd hang them on the bathroom doorknob. Marco's suits and jackets and shirts and slacks take up an entire wall, then meet his belts and shoes and three pairs of suspenders on the adjacent wall. She has dresses and jackets and pants, all of similar fabric and dark hued. They're here for good – not running – Marco is present for his wife, for his son, his parents, his neighbors. His memory drives him. It's fuel for ambition; two fingers on a concrete slab, gangster movies, and acetylene torches. I've heard other parents at school functions butcher his name, *'Maar-coh!'* as though they were proclaiming to him *his* perceived exoticism. Marco is driven, his memory neatly apportioned and in support of his plan. A plan. That's all she asked me to do, make a plan. I should've been honest. I should've asked her, what – suicide or flight? I pull the ladder down and go up the hatch.

The moon has shrunk, risen, and dimmed to a cool yellow. The sky has lost its depth of blue. It's gone whitish, tinted by the clouds, once thick and heavy, now stretched and almost sheer, making the night lilac and yellow with pink highlights – the source of which I can't discern – maybe natural, maybe not. The Manhattan skyline is obscured by the taller buildings on Court Street, but in the northeast I can see the Chase Building, odd in its aloneness, too big for lower Flatbush and its car washes and bodegas.

It's about twenty feet to the parapet, but the roof is pitched back, away from the street. It would be difficult to make it seem as though I stumbled uphill and fell. Marco's building is only thirty-five feet to the top of the cornice – perhaps not a lethal height. There's a good chance that things wouldn't work out. Or, have they not *worked out* already. I may have reached my terminus – an unknown destination. I have a million-dollar term life insurance policy. I don't think it's lapsed. I don't remember what the policy says, who the carrier is.

Claire and I decided that the two of us needed to be covered after C was born, because while looking at our newborn lying between us on the bed, we both considered our deaths. A nurse came to visit us at home and took various samples. Claire had been preeclamptic in the last two weeks of her pregnancy and her pressure hadn't gone down. '*Relax, hon,*' the nurse had said. '*This ain't*

93

nothing.' Claire was nervous. '*I'm sorry,*' she said weakly. '*Nothing to be sorry about.*'

I pressed our agent as to what a preexisting condition was, but in the end, Claire's premium was too much. He suggested that we double mine – because I was the man. At the time his idea made sense. Because I was making money – at least what we thought to be money. I was in school and it seemed that I was destined to make more.

And it seemed to make sense now, to me at least, to have paid out all that money in premiums. The transition had occurred, quick and silent – savings turned into debt. Claire and I sat at the kitchen table one night this past spring with the credit card statements and Marta's new lease and the boys' tuition bills. Over the course of an hour she went from pragmatic to desperate – pushing the papers around the table as though rearranging them would make them read benevolent and new – then from desperate to sorrowful. She tried to stop her tears by curling her long lips in, but that made her look angry, which made me defensive, which made me angry.

'What?'

'What yourself?'

'We need to make more money.'

'You mean *I* need to make *some* money.'

She stood up, frustrated, angry, but Claire's never been good with anger. She's never known what to do with it. She cries.

'So I'll work, too.'

'Doing what? Can you make more than a full-time sitter?'

She fumbled.'

'It shouldn't be so hard. You're smart. You're talented . . .'

'Assuming what you say is true, that's still a long way from money, honey.'

'Why?'

'I don't make the rules.'

'Why don't you? She slammed the table with her hand and went to kick it, too, but she stopped. I fingered my sternum.'

'I'm the problem, right?'

'You're not a problem.'

'*The* problem. Look, I figure, to deal with all this, we have two choices. I leave and you can marry someone rich. Or I die and then you'll be rich and can do whatever you want.'

'Fuck you!'

'Fuck me?'

'You just think I'm some greedy, shallow, spoiled . . .'

'I didn't say anything about you. I'm just saying that I'm probably worth a lot more dead.'

She slapped me. I could see it coming. She had to get around the table, line me up, and then decide whether or not she really wanted to do it. And when she finally did let go, it was the most noncommittal blow I'd ever received. It wasn't like my mother's eighty-foot iron tentacle slap.

Her wrist folded and her hand went limp on impact. We were in trouble because I knew she could never make me do anything I didn't want to do.

Then the debate returns: private or public. New York or elsewhere, and can we afford to live in a town that has good public schools. Then she looks at me and considers herself and can't come up with anyplace else. And then I tell her something about my past, that there weren't any ski trips or beaches or whatever people do to luxuriate and that the only thing I came out of those years with intact was the dim notion that I wasn't quite ready to resign myself to any fate prescribed for me because of melanin or money – that I'd put off death for a while and dream. So back to the school debate: *'Imagine if you and Gavin had gone to private school . . .'* Claire has always loved what she's perceived as my *high mindedness*, until, of course, it's turned on her. Then it's just scary and mean. And I had many responses – from *'I would've hated those people'* to *'I do, all the time.'* And even that light cuff drew tears. I can't stand it when she cries, when that mouth turns down into an exaggerated frown. I used to do anything to stop it.

Marco's phone rings. I answer. He speaks before I can.

'Hey, you up there?'

'Yeah.'

'Do you see the numbers on the side? Shit, is there a flashlight there?'

'I'm good.'

'All right, it should be tilted at a thirty-five-degree angle – is it?'

'No. It's about thirty-seven.'

'Okay, so make sure the arrow is pointing to thirty-five.'

I do it.

'Great. It's in. Lock it down.'

I do and make sure all the bolts are tight.

'Fuck. It's three-nothing already. What the fuck happened? All right. Come down.'

His command annoys me so I sit. Then I lie down on the silver-topped roof. It's still warm from the day, soft, almost tacky, but the sun sank before the rubber began to melt. No stars tonight, just the pale sky and the pink. I don't want the memory of Claire's frightened face. I'd rather it be calm, at least, that long mouth like the stretched clouds above. It doesn't come. The night won't conform; it whispers a memory, instead: *'No one can touch your immortal soul.'* My mother used to say, sometimes before walking out the door for the day, sometimes before drifting into sleep, *'You are the light of the world . . . you are the salt of the earth . . . and when the world has lost its taste for you . . . ,'* in such a way, with such conviction and good timing, that I thought she'd made it up on her own. My father, although he was an atheist, seemed to agree. Whatever my soul's nature, they both believed it needed edification. They took advantage of my early reading skills and comprehension and had me memorize things: he, song lyrics, poems, long prosaic passages, and sports stats along with band and team rosters; she, important civil rights events and the dates of assassinations.

They met over a tray of Salisbury steak in the main Boston University cafeteria. She was rear-ranging the meat. He was waiting with his tray. Neither one of them ever went much deeper than that – how the senior class president and the semiliterate drifter went on to get married and have me. I suppose it would be simple to say that he was on his way up and she was gorgeous, and they were both unlike anyone the other had previously met.

I hear the brakes of a car down on the street, followed by a string of curses uttered by a young person. They're more plaintive than aggressive. Someone else giggles. 'We weren't bad,' I say out loud. *We were never bad.* Alcoholic? Yes. Damaged? Certainly. Lost? Perhaps. But never *bad.* And, I mean, they got us early, the next greatest gener-ation. They got us – the Harvard sociologists, PhDs, Eds, swarming out of Cambridge to the bedroom communities west of Boston; the aspiring and lapsed Jesuit priests, the transcen-dental remnants, the hippie holdouts, the civil rights holdovers, the art freaks, no-nukes and Greenpeace, the pacifists, the liberal Jewish intellectuals with their intoxicating gravitas.

I tried to stop smoking weed before I was

seventeen – came up sober for a breath – but, but what? – I, we, went back down for the cool air of sleep, the wind through a summer day's screen: ill-advised runs to New York to the head shops on Macdougal for canisters of nitrous, the stop in Washington Square for the squirrelly brown buds of shit weed sold by a guy named Willie, who looked black, save for the eyes and the violent Spanish flourishes thrown at the impatient junkies trying to cut in. Then back to Boston. We graduated from whippets to whole tanks of gas. We rode around in Brian's father's car, filled balloons, put on Jimi Hendrix, and were slapped to other realms of being.

Perhaps we princes were only dreaming. How else do rogues get the chance, either together or alone, to turn everyone on and free the world? The first true children of integration; up south, over pond, peeking out of ghettos; no factories or fisheries or railroad yards for us to languish in – set for dreaming. We slept too long. Everything passed us by.

I remember the first time I tried to get sober. Sally had just dumped me and I had seen her at a party listening closely in the rec-room basement to a rich boy I despised. I'd promised myself before arriving, alone, that I wouldn't drink. I went upstairs to the bathroom, touched all the towels, looked into the expensive vanity at the foreign ointments and pills. I thought about popping some, but I closed the door and looked in the mirror. I couldn't see what Sally saw in my face – what spooked her so. I had seen my father that morning, the first time in some time, hunted him down on my own – surprised him. I guess I was a little bit desperate. I couldn't talk to my mother about anything, really, certainly not about being dumped by a poor, freckly white girl – any white girl, for that matter. Shake and Brian had already been with too many girls, and Gavin hadn't been with any. So I went to my father, and I don't know why I expected him to be anything besides a stranger. I kept pretty quiet, pushed an uneaten sandwich and coffee mug around a diner counter. He didn't say much, either, just clicked his teeth. A couple of times he looked out in front of him, toward the open kitchen into nowhere, and smiled. When I was getting money out for the check, I'd looked up and caught him shaking his head at me. 'When you were a little boy, you were so full of light . . . ,' he'd started. He thanked me for lunch and the opportunity to see me and left.

Even locked in the bathroom, I could hear Gavin from downstairs, exclaiming over some bad eighties rock in his most exalted tone that '. . . indeed, the party has just arrived.' By the time I got downstairs the negotiations had begun – Brian and Shake were welcome, but Gavin had to go. When he saw me, he bellowed drunkenly. 'Mu brathir – *Eire nua!*' He snatched a bottle of fancy whiskey off the bar and tossed it to me dramatically like it was my confiscated sword. 'Sar! Ho!'

he bellowed and then ran out the door into the night. I held the fifth by the neck, looked around at the ring of rich boys, had a quick mind – tried to calculate how many I could crack with the bottle. Then I drank and followed.

We went cruising around downtown in Shake's new used car – out and aimless. Brian had just dropped two hits of blotter – goony-birds, I think. Shake's tape deck had just eaten his latest party mix, so we were listening to the radio. Even though it was his car, he thought it fair for everyone to have equal time on the dial. Brian chose first.

'Classics, dude.'

'Whose classics?'

'Come on, dude. One hundred point seven.'

Shake pulled the car over. We were in Chinatown, on the edge of the Combat Zone – Boston's tiny red-light district. He shut the motor off and turned to Brian, who was slumping in the back seat, and stared at him coldly. Shake was about as close as any of us could come to being a bully. He was already fully grown and dark. He was already a very good writer. He'd graduated midyear and was on his way that summer to New York to serve as an intern for some well-known director that none of us had ever heard of. I asked him once about his writing, how he did it. 'I see things and I write them down – connect the dots to here,' he snapped. I thought that I'd annoyed him so I didn't push it. I hadn't known that his anger was targeting something else, the visions,

101

an awakening schizophrenia, which was soon to leave him shaking and alone.

'What, dude?'

'I'm in no mood for your shit,' he shot back crisply. All three of his accents – urban black, Jamaican patois, and his father's high-brow Londonese – were confounding to listeners. He could scare almost any white boy at will.

'What?'

'G'wan claat!'

'Sorry, bro.'

'I ain't your brother.'

'Sorry.'

He switched on the juice and tuned the station in. Van Morrison was on, singing 'Into the Mystic.' Shake nodded to the music and turned it up.

'This tune's all right.'

Brian slouched more, relaxed, and looked out the window. I followed his eyes down an alley where a transaction was going on between a black hooker and a white john. The first few snowflakes were starting to fall. He muttered, 'Merry Christmas.' She was pushing him back against the brick wall and behind a four-foot stack of milk cartons, which was their only cover. Brian grinned. His eyebrows twitched involuntarily. What was he doing here? His parents had gotten out of their immigrant ghettos – better diet, better education, and – *gestalt*. Brian left his academic folks befuddled, sped around drunk in his old man's car like a broke, rebellious teen trapped in some dying mine or mill town. Brian, the stoned auditor; now he was stuck with us. In slumming, he had gotten a little dose of the void, if only vicariously, but now he was hooked, a true oblivion junkie. Morrison cried about some girl's 'gypsy soul.' Brian fingered an imaginary saxophone and then looked at me, still slouching, caninelike. He looked back down the alley, then back to me. He leaned in smiling crazily from his mounting adrenaline. He tried to make his face look serious and concerned, but he just looked scary and high. He placed his hand on my thigh.

'Dude,' he whispered, as though he was about to tell me a secret. I didn't respond. I was too busy trying to fight off the growing sounds in my head of the rich boy's murmurs and Sally's breath.

'Dude. Is your dad white?'

'Don't answer that.' Shake was glaring at him in the rearview. 'Fuck you, Brian!'

Brian threw himself away from me and into the corner of the car as though Shake had lobbed a grenade into the back seat.

'Dude, it's just a question.'

'Fuck that!' He found Brian in the mirror again.

I looked past Brian into the alley. She was now on her knees. He'd knocked over the cartons with the spastic swing of his hand.

'I just want to know.'

'Why?'

'Cause he's my friend.'

'No. It's because you want to know why you

have tutors and he doesn't. Why he's a letterman and you can't make any squad.'

'But you're in AP math.'

'Yeah, but we have the same tutor. You see how I work.' He thumbed at Gavin, who was in the passenger seat. 'I don't see you asking him what color his father is.'

'But I know Gav's father. I mean, I've seen him.'

Gavin cleared his throat, waved a hand in the air, and assumed his highbrow accent.

'Must you two do this all the time?'

'Do what?'

'Disguise your genuine contempt for each other with racial gobbledygook?'

'Gobbledygook?' Shake wanted to laugh, just because of the word, and that made him angrier.

'Yes. Well, I don't know what either one of you is talking about. It just seems as though *you're* looking for an excuse to beat his head in and *he's* looking for justification to have his head beaten in.'

'What do you know?' asked Shake, still watching Brian.

'About what you're talking about?'

'Yeah.'

'I just told you, absolutely nothing.' He emptied his beer, cranked down the window, and finger rolled it into a heap of garbage bags across the narrow street. He produced a pint of vodka from his breast pocket, took a pull, and without looking, offered it to me. I drank and held on to it – something else to focus on. He started rolling his window up. It stuck a bit, moved unevenly, so he guided the glass with his free hand. Shake watched closely. He bit his lip, shook his head slightly and then more and more. 'What I suggest is, if you really want to fight, let's go back to that so-called party.'

Shake ignored him. He was fixed on something else.

'You know what I know?'

'No.'

'I know busing. I know white flight. I know glass ceilings. I know higher interest rates on mortgages. I know being put in the remedial reading group – when you've already read Chekhov. I know our high school drama department and how they'll never cast me in a lead. I know how, when I do move to New York, no one will ever produce one of my plays unless I get a bunch of overall-wearing feel-good niggers jumping around the stage singing about how 'the sun's coming up on their black asses some day.' I know what color his daddy was or is but I ain't telling that muthafucka nothin' and neither is he.'

Shake watched Gavin slump in his seat. For a moment he looked as though he wanted to apologize. They liked each other. They just couldn't seem to talk to each other – as one was too jaded in the areas in which the other was naive. Gavin kept sinking. I don't think it was because he'd been yelled at, but because he hadn't been heard.

'*We can't do anything for the boy – that's what they said,*' his mother told me the first time we were alone. I always liked his mom, Mary – the only parent who demanded that I call her by her first name. She was much younger than my mother, but she carried the same fatigue. An ex-hippie gone hard and sober. She was a hitter and a screamer and I found those familiar traits comforting. And although she said I was like a son to her. I still wasn't her boy. She yelled at me but didn't come after me in that terrified, maternal panic. We had some quiet moments together, usually on car rides home from emergency detox runs. '*In first grade they wanted to move him up to seventh. I said no. I didn't want my boy to be some freak.*'

'*We can't do anything for the boy.*' Gavin is one of those people you can't stand to see sad. He thinks, has always thought, that he wears it well, but he doesn't. It kills the light in his face, makes him look, rather than hurt or even desperate, like a dead boy – the face resigned to despair. I could see in Shake and in Gavin that I had to do something. I instinctively tapped him with the pint. He turned, saw the bottle, and sighed. I might as well have been handing him a pistol.

'*Mr Sandman . . .*' I pulled the bottle back and started singing. He kept his head turned, his face not changing but no longer descending. He waited like that until I sang the wispy call and he responded, crooning, 'Mmmyyesss.' Then

106

he smiled, the freckles like so many tiny Christmas lights turning on cluster by cluster.

'You guys are freaks,' mumbled Brian.

'Mmmyyesss,' Gavin repeated.

I could tell that Brian was beginning to trip: He was twiddling his fingers in his lap. He went back to looking at the pair down the alley, watching the indifferent giving and receiving of a December blow job. It was freezing outside. The harbor wind seemed to have found its way into the alley, too, and was blowing the thickening snow side-ways and around. The cold was creeping into the car.

It's a strange thing to go through life as a social experiment – bused, tested, and bused elsewhere, groomed for leadership. When I was a boy, my room was full of great men's images – posters on one wall of Gandhi, King, Jackie Robinson, Malcolm X, Tommie Smith and John Carlos, Stokely Carmichael, a pen-and-ink drawing of Frederick Douglass, The Jackson 5, Crazy Horse, a W. E. B. DuBois bank, and a Booker T. Washington mural. And on another wall the '67 Red Sox, Ted Williams, a Shakespeare collage, a family tree of the Greek deities, Oscar the Grouch, Bill Russell. And I remember trying to understand the segregation of the images. The best I could come up with was that one wall was my mother's and the other was my father's, but even then it was difficult to keep straight; each individual image reflected and rejected the alleged virtues of each group and person.

That room. Those walls. Gone – cash from a second mortgage invested in some buddy's business venture. In the summer of '72 my father had been either laid off or fired. My mother went to work, so he had to take care of me. In the midmornings he'd call up the stairs for me to wake. She would've already tried and failed – first by moving things around the room roughly and noisily; then she'd leave and I'd hear the tub running. She'd come back when she was done. I'd open my eyes a crack. She'd be wrapped in a towel, hair in rollers and scarf, hissing, *'Get up!'* She would leave again, dress, reenter, and rip my covers off with an inscrutable hiss, standing there with my blankets – the freckled Celtic/Black/Indian – red armed, yellow faced, eagle nosed. One eye amber and one eye green. The progeny of, to name only a few, an Irish boat caulker, Cherokee drifter, and quadroon slave – *'Get up!'* And then she would go, and I'd drift off until my father ascended the stairs and with his stinky instant coffee breath nudged me and whispered my name.

We'd cook bacon or sausage and eggs, and after we finished I'd clear the table and he'd give me the *Boston Globe* or a book to read while he washed the dishes. He'd turn on the radio – to the big bands on the AM dial; Glenn Miller, Benny Goodman – pointing at the radio during a Charlie

Christian solo: half dressed, suit pants and shirt, and almost always with a slight grin. I rarely saw him frown, even when I'd go to meet him at work after school, even when I began frowning at him. He'd gone from philosophy to drugstore chains to department stores to random mercantile outposts – always some friend's idea that most people could tell was preselected for failure. And while my mother never tried to hide the fact that we, as a family, had been preselected for failure, he did.

We'd go out in the late morning on errands – usually to the corner store owned by the Italian boys he'd grown up with – get staples and he'd chat with them, and they'd ask him how my mother was, because she never shopped there. She went a few blocks farther to where a black couple had opened up a superette. Then we'd walk back with the bread and crackers, the peanut butter, the beer, cold cuts, and cigarettes.

Sometimes we'd play catch. Sometimes we'd perform some kind of chore until the early afternoon, when I'd make lunch: peanut butter and saltines for me, hard salami and Kraft singles for him. He'd set up the folding TV tables in the living room, and I'd bring the trays of food. He'd turn the television on to *The World at War* and we'd sit and eat – he with his bottle of Miller, me with my milk or water. We'd watch the WWII footage – explosions in the South Pacific, tanks rolling through Italy. He'd leave about an eighth of his beer for me and place it on my table. *'Take it easy,'* he'd say when I'd pick it up. *'Take it easy, pal.'*

When the war show was over, he'd tune in to a game show or Merv Griffin or Mike Douglas – still drinking. When they were over, he'd turn it off – a break before the nightly news – and he'd put the stereo on. I think it was mahogany. It seemed old to me and was enormous, even for an adult – like some giant basement freezer you'd find at your grandmother's – packed with LPs and 45s and even 78s. The receiver no longer worked, but the turntable did. It was black and heavy looking – wood, metal, and rubber with the solid arm that held the records aloft above the spinning disc below. There were two sliding panels on top, one for the record storage and one for the works, and when he opened it, I could smell the old cardboard covers, the warm vinyl, the wood, the Lemon Pledge. They were all almost too faint, like the imagined smells that emanate from a deep freeze belonging to the colored labels, frosted shapes, and colors of popsicles and waffles and ancient meats and sauces. Later, when I was older and he was gone and the turntable broken, I would still crack it open for that warming scent.

I'd hear the scratch of the first LP – my father's perma-grin, now wide, showing his wobbly teeth. He'd smile at me. *'Doo doo diddly-ah ya doo-ah ooh.'* First, a dose of Ella, maybe Satchmo, then Tony Bennett or Sinatra. He'd usually choose the crooners, or the swingers, though sometimes he'd play Bird or Miles or even Coltrane. Invariably though, he'd finish with Glen Campbell's 'Elusive Butterfly of Love.' He'd never sing along because he thought his voice was rotten. He'd just snap and clap by the stereo, watching me. I'd be beer addled and happy, elated because of the music and his obvious joy, but careful to stay away from his lit cigarettes, although obliging when he'd say, *'Light me.'* The pop of the match and the sulfur smell, the beer smell, the salami and peanut butter and the butterfly of love. Summer's urban afternoon slowly losing its sharpness. The rush-hour traffic out on Cambridge Street. The beeps and the exhaust through the holey screens. Then no more music on the big stereo – the absent songs hissing in the speakers. He'd clean the bottles and the dishes and hide the tables. Then he'd give me a pen and pad and sit me in the dining room at the table. He'd turn on the television again. I could hear the anchorman talking while I'd write and draw, about the shrinking Massachusetts economy and the expanding Vietnam war.

When my mother came home, we'd both be in our fogs of the prehangover that comes from drinking in the afternoon. She'd walk by me and ask him, *'Did you get a job?'* He'd sit back in the couch and sigh, *'Lila . . .'* And she would try to start a fight, but he wouldn't bite. She'd turn off the TV, walk by me again mumbling just loud enough to hear, *'You should be in summer school,'* and into the kitchen, where she'd bang pots and

111

pans around, hissing and mumbling in the same inscrutable way. My father would croon back to her in his baritone, *'Lila, he's only five.'*

She'd call me into the kitchen, and there'd be a plate waiting for me and a scotch and water for her. The radio would be on but tuned all the way down to the right end of the dial, where there was soul. I'd eat – stewed meat, boiled potatoes, fry bread. She wouldn't. It seemed she never did. She'd move around, busy but slow, doing things and mouthing the words of the songs that came on. I remember them, of course. I listen to them now, but I was a boy then, and although they were so beautiful to hear, they were also so troubling in the same amount – songs of resistance, of loss, of just holding on: love songs, music both sacred and profane, church music evoking sexy fathom-less grinds, sexy music calling on God. When she was done with her busyness, she'd sit down. Sometimes she'd sing, *'People get ready . . .'* Her voice was lovely, but she'd only sing a line or two, then perhaps hum, then go quiet and sip and swallow. She was usually so hard to look at: the eagle nose, the freckles, the green eye, the amber eye. For me, my mother's face seemed like a void, a historical abyss, an emptiness from which, if I ventured, I would never return. But really, it was rich with artifacts, made of memory and blood, things that could be regarded only in the past, never in the present. Perhaps it was the old beer in my little head that would make her face close, and I'd see it, I'd see her – just her eyes, her skin, below the buggy fluorescent and above the tap water and rye vapors, a song on her lips – she was beautiful.

We'd hear the front door open and click quietly shut, and we'd know he was gone. While I got ready for bed, she'd pick out a book for me, and in the lamplight, surrounded by the pictures of great men, some shadowed, but because of the busted shade, some still with a hint of glistening, I'd read to her until I fell asleep.

'Why is it called the oldest profession?'

We ignored Brian. Shake turned the car on, startling the woman. She was alone in the alleyway, looking at us. She was short, chubby, and wearing the obligatory blonde trick wig. Brian was watching her as though he would call on her, if he could've found his pecker through his lysergic haze. He started to roll down the window. Shake stopped him cold.

'You roll down that window and I'll break your fuckin' arms.'

'I just want to ask her something, man.'

'Leave her the fuck alone.'

'I just want to ask her something.'

'Ask her what?'

'Why she does it.'

Gavin fogged up his window with his breath and quickly drew a cartoonish eagle – tongue out and cross-eyed, like some rascal had just brained it with a mallet. The horns introduced the Beatles. Gavin wrote, 'Love, love, love' under his sketch. She walked out of the alley, past the car, and down the street. I could see that Brian wanted to defy Shake, but he was starting to hallucinate. He began to stare at the carburetor's hump as though he was a herpetologist and it was an anaconda sleeping on the floor. She disappeared into one of the strip clubs on the street.

The snake disappeared, and he jerked his head up. 'You'd think that it would stop.'

'What would stop?' asked Shake, annoyed.

'Prostitution – sex for sale.'

'What are you, high?'

'No, Shake, hear him out.' Gavin turned to Brian, who was now fiddling with his coat zipper.

'I mean, why isn't something else the oldest, like selling bread or wheat or water? What about wisdom? Haven't people needed knowledge as long as they've needed sex?'

'I thought you said wisdom,' said Gavin.

'You know what I mean.'

'No, I don't.' He opened a beer and looked into the hole as if it was an imploded star. 'You're confusing your terms – your argument. You're confusing me.'

Shake started to laugh. Gavin tried to hush him.

'You guys are just fucking with me because you think I'm fucked up.'

Brian snorted and grunted like an angry two-year-old. The acid seemed to be making his face

114

distort – for me. He settled himself and looked out his window back down the alley, then out the front, down the street, at the row of strip clubs on both sides. He sighed, 'Why doesn't someone do something?' He shook his head, gestured in front of his mouth to conjure the words – 'Something heroic.' He pointed out the front window. 'Look, there's at least six strip clubs on this block alone and I don't know how many hookers and pimps in alleys, man.' He sipped at his beer and made a face as though it should've tasted different. 'I mean, I thought technology was supposed to be the great liberator.'

'Technology?' spat Shake. 'What technology?'

'*Technology*,' he stressed, as though changing the intonation would provide clarity. He waited. No one responded. 'Like cars, bombs, indoor plumbing, *electronic radios*.'

'Maybe,' said Gavin, 'technology just turned out to be a more advanced oppressor – each advancement that much less humane.'

'Aw, fuck it, dudes – fuck it. Forget it. I'm just tripping.'

'Nah, Bri,' said Shake, turning, suddenly taking him seriously. 'But you've got to understand that *this*,' he gestured out the windshield, 'this is just a microcosm – for capitalism.'

'Dude, you sound like *you're* high.'

'Capitalism?' asked Gavin. He erased the crazy bird, finished his beer, and opened another. 'Capitalism – hah – we need more beer.'

'Yeah, Gav,' warbled Brian. The drugs were working on his voice. 'How many beers do you have stashed in your coat, man?'

'Enough.'

'You gonna sell your surplus back to us later on?'

'My good man, with beer, there is no such thing as surplus.'

'See, dude – they got you right where they want you.'

'Who?'

'The beer companies.'

'Yes, they do, underage and chemically dependent.'

Brian propped himself up and clenched his jaw like he was either summoning all his courage or trying to suppress a violent stutter. He threw in a finger point, too. 'So who's the pimp and who's the ho?'

'Pal,' Gavin chuckled, 'I'm afraid your analogy isn't analogous.'

'Yes it is.'

'No, sir, it is not.'

Shake jumped in. Still strangely interested. 'Anheuser-Busch is the pimp. Budweiser or Michelob or whatever product is the ho, and the drinker is the john.'

'No,' said Gavin.

'No?'

'No.' He took a long pull. 'You've misnamed some players and omitted others.'

'Go on then.'

He pointed at his can. 'Anheuser-Busch is a company, made up of employees, many of whom don't share in the company's profit. Augustus Busch – whichever number they're on – and his family, are the only pimps, and everyone and everything assisting in the delivery of the product to the consumer, who in turn is not substantially enriched by the process – anyone who truly labors is the whore.' He took another pull and exhaled in mock satisfaction. 'You are correct in saying that I, the consumer, am the john, but alas, *you've forgotten the product,* which is the buzz, the high, that swirling in my heart and head that makes me feel a part, that makes me continue on, babbling in this most idiotic manner about this idiotic topic, that makes me carnal and stupid. Gentlemen, yes, indeed, they have managed to distill, package, and market sex, good times, and death in a tin can.'

'Dude, you're tripping.'

'No. You are. I'm drunk. But I'll tell you something.'

'What?'

'As soon as I wean myself off this cosmic barley tit, I'm going to turn Augie Busch's little ash can out into the streets of East Saint Louis. *Hah!* Trick or treat, Bud Man!' He crushed the can and, forgetting that he'd rolled it up, bounced it off the window.

'Dude, you've lost it.'

'Fuckin' Brian. What kind of Irishman are you?'

117

'I'm half Greek.'

'Oh fuck you, asshole – Greek – you believe in Santa Claus and the Easter Bunny.'

'Okay,' said Shake. 'But until Lorna Doone and his great wave of heroes dry out, what gets done in the meantime?'

'Yes,' said Gavin, still agitated, pointing a finger in the air. 'There needs to be a plan in the interim.'

'What?' asked Shake.

'Love,' said Brian.

'Love. Shut up. The closest thing I've seen to being an act of love has been my dad's three jobs – how much he did work, works, and will continue to work.'

'Why, so he can buy you a car?' Gavin scoffed.

'I bought this. I see you riding in it, too.'

'I know. I know,' sang Gavin. 'I wish my old man worked like yours.'

Shake went back to Brian. 'So an act of love is going to stop tricks from getting turned, or these guys from drinking, or you from getting high every day?'

Brian pointed at the largest club, the Naked Eye. 'There are women, and men, in there being exploited.'

'They want to be there,' said Shake.

'No, they don't.'

'You ever been in a strip joint?'

'No.'

'Then shut up.'

Brian snorted again. His eyes were spinning

118

crazily in his head. He rubbed them to get whatever it was that was flashing before him to stop.
When he uncovered them, they were still.

'What's the antithesis of love?'

'Hate.'

'No, fear.' He propped himself up in his seat –
proud for a moment. 'And if you refuse to perform
or receive an act of love, it's because you live in
fear and are therefore subject to all fear encom-
passes.'

'Who do you think you're talking to?' asked
Shake.

'All of us.'

'You'd better back the fuck up.'

Brian shrank again, but Shake kept going.
'You're like a bad cover song, man – Pat Boone
or some shit – fucking establishment mouthpiece
talking to me about love.'

Gavin fogged up his window again and drew a
house with a smoking chimney. He took a dip of
Skoal and reached back for the pint. I gave it to
him. He rolled down the window and spat.
'Odorless, colorless . . .' he breathed. He held the
bottle aloft for a second, looking through the clear
liquor. 'This is a fucking disaster,' he mumbled,
had a drink, and pocketed it.

'Gav,' I asked. 'Can I get some?'

'Of course, my friend.'

I drank. I could taste the tobacco in the sip. I
felt a slight flutter in my guts, wondered what it
was, then remembered the promise I'd made

earlier. I wondered what the pang would've been had I promised anyone but myself. The fab four faded out while trying to reassure us all of a nameless girl's affections. I took another drink, sat up, and realized I was blasted.

'I don't think it matters – who says it,' I mumbled.

'Who says what?' said Shake, trying to rekindle his interest.

'Love.'

'Uh-huh.'

Gavin was my best friend. Everybody knew that. Shake and I had been enemies – or positioned as such – two black boys growing up in a white world, who were really nothing alike. We got past it, I suppose. When we ended our strange competition, Shake had walked away with the *blackness* crown. The mantle he'd lorded over me before we became friends – that which had come to imprison him as a type he resented, but still mined. I suppose he tried to take care of me – assumed things; for me a naïveté and for him an overarching practical knowledge. And in part he was right, I needed a brother who knew, but neither of us liked it.

He was never good at being gentle, so he cut the silence. 'So what, is there a whole lotta shakin' goin' on in there? Do the Naked Eye and places like it exploit?'

'Yes,' I said.

'Yes?'

'Yes.'

'But is it any worse than anyplace else?'

'That doesn't matter.' I took another pull. It seemed to fix my head, yank me back toward clarity. I tapped Gavin on the back with the bottle. He took it from me.

'Why not?'

'Because you have to pick your battles – so pick a battle.'

'So this is our battle?'

'It is today.'

'Why this?'

'*If a man hasn't found something he's willing to die for* . . .'

'Spare me.' Shake patted his chest. 'I know it as well as you.' He shook his head repeatedly, trying to force a smile. He closed his eyes. 'You're like that other kind of bad song,' he thumbed at the radio. 'Original, but still bad.'

'*Love, love,*' Gavin cooed from the front, over the commercial. He laughed and finished the pint. He reached into his coat again and produced two nip bottles.

Shake laughed, too, but seemingly at me. 'I can't believe people get suckered by the whole whore-Madonna thing. I can't believe *you* fell for it.'

Gavin turned to Shake, opening one of the nips as he did.

'Somebody had to.' He offered him the drink. Shake shook his head but took the bottle. He stared at the windshield and muttered to himself, like a man going through a checklist before skydiving. He jerked his head to the side as though he heard

121

something. He closed his eyes again. His face went blank and he shook his head again, this time slowly, as if he was gravely accepting what he saw. He opened one eye and stared, both outside and in, as if reconciling his vision with the night. He drank.

'Let's do this then.'

We locked Brian in the car. Shake said it out loud, and Gavin and I agreed that he'd be a liability. He shouted out advice to us through the closed window – 'Guys, no one buy a lady a drink!' We all flashed our fake ID's and went into the Eye. Neither Gavin nor I looked a day over sixteen, but we were waved in. It wasn't as seedy as I'd thought it would be. It was like a high-end diner, which made me think *woman burger*, which made me wish it had been seedy, after all. They were playing heavy metal music, but not too loud. There were three small stages to one side, a bar to the other, and a dark velvet curtain in the back, above which read, VIPS ONLY. There were only about twenty people scattered about, a cigarette girl and a male bartender. I heard one woman in a gold lamé leotard and tiara say to a man at the bar that she was Cleopatra. In the middle of the room were two giant men, former third-string NFL defensive linemen packed into cheap double-breasted suits. Gavin and Shake went to the bar. I went to the center stage, as the other ones were dark and empty. Five men were sitting in front of it on stools, waiting for the next show. A voice boomed over the PA, *'Ladies and gentlemen – Diana.'*

Diana appeared from behind a heavy curtain. She was tinted orange by the gelled Fresnels that hung above the ramp and the stage. Some loud disco came on, drowning out an effects-laden guitar solo. The music bounced and then so did she – across the ramp to the little round stage in front us. She was dressed like a jazz dancer going to an aerobics class, and it looked like she'd been wearing the outfit while being attacked by a bobcat. Her hair was dyed jet black – too dark to be altered by the lights. She wore heavy black and red makeup – a gothic fitness guru. She tore her top off and threw it at us. A man in front of me snagged it before it hit my face.

Someone sat down next to me.

'You're too young.'

I turned. It was a woman – a girl – another stripper, I gathered from her makeup. She wore leather and bandannas and didn't seem much older than me. She was very blonde and tan – too tan for anytime in New England, especially early winter. I wanted to respond to her quickly with something I supposed a normal person would say – *'Too young for what?'* – but I missed my chance. I just looked at her. She raised an eyebrow, perhaps provocatively, perhaps only a signal of her growing scrutiny.

'How old are you?'

'Twenty-three.'

'Hah.' Her laugh was forced, like it should've been a giggle but she was running an age game on me, holding her alleged experience over my head. She leaned in. Her face was inches away from mine. She exhaled. She had cool tic tac breath. I had kissed a girl once, under pressure from Brian. Word had gotten out that Sally was on the pill, and one day between classes he'd waited to congratulate me. I told him the truth – that she'd gotten the prescription to dissolve cysts on her ovaries. He'd taken a step back when I told him, as if I'd tried to kiss him in the locker row.

'Dude, your sex life is none of my business.'

'I don't have a sex life, Brian.'

'I know. Is there a problem?'

He told me he'd pick me up that evening and take me to the big party at Nate Gladstone's, that we'd discuss strategy on the way there – how to get Sally alone downstairs and then how to get her alone upstairs and what would follow. I'd been alone with her before – she was my girlfriend, after all, and her mother was a nurse, who often worked at night. I'd been alone with her before, and I think I'd wanted to kiss her – I just never figured out how. I could never tell if she was damaged, too. I always thought I detected a hint of it, no matter, I stank enough for the both of us. I was worried she could smell it, too.

We'd parked outside the party and drank a few beers. I showed him my book of poems.

'What's this?'

'I'm going to give them to her.'

He turned to one and then another. 'No, dude. No.'

'Why not?'

He flipped through the pages, shaking his head. 'Dude, they're dark. Have you shown these to anyone?'

'Gavin.'

He rolled his eyes. 'What did the altar boy say to the choir boy?'

'He thought they were very powerful – very mature. He said any girl would be lucky to have them.'

'Oh, I'm not arguing against that, they're powerful.' He looked at me as though he could assume some kind of patriarchic authority over me, as though the look alone granted him that.

'You guys are intense. You're kind of like a part of a shotgun blast.'

'So give them to her?'

'No.'

'Why not?'

'You're the part of the blast that misses.'

So inside Gladstone's party I kept careful count of my drinks – four to be human, six to be sociable, eight to be interesting but not scary, and the window between ten and fourteen when I was in control. When everyone else had had too much to drink and were willing to do almost anything, I'd coaxed her into Nate's sister's lightless room and sat her on the floor, the deep pile carpet, with our backs against the bed. I brushed her straight blonde bangs away from her face. Her lids were drooping over her moon eyes.

'Hey,' she whispered.

'Hey,' I whispered back. And it seemed quite natural to take her cheeks in my hands and guide her face to mine. There'd been times before – many – when my world had seemed to either stop or spin wildly or be detonated or implode. When time seemed irrelevant and then was discarded, and good or bad there seemed to be a bridge between me and the action, and I could see myself walk over and disappear, dissolve like a bouillon cube in my mother's stew, or times when I could see myself regarding that bridge's absence – watching from the stage or from center field as my mother moved in the all-white audience at my recitals and ball games, her awkward form scaling the bleachers; a cop car trailing me while walking home from school; the opening strands of a favorite song or the first beer of the evening, watching curbside, with all the white kids chattering indoors, then opening another and watching the stars align, smelling the rush of hops in my nose and the night sky becoming fixed and recognizable. Sally's lips were warm and dry and when she opened them she inhaled. I felt myself go in and in as though I was a ceaseless breath. She felt it, too. She gasped and shut her mouth tight and pulled away.

'What's wrong?'

'I think I'm going to be sick.'

'I'm sorry.'

'No, I'm sorry.'

She covered her face, drew up her knees, and put her head down.

'It's not you.'

She shrank, into the bedside, into the rug, into wherever she needed to go, and disappeared. For a moment the room seemed completely dark, like between the scenes on a stage, and I waited for something to limp or crawl out from an even darker place and take that space, draw attention to itself, call for light. I waited. Nothing came. Then out of the quasi void.

'Hey?'

'Yes.'

'Are you angry?'

'No, Sally.'

'Are you sure?'

'Yes. I love you, Sally.'

I saw a horse collar in my mind, and then I saw it in the dark room, descending in slow motion, spinning as it did. It dropped on her girl shoulders. I could hear its weight in her voice.

'I love you, too.'

She took one hand from her face and in the dark searched for mine. She found it, slipped hers in between it and the rug, not squeezing, but waiting for hers to be held. I did – her little hand in my already giant one. She squeezed back as best she could and sighed long, almost inaudibly, as though she wanted to dispel what little of me she'd inhaled, but discreetly, so as not to let me know.

★   ★   ★

127

'I'm Natalie.'

'Hello, Natalie.'

'Do you want to get to know me better?'

'Sure.'

'Here is twenty-five. Private is fifty.'

I couldn't get a bead on her. She wore big hoop earrings and her hair was piled on top of her head. It ended in a ponytail tied off with a black bandanna. She'd just painted on a lot of blue mascara and black eyeliner. The makeup glowed wet. She wore a leather skirt, leather biker jacket. I don't think she had anything on underneath them. Her body smelled like smoke and deodorant and Oreo cookies. Someone was working the Fresnels – opening and closing the shutters, toggling between the differently gelled lights.

'Hello, Natalie.'

'You already said that.'

'I'm sorry.'

'Are you baked?'

'No.'

'You look baked.'

'I'm detached.'

'That's a good one. I'll have to use that someday.' She popped the gum in her mouth, sending a blast of Juicy Fruit at me. I remember thinking that I liked Natalie and that I thought she was pretty.

'So what do you want to do?'

'I want to get you out of here.'

'I don't do that.'

'Do what?'

128

'I'm not a hooker.'

'I know that. That's not what I meant.'

'Good. But I don't date customers anyway. You're cute, though. You seem sweet.'

'I'm not a customer.'

She scowled, drew back, then let it go. She smiled again, vacantly.

I pressed. 'Don't you want to stop?'

Natalie crushed her smile into a nasty little pucker and turned away from me.

'What's wrong?'

'Don't waste my time.'

'I'm not . . .'

She cocked her head to the side and barked, 'You think you're better than me?'

'No.'

'Then don't waste my time.'

'I didn't mean anything bad.'

'Go save someone else's world, faggot.'

I must have missed the signal, but the two football rejects started over. I went to stand, but a third, surprisingly enough because he was enormous, had sneaked up behind me and dropped his hands on my shoulders and held me still until his partners got to us. I heard his voice, high pitched, come from way over my head.

'Is he bothering you?'

I raised an eyebrow to her in an appeal for her to remember what she'd just said to me.

'Yeah.'

They picked me up – one by the neck, the other

two by each leg – lifted me over their heads and began the bum's rush. The music continued, as did Diana, who was down to a terry cloth G-string. It was stuffed with bills. She was upside down, clinging to the steel pole in the center stage. Shake was walking hand in hand with the Egyptian princess toward the back. Gavin was engaged in a tug-of-war with the bartender over a can of smuggled beer.

They opened the door with my head and walked me down the street, toward the alley, still in the air. When we reached Shake's car, they threw me into the swirl of wind and snow. I tried to right myself – catlike – but I landed headfirst on the windshield. Both cracked. Inside, Brian was having a bad trip. He was writhing in the back seat, covered in puke. It took a while for the sound of my impact to reach him. When he finally did hear, he looked up at me through the glass. A look of messianic terror spread across his face. Later, much later, he would tell me that I had appeared like some demon moth on the wind-shield – splattered – but now he pointed and screamed. It was muted to me outside the car, in the loud wind.

I slid off the hood, found my feet, and walked toward the bouncers. They were almost at the door. I called to them.

'Excuse me!'

The sneaky one turned. He shook his head and pointed back down the street.

'Excuse me,' I continued toward them. 'I left my coat inside.'

They ignored me and went in. The hooker came out of the neighboring club with another guy – big, white, going to fat, and strangely sweaty. The snow had taken hold on the ground. He slipped a little and she caught him. Then they both saw me. He snickered.

'Season's greetings, sucker.'

She slapped his arm as if to shame him. I kept heading to the Eye. They intercepted me in the street, ten yards from the door.

'Sss – baby, they fucked you up!'

She cringed as though she'd never seen blood before. He craned his neck, making his jowls collect against each other. He squinted and shook his head.

'Chief, you'd better get that taken care of.'

'Fuck you.' I stepped to them, closing the distance to an arm's length. I saw my blood on the snow.

'Whoa, chief,' he leaned away. 'You don't know who you're fucking with.'

When I hit him in the stomach, he gagged and crumpled. When I hit him in the head, he made no sound, not even his big body landing on the street. She screamed. It must have been all the snow muffling everything that kept most of the sound from me because even the collective roars of the V-8s in the Ford LTDs seemed quiet. Metro cops, the worst. I don't think they turned on the

131

sirens, but the rollers were flashing and their red and blue tainted the new snow. The high beams were flashing, too. They spotlit the fat man, who had made it to his knees. The hooker, now a good samaritan, was pointing at me, screaming, 'Him! Him!' The cops got out of their cars, grasping their sticks. Their radios squawked and beeped and spat fuzzy nonsense. The door of the Eye remained closed. And like my mother had taught me, as it had been taught to her, I kept my head down. I walked toward the door with my head down, and so the blood from my brow dripped in front of me, and like a carrot on a stick led me on.

When I picture the Charles Street Jail, the image in my mind is always wrong. I see the bridge. If you look at it from the south, from the drugstore when you come out after buying cigarettes, or from one of the paths you can run on along the river, you see the train stop on the big metal and concrete bridge – the Red Line bound for Quincy, bound for Alewife. It obscures the hospital – Mass General – across the street. And Buzzy's Roast Beef is below it, where you can park on the sidewalk and get a late-night sandwich when you're high. I can't see the jail – the outside, anyway – it's set back, off the main drag. I don't remember if you can see it from anywhere.

Pinky had one of those faces pocked by years of

junk and old acne scars. He was jaundiced – yellow eyeballs, yellow skin, and dirty, nicotine-gray hair. He made me think of a twisted old belt. He was shirtless, struggling on the toilet across from me. He'd been watching me. He had blue eyes. They were huge and unblinking as though he'd been on speed forever.

'Harder and harder to pinch one off.'

'Fuck, man,' barked someone I couldn't see but who sounded very evil. 'You been eatin' poison?'

Pinky still stared at me.

'Ray's shit don't stink – you know, little brother.'

He stood, flushed, and slid his camouflage pants up. 'I'll get back to that later.' He zipped, doing a little jump at the end as though he'd torqued himself off the ground. 'Rough night, little brother?'

'Tchh!' Ray sucked his teeth hard and walked into my view. He was old, too, but not nearly as worn as Pinky. He was squat, bald, and light skinned. He had washed-out hazel eyes, a hippo-like nose, and an enormous gap between his upper bicuspids. He stuck his tongue through it and snapped off a louder 'Tchh!'

He was above me, and I realized that I was on the floor, leaning against the cinder-block wall. It was cold, but it felt strangely soothing. I thought some ribs might be broken. He bent at the waist, looked me over, and turned away to Pinky.

'Fucked that nigger up right. Fucked him up good.'

133

Pinky shuffled over. 'Cops do that to you?'

I nodded.

'You're a good-lookin' kid under all that mess.' He crunched up his face and hissed as though he was in pain. Everything but his eyes collapsed. I went to touch my head and saw my hand as it went past my eyes. The top segment of my ring finger was pointing the wrong way. It started to hurt. I touched my forehead. It felt like one scab.

'You're a good-lookin' kid,' he repeated. 'You'll do all right.' He shuffled over to Ray, who was now leaning against the bars. Ray lit a cigarette and offered one to Pinky, who took the smoke but refused the light. He looked across the hall at the blank, white cinder-block wall. He stared at it for a moment, then turned for a light. 'Mornin' soon.' He turned to me and exhaled. I wanted a cigarette. 'Hang in there, kid – you'll be okay.'

I kept looking around the cell – the bars, the toilet, the cinder blocks, Pinky and Ray. It wasn't my first time in a tank, but that didn't seem to matter. And I remembered my missing coat and wondered whether Gavin or Shake had gotten it. And then I remembered having worn a sweater, a black wool one – like a sailor's – but it was gone. What I had left was my thermal shirt. It was bloody and nearly torn off. I went back to the bars and then the toilet and the wall and the men, scanning the scene again and again. And I tried to spin it – turn it over in my mind. Then for an instant I thought that the otherness of the objects and the men was a good thing, and that I hadn't become inured. I shook that notion off and I kept on trying to spin it, flip the image over and over in my head, but it still kept coming up wrong.

Ray snapped his tongue through his teeth again. 'Don't bother talkin' to him. He ain't goin' nowhere – shit – you just trying to butter him up and roll him over.' He pinched the cigarette and pointed it at me, then at the wall and perhaps the world outside.

'Headstrong niggers these days don't know shit. He ain't goin' nowhere.' He took another deep drag. I watched him blow it out through his big nostrils.

'What, nigger, you want something?'

There was a bench next to me attached to the wall. I used it to press myself up, and I managed to sit on it. Ray shook his head and threw his butt in my direction.

'Nigger thinks he's cute.'

I straightened myself on the bench, flattened my back against the cold stone, and, staring back at the squat yellow man, now scratching his thick knuckles, said, 'I'm not a nigger.'

The F booms a few blocks away from the southeast as it comes up from underground. I scan the empty night. No audience up here, only me.

135

There shouldn't be any ironies when you narrate to yourself, no secret distances or disconnects, prophecies or deep levels of interiority: *And I will be true to the boy who is me* . . . I'm surprised I never realized that while we were being groomed to become leaders of the next great enlightenment – student-athletes, scholar-artists, and philosopher-kings – we were training ourselves to be Wino Henries, Hobo Bobs, and Boxcar Willies. No true idealist has a solid backup plan. *A train, a train; to be on a train.* To tramp about with a nation sack and guitar and the bitter bitter past on your ass. With rushing air and iron wheels to accompany your blues. *Suicide or flight. Suicide and flight. Suicide in flight.* I think, though, that it would be hard to be a twenty-first-century hobo, especially one who was badly injured. I should've been born somewhere else, sometime else, when I could walk and ride the rails in any direction. But the F only runs from Queens to Coney Island and perhaps not even the blues could sing of or heal the damage incurred in a failed escape, a botched suicide – broke limbed, frozen, and mute. And that would matter, being unable to sing but still remembering – riding the F inbound and out.

I get up and walk to the back of the building. There's a three-foot length of electrical conduit and an Astroturf mat. Next to it is a bucket of golf balls and Marco's newest driver. He's set up to shoot out at the river, although it would take a drive of well over a thousand yards, carrying over blocks of brownstones, parked cars, and pedestrians to reach it. I pick up the club and set up on the mat. I like to stand tall at address and get my hands as far away from my body as I can at the top of my backswing. I let it go. The club head whistles down and around and over and up. I stand tall again in my follow-through and bring the club back down in front of me. I wonder if Marco keeps track of how many windows he's shattered.

I put the club down, pick up the conduit, and rest it on my shoulder. Gavin got *The Science of Hitting* for his fourteenth birthday. I was just getting to know him and we'd meet in the park with only a bat and the book and take turns studying each other's swings, making sure the other was doing exactly what Williams said. *'He was a monster,'* Gavin told me the first time, bat behind his left ear, uncoiled in his follow-through, watching the arc of his imaginary blast. 'He was a monster of obsession, discipline, and knowledge.' I turn on an inside fastball and send it off into the night sky. In my mind I can't stop it. I've knocked it clear off the planet, only to be caught by some ionospheric netting. I swing again – another blast. *You blew it. You threw away a good one.* I turn the bat into a guitar and start strumming. I try to make it a song – a blues song. I hum random notes, hoping something in the night sky will hear it, structure it, and sing it back. Nothing comes. I wave one hand in the air, fingers spread, trolling the night for a song: 'Hmmm-hmmm, hmmm-hmmmm . . . Trains are gone . . . hmmm-hmmm, hmmm-hmmmm . . . Baseball is, too . . . hmmm-hmmm, hmmm-hmm-hmm . . . But it's all right . . . hmm-hmmm, hmm-hmm . . . I ain't blue . . .' Then, 'You better come on, in my kitchen. It's gonna be rainin' outdoors.' It's not my song. But it's a song nonetheless – good enough for now. I'm sure Marco is passed out on the couch. I go back inside.

Thomas is awake and seems agitated. He's near the surface, pivoting on an invisible vertical axis with aggressive fin flicks. I've seen him do this before, usually late at night when one of the boys has to be put back to sleep after a nightmare. I'd lie, depending on who it was, on the top or bottom bunk. The hallway light was always on for them, and Thomas would flick left and right in its glow. I'd watch that fish. I'd listen to the boys' breaths. None of them possessed the language to describe what had made them shoot out of bed crying, or twitch, wide-eyed under water. C or X, panting, quieting, then wiping his eyes and lying back down, without determining whether it had been a noise or a shadow. Neither boy speaking words: Neither boy believing that words – anyone's – could unburden him of his shapeless and seemingly nameless fears. And so I would stay until I heard his soft snores, wait for them to deepen, and imagine that the fish's scales were reflective and luminous and spread light all around the dark little room.

CHAPTER 5

It's a strange thing to go through life as a social experiment, especially when the ones who conceived the experiment, the visionaries with sight of the end, with an understanding of the means, are all gone. No more DuBois. No more Locke. No more Gandhi. No more King. No more groovy social theorists or hippies or activists or anthems.

For some reason I believed that when someone sang about love, that's what they were singing about. I thought that I was a poet when I was younger – that I was deep. Perhaps I'd always been the one who'd been too fixed, too literal, and missed out on all the subtleties one could mine a work of art for – to get laid, to get paid. That if you quoted someone, or turned on the right song, with the lights just so, money could change hands or clothes could come off. Perhaps that's why Sally balled the first guy she met after me. And Sally wasn't a tart, wasn't a denizen of casual sex. I'd watched her regard us, consider forever with me, and say to herself, 'No.'

It's a strange thing to go through life as a social

experiment. If you were born of ideas, then all you have are ideas. Sitting on the floor of some dark room playing 'Lay Lady Lay.' Strum-plucking my guitar, singing softly. Wondering when the *world would begin*. I could never get close enough. Not with his words, not with mine. I used to think that the failure was hers. Now, I think, perhaps it's mine. There's a world where young girls blush and sigh when they are touched, and it may be that it is good and quiet.

I suppose I should've been a superhero or an agent with no mission – AWOL, lost, forgotten, like a cold war relic, the laboratory, the training camp blown-up, the notes destroyed, my creator insane or in ashes. There would be, of course, those who knew of my existence. Perhaps they're watching me, or looking for me. I should have been a vampire or a werewolf. But if that were the case, then there would be some kind of unbroken blood-line tracing back to the original. I feel artificial, manmade, like saccharin or LSD, something synthetic that was fucked up but issued nonethe-less. I should have been something inexplicable, but at the same time nameable – a tolerable paradox, a recognizable dichotomy – like the Silver Surfer, both blessed and cursed; protector of the innocent, the ignorant, the stupid, the cruel; guardian of the land of the obvious; and, obvi-ously, phenotypically different. My internal conflicts need be expressed not in words but through the *power cosmic* – bolts of pure space

141

funk and blues blasting from my fingertips. Then love me or hate me, you'd at least see.

If I have the power cosmic surging through me, it seems only to give me angina and a nasty paranoid streak. I turn my gait up a notch. It hurts, but Brooklyn is dark and the streets are mine. There are no cops, no nervous pedestrians. I run and think, or I think and run – either way, I meander through the treed streets in the Heights: ginkgo, birch, oak, American elm. Their thick leaves sheath the streets, delineating a distinct border between earth and sky. They are healthy trees. Most of them have neat beds of perennials at their base, or ivy – Boston or English – and are fenced by wrought-iron painted black, or unfinished cedar. It's a wealthy neighborhood. The houses are even bigger than Marco's. They are old, kept old with the detailing – crown molding, sconces and chandeliers, dark oak floors, antique dining rooms, shutters, and mahogany doors.

I know I'm drifting, in widening concentric circles, toward the bridge – and then back south down Clinton to Atlantic Ave, the divide between old and new, with the North African and Middle Eastern stores, in which there are jugs of olive oil; bins of grain, coffee, and dried fruit; spices and dried herbs; olive-filled buckets; and in the afternoon, especially Saturdays, white people. I suppose there shouldn't be anything wrong with that, but there is, for me, and when I shop, for them. I stand in line and they stare at me until, of course, I stare back. Then they look away. It's strange that it should require an imagination to understand that I like olive oil and the bargain prices on Bulgarian feta, too. And stranger that they don't seem to possess imagination in even that tiny amount. At times I've chosen to extrapolate, generalize – a widespread condemnation of an entire people based on the observation of a nervous few. When he first moved to New York, Shake applied for grants to study the habits of Upper East Side white people – their rituals, their culture. It was, of course, rejected.

I turn north, up Henry Street, and finally break a sweat. Even on this hot night it's taken me over half an hour to get warm. It's an awful feeling, running cold. Sometimes it's what keeps me from running. Things bind up and creak and grind. I breathe short and shallow. My sternum aches and I remember my father and his father and prepare to die alone, late night on the asphalt. I've been told that I have a death wish. When my chest aches and my stomach acid rises up my esophagus to my larynx, I know it's not angina, but I can't believe it's anything else. I speed up to run through it and then belch or gag up a bit of bile; my sternum pops like a rude knuckle. I wipe my forehead, spit, and I'm free.

I haven't run in three days – just enough time off to be fresh, fast. The temperatures of the air outside and my musculature seem the same.

I lengthen my stride a bit. Whatever the disaster of my past life, or the low-calorie days and sleepless nights, I can still run, which is something that Claire and many other people, being neither ex-junkies nor ex-athletes, cannot understand. She would say, when she thought I was angry, *'You should run,'* as though it would be some cathartic event. Her suggestion would *make* me angry.

Gavin's father would sometimes show up at his mom's apartment ready to run. He'd point at us and say, 'Up,' and then he'd walk out and bark back to us, 'Suit up.' He was still young – about five years past his prime – just twenty years our senior, dragging two hungover, hairless late bloomers through a world-class workout. He'd run us hard until one of us puked, and then he'd shut it down and we'd coast back to Gavin's, his old man quiet and content for the moment – he still had it. Then he'd disappear and come back with meatball subs, beer, and cigarettes. We'd absent-mindedly shoot baskets in the driveway until the food was gone, and then we'd play hustle and there'd be a hard foul, and then a fight. Gavin, by that time, probably could've held his own against the old man, but he never did. He'd just jab at him to keep him at bay. Then his dad would charge and they'd wrestle. The old man would sneak a rabbit punch in, and I'd pull him off and throw him down on the driveway. He'd call us pussies and weave off in his latest jalopy. I think that we each realized for ourselves that talent and potential were both, in the end, irrelevant, and that winning, and winning big, which required some dark manipulation of mind, body, and soul, was all that mattered. Gavin will not run with me anymore. I suppose I don't want to run with him, either. I don't know if I will run with my children. It has become a solitary endeavor.

Ahead of me are two cyclists. They're riding the wrong way. This always peeves me – you walk and run against the traffic; you ride with it. They're wobbly, struggling, almost the same amount, up the incline. And this isn't a hill. New York City, for the most part, doesn't have any – not like Boston. I drop it in gear and begin to reel them in. I can't tell if they're wobbling from the effort, or if they're drunk. They look to be stuck in too high a gear. They come back to me. By the time we get to Remsen Street, they're mine. I pass them. The man dismounts, startled. This is going to be a good one. I have no internal organs, only gears, which drive steel-spring legs and suction feet that grip the road and release. I'm like some high-tech primordial machine.

For the last ten months I've been drifting back to the bridge though never attempting to cross it. As I get closer, the day comes up, rolling through my head like some conspicuously edited newsreel: I've just finished running and I'm walking home from my then favorite coffee shop – now closed – with a pound of freshly roasted beans and the *Times*,

145

and I smell a strange chemical taint in the air. There's what seems to be a snow flurry over the East River. I run into one of Claire's pals on the corner: she's taking her two kids to school.

'Hey.'

'What's going on?' I ask, looking around in the sky.

'I heard there was an explosion in the Trade Center.'

'An explosion?' I look west, over the docks, up to the north tower. It's smoking up top.

'Someone told me a prop plane hit it.'

'That's impossible.'

'Apparently not,' she asserts, as though she's annoyed by my faith in pilots and air traffic controllers.

'No, look.' I point. 'Do you know how wide that building is?'

She doesn't seem to understand – the physics of it. I run. The streets are full of parents and children. Some watch me sprint up the street. I open my building's gate and bang on Marta's door. She peers through her diamond window.

'Close all your windows, now!'

Up the stairs to the top, banging on the other doors. Claire's preparing the recycling. The apartment door's open. She's smiling. Things are going well. The kids are dressed and fed and ready to go – a plan she's had ready since mid-August. She looks up.

'What's up, hon?'

146

I think I'm breathless, but I'm not, so it comes out as a roar.

'Close the windows!'

She keeps wrapping the packing tape around the newspaper and pizza box – still happy – not wanting to change her expression, not wanting to heed mine. For once, for a moment, things seem to be going well in our lives and there's no reason to let it go.

'Get inside, now!'

I never raise my voice at Claire; now I've done it twice in ten seconds. It crushes her smile. Her long mouth makes the transition dramatic. She drops the taped bundle and backs inside. The windows are closed. The AC is on. I shut it off.

'It'll get hot.'

I bark something at her. X and the girl are on the floor, playing with toys – dinosaurs, trains, and farm animals.

'Where's C?'

'In his room.'

The boy's room is a half flight up, and just as I'm about to push off the landing and go through the door, he yells.

'Daddy! Daddy!'

The second plane comes and it hits like the news of a loved-one's death, shapeless, soundless, but reverberating, bassy, like the echo of a giant vault door slamming shut – but it's on my insides. The shock stops my heart. I'm frozen, one foot in the air, one foot on the ground. Then everything

147

begins again – my heart, doubly so, making up for lost beats. I crash into the hollow-core door. C's on his bunk, looking out the window. I see his face. He's a child, then he's not, at least not in his face: It's wiped clear – no chocolate, no jam smears, no innocence. Then the child returns, which is worse, because that face can't absorb the horror of the fire across the river.

I land and then I have him, and even descending the stairs, wrapped in my arms, he's still looking out. Then I'm back in the living room, holding him. He wriggles free and slides to the floor to join his siblings. Then we just seem to stare at each other – Claire and me – alternately asking if the other is okay. Looking at our kids on the floor. Walking to the kitchen to listen to the news – kept low so as not to let them hear. Picking up the receiver, listening for a dial tone.

Gavin finally gets through on the phone.

'You guys okay?'

'We're fine.'

'You got wheels?'

'We can't go anywhere.'

'How many people are in those buildings? Is Brian up there?' I don't answer.

'Dude, get out of there. Do you know what's going on? Bush is six miles high on Air Force One running to some bunker in the Midwest. I'm getting a car, somehow. Fuck! They closed the bridge.'

C's gone. On the floor he's left several pictures –

planes, towers, fire-balls – some the separate objects, some the entire event synthesized in colored pencil and water paints. I find him back in his room, on his bunk, pressed against the window as though he'd be sucked out if it were opened.

'C, get down.'

'People are jumping.'

'No.'

'Then how are they getting down?'

'Come downstairs with me.'

The first tower falls. This time his face doesn't change, as though he's already adapted to it. Across the river a cloud rises – ash – gray and white. It unfolds from itself and unfolds again and again, crossing the water, coming to us like a late-Cretaceous plume of postfire. And then we are in it and can no longer see.

I come up the back way, around Cadman Plaza Park, behind the shell of the in-progress Federal Building. Through the windows I can see the hundreds of light bulbs at the ends of hundreds of pigtails, temporary lighting that stretches up and up through a void in the building's diaphragm, twisting and seemingly replicating itself as it goes to the top. I catch my reflection in the glass of the first floor, and I remember why I haven't been running. I've dropped weight, enough since I last saw Claire for her to notice, to worry.

I don't wear a watch, but I know the checkpoints

for my splits. I base my progress on feeling. I feel I'm moving fast when I hit the concrete runway – the approach for the bridge – which isn't really a runway, but it seems like it to me so I have to build up speed for liftoff. Even at this late hour there are cars backed up at the light. Their exhaust stinks and they throw off thick heat, which makes them bend in the wash of headlights and street-lights. People stare as I run by their windows. I run on the divide, the embossed yellow line, which separates cyclist side from pedestrian, and then I'm past the cars, bending left toward the bridge. The concrete turns to wooden planks and I rise above the heat and fumes, into the cooler air and headwinds above the river.

It's 1:25 a.m. and all is well. The electric lights line either side of the wide wooden path and evoke gas lamps, their lenses frosted or etched – I can't tell, but their light is diffused, making the path ahead always look like a glowing entrance. Up above the lamps is clear. The sky is lacquered azure. No stars here. The moon is behind me. The clouds have gathered again, gray and fat over the mouth of the river, over Lady Liberty. And when I see them, I notice the air's thickness, the density of the water in it. The bridge cables rise and cross and attach to the highest cross span. It seems impossible, their suspension, their heft, glazed by subtle lights, slack and taut, delicate, heavy, twisted steel – now bonelike, now like sinew and back to braided steel. My list – Claire's list – seems small, manageable, unremarkable, no different from what any other family contends with, and it is, after all, *only money*. *'There but for the grace of God go I'* – up the planks, loosely through the night. I like the greasy slip of my arms, going back and forth against my sides, my sweat evaporating in the night air. Plank after plank goes under me as though the bridge is a giant conveyor belt that I run against.

I wonder how my wife is and I feel like a bastard for not having wondered before, that my latest thoughts had been to sneakily indict her as an architect of my demise. I wonder how her nose is, if Edith would cough up the dough for a surgeon to reset it, or if Claire will finally be blemished. I can't see her transformed face, but I do see her – young woman, young mother, then mother, ringed by her babies on the beach. Low tide. Sunset. Happy to see me as I appear on the dunes.

There must be wind down on the river, too. The dark water has low crests, which reflect the dim light they gather. They look like hands, and the lapping of the river against the stone pilings sounds like slow claps. Above, the D-train wheels spark against their track, lighting up the Manhattan Bridge's steel. And after the light there is shadow, dark forms of ghost welders on the beams, and the memory of the train wheels' spark allows me to see their old torches. The steel, the stone pilings, the dark water all know their own stories, and they reveal them in their own way, the bridges through their solidness, the river with its ceaseless motion – lapping. But also, they are in audience.

A river is a good place for ghosts. Perhaps ghosts believe they are like rivers. Or perhaps they feel they're like bridges, that they are useful in that way. My mother is a ghost and I hope for both our sakes she finds a river to haunt. I think she may have made some ghosts of her own, flushed some babies down before me, and perhaps some after, and I think, now, I know why. It wasn't because she didn't want children, but because her children would never be children. In the end, they would fail, and so would she. So standing at the top of her diasporic arc, she flushed. I wave out to the dark water, if she is there, to tell her I'm okay.

It's a strange thing, indeed, to go through life as a social experiment. I've been to Dublin and London, walked in tobacco and cotton fields. I've been to the Oklahoma reservation Minette walked away from, and I've seen the Mississippi dump into the Gulf. And I've seen a faded rainbow, like the parabolic wake of an arrow, shot through the center of them all. Ellis Island is to my left, and I scan back, south to north from the mouth of the river to the Empire State, red, white, and blue, and back again then up the rising central tower of the bridge to Old Glory. I'm on the flat now, around the back of the tower.

When you do something three hundred times a year for a decade, it becomes, even for me, habitual. So when I look down to where the towers should be, the cognitive dissonance hits me like a punch to the inner ear. I go down as though someone has taken my legs, and then my body, and I'm only a head that drops. Then I'm up again – vain, a cosmic vanity because no one's there to see it. There's blood in my mouth.

Brian is buried in a mass grave down there. I know it. Incinerated in an enormous oven. I feel I should call out to him but I know he won't respond. Just as he never called – returned my stupid message on his machine: *How are you doing?* – *'Not well. I'm dead.'* I see him with his shaved head and eyebrows, his saffron robes and alms bowl. He's sitting at his desk next to the window. I see him on the soccer field, on the baseball field – awkward – then leaning against a locker, talking close and cool with yet another girl. His hair was black, thick and loopy then. I remember him watching *Dirty Harry* and thinking he could fight and then getting his ass beat. I wonder what the woman he'd told me about, when he first disrobed and moved back, was doing. Did they stay together? Was she dead, too? I wonder what he'd say to me. Do the dead cry out for retribution? Some said they do – but did they really ask the dead?

The television, the radio, the newspaper – I heard and read that there were no words to describe what had happened. It was said that it was tragic. It was said that the people who had died were heroes. And I heard some try to evoke the spirit of the heroes by speaking their names, as though their evocation would, in turn, make them heroic, too. I don't know what happened on that day, at his desk. I don't know if he was buying or selling puts or calls. I don't know who he saved or who he may have abandoned before he was crushed or burned. I do know that if I call his name into the air, it does not imbue me with his spirit, nor absolve me of the guilt I feel: Ass and fool that he was, I didn't mourn my old friend. I know that when I heard the corporate-speak, the market-speak, the military-speak, the politico-speak – I know that when I heard all the speak and watched the markets tank while people spoke of patriotism and unity, it made me lonely. It made me sad. It made me seethe.

Beyond my arm extended is a mass grave. Why is it that those least equipped to speak, speak – the most, the loudest, in sound-bite, reductive, in attempts to name and dichotomize, to clarify with words that are general and misused, with phrases that are hackneyed? With anthemic statements that do little to cloak the next agenda – more death. Why more death? I don't recall any symbols or ideas buried under the debris – just people. Mothers and fathers, siblings and friends, lovers and beloved, who were caught in the whirl of the bartering and the bloodshed of nations – the ill will of men. Men who have claimed the position of God, to deal death with impunity: their people, asleep or tranquil and full of their opiates. Yes, in some way complicit in their own slaughter, but how could they have known? How could anyone have known that one morning they'd awake to be ripped by fire?

And the leaders call to the dead. They call on the dead, and then say the dead call out for retribution. It all seems too convenient – that the chorus from a mass grave would rise up and sing for another and another and another. Genocide wrapped in some rationalization that someone is owed something. The continued body count, millennia old and miles long. My old friend Brian is ash. Fuck you.

And then it was time to get past it – move on. I hadn't gotten past the last slaughter or the one before it. And I knew I was wrong, because I crashed around, ranting and angry when I knew I was just sad, just a sad coward. Too scared to mourn, to deal with grief, so I took it out on my children. I made sure that they were okay. I made sure that they were healing, all the while knowing that my motives were flawed. Premeditated acts of heroism usually are.

I turned off the radio and the television for a long time. I stopped reading the newspaper. I missed the war. When I thought it was safe to tune back in – back to those who'd moved on – I found that it wasn't. It was back to the same old shit – bulldozers and human bombs, corporate scandals – people advancing what they thought they deserved. Racial ideology. One day I heard a man posit the same tired argument promoting *black entrepreneurship:* Money. Power. It's always struck me as odd – turning one's back on resistance. If you and yours have been exploited for capital, then why, in turn, would you covet that capital?

I used to sit on the curb on hot summer days, music on the transistor radio hung on the cyclone fence. The singers would preach the gospel of love and redemption – like a sermon on the slab. Even the teenagers, the junior pimps and loan sharks, would stop and listen. And when the cops would cruise up looking for someone's brother or someone's daddy, or the owner of the fence, and would threaten to 'smash that damn thing' if we didn't shut it off and move, we'd all quietly stand and stare and turn off the radio and take it off the fence. I don't know, but to me, even as a small boy, I thought we'd done something. I thought we'd won. And some of those boys are dead now, some are locked up and some made money and bought houses with fences to remind a new generation about property. But the caller on the radio, a doctor, successful, he claimed, was angry – his Hippocratic oath lost in some cellar box. He shouted that the last thing *we* needed to be was spiritual. Would that be changing the system from within – buying your freedom? As though freedom had a price that could be expressed monetarily.

The man gives you a dollar and a title and everything's cool, or on the way to being cool, or cool enough for you. But what would I know? My father is toothless and impotent. My mother died broke and alone, listening to yet another soul single. Looks like I will, too.

There's a noise on the bridge. There's something up here with me and for an instant I let myself think it's something evil, something after me. I jump and I run. I'm gone, downhill – as though Mrs McDougal's sicced her Doberman on me and I'm just trying to make it to my door, but I'm running the wrong way, into Manhattan and I don't know what's behind: dog, dog pack, bike gang. All I can hear is my breathing, my feet on the planks. There's no cover downtown, nothing until Tribeca or Chinatown. I'm on the concrete. The descent flattens. I tear through the turn at the bottom and try to sneak a look. There's something behind me, just far enough away to be a blob, but still menacing. The whole bridge seems to move. The air around it, the glossy, blue starless night separates from itself: great blue body, great blue sea. I search for another gear as I zig off Centre to Duane – it's not there.

I turn up Church. My spit tastes bitter and I'm beginning to feel my body, its limits. My legs will cover only so much ground. My feet will turn over only so fast and it doesn't seem fast enough. Gavin's father had always drilled us never to look back, that looking back robs you of your inertia. *'Be like Lot.'* I start seeing colors in the periphery at Spring Street. The streetlights blur and form permanent dots in the air. I'm going catabolic. Protein is shitty fuel but I suck on my bleeding lip anyway, trying to recycle something.

It's a strange thing to go through life as a social experiment. Mama never told me there'd be days like this, that the God she'd evoked would be gone, his disciples dead, mad, vanished, or corrupted, that those who were left would be running for their lives. I wonder if God stayed my mother's hand above the toilet bowl. I see me swirling down. A sheet of lightning blows up Sixth Avenue. It's outflanked me. I turn east on Houston. Two women at the corner clap as I go by. The blocks seem to elongate and then suddenly I'm at the end of them. More lightning over the river. I run south down Lafayette. There's still a chance. Somewhere on a side street a truck runs over a steel plate. The thunder responds. Then the sky explodes with noise and light and water. The rain on my face mixes with my sweat and I taste brine and blood on my lips. The wind throws garbage at me. My heart thumps like a manic donkey's hoof against my chest. It too will explode soon. I'm still three miles away from Marco's.

I make the bridge. I watch it rise, long and steadily and I realize I've been running downhill for the last mile. I make it halfway up the wood and the bile comes – an olive green blast that cuts through the wind. I stumble forward, still puking, and then I go down. My gagging is so loud and so external I can't believe it's me.

Finally I stop. The rain may have stopped before, I don't know. I'm on my knees, the last wave of heaves gone. The bridge cables rise and seem to bend over me like ribs. I'm inside a mile of skeleton. Inside. I've been inside all along. Swallowed long ago. I never knew. I never wanted to know. I've been dumb and wanting inside a giant sea belly. The sky is calm. The world has cooled because I'm inside – no weather. The city sprawls endlessly in every direction.

There's someone ahead of me on the bridge, not too far away. Close enough to see the bob-bob of her ponytail as she ascends. She runs like Claire. She looks as though she's moving quickly, but she isn't covering much ground at all. She must have been close when I went down. It's too late for her to be alone on the bridge. It's not safe. I stand up and start running again – just fast enough to close the gap a bit. Just close enough to keep an eye on her.

I close on her quickly. She bounces up and down, going through the motions of running without really doing so. Black sport bra. Black short shorts. Blonde hair. She's long legged, and as I close I see her hamstrings and calves contract and release.

I'm on her hip and she turns. She doesn't startle. She smiles and waves in time with her gait. She speeds up and tries to stay with me. We run together, make the plateau and wind around the center pillar, me every few steps pushing the pace just a hint. She breathes heavily and lengthens her stride – less bounce. She exhales through her mouth, pursing her lips as if to focus her overall effort. We hit the downhill. She shakes her head, whipping her hair across her face like a horsetail.

'Go.'

She waves toward Brooklyn. She pats her sternum and feigns a wheeze.

'I'm okay. Go.'

She waves again. I find a new gear, and then another. And I'm fast again. But now I feel solid, like one muscle exerting one effort with no memory of the effort before. I make a promise, out loud, to whoever may be listening. *I will do it. I will get the money. Then I will go. I swear it.'*

Tomorrow I will go to work and do whatever it is I need to do. The vertical iron rails flash by quickly, giving fleeting glimpses of the road below and the river beyond. I remember riding the street-cars with my mother after work and how the fences would start to blur as the train gathered speed. The metal would flicker with light and the images of the world beyond as though I was looking into the lens of some old, dimmed projector. She'd shift her legs and the grocery bags at her feet would complain. And not knowing I was watching her, she'd sigh, and her miles and her age would show in her face and sit on her shoulders. She'd involuntarily start to hum or even sing, *'People get Ready.'* The memory fades back to the black water, the rails – so real that I reach out for them. And it's just me going fast and the bridge and the water, sleeping Brooklyn in front and tomorrow in my head. The dead are quiet now, soon they will be gone, for that is the price of empire.

PART II

BIG NIG

If you came this way,
Taking any route, starting from anywhere,
At any time or at any season,
It would always be the same: you would
   have to put off
Sense and notion. You are not here to verify,
Instruct yourself, or inform curiosity
Or carry report. You are here to kneel
Where prayer has been valid. And prayer is
   more
Than an order of words, the conscious occu-
   pation
Of the praying mind, or the sound of the
   voice praying.
And what the dead had no speech for, when
   living,
They can tell you, being dead: the communi-
   cation
Of the dead is tongued with fire beyond the
   language of the living.

   —T. S. Eliot, 'Little Gidding' I

CHAPTER 6

C had looked at my knees one morning. We were staying at an inn and had gotten up early to watch the World Cup final from Korea. I was trying to walk quietly down the groaning steps. My legs were stiff, having danced with Claire the night before at her cousin's wedding, and I had to use the rail. There's not much worse, socially, than being a brown person on the dance floor at an otherwise all-white event. I don't like dancing anywhere, certainly not sober. And to have them watch me shift my weight, conservatively on creaking knees and ankles, emulating the sexual act with their Brahmin jewel while flanked by my children, X every so often slamming into me like a blitzing linebacker. Claire thought it was fun.

C watched me struggling and wondered aloud if Ronaldo's injuries had been worse than mine.

'Worse. Much worse.'

'What did he do?'

'One year a fractured tibia. Ruptured patellar tendon the next.'

'That's bad?'

'Yes.'

'But he's better now?'

'Yes.'

'Good. They need him.'

We were alone at the start – seven o'clock. It was a chilly New Hampshire mountain morning. And as the den began to fill with guests and the morning warmed, C left his sweater on, sensing from the crowd that they, for a reason he couldn't understand, were rooting for Germany. It was tense going – more people entered, sat, voiced their opinions, and talked about their children's teams or their own former athletic glory. And even when his hero broke the scoreless tie, he remained silent. He looked around nervously and pressed a bit closer to me on the couch – trying to read my expression. I patted his head. One woman kept looking from C to the television, trying to link him to the Brazilian players who celebrated. She wouldn't look at me. When Ronaldo scored the second goal to seal the victory, C couldn't help himself. He jumped up, tore his sweater off to reveal the homemade shirt. He pointed into the air, waving the index finger slightly – just like the man on the TV – and ran out of the room, triumphant.

Still no sleep. It's amazing what happens when the adrenaline tapers off, the endorphins disappear. I sit on the bed in the dark kiddie room and feel the pulsing, dull ache of twenty years of long distance running, hundreds of soccer games, hundreds of slides on hard-packed infields, fence jumping, sprints down alleys, nightsticks to the ribs and handcuffs, knees threatening to collapse while playing with the kids on a Brooklyn school-yard's asphalt top. They, unknowingly undercutting me, me not wanting to trample them. Then later, C watching me pop Motrin and sit on the floor strapped in ice.

I get ready to leave before Claire can call to wish me a happy birthday – to ask me what I'm doing. I feed Thomas three pellets. He's slow to react. They start to sink into the bowl. I want to give him more. The food instructions say that he should eat fresh pellets taken from the surface of the water, but they also warn against overfeeding. I'll give him more later if those aren't gone.

Because of its southern exposure, the great window room is already bright. Marco is asleep on the couch. His laptop is next to him and the brief in question is spread across his knees. The television is on – *Cool Hand Luke*. He's preaching his gospel to George Kennedy, just before they shoot him. I shut it off. He stirs, kicking the paper in the air. He gropes the couch for his glasses.

'What time is it?'

'Six thirty.'

'You're out early.'

'Meeting.'

'Right.'

He closes his eyes again. I think that I should

167

make sure he's up for good, but he's the boss. He can be late. I go down to the cellar to where my tools are stashed. I open the gang box and proceed to lay the items I want to take on the floor. I don't know who I'm working for or what I'll be doing so I take out my 3/8 cordless and my half-inch drill. I take out my twenty-ounce hammer, five pencils, try square, twenty-five-foot tape, speed square, chalk line and extra chalk, grease pencil, Sharpie, utility knife, extra bits, #2, and #3 Phillips, #1 and #2 trim square, slot-head bits, 5/16 hex head, channel locks, tin snips, needlenose, small C-clamps, Besseys, speed-bore set, masonry and metal bits, plumb bob and line, torpedo level, wooden rule with depth gauge, five-in-one, battery charger and extra battery for the cordless. I leave the ratchet set, pipe wrench, and the remaining power tools behind. I look over the assemblage – call each tool out by name. I do it again, touching each one, as well. Then I put them, one by one, into my large canvas bag. I stuff my tool belt in last and sling the bag over my shoulder.

Marco's still on the couch, but he's awake, sitting up, rubbing his eyes. He stops and looks my way. He's too nearsighted to see me from across the house. He waves to the sounds of the street coming through the open door.

I set off. It's already hot outside. The air's loaded with water. On the corner of Wyckoff and Court is a Chinese takeout booth. As I pass, someone turns on the exhaust fan and I get a blast of celery and ancient chicken in my face along with the rust tint of the fan blade and whatever greasy filth is trapped in the housing. I turn right – north – up the slight grade. I walk past the travel agent, the gourmet shop, past the coffee shop in which, ten years ago the kid at the counter checked to see if the ten I had given him was counterfeit. I walk past the realtor who never seemed to be able to find Claire and me an apartment when we first looked at the neighborhood. Past the closed Taqueria. I cross Bergen Street, looking down the hill to the F-train stop at the bottom.

A kid from the bagel store is hosing down the concrete, washing the scum left behind from last night's trash. He stops the water so I can pass. He's used bleach. It burns my eyes and nostrils as I walk by, but it's failed to kill all the stink. The milky, oily water collects in the gutter because there's a slight depression in the road. The sun will have to dry it all up.

I pass and hear him turn the spray on again. I walk past the vet and wait at the corner of Dean, where cars always make the illegal dogleg turn against the traffic on Court. They've finished the facade of the funeral home. Instead of stucco they used Styrofoam sheathing and epoxy paint. Down the hill is the gym I used to go to. A couple walks up past the little firehouse toward me. They're both very tall and thin. I've seen them for years. They're both graying. They walk with their squash racquets poking out from their bags. He, as always, is still wearing his safety goggles. He sees me and shoots a quick, high wave. She doesn't. I wave back.

A neighborhood mom I recognize from the playground passes them. She jogs slowly. She's sweaty and heavy. She wears big shorts and a tentlike T-shirt. She nears, does a double take, and waves. She looks at my tool bag and nods as though it's answered a question for her. She passes and I recall her face – little eyes, rodentine, lidless, and her pinched nose. I turn to look at her. I've overheard her talking about her battles with her weight with her pals. She's been shuffling in the early morn for a half decade now. She's dieted, fasted. Nothing's changed. Now, she's just older.

There used to be a café – Roberto's – owned by a screwball Puerto Rican who passed himself off as Italian. He made the best coffee, nice little sandwiches, too. No cell phones allowed. No laptops. He had iron lawn chairs and an oak church pew and two long plywood tables. One day he got sick of breaking even, serving the privileged stroller brigade, and left the shutter down.

It surprises some people that I go to a chain store for my coffee, but I won't support the incompetent mom-and-pop operations that keep springing up around the neighborhood, subsidize half-wit entrepreneurial fantasies by agreeing to their criminal markups. Besides, black girls work in the Starbucks. Sometimes I even call them *my girls*.

I don't know if their personal stakes in the company are myth or fact, but they always brew a good strong cup and treat me well. Besides, my girls have taken over this outpost – shed the caps and shirts. Shed the greetings. I never have to order. They always slide my large black to me with six ice cubes dropped in on top so as to take the coffee out of the lawsuit temperature range.

Kelly is short and round faced, with dark chocolate skin. She waves me off when I go for my money.

'How are the babies?'

'Babies are good – good. You?'

'I'm good. It's all good. You look tired.'

The others in line are perplexed by our exchange. Kelly takes the next order. I drop some of Marco's change into the tip jar and leave.

Across the street the ice cream store is closed, as well as the two pubs I've never been to. One, Coopers, has a blackboard in the window advertising an open-mike night Wednesdays at nine. Farther down the block the church steeple rises up above the adolescent trees and low buildings. It's newly clad with brown sheet metal, but the old copper trim and gutters are oxidized. It can't, from the way the seams appear to be bent, be watertight. Behind the big louvered panels is the broken bell. I missed its last sounding. I figure I'll wait until the next clang and slowly make my way to work – eight to four. Then at four I'll call on Marta for our check, perhaps even make it up to school to plead my case for the boy's tuition installments. If I get paid in cash, four days of work will net me a thousand. Then I'll have two weeks till Labor Day: tuition, new apartment deposit, miscellaneous bills, the bus ticket, the Ronaldo shirt – not likely but possible.

A paddy wagon pulls up and one of the cops gets out, repeats his partner's coffee order twice, and goes inside. Somebody yells something from the back and the cop without turning snickers, 'Sorry, the AC's broken.' He listens to another complaint and replies, 'I'll give you my badge number now.' The 'brown like poop' kid's mother power walks toward me. She's holding little dumb-bells. She sees me. I can tell she'd like to avoid me, but that would require a change of pace and a turn into the street. She readjusts her face to look happy – surprised but happy.

'You're up early.'

'Sure.'

'What are you doing? Are you having a good summer?'

'Sure.'

'How's everyone?'

'Great. Yours?'

'They're great. We signed Eli up for German lessons. He loves it.'

'German, huh?'

'Well, I'm half German.'

She's wearing a mauve sport bra and long, black

172

tights that would seem to be suffocating in the wet August heat. The elastic bands of both are too tight. They cut into her ribs, her waist, creasing her flesh, intensifying the shapelessness of her exposed gut – one big fleshy roll on display – pink and peach and white and sweaty. I don't want to stare at it so I look at her face. She has a little head even for a small person, but she's tall, about five-ten. She has chestnut hair. It's short, but she wears it pulled back, revealing her ears, which would fit the head size she should have. Her nose is large, too, and her eyes seem to cross a bit – forever inclined to follow its length. She wipes her cheek with the back of her hand.

'What's Cecil up to?'

'He's at the beach.'

'That's great. Did you guys find a place?' She asks cautiously, as though she's unsure whether our problems are common knowledge.

'Not yet.'

She shifts her right side forward. Her shoulders and arms are skinny but shapeless. Her body doesn't start to widen until her navel – that wide ring of flesh – then it keeps expanding. She's bottom heavy, but she tapers toward the knee. Her calves are thin. Her feet are tiny.

'I'll keep my ears open.'

'Great. Thanks.'

'Good to see you.' She leaves but waits half a block to resume her power walk. I sip my coffee and watch her – hands high, head forward, ass

173

out, like some poorly conceived bird, a problematic emu, lost in Brooklyn.

I feel mean as I watch her disappear down the street. I had a knack once, for a short while, of talking to her – people like her – or, at least, listening. That's gone now, too. Before Claire left, we'd walk these streets as a family. She'd stop and talk or give a bright smile and wave, without breaking stride but slowing down and turning just enough to make the greeting seem customized and sincere.

When I walked these streets alone, before anyone knew anything about me, I was afforded the respect reserved for large dark men: Other dark men would nod gravely; dark women would roll their eyes up and smile or just ignore; the cops would slow down but pass on, somehow discriminating between me and those men in the van, whom they would stop and question. The white people scattered – not the ones who'd been here – the old Italians and their children and the pre-crack whites to whom this neighborhood belonged. They didn't flinch. It was the neopioneers – a strange breed of professional liberal whites, bankers and lawyers and midlevel media folk who'd first rejected their suburban origins then rejected Manhattan's crush and bustle. Things changed – a restaurant, a shop, a gut renovation. Then they were in, cramming into the old butcher, the green grocer, the coffee roaster, perturbed by the lack of service.

174

Playgrounds were suddenly clean. Trash cans appeared on corners and young white girls scurried about, pretending the Arab and Latino boys who drank soda, leaned on mailboxes, and called each other nigger weren't there.

'I used to be king here,' I said to Claire once after coming home from shopping. 'Now I get eyeballed like I don't belong.'

She shook her head and smiled. 'People look at you like that because they like what they see.' She rubbed my cheeks. 'My husband.'

I pointed to my scar – two inches long, raised and jagged. 'Some people stare at this,' I rubbed my forehead. 'But most people stare at this – and when they aren't, they're staring hard away.'

'I just think you're handsome.'

'Well, you're not them.'

It changed when I was with her. *I* changed – to them – seen through the lens of my wife. I was no longer frightening, perhaps intimidating but in an exotic kind of way, for the women at least. The men reacted with a timid acceptance, tolerating their wives' open curiosity when they passed on the street.

Then the children came. 'They' had always considered Claire as one of their own, and perhaps, after I became a father, they considered me that, too. Somehow they let us in – they let me in. And although I don't think that I changed a bit, we became a part of the 'us,' that seemingly abstract and arbitrary grouping that is able to

175

specifically manifest itself: the right school, the right playground, the right stores and eateries, the right strollers, the right books and movies, the right politics, and the right jobs to bankroll all the rightness and distance them from asking whether it was perhaps all wrong. And yes, there were subdivisions of the us, but the only relevant divide was those who could afford to pay and those who could not – an us and a them. Somehow that became a measure of 'good.' I heard it in quick snatches – on line getting coffee – those quick, small judgments: *They had to pull their kid out. I think they defaulted. He hasn't worked in over a year. And this one knows the best real estate broker. And that one's a trustee. And his father owns the western world. And if you're good, you can be a part.*

I've met many people who think that what they believe in, just because of the fact they believe it, is good. And so those who are of a different credo are bad – or, at least, difficult – and any kind of proximity to 'them' requires some act of goodness on their part, conforming their moral superiority in their minds. And perhaps I'm no different. I look at them, their strange conformities, and I judge. So, for a moment, it seems fair – equal assumptions – but I look around and *I* don't see an us. And they never lived in a world where their notions of good aren't constantly validated. Even this strip is like a shrine to the local, the mundane. *The good.* Liberal, spending, complacent, in ever growing numbers – the *us*.

Now they don't stare, they avoid. Somehow, it changed. I don't know exactly how or when. Maybe I criticized a film or didn't like a book, refused too many cocktails and stayed quiet in a corner – watching. Maybe it was all those things. I don't think it was purely race (although I know most of them are racists: they believe they're good; they believe they're better). There were other dark people who became a part of the us, people who, strangely enough, arrived on the scene at the tail end of the gentrification. But I never considered myself a part of them, either. Shake had a conspiracy theory about the reason we were thrown together when we were kids: They put budding alphas in a pack, hedging that we'd either kill each other or waste too much time trying to figure out how to live. And if we made it out, it wouldn't matter: *'The creation of the lone wolf – can't do shit flying solo except make the settlers afraid.'* Maybe that was it – they were just afraid. Strange, they have me outnumbered and outgunned, but they're still so afraid. It's amazing the amount of cowardice privilege can afford.

Them. I spit-chide myself for using the word – how I let that woman become a them. I wonder what the emu – Cynthia – sees, if she has any inkling of an us. I wonder if she wanders around feeling misplaced and alone. I wish I could do as Claire would've. I would do well to exhibit some of her kindness – even now – her charity, not to confront, even internally, any of these matters.

I know that I'm not better. I know that drunks, madmen, and corpses make for lousy dinner guests. But I also believe that there's a them and they believe that they are good, and I know that if I had what they have – privilege, money, and numbers – I'd tear this fucking place down.

But I don't and it's late and someone kicks the paddy wagon wall from inside. I walk extra blocks east so I can avoid the commuters on the main drag. I finally turn south on Third Ave, and walk all the way down it to the little plank bridge that spans the Gowanus Canal. I can smell the water. It's extra poisonous from two months of cooking in the Brooklyn heat. I've always liked this spot, though. I like the sound car tires make on the old wood. I like the promise of the open ocean to the south and the hint of the past centuries' barges bringing in their truck. The oyster men. It seems like New England, a little patch of it, here between the sprawl of failed industry – more empty ware-houses, the auto shops, the chop shops – where the desirable neighborhood ends. Gowanus: There have been reports of a one-eyed seal living in the oily waters. I've even heard some say that he likes it there – happy to make the muck banks and rusted car chassis his rookery should he ever coax a mate up the man-made black water.

I lean against the railing and contemplate the promise and the plan for the day. No romping, at least not until I've earned it. But I have time, so I wait a moment for the seal. A harbor seal? A spotted seal? *'What kind?'* X would like to know that specific information. Boogums the harbor seal. I saw him on my first walk along the Irish coast. I spent a sober week in Dingle. I had made enough money doing odd summer jobs and taken off. I remember saving the specific dollar amount, racing against the countdown of days. I did it and then wandered along the coast looking for my family. No one took me seriously. *'Do you know how many Murpheys there are in the Dingle, lad?'* And finally I had a couple of pints, which degenerated into a couple of days waiting for some cousin or that fucking seal to come walking out of the water.

I close my eyes in the strong sun and try to focus on the money it took to get there – the exchange, cash for the ticket, cash for the room. I was only eighteen, but at least I got the transaction right. The image is erased by light. I cover my lids with my hands. They go cool, but I'm left with the paths, temporarily burned into my retina, of the beams returning to the sun.

I open my eyes, wait for them to readjust, and look north toward Manhattan and then south out to sea. Smaller bodies of water are much easier to navigate – smaller bridges, smaller boats. I go to scan the water once more, but even from this far off I hear the sick clang of the 7:30 bell. I shoulder my bag and go.

I forgot my pry bar. I turn on Carroll. The building is two lots in, across the street. I'm still fifteen minutes early, so I wait on the corner. It's a brick town house – narrow – only about seventeen feet wide. The facade is a mess. It's covered by peeling goldenrod paint. The bricks that are exposed need to be repointed. There isn't a straight row to be found. The wall seems to ripple from top to bottom even in this still air like a tent side in the wind. The cornice is about to fall off. I'm surprised the whole thing hasn't tumbled down already.

The windows are boarded up, so I can't see what they've done inside, but it seems to me that the first thing we need to do is get a scaffolding set up in case it does decide to fall. If not that, then we'll have to shore it up from the sidewalk – 2x12s on toeplates, leaning at a sixty-degree angle, pushing against more 2x12 plates placed horizontally against the brick. It seems a bit rigged, but maybe they're trying to save money. Regardless, it's incredibly careless to leave a two-ton pile of loose bricks waiting to fall. Perhaps they're going to knock the whole thing down. If that's the case, I don't know why I'm here.

A flatbed turns the corner and stops in front of the building. It's carrying a forty-yard dumpster, ROLLOUT CARTING stenciled on its side. The driver hangs an enormous tattooed arm out the window – flames and dragons, from what I can see. He's got a blond King Tut beard shooting from his chin, long sideburns, and a shaved head. He's wearing wraparound sunglasses. He leaves

the truck running, radio blasting the Stones –
'When the Whip Comes Down.'

He sees me and shuts everything off. He waves
me over while opening the door.

'What's up, brother?'

I nod back. He jumps out of the cab. He's
massive – big headed, thick necked, simianlike
torso and arms. He beckons to me again but
crosses to my side while doing so.

'Hey, brother!'

I nod again.

'¿Yo hablo inglés?'

'Yes.'

'This your job?'

'No.'

'Cool. Cool. I thought I'd be late. What time
you got, brother?'

'About ten of.'

'Shit. Maybe I am late.'

He reaches into his back pocket and produces
a multisheet invoice.

'Brother, do me one. Sign this so I can get the
fuck outta here.'

I look at it, not to read it, but to kill time.

'Ain't nothin' – just something saying that I got
here with my shit and everything's okay.'

I look at the dumpster. Five hundred and fifty
bucks for a dirty steel box, suitable only for hauling
crap.

An old van pulls up. It looks like an auctioned-
off cop van. It still has some of the old NYPD

markings on it, but there's a rack with ladders on the roof and a big padlock on the back. Two men slide out of the passenger door. I recognize them from old jobs – Vlad the Toothless and Roman the Scarred. Vlad stops on the sidewalk and looks up the wall. Roman heads to the back of the van. The driver points at him.

'That the chief?'

I shrug. He nods and does his ape strut over to Roman, who's unlocking the back. 'Hey, brother!' He waves the sheets at Roman, who ignores him and opens the doors. One by one, small brown men climb out of the back and gather around the stoop. Roman claps his hands like he's introducing a troop of performers. When they're all by the stoop, he points to one, whistles, and dangles keys in the air. The man takes them. Roman points at the makeshift plywood door up the stairs, whistles, and waves him up. He points to two more men, then to the van. He barks, 'Let's go!' They break rank and disappear into the van.

I hear the distant church bell clang. It's eight. No carpenters. No foreman, just the masons. I cross the street and head for the stoop. Vlad greets me.

'My friend, can I help you?'

'I'm here to work.'

'You need job. You need work?'

His voice is remarkably gruff, a smoky belch-bark, but he smiles, wide. He only has a few molars left, and his gums are gray but for some reason

182

it's not unpleasant to look at. The soft flesh tempers his voice, almost makes me believe that there is good nature in his smile.

'I have work.' I point at the wavering facade.

Vlad shrugs his shoulders and looks away. 'I don't know, amigo.' He whistles at Roman, who's fumbling with keys, trying to lock the back of the van. They meet beside it, then walk a few paces, whispering in Polish as though I understand what they're saying. They break. Roman whistles at me. Vlad walks past me – no smile – and slides across the front of the van into the driver's seat.

'My friend! Amigo!' Roman stands in his place, waving to me, ever quickening.

'Inglés? English?' I remember now. He shouts everything. No one can move fast enough for him – not even himself. He has a wide keloid scar that starts at the inside of his right eyebrow and travels diagonally across his nose, his cheek, down to his neck, then turns back, stopping atop his Adam's apple. *'Cancer!'* He'd told me years ago. *'I go home, they take it out!'*

He pats his clothes for his cigarettes. He doesn't find them. He grimaces, stretching the skin on his face, making his scar look like it will tear open. He relaxes, squints, trying to remember what he did with them. His eyes open again, wide, as though he didn't know I was there. He waves me off.

'Go in! Work!'

I climb the stairs to the top of the stoop and look into the open doorway. There's nothing inside – no framing, no stairs, no roof, no back wall. Just a ditch with three rotten joists below and a rigged extension ladder going down two stories to a rough cellar slab. The small brown men are already down there with shovels, a pick, and a sledge. Roman comes up the stairs behind me.

'What? Get down! You want to work, go down!'

He's carrying empty joint compound buckets, two stacks of four. He pushes them to me.

'Throw them down, amigo!'

I take them, turn, and feel for the first rung with my foot.

'My friend, no!'

I look up at him. He spreads his arms in mock exasperation and hisses a short blast of breath.

I climb down with the buckets, with my bag. It doesn't seem like a true descent because of the missing back wall. The big sun has already risen above the young sumacs and the one-story warehouse. It's gotten about ten degrees hotter than when I first stepped outside. There aren't any clouds to be seen.

When I reach the slab, Roman barks something incoherent from above. He's found his cigarettes. He lights one with a Zippo – that was it, he used to always watch his men work while playing with his lighter. He was always preceded by its clicking and the butane smell. I can't smell it down in the hole, not only because it rises, but because the ditch is an amphitheater of stench: the mustiness of the walls – years of water seeping or evaporating out of the failed mortar joints – the dank foundation wall, and the stink of the urine-stained weeds in the back garden.

'Okay, amigos! Vamanos!' yells Roman, checking his watch. 'The truck comes to pour at three!'

I look up at the wavering front wall. I wonder how I will breathe down here. I look at the other men. They don't seem concerned with anything, and this momentarily dispels the sense of danger. There are six of them, ranging in size from small to tiny. They seem familiar with each other, but they don't seem to be friends, countrymen even, just coworkers, set to dig in an airless ditch in the summer heat. If they do share anything, it is a culture of bravery. And since I find myself wavering, eyeballing my escape – up the rickety ladder – I figure I could use a dose of that culture. We're all brown and we are all, at least in part, New World Indians. We have that. That is where we begin.

The remaining joists are about five and a half feet above the existing slab. I imagine that they'd want seven feet clear from floor to ceiling. Four inches of concrete and a foot and a half of dirt in a seventeen-by-forty lot – fifty-one cubic yards of shit in seven hours. Mr Simian drops the container outside on the street. The front wall shakes. Dust and bits of mortar fall down on us. I look up. Although the exterior course of bricks bellies out toward the street, the interior course bellies in.

185

He drops the front end of the dumpster. A piece of brick about the size of a walnut lands at my feet. The six men look at each other. One very young-looking one looks up at me.

'Big man.'

He sucks his teeth and shakes his head. He's very slender, jockey sized but without that wiry toughness. He has a little round brown face and the faintest trace of a mustache. His black hair is close cropped, almost military.

'Big man.' He's an alto. His voice is unaffected by smoke or yelling. It's thin and soft like his body. He throws me an open-mouthed smile. His teeth look like uncooked arborio rice – ovaline, pearlescent, and little – spaced too far apart.

'Mithter big man . . . ,' another says. I can't see his face very well. His back is to the light. He's painfully small. I stoop and squint. They all laugh like we're in some spaghetti western. I'm the bastardized Eastwood – Blondie, that's what Tuco called him in one – and I'm about to be initiated into a band of desperadoes, Mexican banditos. But I don't know where these men, if they do have a common nationality, are from. They're all short. None of them is taller than my shoulder. They're all brown with dark hair. They're all in a filthy, dark, hot hole looking at me. They've named me. I must name them now. He Has Rice Teeth. I concentrate on the four remaining: He Has One Eyebrow, He Has Big Boots, He Is So Small – Too Tiny. The last one is the largest. He has a goatee and he scowls at me and at the ditch as though he has a stomachache and we're the cause. He Who Must Grimace. We've schematized each other. The naming is complete; although I know the names are too long, too formal, they will do for now. What's the harm in labeling for expedience's sake, anyway?

'Hey!' Roman bellows from the stoop, accompanying himself with crisp claps. 'Amigo!' He points in my general direction. 'Yes you! Use the hammer!' He claps again, then gestures to the rest. 'Take it away!' He whistles while pointing at the door below the stoop. 'Take it out here! I open! Start!'

Rice Tooth thumbs at the sledge that is lying on the slab.

'Amigo, we start. Hablo español?'

'Un picitto.'

'Okay. You.' He walks away from me to the south-west corner of the lot and stands in a strip of light about two feet wide. 'Hit here.'

I pick up the hammer. Surprisingly enough, it's new. It has a yellow fiberglass handle and a shiny black head. The label is still on the top – 'Collins Axe, 10 lbs.' Rice Tooth waves me over to the spot.

'Okay, here.' The others move in and ring me, some in the dark, some push their way into the piss bush outside. I raise the hammer and let it fall. Nothing. Not a crack or even a broken bit, only a light click on impact. No one reacts. We all agree that it was only a test.

I slide my hands down the handle toward the bottom and narrow the gap between them. I swing again and get the resonate thud we all expect. I've cracked the slab, but they seem, especially Rice Tooth, disappointed, as though they'd wanted something more from me. I want to tell them that I haven't swung a hammer in a while, and that in a batting cage or at the driving range, your first few swings are bound to be somewhat wanting. I don't say anything. I lift the hammer again and bring it down harder. It doesn't seem to do anything to lift their spirits so I put a little body behind the next one. It hits with considerably more force, but they still don't give me anything. I wave them away from me. I lean the handle against my leg and wipe my hands on my shorts, then rub them together. I grab the end of the shaft with my left hand, stretch down low and choke the neck with my right. I pull it behind me, standing up as I do, letting the momentum almost lift me off my feet. As I start my downswing, I let my right hand slide down the shaft to meet my right. The lot booms on impact and the slab cracks for three feet.

'Good, amigo.' Rice Tooth directs me to the end of the crack and points. 'Hit it there.' I do. The crack continues. He goes to point to the next spot but I wave him off and bring the hammer down. I go back to the beginning. Grimace is waiting with a pry bar.

We move east to west across the width of the building, always just ahead of the light. I hit, they pry, gather, and haul. I've acclimated to the stink, the heat, the lack of oxygen. Rice Tooth and Grimace pull the chunks away. I keep a consistent line going, then break off a chunk every two feet. It's important not to pulverize the slab because they'd have to stop and take the time to shovel the bits away. I can hear the blocks thud against the steel bottom of the container. They seem comfortable with my tempo, that my aim won't waiver, that I'll hit the right spot, not their hands, not their heads. They must trust me with their bodies, and so I lock into the rhythm – I give them three seconds to clear before I swing; they wait three to dive in.

We reach the midpoint. Rice Tooth comes out of his crouch and holds a hand up for me to stop. Eyebrow's just gotten off the ladder, and he whistles over to him. He points to a hose attached to a spigot on the front wall. Everyone else stops and drifts over to the water. I don't. I can feel the sun on my calves. I swing again, moving faster than before because I don't have to wait for the others. It's bad form, I know, to work during a scheduled break, but I need to keep going. I'll stop when I reach the north wall. Then there will be another task, and perhaps another to keep the day moving and my mind still – locked into duty. I feel the weight of the hammer and swing, hear its no-sound as it goes by my ear – just movement – and then the crack-boom as it meets the slab. I hear the dribbling of water from their mouths, louder still when they pass the hose along to the next man.

Someone mutters something in Spanish, and they all chuckle in a nasty way, like people who claim to mean no harm but still want to have their fun – briefly and without zeal. I throw my hips into the next swing and the greater impact shuts them up. I let go with another and another and I'm up against the west wall. I take a step forward onto the rubble. I can't get a footing so I keep moving north – to the corner. I raise the hammer, forgetting about the joists above, and catch it on the backswing. It skips back a tick on the foundation. A cloud of splintery dust surrounds me. After it's apparent that the beam won't fall, they laugh, this time with greater commitment. I turn sideways to swing along the length of the beams. I don't think. I just somehow know that the hammer is going up then down. It meets the ground, seemingly without impact, like one of those little league swings when you think that you've closed your eyes but you haven't, and you don't feel the bat hitting the ball. The ax head bounces off the slab. I catch it, cocked and ready to swing again. There's a crash behind me. I turn. We all see a pile of bricks. We look up, scanning the interior course until the void is found – above the center window, three stories up. I smell butane.

'Amigo.'

Roman leans in the door under the stoop one

flight above me. He surveys the wall, up and down, reliving the brick's descent.

'Amigo, don't do that.'

He looks over the uncovered earth, nods to himself, then looks at Rice Tooth.

'Why do you stop?'

'Agua. Mui caliente.'

'Agua. Agua.' Roman waves his hand as though shooing away a pest. 'More agua?'

'No, boss.'

'Okay. Vamanos!' He whistles and points at me, then to my tool bag. 'You have drill? Hammer?'

I nod. He points out to the former garden, beyond the first row of pissweeds.

'Wood!' He gestures, pulling his arms into his gut, then spreading them out as though smoothing out a tablecloth over the area of the joists. He snaps at Rice Tooth, then points to the pick and shovels. He whistles and waves his arms in the air, the signal for work to begin again.

It smells worse out in the open air. Even the sunlight seems to stink. The first line of weeds is about ten feet deep, then there's a pile of trash – dirt, drywall, insulation, bottles, cans, cardboard, and newspaper. A mattress – rain soaked and dried and resoaked many times over. I collect what usable wood I find – jagged 2x4s and 2x6s, soggy and ridden with twisted and rusty nails; random plywood shapes – and bring them back in.

If I remember anything about Roman it's that it would be stupid to ask him about screws, so I

191

salvage what nails I can, bend them straight. His crew used to show up on jobs needing to build concrete forms without tools or fasteners or wood. Most of the carpenters would grumble when the masons asked to borrow something, but fuck, it was rumored that even the Polish guys, the skilled masons, got only room, board, and a few bucks a day to live on. I can't imagine that these men could have received tool-buying wages. Why would they invest in their careers? An old-timer once explained that their standard of living had been so low that anything they dealt with here was better than what they had had – wherever it was they'd come from – and that they were sending it back or hoarding it here to take back when they left for good. I look at Grimace filling the first bucket. I try to imagine him living on, let alone investing in his future with, ten bucks a day. I do my best to tie the three joists together so they won't roll. I find more nails in the beams and pull them out. Then I lay what remaining lumber I have perpendicular to the first row and cover it with all the irregular sections of plywood – about fifteen square feet altogether. Roman clicks his lighter in the doorway as I sink the last nail; this time he lights a cigarette.

'Is it good, finished?'

I nod and extend my arm, inviting him out onto the staging. He sticks his head in the doorway, looks the platform over, and toes it.

'Okay!'

He gives me a wrinkled chin nod. Then he checks his watch and taps it.

'Okay, go down.' He pats my shoulder and then makes a flicking motion with his hand at the ladder. I climb down. Five of the buckets are full at the bottom. Tiny and Eyebrow scramble up. Roman whistles at me, gives a thumbs-up sign, then shoots it over his shoulder.

'Let's go!'

I press a bucket up. Tiny grabs the handle, but it tips forward as he lifts, dumping a good shovel full of dirt in my face.

'Sorry, mithter.' He does look sorry. It's not a joke to him. His brow is wrinkled with concern, making his already little face seem to shrink into its center. I shouldn't call him Tiny. I'll call him Lispy, short for Speaks with Lisp. I press a second bucket up. Eyebrow grabs it – more spilled dirt, although I realize now that it's not really dirt; it's more like clay. It's damp and reddish and has a distinct odor, though I can't place it. It doesn't belong here, not with the rat and must and ammonia and rotting vegetation.

I pick up a bucket, but Lispy isn't back from dumping the first one, so I slide it onto the plywood. I put the remaining two up. Rice Tooth drops another one at my feet, which I immediately lift and place. Lispy comes back and sighs at the work waiting for him. It doesn't pay, really, for any of us to be efficient, to work any harder than we need. It's just that I haven't established

193

that line of need. Vlad has given us an ultimatum, but the brown men don't seem to be taking it all too seriously. Grimace and the lads have barely shoveled anything. I do the math. A five-gallon bucket holds .785 cubic feet of dirt, which means there's about thirty-four and a half buckets per cubic yard, one thousand three hundred seventy-six or so to fill a forty-yard dumpster. At one minute per bucket, it would take twenty-two hours to fill the container. We're moving about one bucket every ninety seconds. Eight buckets. Nine. If I stand to the side and push it up over one shoulder, Eyebrow and Lispy let the dirt fall only to the side I'm not on – it's a tacit agreement. I slow down, let the buckets collect at my feet, a small concession, but it seems to do a lot for them. Their pace evens out, so much so that I don't have to look or even listen for them. I count their steps in my head, eighteen for Eyebrow, twenty-one for Lispy, then into the container where they each set their bucket down, lift again, and dump. They rest. Then back inside, out of the sun, and onto the platform from which they drop their bucket onto the damp clay beside me, where Rice Tooth picks it up, brings it back to the diggers, picks up a filled one, brings it to me; I hoist it. Thirty buckets. It seems we're moving faster now. The sun is full on their backs. Grimace wields the pick, loosening the clay for Bigboots, who chops and scoops and drops it into the bucket. He works cleanly, squaring the earth as he goes. They all

194

work with an economy, without desperation, little bend in their backs – the eugenics of excavation. I lift another bucket, number forty.

Bigboots stabs his spade into a pile of dirt but doesn't pick it up. Rice Tooth turns away from his bucket. Grimace buries the pick head and starts beating the dust off his pant legs. Lispy and then Eyebrow come down. Lispy turns on the spigot. The hose lurches, filled with water. He picks it up and holds it for the others as they, one by one, rinse their faces and hands. Rice Tooth turns to me.

'Big man. Mange?'

Lispy pushes the hose at me, signaling that he'll keep holding it. I walk over and extend my hands. He splashes my forearms, then my palms. Under the water the clay gets gooey and sticks to my skin, then loosens and runs off. It's now more like fine silt, noticeably discrete particles. I wash my face. The water is cold, and it seems to erase the morning's work. I take the hose from Lispy and hold it for him. He washes, nods thanks, and shuts the water off.

We all climb up and out and enter the light one by one. We gather on the sidewalk, squinting. Grimace shoots his thumb in the direction of Third Avenue and starts walking. They all follow. I don't. They pass Roman, who's leaning against a street sign a few houses down. I sit on the stoop. I look at my arms. I didn't do a very good job cleaning – no matter, I'm not eating. I try to picture Delilah's face, what it would've done if I hadn't gotten her drinks last night. What it would've done if I hadn't walked her home. It doesn't come. Claire's voice does – over the phone, singing 'Happy Birthday' with the kids, then taking the phone for herself and saying, 'Happy birthday. We all love you,' and then the pause. It must be some kind of defense mechanism I have that prevents me from seeing her face – the face she makes when I tell her everything's cool, the face she'd make when I tell her I'm digging a ditch for Roman and Vlad.

I know it's Johnny Little Nancyboy because of the truck. It's a dark blue pickup and it's new, but it's just like the one he used to have. It's clean and he parks it in the same way – up on the curb, as though he's on official business and has a permit to do so.

He gets out. He's aged since I last saw him. He wears his cap forward now, and it's no longer the Mets – just a logo. He's put on weight, about fifteen extra pounds, and it doesn't suit him well. He's short, but he used to be wiry and hard, like an angry weasel. Now he looks more like a well-fed squirrel, until he opens his mouth. He still sounds like an angry little bastard.

'Qué pasa, homey? The Polaki treatin' you right?' Johnny always seemed to think that because of who and what he was – an Irish Puerto Rican from Queens – he could spit out racial epithets

196

and ethnic slurs with impunity, although around me, he stayed away from the ones that disparaged blacks.

'Just shittin' ya.' He takes his phone out of its holster and flips it open. He stares at the screen, whatever's on it, closes it, and puts it back.

'So, professor, I was just stopping by to check in. Things going all right?' He doesn't wait for an answer. He walks up the stoop and pokes his head in.

'Professor. You're gonna be a professor. That's cool.'

He had been my assistant on the old crew. We'd just installed a door jamb – trimless mahogany – and he was bringing the door over.

'So what will they call you?'

'Who?'

'Your students.'

'Professor.'

'What, that's like one up from mister and one under doctor?'

'I suppose.'

'Do I have to call you professor?'

That was what I thought to be my last day in construction. I gave him my old chisel set.

'Looks okay.' I find it hard to believe that he, in the years since I last saw him, back when he had difficulty cutting lumber square, had learned much at all. He was a high-strung little pothead, ready to fight with anyone. I guess the kids in his neighborhood had picked on him, given him his nickname.

'You free tomorrow, you got anything going on?'

'Yeah, I'm free.'

'Cool. Cool. Call you at that same number? You got a cell?'

'That number's fine.'

He goes to pat me on the shoulder but thinks better of it.

'Let me know if I can do anything.'

I don't say anything. He has his back to me. He does a quarter turn and picks up his phone again.

'How's the old lady? You still . . .'

'She's fine.'

He looks up from the phone and flips it shut. He looks down at me under the visor as though he's my baseball coach and I'm back on the bench after taking a called third strike down the middle. He gets back in his truck, starts it up, and rolls down the window. He shoots me a salute.

'All right, professor.'

He eases off the curb and drives away.

I see the crew returning with lunch. I go back inside and drink. The water takes the edge off my hunger. Someone outside starts beeping maniacally. Now that I'm alone, I look at the west wall, the rubble foundation and the bricks stacked atop it. The brick rows are stratified and look like a fossil record – the horizontal joints and old floor lines – but one that's been upset, the history scattered about in seemingly random sections delineated by mold and watermarks. That which was once uniform and strong is now a patchwork of stain and erosion.

A realtor once showed us a house nearby, much the same as this. The only question she'd asked me was *'Are you Native American?'* I didn't respond. Claire did, with a question. *'Why?'* she'd asked in high defense mode, ready to become as offensive as she possibly could. *'Because Native Americans built these homes. They built a good amount of the Heights and Lower Manhattan. They built these row houses to live in.'* Claire hadn't believed her but asked, *'Which tribe?'* to be polite. She seemed relieved somewhat that the woman, a mousy little WASP, had at least some story to support her curiosity. *'Mohawk. The Mohawk Indians built these.'* Claire spoke for me again, *'He's Cherokee and Apache,'* taking my wrist and squeezing it, then sliding her hand into mine. *'Wow,'* the broker looked up at me and let me watch her watch me as though she'd suddenly understood something about me, something that allowed her to stare. When we got outside, Claire stopped, pulled my head down to her, and kissed me long and unrepentantly. *'Dumb bunny – don't mind her.'* And she did it again and pressed herself against me. We didn't know it then, but C was about the size of a kidney bean inside of her. We walked to the pizzeria, and she bought lemon ices for us. And when that didn't seem to cheer me up, she asked,

'*What's wrong with my guy?*' and then not waited for an answer.

We walked back to the house and she asked, '*Do you think we'll be able to buy a place someday?*' She looked up at the crooked facade, perhaps dreaming. '*Sure,*' I said. And she smiled. That was it. That was all it seemed to take to make her happy – my word. I've always felt afraid for my wife because she could never understand how empty the spoken word is, how lacking her remedial care was – that the flavored ice in the little cup did nothing for me.

She was not the girl – not the girl I'd been expecting, not the girl I'd imagined, not the one who would love me. She was white and full of the courage, confidence, and apprehension that only white girls can have – nonempirical, ignorant of the stakes. I was only a year sober when I met her. Gavin and I had just finished performing – he read some poems; I played some of my songs – and the two of us were feeling fairly invincible, so we walked into a bar – not to drink, only to be around people our age. She was sitting with her friends in a chocolate brown banquette – epiphanic. She looked back at me. Gavin whispered under his breath, '*Uh-oh,*' and everything in her face told me no. She was not the one. I'd thought about it quite a bit as a boy. And although I didn't know what she looked like, I knew she wasn't white, wasn't soft, didn't cry – at least, not so easily. Perhaps she drank a bit and sang. Okay, yes, like my mother, but literate, free. And when I was older and started to wonder if that girl existed, I found liquor and Gavin. Alcoholism and fraternal love seemed to suit me better, perhaps because with a best friend, when you're drunk, you don't have to do anything. You can just, if you like, watch it all go by.

She was not the one. I kept telling myself that after we joined her and her friends and made them laugh with PG-rated versions of our childhoods. It was really quite awful, that evening, the sober ethnics entertaining the tipsy WASPs in a dive bar. We closed the place and then lingered out on Third Avenue, trying to keep the night alive. We exchanged phone numbers. She called me a few days later from the street and said she would pick up lunch and stop by. For some reason, I allowed it. Claire's eyes are oxidized lime green. They're oversized, oval, and slant slightly from the outside corners to the bridge of her nose. They're the first things anyone notices. They're ridiculous, actually, how obvious they are. But her face is girlish, open, juxtaposed to that cool, electric green. The charge they have seems to come from a place that's ancient and far away, but she isn't distant. The rose hue of her cheeks, her long, crooked lips warm her – I can smell them. She is present, and that, to me, has always made her seem good. 'Hello,' she said so quietly, but clearly, barely moving her mouth. She was not the one, not the one that I'd imag-ined, not the face of love – standing in the dim hallway of my tenement walk-up, or on the street carrying our child. I still don't know if it was her eyes or her face that made me let her into my rooms, or made me take her by the hand, look to the wall, the twisted door and window openings, and say, *'Us Indians sure make crappy homes.'*

The crew comes back inside. Inca. Aztec, Mayan – who knew? We're building someone else's house.

'Amigo,' says Rice Tooth. 'Amigo, you hungry?'

He offers me a foil dish full of rice and beans, perhaps a collection of everybody's leftovers. And even though I can't stand pinto beans, I salivate. But I like my food to be segregated into discrete portions, and I can't eat around strangers.

'Gracias, no.'

He shrugs and puts it by the hose. Everyone seems to be sleepy, and they drag slowly to their stations. Roman clicks from above.

'Not good, amigos.' He walks back out muttering, 'Now I have to cancel truck.'

'Hey, big man.' It's Grimace. I don't move quickly enough for him. He gives a shrill whistle. I turn slowly, hoping that by the time I'm facing him I won't snatch the shovel from him and bust his head with it.

'Hey, big man.' He taps on something hard. It's a rock, half buried. It looks like the partially excavated skull of an ancient giant.

'Can you lift?'

I shrug my shoulders. I forget my size – how others must see me. He taps at the dirt around it. The others start to gather. He points at Big Boots to pick around the stone. Together they clear enough of it to get a pry bar and spade under it. They roll it out of its hole and onto the clay. Big Boots drops the bar, bends down, and tries once to roll it with his hands. It's almost the size of his torso. It doesn't budge. He stands up shaking his head and backs off.

'Big man.' Grimace inhales and flexes, then mimes pressing it over his head and throwing it out into the pissweeds. 'Diez dineros.' He whistles softly and cocks his head to the back. Lispy has moved beside me. He starts nodding his head, slowly at first, then with growing earnest. '*Si. Si.*' He sizes up the stone and looks up at me.

'Mui grande,' says Grimace, trying to bait me. I don't know what kind of stone it is, how dense it is. It's light gray. I bend and touch it. It's cool and silt covered – nothing to really grab hold of. I dig my hands into the clay to get them underneath. Grimace chuckles. The rest begin the obligatory audience murmur. I get it up to my waist and stand erect. My grip is awkward, though – flat palmed. I try to wrap my forearms under it, but it doesn't work. I start to feel the strain in my lower back. My biceps start to burn. I roll it a quarter turn and rest it against my stomach. It's better on the back for the moment, but now, because of the silt, it threatens to slide

203

between my arms and crush a knee or a foot. I get my hands, one at a time, back around to the outsides, bend, and press. The murmurs turn to yelps. *'Over your head!'* demands Grimace, and so I press – up, up – until I can lock my elbows. *'Throw!'* squeals Lispy. I start shuffling across the clay to the back. I make it to the edge of the piss-weeds and push it in. The lads give a cheer – even Grimace. He walks up to me, nodding his bowed head. He straightens, reaches in his pocket, and pulls out a sweaty ten.

'You are very strong.' He flexes again and hands me the money.

'Gracias.'

He waves his hand, puckers his mouth, shakes his head, and returns to his spade. I look out to the piss weeds – the break in them caused by my missile. I wonder what the rock would've done to my skull if I'd dropped it, and I wonder who would've been able to tell my kids, my wife. 'Vamanos!' bellows Roman from the stoop. He walks out again. Lispy gives him the finger. The others laugh, and then we all go back to work.

The sun has caught the east wall. I'm sure whatever it reveals is much the same as what it had shown before on the other wall. I don't want to look. It's time to go. Half the cellar has been excavated. They wash. I don't.

'Okay, amigos,' says Lispy, taking the lead. I shake all their hands, even Grimace's, and climb out. Vlad has arrived. He's standing behind the van with the doors open, waiting for his cargo. I go to him.

'Anything for me?'

'No, amigo.'

I look at him, questioning. He shakes his head as if to strengthen his denial. Roman joins in. They both shift and shake and look as concerned and friendly as they can.

'You need to see the boss,' says Roman. 'You need to see Johnny. He knows.'

'He knows?'

Now they both nod in unison, smiling – Roman with his expanding scar, Vlad with his gray gums. I shoulder my bag and leave.

I have gas pains from not eating. I have enough change for coffee and, if they give it to me, some kind of biscuit. The coffee shop's bagels and muffins are inedible; the bagel store's coffee is undrinkable. If I buy a bagel first and I'm not offered a coffee later . . . but if I buy a coffee first, I'll have to bring it to the bagel store, which would be rude. I like the people who work there, and I don't want to offend. I decide to get coffee. Then I remember the ten I just won. I should eat something. I go to the bodega behind the projects. A blonde pillhead is outside.

'Hey, papi.'

She tries to open the door for me, but she's too shaky. It's hard for her to grab the handle, and when she finally does, she hasn't the strength to move it. She's detoxing hard. I can see her skull through her translucent skin. All the blood seems to be collecting there. It's about to burst.

I nod to her, go in, and make my way to the coolers in the back. Bud is on sale. Six bucks for a rack of talls. I grab one and go to tear a can off. The sensation of the cold metal shoots up my arm like a fix. I take my one can and back away. A voice calls from the front.

'Can you keep that closed?'

I come out of my shock and peer down the aisle to the front. Airborne dust lingers in what little light that has made it through the fogged-out storefront. The old linoleum is gritty. There isn't much for sale here – cold beer, warm beer, soda, bottled juice from concentrate, junk food that may have reached the end of its long shelf life on which the dust has settled. I see the clerk now. Hiding behind a rack of gum and candy. I take a single and bring it quickly to the front.

He comes out of hiding. He's only a teen – light skinned and chubby. Behind him is a Budweiser clock and a painting of the crucifixion. Jesus is white, blond. He looks more bored than pained. Next to him is an outdated promotional poster for a liqueur in which a honey-skinned, green-eyed woman in a bikini asks, 'What are you doing tonight?' I take a roll of antacid and place it beside the beer.

'Three.'

I don't do anything – a strategy to make him recalculate my tab. He senses this and cuts to the point. He points at the Rolaids. 'One.' He points at the beer. 'Two.' He taps the counter. 'Three.' I keep staring at the crucifixion. He tries to further explain.

'It's only on sale if you get the six-pack.'

I give him the ten. He drops seven singles on the counter.

He reaches underneath the counter and produces a small bag, which he snaps open and places the beer carefully inside.

'All right, buddy.'

I want to respond, with something highbrow and long-winded, but I think of the girl outside, if her head has exploded. For her sake I let it go.

The pillhead tries to open the door for me again. I let her believe that she has. She backs up to let me step through the small opening. I hold out my hand and show her a dollar bill and some change. She does her best to focus on the money and then looks up at me, questioning. She has a wandering eye – the left one. It looks glass until I see the moisture on it. It finally fixes on something in the sky.

I hand her the beer. The crazy eye snaps down to focus on it.

'Papi.' Her hands are shaking. She has a deep lesion on one of her forearms. I open the beer for her. The ritual freezes the both of us for an instant. I give it to her.

'Thank you.'

'You're welcome.'

Someone, I don't remember who, once said while extending his index finger, 'A normal person's soul is like this.' He bent it and said, 'The soul of an alcoholic is like this. Drinking makes the alcoholic feel that his soul,' straightening his finger again, 'is like this.'

Kali made me feel that way for a little while – right, unbroken – but the few sharp memories I have make me feel wrong. She had the power to make one compelled to act: begin a punishing diet and exercise regime, learn another language, or lose oneself at the bottom of the river. Once, before we were married, Claire found Kali's picture inside a book, and was made to feel so inadequate that she was willing to give me back to her. She gasped – looking from the photo to me, while her face steadily drained of blood – wondering where this woman was and how she would figure in our lives to come.

Kali ruined me. That's what I said to myself after I had taken a drink; the first in some time. I'd just grunted to myself, *I'm not drinking 'cause of some girl.* After I had sex for the first time, I left Kali's room and went down to the river, hoping that the movement of the dark water would replace, in my mind, the tableau that wouldn't leave: Kali and I standing naked, facing each other, my penis in her lightly calloused hands.

I decided after Sally that I would never be with a white girl again. Brian said he thought it was racist. Shake nodded his head in agreement and chuckled to himself. Gavin said, *'That's good, I suppose, if you see the world in that way.'*

The summer after graduating high school I met a girl, a woman – Jenny – *a black woman*. I was working in the stockroom of one of those giant liquor stores, lost in perpetual amazement of the inventory. She was a receptionist at the travel agency next door and was a few years older. She was short, had bright caramel skin and her hair was pulled long by the hot iron. She never needed to twist it with her fingers or look away shyly. She cut my nervous rambles short by abruptly turning away, or stepping, like a boxer, to quickly cut the distance between us, press close to my chest and look up steeply to kiss me.

It was, of course, a disaster. That awful paradox of being good and prodigal: I had been born to lead my people, but also to find a hardworking black woman, like my mother, as she'd been instructing me to do most of my life. Jenny fit, but I wasn't ready. Whenever she got close to me my anus would burn, or I'd think I was choking. I must have seemed insane to her. In a quiet moment when I was closing up, she came to the back of the store and told me that I was a repressed homosexual and that I should do something about it. After Jenny I decided that I would eliminate all race of woman and girl. When I told Gavin about it, he asked me if I might be gay. I told him I didn't think so, I just didn't like being so close to people. He nodded and said that it was probably for the best – '. . . *heard melodies sweet, right?*'

I stuck with that – it's easier than most would think – virginal abstinence. In high school there had been plenty of sex to avoid; in college there was more, and without my friends to hide behind. Shake had left for New York, Brian went away to the Midwest for school, and Gavin went on monthly benders. I had stopped drinking with him, partly out of some quasihonor, but mostly because his ma had screamed at me that I was helping him die. So every once in a while he'd show up, trembling, and we'd go out and consume just about every non-alcoholic beverage in Harvard Square, twitchily reminisce, and watch the students and hipsters our age prepare to fuck. Sometimes we'd be asked to join, but we'd refuse and the inviters would look perplexed. He'd sketch me and I would write a poem about the girl at the next table or the old drunk out in the street. Sometimes we'd go down to the river and I'd play him a song. Gavin always seemed to be able to listen to things deeply – more than a polite audience – he was engaged.

The Halloween night, sophomore year, after an unremarkable first two semesters of academic probation and athletic withdrawal we were on the MIT bridge, looking west up the Charles, listening to the sounds of revelry traveling downstream.

We hadn't said much all evening. He leaned forward over the rail as though he wanted to roll over it, but he only inhaled deeply, straightened, and still looking down said, *'I wonder if the toasts we made were heard and granted – if this is oblivion.'*

Then he had another fall and somehow went from the public detox to a mental hospital, and I didn't see him for months. I avoided everything. I remember the strange feeling of being both conspicuous and peripheral – an outside insider – not at all prepared for claiming and maintaining a place within the loop. I was waiting – test scores and potential aside – to be revealed as a fraud. I went for long runs along the Charles. It had seemed different when I was boy – hopelessly polluted, something to be avoided – but now, traveling it's narrow paths afforded me a quiet timelessness in which I seemed to move freely.

Then I saw Kali. Something had told me to turn. There used to be a little ice cream shop just off the main drag of the square and I watched her go inside – the big window – point at the board and then the flavor in the case like she was in a silent movie scene, but with vivid color. I could even see the faint yellow tint of her lemon sorbet – her first lick. She was a *'terrible beauty'* whose existence confirmed for me that there was both an *immortal hand and eye.* I got caught up in her symmetry and she was gone.

I looked for her, waited across from the ice cream shop, drifted around the perimeter of the yard, waited outside thrift stores I thought she might be browsing in, and searched from my dorm room window, while my roommate, a pimply hockey player from Maine, watched with suspicion. I hated him, but I almost confided in him because I didn't know what to do. I drank and waited; wound up hospitalized for exposure, wandering through the late streets of wintry Cambridge and Boston, trying to figure out what to say to a girl like that, trying to be near her and make her want to be near me.

I tried to imagine her life at school: how she spoke, how she moved. I wondered if she was as alone as I. The other black students. I thought, regarded me with suspicion, because I seemed to have no concrete reason to be there. I wondered how she appeared to them. *Ah, the promised few*: what a horrible burden. There's a limited amount of space for people, any people, anywhere. And on the inside of any powerful institution, especially for people of color, that space gets smaller and stranger. Most white folks believe the reason you've come in is to lift up your people. But you can't bring your people inside, except compressed into a familiar story that's already been sanctioned. And you wouldn't be there in the first place unless you were a recognizable type: the noble savage, Uncle Tom, the Afro-Centric, the Oreo, the fool. Those students made sense, but Kali, I thought, was different – an artist – and her crippling beauty seemed to refract the images around her into new things.

I remember realizing that she may not be a student – may have only been a visitor. The thought made me stop and sit at one of the chess tables in the middle of the square. It was a bleak November afternoon – straining, futile sun – and I was skipping another class, not wanting to hear the mumbling TA paraphrase someone else's thought about Joyce. She appeared on the corner. I saw the blood-red wool hat first, then the long, dark coat, then her face – dark brown and regal. I knew I could never speak to her, or get near her because I would die, but I followed her down the side street and into a coffee house. I sat, waited, and tried not to stare, but she caught me, twice. And the third time she waved me over. '*Sit down,*' she said – liquid alto and quiet. Her chiseled, dark face and wine lips made me float.

She was the one of course. Perhaps I was not: love and demographics. She's asked me about my poetry, but when I met her I had to throw out everything I'd ever written about Sally, because it seemed like boyish gibberish. She was politically radical, artistically progressive. And to others – whether or not they liked what she said or did – she made sense: the affect and content were whole. When I finally let her read the new poems I'd written, and she'd seen my confused reaction to her text-laden paintings; walked through the yard with her and felt the weight of observation on us – that we, as a couple, meant something – a burden we'd experienced alone, but as a couple,

213

exponentially so; when I held her hand on Massachusetts Avenue after three coffee dates, when she kissed my neck that night to say good-bye, I could tell I was no good. I watched how she moved, with ease and elegance through different circles – so unlike my nervous skittering. I know she found that skittering taxing. She couldn't understand why it was so hard for me to make it to classes, or sit on the grass in the green; why I never responded to invitations from instructors or the dean to *come chat.* And in that voice she'd say, *'This place and these things are for you.'* I still wonder if she believed that.

One night in her room she prepared for bed – moving things about, preparing for the next day – but after undressing she stopped, came to me and helped me take off my clothes. I had thought of us naked, but I could never get past the image of tracing the outline of her body with my palms, as though she was protected by an invisible field. *'Such a strange boy.'* She whispered with that voice in the near-dark, almost to herself. I wanted to say something back, but I didn't and went cold. When we lay down kissing, I became metalled. And when I entered her, I pushed in a mechanical way. I didn't move, I jerked in robotic spasm. And when I came, I finally felt our heat, my stillness. And I lay in the quiet horror of having been made flesh.

I did go see someone after that: Dean Richard Ray, and he shook his head faster and faster as if he was trying to give his words momentum before he threw them out at me. My collarbone was broken and I stared at his bloated turkey chin shaking to take my mind off the pain.

'You hit a police officer?'

I kept looking at his jowls as he kept shaking them. I didn't remember. I wanted to tell him. He took his glasses off and rubbed his face while sighing. I'd expected him to be angry, but his expression was blank. He looked at my arm in the sling and then a painting above my head – Sargent, I think. He opened my file, pretended to look at it, scanning it with a pen to guide him.

'We can't do anything for you.'

He closed my file and sat back in his chair. He pressed his hands together, as if in prayer, went back to the painting.

'Do you have anything to say?'

I tried my memory one more time even though I knew it was pointless. All I could come up with was a rushing montage of faces: Kali, Sally, my mother, which then gave way to a dull hum. I remembered the sound of my voice reading the acceptance letter to my mother, and her uncharacteristically jumping and clapping like a little girl. I was late for my visit. I hadn't brushed my teeth. They felt moldy. My mouth was hot and funky and I was trembling, clammy, itchy – worried that I was about to shit my pants with bile. The temperature in the room seemed to dip and rise.

'You don't understand . . .' was all that came

out – and that, although not what he was looking for, was probably the truest thing I could've said. *He didn't understand.* He concurred.

'No, I certainly do not.'

I left his office, left the building and the campus, and walked west along the Charles, growing angrier the whole way. Not that he'd kicked me out, not because he'd refused to understand, but that I had cried in front of him and he hadn't cared. What was that look he'd given me, Dean Ray, the white-haired jowl-beast, when I searched for the words to begin, didn't find them, and did nothing but huffed and wept? It wasn't pity for one of his suffering students, and it wasn't scorn. In the wood-paneled office, the old world had regarded the promise of the new – he looked at me like he had won. One more dumb nigger down.

'Baby, you don't look so good. Is there something wrong?'

My mother had taken to calling me baby since I'd started college. I couldn't let her know. Shake was waiting in the car outside. Most things in her life hadn't gone as she'd planned them, but she believed that I had – or that at least I was on the way. She was sitting in her chair, a teacher's wooden one that she'd gotten years before when one of the schools closed down. It was dark in the little room – winter dark of the late afternoon – but she left the light off, having her whiskey in the dimness. She'd been listening to Marvin Gaye.

And I'd arrived in time to hear his last plaintive wail. The needle was running on the record's blank spot, popping in the speakers. She reached out from her seat, across the room to my arm in the sling.

'Baby, what happened to you?'

'I was playing ball.'

'Well, you don't need to be doing that.' She pulled her arm back, groped for her drink on the table beside her. She found it and took a sip. 'You used to look like your father. Then you looked like me. Now . . .' she exhaled loudly, which made me question if she'd been breathing before. 'You know your friend got back in town awhile ago. He's been raising Cain.'

'I guess I'll go find him.'

'Why you gonna do that?'

'He's my friend.'

'Well, I guess that's what you have, huh? Hah!' Her cackle cracked in the dark. Then she waited for a response from me. 'What, baby? Ain't you gonna sit – stay for a while?' She didn't wait for me to answer. 'You know when you were young, a baby, you were so smiley.' She took another drink. 'What happened?'

When I get to Starbucks, Kelly points at a table in the front by the window and mouths, 'Sit,' to me. I do, bent over to relieve my stomach. I start to feel my body. I'm tired. My hands feel like they're swollen, getting more so all the time, and they want to close into a fist on their own. I flatten them, palms down, on the table.

'You look even tireder.' She sets a coffee down. 'Is that even a word?' I straighten up and think I feel my stomach lining tear. I suppose I grimace because she looks concerned.

'Baby, you all right?'

'Yeah. Just a little beat.'

She looks me over, my unwashed hands and arms and my filthy shirt.

'You're dirty.'

'Yeah.'

'Tsk, tsk, tsk,' she shakes her head. Raises her voice a half octave. 'You shouldn't be out looking like you do.'

'I know.'

'Take a bath.'

'Yes.'

'Get a massage.'

'Okay.'

'Have a nice dinner.'

'Sure.'

'Then go to bed.' She says this while starting to walk away. She stops. 'That's for free – the advice, too.'

'Thank you.'

'You hungry? We have some muffins we're just gonna throw away.'

'I'm good. Thank you.'

'Stop. You know I love you.'

She snaps her towel and leaves me. There's a

line forming. There always seems to be a four-thirty rush – postschool, postcamp, post-nanny. I remember this world, of strollers, cooing mothers, and sporadically employed fathers – alleged writers. I used to write in cafés before I had children.

Someone sneezes, and I sit up. There are two women seated in armchairs. Close to one is a small child sleeping in a stroller. The other woman has a toddler on her lap. He obviously has a cold. He has dried snot trails beneath his nostrils. She absentmindedly feeds him broccoli. He can't breath through his nose, so he inhales deeply with his mouth while pulping the florets.

I turn away. His mother says something that sounds like *'There's a lot of reciprocity in our relationship.'* I look out the big window to Dean Street, then to the corner of Court and beyond, to the south, across the dogleg intersection. There's a minivan waiting at the light. I can tell it's going to make the illegal dash, the wrong way across the intersection instead of turning right. *'Yeah,'* responds the first mother, *'I know exactly what you mean.'* I wonder if it's possible to quantify reciprocity – love. You either give back or you don't. You love or you don't. You drink or you don't. And that's the rub – the either or. I hope her partner excuses her abuse of language, the intellectual masquerade, the self-help quackery. What doesn't she give back? What is she capable of giving other than a limp screw and nonsense. Nonsense.

219

Her kid has climbed off her lap, blown a snot bubble, and now stumbles toward me. He waves at me. She beams as though he's achieved something. She warbles something, and he waddles back to her. She produces a bottle of juice and again is amazed when he takes hold of it and drinks.

'Is it good juice?' she asks, high-pitched and far too loud. He takes a break, nods, and then continues with his snuffle-sucking.

Sometimes my mother had to take me to work. She would put me in a chair, give me a book, and tell me not to move, not to make a sound. She'd do the same in stores and on buses. I listened to her, not because I was scared of being punished; it just always seemed the right thing to do – to make us both okay. Lila's wrath was terrible, but death was even worse, and a failure of wits, of equipoise, of dignity, a lack of quality was death: *Keep your black ass still or thou shalt die and not live.* I wonder if I've been too hard on my boys, especially C: having him sit up straight, chew with his mouth closed, and display a certain amount of dignity – as though he was going to face German shepherds and batons in Selma or cops behind Faneuil Hall. The stakes weren't that high anymore. How had it been passed on? I certainly was proud of him, privately, perhaps too much so – the privacy. They would sit and sip their hot chocolate, but is their fight mine? Was mine my parents? Was there really any fight at all save the fight against throwing oneself in? Claire would always try to intervene – when I'd be demanding that he swing the bat correctly, that he answer my questions clearly in both thought and diction – try to tell me that he was just a little boy. *Brown boy*, I'd grumble in my head. Sometimes he'd weep, and she'd ask me why I needed to drill him so and say this would come back to haunt me. *'He's just a little boy. You're probably halting his progress.'* And I'd say it – unrelenting – *'There is no dignity in progress. The dignity is the progress.'* And C is a *good boy – a sweet boy*. Content with whatever comes his way, which seems to me a fatal flaw. Brown boys have to be more – smarter, tougher, and possess a dignified tenacity.

The boy is back. He's pointing the broccoli-flecked nipple at me as an offering – the viscous trail on his lip. He grunts at me belligerently and makes a face like he's trying to pinch a hard one off. His mother isn't watching. I could probably get four blocks with him before she realized he was gone. I want to speak – *Madam, the boy needs discipline. So do you. You are cruel to the boy, and when he comes to adulthood, he'll realize that you robbed him of his chance to walk with dignity. He'll be snot-faced and wanting, needing to fudge all his data to convince himself he's not – that he is good. And where's the quality in that? No wonder the White House is full of cretins. There's no discipline, no dignity. We welcome the inept. We celebrate the mediocre and run in horror when we realize the effort required to be good and stay good – fuck!*

I'll give the little snot-faced kid this: He's tenacious, still hovering by my table, still pinch faced, waiting for my acknowledgment.

'Hey, kid.' I grunt like an old salt. The women, in unison, coo.

I look up. There's a woman on the corner. There's no traffic, but she's waiting to cross. The light changes. The minivan makes its move – diagonally across Court. When it reaches the opposite cross-walk, she steps off the curb and throws herself over the hood. The van stops. The driver gets out – a little man. Then I see Shaky. He's across the street, in front of the corner pub. He watches the driver with a flat affect. He rubs his hands together, points a finger in the air, and then sprints off the curb toward the scene. He looks like he's screaming, 'Hey, you!' Now he's pointing at the man, who fearfully shifts from his victim to Shaky to the gathering Samaritans, who will claim that they saw everything. Shaky traps him against the van and starts screaming in his face. The women in the easy chairs finally notice. 'What happened?' they ask each other, and then shake their heads in tandem. They look at me but don't ask – content to stare outside ignorantly.

Two firemen run up the hill and tend to the downed woman. A police car comes and stops in the middle of Court Street. The Samaritans recreate the crime with arm gestures. Now Shaky's just nodding – cooled off. The mother of the sleeping child mutters to her friend, 'Wrong way.

222

What an asshole.' Then tries to apologize for cursing with a shrug and a sheepish look.

I shoulder my bag and leave. I cross behind the scene and try to catch Shaky's eye. He doesn't look at me. I keep going.

CHAPTER 7

I hover over the change bowl in the kitchen. Marco has replenished it – dimes and nickels. I take a dollar seventy-five, enough for a slice or a sport bar. I go upstairs. On the desk are two cigars and a note.

> Meet me at 57th and 5th, 8:00. Bring the cigars.
>
> —Happy Birthday,
> M.
>
> p.s.
> If you don't mind, would you drive the car in? It's in the garage on Pacific. They're expecting you.
>
> Thanks,
> p.p.s.
> Claire called.

I'm ashamed for a moment because I'm excited, like a kid promised fast food. I get over it quickly. I shower, shampoo, shave, and leave the bathroom still wet, letting the water drops slowly evaporate in the air conditioning. I wouldn't walk around nude in my own house, but I'm naked in Marco's, naked and dripping water on the hardwood floor, on the wool throw rugs. I search through my bag, knowing I won't find anything. My good clothes are in the basement.

I go downstairs and begin rummaging through our belongings. There are boxes full of crap – notebooks. I pick up an old one, begin to open it, and think better of it. There are photo albums that Claire has put together – the annals of our life together and apart sit contained in boxes. Thirty-two square feet of memory on pallets. There's the warranty for my laptop, disks that are unlabeled. Claire, of course, packed everything according to some kind of organizational logic: computer disks with notebooks and gift pens; our library, sectioned by what appears to be race, then gender, then genre; my old stuff, when I used to buy expensive sketch books to write in; music books; record albums: CDs, which I decide I'll bring upstairs. There are some loose photos, a recent one of Edith holding my girl. Edith looks pained. My girl's about to cry, trying to get free from her grandmother, do anything to get to her mother, who's taking the picture.

There's a box of pillows and towels, at the center of which is a bundle of newspaper. I take it out and unwrap it. It's the urn containing my mother's ashes. It's a simple design, U-shaped, black with a matte finish. I didn't get to pick it.

I thought I would've, but they'd handed it to me already done. And I would've spread them out immediately but I hadn't known where. Boston wasn't right, since it had seemed for her to be only a kind of purgatory, one she never made it out of. I thought about Virginia and then Oklahoma and then Dublin or Dingle. Then I thought that I could divide her among all three. I didn't do anything. When I met Claire, she suggested that when I had a permanent home of my own. I could make a little flower bed of Lila's favorite flower and put them there. I thought that sounded like a good idea, perhaps only because Claire had said it.

I hear someone inhale sharply. I turn to the stairs. It's Laura, Marco's wife. She's staring, frozen by my nakedness. She manages to raise an arm to the stairs, a stop command, but James, her son, walks through it. They both look at me in the center of the cellar. I step behind the boxes.

'Hello, Laura. Hello, James.'

'Hello.' She takes him by the arm. They both look down. 'I'm sorry.'

'Oh, no.' I shuffle behind the boxes. 'Don't be. It's my fault.'

'I came down to look for something. I didn't think anyone was here.'

'Just pretend that there isn't.'

She laughs, a bit nervously, but better than she was before.

'I was just looking for some clothes.'

'Oh.' She finally looks up. He doesn't. 'It's your birthday. Happy birthday.'

'Thank you. I'm sorry about this.'

'Oh, don't worry. We don't use this space for anything.' She pauses for a moment, perhaps wondering if we're talking about the same thing. She points at the urn. 'What's that?'

I hold it away from me. 'This is my mother.'

'I'm sorry.'

'Quite all right.'

'How long . . .'

'Sixteen years.' She looks confused. 'I need to spread them someplace else. How are you? How's your summer been?'

'Great, thanks. It's great to get out of the city. Claire and the kids must be happy.'

'Very.'

'Well, see you after Labor Day.'

I wait to hear the door close, and then I count to two hundred before I start searching again. I find a suit – my father-in-law's, actually: three piece, wool but thin, dark blue with pinstripes. There's a periwinkle shirt and a medium blue tie tucked into it – a ready-made outfit. I find my shoes but no dress socks. I listen for Laura in case I missed her coming back for something. I sprint up the stairs to the kiddie room with the clothes and Lila.

I set her down next to Thomas, who, although he still hasn't eaten his food, looks more alert than this morning. I give him three more pellets.

He ignores them. I think that beside him is a bad spot for her. I move her to the bookcase. I rarely saw her before she died. She was living alone, emaciated, bitter, and, unlike my father, completely lucid – her senses, at least. And unlike his medicinal six-pack, she was drinking hard stuff all the time. The last day I saw her alive had begun with wine at lunch and ended with her calling me a useless mongrel bastard while whipping an empty pint at my head – a microcosm for our legacy. Whatever the case, she is, after all, still my mother and deserves better than being a bookend in a stranger's home.

I get dressed quickly and look at myself in the mirror. I hate to think it, but I look pretty good. The suit – the pattern, color, and cut – is conservative enough to keep me from looking like a pimp, my face and hands *de-automatic* enough to keep me from looking like a stiff. Why can't I be successful? I look successful. I leave the mirror before I can change my mind. I collect the cigars, my CD fold, and leave.

It's still hot. I consider taking off my jacket and throwing it over my shoulder, but it would seem a bit too jaunty so I leave it on. I pass all the shops. Kelly whistles from the doorway as I go by.

'You clean up good, Papi.' I wave back to her, jog across the street to the garage.

'Can I help you?' asks the attendant.

'Andolini, please.' He looks at me like a bird regarding something shiny and new.

'Right. Just a moment.' He picks up a walkie-talkie. 'Send down eighty-nine.' He looks up at me, smiling. 'Sorry. I'm new.' He looks at the clock. 'You're early.'

'I'll be back.' I wander outside. Away from the oil and gas smells and away from the tinny echo of AM talk radio. I stand in the spot where I first saw Shake earlier. I wish he'd spoken to me. I wanted to hear his voice – anything familiar now – however strange it might be. It's been years since we've all been together, years of him passing me, sometimes speaking, sometimes ignoring me. Gavin used to say that he and Shake were the manifestations of my split psyche, and when I wasn't around, they couldn't communicate with each other. I don't know. Shake and me – the bused urban black boy and the newly suburbanized black boy – vying for the spoils of a wrecked kingdom.

The bookstore is full of people browsing. In the window is *How the Hammer Did Fall* by my mentor, the Reverend Dr A. Jasper Pincus. Next to it. *No More Auction Block: The Repossession of the African American Body and Mind* by Karl Nometheus. Both books have spare covers: Pincus's courier type superimposed over railroad tracks. Nometheus a dark face and a dollar bill blown up to near the point of abstraction. Two black cultural criticism books prominently displayed, and it's not even February. I know what Pincus would say if I saw him now – 'Your work should be in this window.'

Pincus of the little mustache. I'd been sent to him, as he was the chair of the philosophy department at City. 'Sisyphean Dilemmas – Among Other Things: Marriage, the Gun, and the Black Aesthete' was the paper my instructor had accused me of plagiarizing. He'd been waiting for me outside his office, so casually that it seemed he didn't belong there. Dressed more like a stylish preacher than an academic, the Hegel scholar turned civil rights leader, turned man of God and professor. He had close-cropped hair, medium brown, medium height. Stocky but with delicate features, lotioned hands and neat nails, the crisp chin and that damn little mustache – groomed like a vain lady's eyebrow.

'We've been waiting for you.'

'I'm sorry . . .'

'No need to apologize, man.'

He led me into his cramped office, made smaller by the lone institutional window, the three walls of books around his metal desk, and his presence, there behind the desk, looking out at me as though I was some favorite nephew of a childless man.

'About the paper, sir . . .'

He waved me off. 'Stop, stop, I know it's yours. Papers that contain ideas and are for the most part free of grammatical errors are rare birds in these parts. The alarm went off.' He looked out the window, clad in brown anodized aluminum, south down Lexington Avenue, and watched the cars rushing downtown. I took the chance to scan his desk, the room. High up on a shelf was a framed photo of what looked to be a very young Pincus sitting in a diner booth with King, Andrew Young, and someone I couldn't recognize. There were empty plates and coffee mugs on the table. They looked tired – powerful tired, like they'd just finished something they'd been working hard at – the tired of the satisfied.

He cleared his throat. 'Sometimes,' he began with a light preacher lilt, pointing out at the cars. 'Sometimes on a wet night the taillights blur together and from up here that road looks like a red stream – like what I imagine a blood vessel to be like. The headlamps' yellow and the red circles, like blood cells, you know.' He opened a file. 'But I see here that you're a *poet*? You're probably offended by my metaphorical stew, eh?'

'No, sir.'

'I used to dabble in the fine arts, too, but I had no skill and it was a different time.' He ran a finger across the mustache. 'What are your plans?'

'My major?'

'No, son, your *plans*.'

'Well, I'm just trying to, I suppose, right the ship.'

'Fine. Fine. We all stray off course a bit.' He leaned in to make the point. 'All of us.'

'I suppose I'd like to get my degree, perhaps teach.'

'Continue writing?'

'Yes, sir.'

'To what end?' He opened my paper and pretended

to read it. 'You've touched on some interesting points in here. *Subversive*, but interesting.' He tapped the sheets, then handed it to me. 'I'm curious; you said something about *righting the ship?*'

'Yes.'

He leaned onto the desktop, brought his head down low but still, somehow, held it erect. 'Is that ship right now?' He waited for a moment, then began shaking his head. He pushed back from the desk. 'I don't mind a poet, man – I don't mind a poet at all. We need them. But I'll have every woolly-headed artist swinging from light poles by morning, just like those damned tennis shoes the kids like to throw up there, if it means getting something done in this world.' He folded his fingers behind his head and reclined.

'That's a joke, son.'

'Yes, sir.'

'Based on a literary reference.'

'I know, sir.'

'It was ironic.'

'Yes, sir.'

'It was funny.'

'Yes, sir.'

'We demagogues can be subversive, too. *Hoo!*' He howled with laughter. Pointed, 'Gotcha!' He leaned forward again. 'You know they took all the fun out of your generation. You watched too much of that damn protest footage in social studies. Everyone's all steely and severe. You know,' he said thumbing in the direction of the photograph. 'Dr King had a great sense of humor.'

'No, sir, I didn't.'

He pushed back, took a big book from the shelf and held it out for me. 'Augustine. Ever read it?'

I scanned the cover, *City of God*, and was stunned somewhat stupid by the selection.

'No, sir.'

'This is for you – *to borrow*. When you're done, come back and see me. We have much to talk about.'

And we did have much to talk about, or, rather, he had much to say to me. He was good to me. He cut a trail through the administrative bush, right into the graduate program without a BA. Nobody fucked with Pincus. Over the years he'd maintained his authority and kept the respect of his peers by not getting *too* big – staying out of the popular discourse and throwing in only with clergy and scholars. Privately swearing that he'd never leave the city school for the *'private and elite spas.'* And having me tacitly swear it, too. It was obvious to everyone that I was being groomed as his heir-apparent. I don't know why it wasn't obvious to him that I wasn't the one. So it came as a shock to him when I started drifting away. First there were the grave looks of disappointment; then he turned cruel, calling my interests *'archaic and therefore frivolous,'* saying that *'a man of my history, background, and talents should know better.'*

★   ★   ★

When I get back to the garage, the attendant is waiting for me outside.

'The keys are in. You're ready to go.'

I tip him five bucks, which gets a few more words out of him. 'Have a good night. See you soon' – other pleasantries. I pretend to be bored by the car until I turn away from him. It's a black Ferrari Modena – one of the things Marco had promised himself if he made good. Modena, where they're made, where he comes from. 'Enzo Ferrari was a genius,' he'd told me before with great national pride. And now, in the driver's seat, looking at the testosterone-mad stallion on the steering wheel, I have to agree. Sitting in the leather-clad seat, I believe that I'm actually in the mind of a raging horse. Enzo, however, was careful to keep the division between man and brute clear. I'm in charge. All I have to do is whisper a command in the center of the animal mind. 'Go!' I turn the key, and the attendant jumps. The engine's sound isn't equine, though; it growls, perhaps the sound a sleeping horse might make when it dreams of being a predator – some demon stud or perverse unicorn. Marco's put only five hundred miles on it. I touch the gas lightly; the tachometer moves. I let it hover at 1,000 rpm and then release. I have to smile. I'm in a leather and steel chariot ready to be yanked by four hundred crazy horses. I drop the horse metaphor. I drop the clutch, shift into first, and then, gas, just a little, and let up on the clutch. Less and less clutch, more gas, and I'm rolling. Enzo Ferrari was indeed a genius. I turn onto the street and pull over to survey the controls. There aren't many of them – sunroof, stereo. I fiddle with them – adjust the mirrors and seat. I load up the jukebox and put it on shuffle, but I wait to push play. Five thirty. I have two hours to get to Midtown. I check the mirrors again, push my ass into the seat, flatten my back. I push play. *'Fellas, things done got too far gone . . .'* Yes, they have, Mr Brown. Yes, they have. Mr Brown calls again and gets the needed response. I put the car in gear and rumble into the traffic.

It's easy to drive in New York. Unlike Boston's winding livestock trails, the roads here are straight. *'This is a man's world . . .'* I ascend the bridge, always so lovely on a late summer day. The sun is strong. The big wheels seem to have found secret tracks on the blacktop in which to ride. I cross the river, staying with the flow of traffic, but it's like I'm on my own personal rail, in second gear, with so much power in reserve.

New York City can be wonderful in August in the late afternoon because there's no one here. I shouldn't say no one; it's left to the *no ones* who haven't the means to escape the heat, stink, and grime. But just the same, there are fewer some-ones to rub your face in it. Things seem open. FDR is free on the northbound side. It's rare to find a speed trap in the city, so I speed, not exces-sively – the car draws enough attention – but just enough to find out what Enzo's folks have done.

235

With the throttle only a quarter down I hit seventy in third gear. And by the time I pass the Thirty-fourth street exit. I realize I should ease off and just cruise.

I circle the city, staying away from the claustrophobia-inducing towers, remembering why, even when living in Manhattan, I stayed away from Midtown and stuck to the edges of the island. I take the river drive across Harlem and then wind my way to Broadway – the great black way up here. I had fantasies about relocating in Harlem, of finding some distressed brownstone or warehouse, buying it on the cheap from the city and then building a home for us. Claire had surprised me by loving the idea, scrutinizing every listing and dragging us uptown every Sunday for what seemed the better part of a year. We'd missed it, of course, another land grab, the day when a dollar down could reserve your empire.

I cruise back east on 125th. I turn off the AC and open the windows and sunroof. There's something splendid about driving a hundred-and-fifty-thousand-dollar car and not having a pot to piss in. Guthrie comes on. *'The winter wind is blowing strong, my hands ain't got no gloves . . .'* There's something splendid about being on the lam, in disguise. *'Don't you remember me, babe, I remember you quite well . . .'* I stop at the light on the corner of Fifth and sing along. *'High sheriff on my trail, boys, high sheriff on my trail . . .'* I've always liked the sound of my voice next to Woody's. Mine is hoarse, heavier. I switch to the harmony. *'All because I'm falling for a curly-headed dark-eyed gal.'* The light turns, but now people begin to cross Fifth. Some turn to look at the low-riding coupe, but more turn for my duet. Woody probably never drove a fine Italian sports car or wore hand-tailored English suits. I wonder if anyone crossing thinks these things are mine.

There's a break in the line of walkers, and I go. *'Who's gonna stroke your coal-black hair and sandy-colored skin?'* I used to sing this song in downtown bars and coffee houses. People were always polite, but no one ever really seemed to like it. *'Who's gonna kiss your red ruby lips when I'm out in the wind?'* Perhaps my performance was poor – I don't think so. Just the same, no one seemed to be able to hear the plea: *'When I'm out in the wind, babe . . .'* Perhaps they couldn't make the jump, couldn't recognize the girl or empathize with his longing for her. Maybe the face in the song didn't match the faces they knew, or his fate seemed too strange next to their own. Claire hadn't liked it but was polite. Perhaps she hadn't wanted to be that girl – heartbreaker of a lawless man. Claire is good: good wife, good mother, good daughter. She weeps instead of rages. She smiles and makes others feel good – the good teeth, good skin, the good word: They are nearly cold – perfect – but softened by the small hint of sorrow.

I've caught her before – mourning – holding a folding picture frame with two photos of her father: one as a little English boy sitting on his mother's lap, feeding doves on a great lawn; in the other he's a man, dancing – thin, long limbs stretched, spinning round a cane – the big finish of a show. It seems impossible that his heart was ready to explode. 'He would've liked you. You really would've gotten along.' Perhaps – me and the noble, weak-hearted, dancing man whose build was not like mine but whose suits fit me so well – the tall Anglican snob. He was the freak of his family – part buttoned-down conservative, part romantic fop. He was handsome, a great story-teller, so I've been told, and Claire said that he was really very much in love – even in the end. He died in Claire's arms— 'Tell your mother I love her. And I love you.' That I know is true. You can tell when someone's been loved; they don't question its presence, nor do they despair when it seems to be gone. The photographs of father and daughter dancing together are sincere, there's nothing coy about the way they look at each other. Now those pictures are packed up in Marco's cellar, away from her, not good for a haunt, espe-cially one who knows how alone she was when he died – how alone she is still. She's too good – never rages at Edith's loss of memory, nor at Edith's ghostless world. But I can see her sorrow when her lip quivers. It's like he's there, in her face, restless, trying either to emerge or to recede, making her visage move. Then some deep sighs, perhaps some tears, but that is all.

'Who's gonna kiss your Memphis mouth, when I'm

out in the wind?' I shoot my cuffs in my late father-in-law's suit. The light turns green, and then up ahead, the rest begin to change. I weave through traffic. There's a storm cloud over Midtown slowly moving to meet me. *'When I'm out in the wind, babe . . .'* I cut across two lanes and turn east. The street is empty, so I push on the throttle. The big engine growls a response. I time the light, cross Madison doing sixty-five and then Park – trying to hit each light. I pick a hole between the pedestrians crossing First and head north again. I check the rearview for cruisers. In Boston I would already have been popped – curbside, with the two cops approaching me warily from either side of the car. If they did come, I don't think I'd wait around for them. They don't want you to explain why your name isn't on the title. I could get to the Bruckner fast – make for the Connecticut border on I-95. I'd be too fast for them there. I check the rearview again. No cops, but the rain is coming. I can tell the green light at Ninety-sixth is going stale. It turns yellow, and I slow down. The Impressions sing out, *'Keep on pushin' . . .'* I shift into neutral and roll, idling to the intersection. The car shudders with its own power. It's too fast for this city. It wants to go. I stop and wonder if Enzo ever thought his horse machine could outrun fate.

At eight, I turn onto Fifty-seventh, Marco's in front of the restaurant – Sky – gesturing for me to simultaneously pull over and roll the window down. I do.

'Valet it.'

Before I can get out, a kid in a crimson blazer and black bow tie opens the door for me.

'Hello, sir. Valet?'

'Sure.'

I pull myself out of the cockpit. The black street glows with moisture, and the tires of the cars going by hiss and drip as they roll. There's a faint hint of sunlight left and for a moment the city seems clean, almost welcoming. I look west down the street and then up in the sky. A mottled pigeon flies by, then passing in the opposite direction but at the same angle of ascent, an airplane. A taxi honks. The valet hands me a ticket. He's been waiting.

'Hey, man, happy birthday.' We shake. I step onto the curb. 'So, have you joined us all on the downward slope?'

'One more year.'

'Well, enjoy it.' He starts inside, then turns. 'Did your wife ever get ahold of you?'

'No.'

'She called around eight this morning.' He produces his phone. 'You want to try her?'

'No, thanks. Later.'

He opens the door for me and I go in. I'm surprised at how simple the room is. The ceiling is at least twenty feet high, but the space is broken up so as not to dwarf a person with its scale. There are four different levels: The main level contains the bar, poured concrete dyed dark gray. To the right, six steps up, is a raised area that extends to the back, where there are more stairs that lead to another level, about ten feet above the main floor, that spans the width of the room. Under it is more seating. Above the bar in what are like opera boxes are more tables and switchback stairs, which lead up to them. The railing is all brushed stainless steel with cable running through it. The room would look like a cross between a spy weapons lab and a high-tech boutique if not for the side-walls, which are deep slate blue Venetian plaster.

'Good evening,' says the host, looking only at Marco.

'Four for Andolini.' Marco leans back into me. 'I had to ask a couple of associates along. Sorry. Do you mind?'

'No. No, not at all.'

'Right this way.' He extends his arm toward a young woman in a tiny black dress who leads us up over the bar to one of the opera boxes, in which is a large, bright red banquette. In it are two women. One is blonde with shoulder-length hair – a layered hairdo – feathered, I suppose, very sophisticated. The other woman is light brown. Her hair is long, black, and in one braid, which disappears behind her back. I stand behind Marco as he tries to introduce us, as though he can hide me. Maggie and Diana – with a long first *a*.

We all sit silently. They seem to be waiting for

a cue from Marco to begin speaking. I have nothing to say. I try not to drift, but I keep going from the blonde's hair to the dark girl's forehead and their juxtaposition to the wall – both hair and skin contrast. I've never seen such a good plaster job. Someone troweled a 20x100-foot wall so well that I can't find a blemish on it.

They start talking, about office things, I suppose. And I suppose that some would consider what Marco has done for me kind – the car, the dinner, the cigars – and I shouldn't be offended that he's doing business. I certainly can have a lovely meal in silence. It must be like this for him all the time, blending the private and public, business and pleasure. They, in fact, may not even be as separate as I imagine. They may never have been, but as I hear their conversation wind down, hear their focus begin to shift, I can't help but think that Marco is trying to teach me a lesson. It's bad enough for him to try and rub my face in his shit. He doesn't need to rub it in my own.

'How was your run last night?'

'You run?' asks the blonde.

I nod. Silence again. The ladies start to fidget. Marco has tried and doesn't seem to want to try again. It seems strange that this is all they can muster, but when they talk in conference rooms, they probably have something to talk about. This silence must be difficult for them. My stomach shoots out another gas blade. I turn directly to the blonde.

'Do you run?'

Everyone's relieved, but only for a moment. I keep looking her in the eye, paying attention to her – engaged. She starts to answer and then looks away. I should cut her some slack, but then I ask myself why. Her martini is almost finished and I can't imagine her carrying this moment, which is at worst awkward, too far into the future with her. Marco is grinning stupidly. The dark one squeezes her glass stem. I look away and rephrase my question.

'Do you like to run?'

She's suspicious. She looks into her glass, then starts to answer slowly.

'Yes. Well, no.' She seems comfortable again. At least I tell myself that.

'Yes and no?' asks Marco. They laugh as though the last three minutes haven't happened. The waiter comes. He's tall, dressed in an immaculate black and white uniform – immaculate face and hands.

'Hello, may I get you drinks?' He looks at the women's glasses, 'More martinis?' They shake their heads. Marco waves them off.

'Yes,' he says, pointing to the glasses. 'Yes.' He points at me but keeps looking at the waiter. 'Sparkling water for the table.' It's not a question, but the inflection makes it seem as though he's asking one. 'Talisker, neat.'

We all study our menus for a while. I hone in on the simplest things there: green salad. Steak. I leave the menu open to deter questions coming my way. They talk – an occasional 'Everything looks so good,' or some approximation thereof. Finally, my ploy backfires.

'See anything?'

'Oh, yes.'

I close it and go back to the hair, the brow, the plaster, and then to Marco, who is trying to mouth something to me from behind his menu. The waiter returns with the drinks.

'So how was your run? You were out for a long time. How far did you go?'

'About eight.'

He takes a sip of his drink. The girls sip theirs. I wonder if that junkie got another beer. I try to imagine what it tastes like. It doesn't take much to do so – like the mineral water I'm drinking only with a dash of sugar, hay, and cosmic certainty. I don't remember, but I think people liked me better when I drank a bit. The waiter comes back and takes our order.

Marco leans back in the booth and exhales.

'Today was ridiculous, huh?'

The girls concur, but they keep their good posture. I look out over the dining room. It's full now, but the clamor is somehow softened – I don't know how with all the hard surfaces. Marco taps my elbow.

'Ten years ago our client paid this guy twenty million to develop product for them.'

'What product?'

'Software.'

244

'Who's your client?'

'Can't tell you.'

I look at him closely. I wonder who he thinks I might tell – how I could possibly compromise the deal.

'Anyway, he finishes. So now he's claiming that he owns the product and that they have to buy it from him, even though the original contract, which he signed, says that he doesn't.'

'So this is an intellectual property issue?'

'Exactly.' He leans forward and takes his glasses off, puts his elbows on the table. I realize that I hardly know Marco. Yes. I know his story, at least some of the highs and lows, the ones, at least, he's told me, but nothing more than his narrative and what I've assumed from it in combination with what I see. In my head I've seen him in his office in a tall building downtown. I've seen the suits he wears when we've walked together to drop our boys off at school and I've seen him disappear down the stairs of the 4-train. My mother wanted me to be a lawyer. She gave me a book on Charles Houston, and I remember being awed by him and wanting to be like him. I wonder where that feeling went – *why wasn't I like him?* As I got older, the idea of being a lawyer was displaced by the dizzying exactitude of actually becoming one. I suppose I began seeing lawyers, as well – the fathers of my schoolmates. They weren't grave men in hats and overcoats with leather bags walking up the steps of the Supreme Court armed with purpose.

'So what do you think?'

'What do I think of what?'

'Do you think our client owes him anything?'

'A deal's a deal, I guess.'

He nods. 'So how was your run?'

'Not so great.'

Maggie joins in. 'Sometimes I go out and I feel tired. I just slog through it.'

Marco smiles. They check him to see if what she said is acceptable. He's said that they're associates, and I don't know what that means. How had he presented the idea of spending an evening out with us to them? In a hallway, at lunch? 'We can close the Johnson and Johnson merger, but it'll have to be in front of a stiff I'm letting crash at my house.'

Diana looks potentially angry. She's not frowning, but she seems to be waiting for me to say something she can disagree with. I'm not sure what she finds so troublesome about me. Perhaps I'm overdressed. Perhaps she's wary because I'm strange and a stranger. She doesn't know what I do, where I'm from, what I think of her. I'm a suspicious character, and I appreciate that – that she hasn't come to any preconceived notions about me. But I can't sit with her uncertainty. I want to tell her something, anything, to set her at ease.

'Yeah, my run was weird.' I hear myself say 'weird,' and I'm sure it wasn't my voice that said it.

'What happened?'

'Well, I got caught in that cloudburst.'

'I didn't even know it rained last night.' She looks at Marco. Her last comment didn't seem to pass muster with the boss.

'I was chased.' I say it plainly so it takes a moment to register with everyone, including me. I've said it without realizing that I'll have to follow with something more.

'Oh, my god,' says Maggie. She checks Marco. I guess she gets the signal to continue. 'By who, what?'

Now I feel like an ass because I have to answer. They're waiting, curious. Even Diana seems interested.

'By the golden calf riding Leviathan bareback.'

They laugh. Marco spits out his drink and slaps the table. 'Sorry.' He wipes his mouth with his hand, offers me his napkin, which I refuse. I suppose that it is funny, especially if you think it's a joke. I let them laugh. Diana is the first one to regain her composure. She looks at me and I smile and it feels good. She smiles back. She's lovely, just a shade darker than honey with black hair that looks like braided silk. Then it fades – the joy – quickly back to the suspicion, which, after I've seen her smile, is all wrong. Her face shouldn't be so closed. Maggie still has her head down and Marco snorts again, a dry one this time.

'No, really,' I say. And they break up again. I try to talk over their laughter. 'I was on the bridge . . .' They won't have it. Marco waves for me to stop.

I show them mercy. I keep quiet, but just looking at me is enough to keep Marco giggling. He slowly returns to form. I wave back to him – recognize our wordless truce. He inhales deeply, wipes his eyes, and checks the girls to see if they think his breakdown was undignified. They do not. They look to me to continue. I don't know what to say, but I feel strangely touched by their attention – their acceptance – but I still haven't anything to say. I look around the table for a launch. I stop at Marco's glass and point.

'Talishire.'

'Talisker.'

'No, it's from *Talishire* – *islet* scotch – from the Isle of Skye.'

He shrugs his shoulders and leans back. The heat of interest has left his face. I should explain, tell the story of how Gruntcakes as a young man used to go with his older brother to be fitted for wool suits and sample the local whiskeys. But first I should tell them why I call Claire's paternal grandfather Gruntcakes. He was a stoic and unreachable English bastard until later in his life, but he always made Claire pancakes – griddle-cakes – taking great care to cut small chips of butter into the batter before cooking.

The last time he went to Skye, before he and his brother fell out, they walked the foothills with flasks of Talisker. They got drunk. They got muddy, so much so that the innkeeper wouldn't take them. They spent the night in a barn. He told me that story more than once, always in some moment when he could get me alone. *'I had a boat once, a sloop. Named it after the scotch. I wanted to sail it with my brother.'* He'd sit in some corner of some large, spare room, a party going on around him, with his whittled, driftwood cane, staring into the void, searching for his lost boat, his dead brother. Taking stock of what remained: him, me, and the dinghy. We'd made it seaworthy that last summer but never got to launch it. There's an old picture of him on the boat, three-quarter profile, sailing in Buzzards Bay. I've always liked to think that he's going to find his wife, somewhere in the middle of the ocean.

'I worked at a bar once, when they first exported it.'

We're back to feeling good again.

'When did you do that?' asks Maggie.

'When I first moved here. When I was a kid.'

Maggie smiles, not at all bothered that I know how young she is, almost relieved that I've recognized the age gap. Perhaps it makes me seem less predatory, more fraternal. She isn't elegant and beautiful like Diana. She doesn't seem at home in the little cocktail dress with her hair down. She should be in shorts, at a burger joint, after playing softball in Central Park. She, in fact, doesn't look as though she should be in this city at all. Her straight hair should be in a ponytail or under the hat of a team she actually roots for. She leans in, eager for more speech. Her dress falls away from her and above her left breast is a tiny, black cross. I suppose if I needed to, I could make her look like Sally – just without the freckles. She smoothes her dress against her flat chest and waits for me to speak.

'What do you do, Maggie?'

She snaps up straight, gestures at Diana. 'We're law students.'

'They have internships at the firm,' adds Marco. I smile. They all smile back. It buys me some time. I try to picture myself, twelve years ago, preparing for life: plucking guitars in the East Village, reciting poems in Chelsea lofts. Even though I know it's wrong for her to be here, there's something re-assuring about Maggie – her unjaded enthusiasm. I like the wiry girl in the black dress. Diana is another case, though. After the laugh she has gone quiet, but not from shyness. She seems aloof and calculating. And her martini seems to be shutting her up rather than relaxing her – reinforcing her superiority. Booze does that sometimes, make you high and mighty, saucy and silent, while you avoid what is really happening – you're scared, black, and young and you believe you can't afford to make a mistake.

Sometimes dinners come down to being merely exercises – accumulating experiences and killing time, until the food arrives, until it's time to go: filling the time unerringly, without spoiling appetites or hurting feelings. Without playing the fool. To be able to say 'I did this' or 'I saw them.' Diana stares out over the dining room. I direct the next question at her.

'Do you know each other from school?'

'No, we don't. We met this summer.' She finally speaks. Her voice is deep and soft and clear. Her mouth, like Claire's, hardly moves.

'I'm at NYU,' peeps Maggie. I turn to her, nod, and then go back to Diana.

'And you?'

'Harvard.'

'Really. What brings you to New York?'

'I'm from New York,' she answers with a hint of condescension. She turns slightly to Marco, 'And the opportunity to work at Jancy.'

'I'm from Boston,' I pat the table. I don't like my tone – too syrupy, but I'm not sure how to speak. I don't want to match hers. I don't want to turn this into another competition, but I don't know what she wants to hear. I stick with the syrup.

'Do you like being there?'

'No, not particularly.'

I nod.

'No offense.'

'None taken.'

Marco jumps in. 'Didn't you go to Harvard?' The girls turn to me with involuntary curiosity. Diana's face relaxes for a moment. She feels this

251

and tightens it again. I want to kick Marco, but then I wonder what he knows. There's very little he does know about me – so I think. I don't know what Claire, in a weak, confessional moment has put out there in the channels – the gossip that came to him as fact. Whatever the case, he has always been gracious to me and remembered, as much as I'd like to forget it, my birthday. I suppose over the last few years of analyzing starting pitchers and raising discreet eyebrows at cocktail parties Marco has seen the both of us as outsiders. He knows he is. He doesn't apologize, nor does he deny it. Marco's an outsider and everybody knows it – even he. What they don't know is how and why. He's not one of the men in the storefront social clubs, which, though dwindling, still exist. He's not a grumpy landlord's son, nor the corner merchant. He's not a gangster or a steamy lover. What I know is that he appeared one day in a second-grade classroom in a dead mill town north of Boston and he didn't speak a word of English. His father roamed the north shore for day work. His mother stitched shoes. He became a millionaire by thirty.

'Yes, I did,' I respond, nodding too earnestly as if to warn them of what's to follow.

'What house?'

'Adams.'

'What year?'

'I left.'

No one wants to ask the question – 'What

happened?' So they are silent for a moment. Maggie's face goes sad, concerned. I don't like it this way.

'I moved here. I wanted to try something new.'

'Acting?' Maggie's up again.

'Music.'

'Are you a musician?' I can see her picturing me at Lincoln Center, in my tux, tuning up in the horn section. It seems a shame to mar the image.

'No.' They're puzzled, but Marco seems to be enjoying himself, the budding story – if you can call it that. To me a list of events, well detailed or not, has never been one.

'I chickened out. I was playing around the city, working construction, too. I went back to school.'

'Where?' asks Maggie.

'Hunter. It's a city school.' Maggie stays spunky. Diana nods to herself as though she's figured something out.

'How was that?'

The food comes. My steak, though plated beautifully, looks inedible – a dense slab of flesh. I'm not hungry and my gas pains have stopped. In fact, it seems that my stomach has disappeared.

Marco stops his fork at his mouth.

'Do we need wine?'

The girls refuse. I wait for everyone to begin and then I cut off a piece. I chew and swallow. The meat seems to free fall, as though I'm throatless, returning to its original shape as it does. It finally hits bottom. My stomach comes alive, rigid and unhappy.

'So what do you do?' asks Diana, no longer so formal. I'm not sure why. Perhaps the food and drink have started working. Perhaps she, because I can't match her résumé, is no longer threatened. Perhaps she likes me. Maggie seems very interested, not in my response, but in Diana's response to me. She's lost her smile, chewing slowly. Marco is consumed by his food.

'You teach, right?' More of Marco's faulty intelligence, but it's okay. I start nodding, not to her question but to some internal beat I can't seem to refuse. Her syntax is slipping. Her jaw muscles relax. She puts her fork down and spreads her long fingers on the white tablecloth. Her hands are fine and ringless. She gently pushes her palms into the linen. Her calm makes Maggie change – drop the rosy-cheeked smile. They're not so young anymore. They both exhale and seem to, right there in their seats, become women.

Marco hears the silence and stops. We all exhale together and look to one another. I feel tired and it seems okay to show it. I cover my face with my hands, rub my palms into my eyes as though I'm just waking up. When I take them off my face, Maggie and Marco are eating again. Diana watches me. Everyone has a new face, born from a tacit agreement that the old bald white guy isn't here: The Irish Catholic girl doesn't have to pretend to be a WASP; the black girl doesn't have to out-WASP her. And Marco can stop trying to guess at who's mocking him – all manner of *thing* well.

I'm still nodding. And it must seem to her a profound response – that I'm contemplating my years, my road to here. Perhaps I am, but I can't tell. The nod becomes a slow rocking. She joins me, rocking. Poor Diana, trapped in oak-paneled rooms and towers of glass and steel, never an error in diction, tone, or pronunciation, but never arrogant, never haughty. Poor Diana, some twenty-first century princess. For her sake, I lie.

'Yes.' We both stop rocking.

'Where?'

'Hunter College.' Another lie.

She nods, once. 'That's great.' Maggie nods, too. 'My mom went there, back when it was free.'

'It was a teacher's college.'

'Yep.' The three of us take it in.

Marco gestures at my plate with his fork. 'How is it, man?'

I look down at my half-eaten steak and wonder how I'll finish it. I cannot. Maggie pushes rice around her plate. Diana picks at her vegetable concoction. Her jaws move slowly and evenly. I cut another piece and wonder if I should bother chewing it before dropping it into the pit.

'I inhaled mine.'

'Was it good?'

'Great.'

He's buzzed. There's more red in his face than usual, along with a hint of moisture. I never figured him for a lightweight. He excuses himself. Maggie looks at me as though she's a child, waiting for a bedtime story. I would like to tell her one – tell her something – but I have nothing to say. I look at my plate; the blood from the endless meat has contaminated my potatoes. I cut a big slab and swallow it. It lands heavily, making me wince. I look at the girls. They've pushed their plates away. Maggie still wants her story. Diana wants one, too.

'What kind of law are you interested in?'

Maggie starts to answer but stops and gives way to Diana.

'Corporate. IP and such.' Maggie nods in agreement. And I must give something away with my face or body, an eye roll or slight sag, because she holds up a hand as though to hold off my judgment.

'I'm not going to lie. I want to make money,' she nudges Maggie. They both grin. Then she grows serious. 'I owe my parents that.' She tries to find agreement in my eyes – as though I would understand. Whatever she sees allows her to continue. 'And I don't want to have to worry about money. I want to be able to travel, and when I have kids, be able to take them places, as well – give them things, not spoil them. I mean I'll want my kids to have jobs, but I also want to give them every advantage.'

Diana can't possibly know how many times in the last twelve years, I've heard this speech – how much I continue to hear it from those who believed themselves to be entitled but haven't achieved it yet. *They don't want much . . .* only what they want – some minimum of comfort and privilege. But there's something about her that makes me listen, more than her beauty. She seems to believe what she's saying.

'How much personal wealth does someone need?'

I shrug.

'Both of my parents were teachers. Don't get me wrong. They did wonderful work. They touched a lot of people, but how many CEOs did they meet?' She points at Marco's empty seat repeatedly, like the gesture's a stutter, until she finds the words. 'Do you know who *he's* had lunch with this summer?' She almost stands. Thankfully, she doesn't. Militancy doesn't become her. I think she knows that. She regroups but doesn't recant the 'he,' as though Marco was a 'he' to me, as well.

'I get it from two sides – race *and* gender.' She stops, seems to search for something inside and begins again. I look at the blue wall again and think of whales, great fish, sea beasts, and what a swallowed man would find in their bellies: whole civilizations, perhaps wicked, perhaps good, but full of people who have long forgotten they were once in flight at sea.

'As an African American woman, I think I'm charged to do something.' She presses those palms into the linen again. 'I just think I'll do more in a board room than in a classroom.' She says it and regrets it instantly. I see her ashamed for the first time. She doesn't wear it well, either.

'Oh, my god, I'm so sorry.'

'It's okay.' She presses her hands harder and tries a pained look, like she's looking at a dead puppy. It's better, but still not good. I rub the table, too. 'It's okay. I know what you mean.'

Marco returns and stands over the table.

'What should we do?' he asks. And it comes to me, the rest of the evening – more drinks, more clichés, more strange-faced performances. He looks around the table. It seems as though between the bathroom and the table he's lost his authority and he's nervous because of this. He finally, after shifting a few times, sits. He extends his arm along the seatback; his hand rests dangerously close to Maggie's shoulder.

'What should we do?' he asks again, still nervous. He won't look at anyone in particular. Maggie has dropped her head in resignation as though she knew this moment would come. I wonder if when she arrived on her first day she foresaw this or any of the other compromises she will have to make. It's awful to see now, bonnie Maggie, her face fallen. Marco tries to look at her in secret, but we all see it. She feels it, tries to steel herself, not to resist him, but to resist the notion that there may be another way. There isn't even lust, nothing between them, but she's convinced of her obligation to this dance.

The waiter returns with a tray of small rocks glasses half filled with a clear but bright liquid. He sets one before each of us – Marco last.

'These are from us.'

Marco isn't an ambidextrous drinker so he has to take his arm down to hold his glass. Maggie reshifts, straightens, thinks of moving close, thinks of moving away, searches blindly for Diana's hand, doesn't find it. She takes her glass as well, circles it with both hands. Diana follows suit. Marco raises his glass, as do they. I raise my water. I can't let this continue, not sober, but I don't want to drink – not for the girls, not for Marco or our 'friendship,' not to grease the path, lube it for Marco's entry to disaster.

'Cheers.' No one echoes him, but we all drink. He sips at the strange booze. Then nods his approval. He sets the glass down. Maggie tenses and awkwardly leans toward him, but he leaves his hand on the table.

'You don't drink?' asks Diana.

I ignore her and turn to Marco. 'So James fancies himself a goalkeeper this fall?'

He shakes his head to jump into the new context. 'Goalie, yes.'

'James is?' asks Diana.

'My son.'

Maggie's face is lightless. Perhaps the face she reserves for the morning after.

'Do you have kids?'

'Yes, I do, three.'

'Wow, that's a lot.'

'I suppose.'

She sneaks a look at my untouched glass. 'And you don't drink.'

'Would you like mine?'

'Oh, no. I was . . .'

'I'm a recovering alcoholic – sixteen years sober.'

'That's amazing.'

'Not really.'

'You should be proud.'

'Proud of what?'

'What you've accomplished.'

'And that is?'

She exhales sharply to break the cadence. Maggie has drifted off, scanning the lower room for a way out. Marco wrings his hands. Diana leans in, lowers her voice, as if to tell me a secret. 'We need people like you.' Then lower still, 'Strong black men.' She straightens again, ready to share with the others, who are pretending not to listen – regardless, they don't seem to care. She speaks to me as though she's suddenly become my mentor. 'Educator. Father. Role model. You should be proud.' She looks at my glass again, openly this time. 'It takes a lot of willpower – what you're doing.'

'Willpower really has nothing to do with it.'

She snorts – a violent little laugh. I snap up in my seat and bark back to match her tone.

'And I don't see what my sobriety has to do with my melanin count – other than a predisposition

to drink. What is it other than another mani-
festation of my genetics?' It throws her, brings
Maggie back to us, and stops Marco's wringing.
I wonder what he's heard when I speak. 'And
insofar as will, I find it harder to drink than
not.'

I start wringing my own hands under the table.
To stop, I present them to the others. I extend
my left index finger to the ceiling, then slowly flex
and straighten it again.

They're silent – dormant. My powers have
grown over the years. I've put them all to sleep.

A taxi takes the girls west. The valet holds the
door open for Marco. He tips him and we get in.
Marco tries to hide the fact that he's smashed.
He rides the clutch, lurches from stoplights. He
makes it to the FDR without rear-ending anyone
and begins to weave through the traffic. I wonder
if I can sue him if he crashes.

'Got the cigars?' I give him one. He bites the
end off and spits it out the window. 'Matches?'

'No.'

He jumps across two lanes and gets off on
Twenty-third. He pulls over and points at a
bodega.

'Would you mind?'

When I come back out, he's leaning against the
car chewing on his cigar. His face has changed.
It's sharper, somber. I've never seen him this way
before – introspective, perhaps. I strike the match

and the pop and sulfur bring him out for a moment. But after I light him and he thanks me, he goes back to that face.

'You know, I always wanted one of these.' He shakes his head. 'And now I realize that it's just a car.' He stands straight and walks away from it and starts to pace the sidewalk. I light my cigar. The smoke tastes like chocolate, leather, and wood. He calls from across the sidewalk. My smoking seems to have signed some unknown pact with him.

'What happened back there?' He draws a circle in the air with the cigar.

'I don't know.'

'Really?' He asks as though I'm being deposed. 'Everything seemed to . . . everyone seemed to be having a good time.'

'Sorry.'

'No, no.' He waves at me while looking down at the street. 'You did the right thing.'

'I did.'

'Yeah.' He looks at me with the grave face, almost angered that I would question him when he was so sure of himself. He goes to take a drag and stops. He walks to me, eyes wide and blazing. He points at his chest, defiantly, then he starts to speak, then softens as though he's just seen something delicate flash in his mind.

'I've never cheated on my wife.' He says it as though he's now on the stand. 'Not even when we were just dating.'

'That's good.'

'No.'

'Why no?'

'Well, I've never been sure why. I do love her, but it's not because of that. Your wife, if you don't mind me saying, is a beautiful woman.'

'Thanks.'

'You ever cheat on her – probably not, huh?'

'No.'

'What about her? She ever cheat on you?'

'No.'

'How do you know?' He drags on his cigar and checks his watch. 'You never called her back. Too late now.' The thunder punctuates his words. He rolls his eyeballs up. The steak is now whole again in my belly. 'Fuck, let's get out of here.' He circles the car, opens his door, and looks across the roof at me.

'You all right, man?'

'I'm fine.'

She was not the one, not the girl. *'I don't need much,'* she always used to say and I hadn't believed her at first so I tried to give her everything I could, but she kept saying it: *'I don't need much.'* I never figured out what that little bit was.

Marco starts the engine. I hadn't noticed that the rear window extends down over it, revealing the big aluminum V-8. Transparency – a heart on display. Even so, few know what makes it go.

Claire had said that she loved me, was still saying it with electric eyes and girlish cheeks – *'I love you'* – handing out the words like two-bit lemon ices.

CHAPTER 8

Like Ahab I do not sleep but unlike him I don't die – I dream. I dream of Claire with someone else. It makes it easier I suppose, to say good-bye. Money. Plans. Johnny Little Nancyboy left a message for me to go to Greene Street, the corner of Broome. He'd said that there would be better work.

I get up and feed Thomas. He eats. He looks better than yesterday. I wonder who will take care of the fish when I go. I suppose I could leave a note for Marco with care instructions and they could pick him up when they get back. Maybe they won't come back. Maybe she'll stay with Edith. It would be better, cheaper. The kids could go to public school. The house is paid for and they would have all that space. They can just open up the door and run outside with a ball by themselves. I don't think Claire even wants to live in New York any longer, anyway. She hasn't danced in years and the people she's met since then, the mothers she's befriended, the ones she actually liked are all leaving. They can't afford it, either.

Having grown up poor, I never understood what

it cost to be rich: how much a home cost, how much tuition cost, how much it cost to run in certain circles, to maintain a lifestyle. We had cheap rent, and we lived in a small, naive world.

I think I remember coming to New York to become rich – to make a name for myself, with a guitar and notebooks in tow, but it didn't work. I don't know why we'd expected it to, and we never made a contingency plan in case it didn't. I see Claire and myself, twelve years ago, young and stupid – rube-like – making plans to succeed, plans that were really closer to fantasies than anything else.

Most things fail. Most people fail. Most ideas go bad; movements, marriages. I strum the guitar. It's out of tune, but I keep playing anyway – nothing in particular, just random chords I come to finger. *It's only money*. That's all I really need now for damage control. I put the guitar down and sit up. I get a clean sheet of paper and write a list.

Today:
    Go to SoHo
    Go to school
    Go to Marta – get check
    Find some way to make money tonight
    Find apartment for them

Not specific but good enough because it's written down – doable, practical tasks. Things I will do.

266

Things I choose to do. A contract, that sober and of age and consenting, I freely enter. I get up and get dressed. I go downstairs. Marco is standing in the kitchen, dressed and reading the *Times*. The phone rings. He answers and hands it to me.

'Hey. Morning.'

I take the phone from him.

'Hello.'

No one responds, but I know it's her. I believe I can hear her breathing and I know her breaths – each one of them – elated, angry, sad. This is how she breathes when she doesn't know what to say, when in the moment before speaking she realizes how very different we are, how enormous a gap there is between us two and that she hasn't the power to cross it, that I have given up trying. In this breath there is an assessment, a reassessment of me, of her, of us. There is a hint of shame – that she believed in something between us, first without prudence, then without wisdom. Now there's only breath as a symbol – an expression of loneliness.

'Hello,' I say again.

'Where were you?' She lets her voice waver on the verge of crying. The kids must still be asleep.

'I worked yesterday.' Marco leaves, allowing me to lie about his message. 'I didn't know you called until late.'

'Of course I called.' More breaths; these are more frustrated, hurt – which means that somewhere in them is a hope. It makes them worse for me to hear than the lonely ones. 'You went *out?*' Which is an accusation of me spending money.

'Marco took me out to dinner. I met him in the city.'

'I had everyone by the phone. Everyone wanted to sing to you. They were so disappointed.'

'I'm sorry.'

'It's okay.' Like a fool, I believe her – that it is okay, that she has hope that things will turn out okay. I can't imagine her remarrying, but I can't imagine her alone, but like last night I cannot see the face of the man who would replace me, and I wonder if I've damaged her too much for her to ever love or trust again.

'Did you find anything for today?' It's a simple enough question, but it sounds ridiculous coming from her – Claire as the hardscrabble wife of a day laborer.

'Yeah.'

'What are you doing?'

'Something for Johnny – I don't know.'

'Ick. That guy gets jobs?'

'I guess so.'

'Maybe you can start getting your own jobs?'

'Maybe.'

'You talk to Marta?'

'Today.'

'Great. School?'

'After work.'

'Will anyone be there?'

'I get out at four.'

'Oh, okay. I'm sorry.' She wants to stop asking these sorts of questions, but she can't help herself. 'What about apartments?'

'Tomorrow.'

'We don't have much time.'

'I know.'

She brightens. 'What about Pincus?'

'What *about* Pincus?'

'I saw his new book. It got great reviews.'

'Did it?'

'I'm sorry.'

'Why are you sorry?'

'I keep bugging you. I'm putting it all on you.'

'No. It's fine.'

'Things'll work out.'

'Yeah.'

She sighs. 'I feel better. I'm sorry.'

'Shh.'

'Are you coming this weekend? The kids miss you. I miss you.'

'I'll try.' It doesn't sound genuine to me.

'Happy birthday.'

'Thanks.'

'I love you.'

'I love you, too.'

She seems to wait on the line as though she's expecting me to say more, but she hangs up before I can disappoint.

The stink and dread of the subway when you are going to work isn't like the stink and dread of the subway when you're going out to the movies or lunch. It's not the funk, or the idea that you'll be trapped underground, it's the stink of your dreams rotting somewhere along the rails. It's the dread of knowing that you're being carted off – complicitly – to the slaughter. Two hundred and fifty dollars a day in New York City will never get me out from under. Next stop – Satan's lair. It's seven thirty in the morning and I'm on the F-train, SoHo bound.

I try to account for every dollar I've spent in an attempt to figure out how it all came to this. *I made money.* And for a while, at least, we were operating at a surplus. Claire's cousin Linus started a dot-com and hired me to write their copy. It was the first time in my life, since being a stock clerk during high school, that I'd brought home a regular check. It made our rent seem trivial, our monthly nut seem like nothing. We saved. I had an office and someone to direct my incoming calls. I didn't have to do much, either. Linus used to come visit me and ask why I didn't move his cousin out of that crawlspace we were in. He'd sit on my desk, sipping a coffee. He did the same thing when he presented me with my stock in the company. He did the same, only with a cigar, when his shares made him a millionaire. He also did it when he asked me not to sell. But not when all I had left were penny stocks, a little cash in the bank, and an odd entry on my résumé.

★   ★   ★

270

When I come back above ground on Houston, it's pouring. I should've taken the A. I wander down Greene and stop at the address. I look up. There doesn't seem to be anything happening on the third floor. I press the bell and wait – nothing. I wait under the cornice until I figure out that the runoff from it is denser than the rain itself.

Across the street is a store – Lucky Jeans. The gates are down. Claire has mentioned this place. I didn't think jeans could be lucky unless they were some old ratty pair that had seen you through some days, enough days to prove that it really is luck you've experienced with them, rather than coincidence. The shop, even though I can't see in, seems too high-end to be pushing used truck. It's the entire corner, two stories of glass and logo. And how would they get the lucky jeans away from the original owner? Perhaps someone who was down on their luck. Pawn shop or other, it seems wrong. When we were kids, Gavin probably would have chucked a rock through one of the big windows and then stood around as if he hadn't done anything. I miss my friend. I wonder how he's doing. His last slip, what had it been? Not that it mattered. I miss Gavin. I haven't been a good friend to him lately. I haven't really been a friend at all. *'I don't know,'* he used to say. *'My people, when they don't like something, they just blow it up.'* Then he'd look at me, have a smoke or something, and then speak with that highbrow tone, opening his hand to me. *'Your people wouldn't think*

271

that right of you talented tenth. They should teach you how to make bombs or something.' Gavin was the best fighter in town. He could provoke better than anyone. People would look at his skinny body, his freckle puss, the expression in his impish eyes – shy intelligence bordering on outrageous arrogance. He would never throw a punch, only take them. I once saw someone smash a beer bottle over his skull. He went down and bounced right back up. That was Gavin – taking hits, going down, getting back up, going down again. It used to scare me horribly – to watch his father beat him, his so-called friends, the police. And the times when I'd step in, when I thought he'd be killed, he'd say *no*. I guess I got used to it. But now, wishing him here, I wonder how many bounce-backs he has left, or if one really does bounce back – my only real friend left on earth, whom I have let fall.

The door opens and I jump into the street to face it. A woman is in the doorway. She's not startled. Her head's down, as though she hasn't seen me or doesn't care. She opens her umbrella and looks up. She knew I was there all along. She starts out but goes only so far as to still be able to hold the door open – for me. She nods back at the opening, almost imperceptibly. I don't move.

'Do you want to wait inside?'

I keep still – still looking. Her umbrella and raincoat are both transparent. Her hair is long, dark, and loopy. She looks as though she meticulously threw something on and then rushed out.

'Are you working upstairs? You can wait inside.' It goes against my programming to have a strange white woman, alone on a deserted street, show me trust – not that it hadn't happened before, strange that it had happened many times. What is even more ridiculous is that I'm still in the street refusing shelter and it makes sense – to me and to her.

'Have a good day.' She lets the door close. She doesn't wave. She doesn't give me another look. She goes away, south on Greene, around the corner, west on Broome, and is gone.

I find a Sharpie in my bag and a scrap of sandpaper. I hunch over to protect it from the rain, and on the back I begin another list: *Call Gavin. Real estate broker on Atlantic. Security deposit. Change guitar strings.* They had seemed muddy this morning, as though one of the kids had been strumming them with syrupy hands. I remember a demo tape of songs I wrote. I guess I made it some time ago and I want to hear them. I remember them, the performance, too, as being quite good. I started playing on a whim, listening to Dylan, strumming along, then realizing he wasn't just strumming. I had realized earlier that I wasn't going to be able to plead like Marvin, demand like Otis, or croon like Johnny Hartman. My voice is odd – low and nasal, pinched at times. I always liked listening to him search for the tune, bending notes the other way, up out of blue. *'What's your angle?'* Shake asked me once after a set. *'I'm going to be the first big black man to sing like a skinny white guy.'* I wonder if any of my old tapes are still around. I sweep Marco's basement to figure out which box they're in, but the picture doesn't come. I try and focus harder, but all that comes up is a random cassette case stuffed under some papers. My voice has changed since then. I should make another.

She's back. She's carrying a bag. She doesn't look at me. She opens the door and holds it in place with her back.

'Go in.'

I don't.

'This is just silly. You're going to catch your death out here.' She nods her head in the direction of the entrance, this time in a very deliberate way while making a strange sucking sound with her mouth. 'All right then, go on.'

I go in. She lets the heavy metal door slam shut. Then without putting her bag down she opens the gate of the freight elevator, then the up-and-down doors. She moves powerfully, gracefully. She's long, tall. There's no hesitation or awkwardness to her.

'Go ahead,' she says. I shake my head. 'They work on the third floor. You can go in.' I shake again, but she leans toward the opening and that seems to pull me in. We ride up, jerkily thankfully, because it gives me something other than her to consider.

'I think it's illegal,' she says as we stop with a

boom. She goes for the door. 'It's not at all to code, but does anyone really inspect elevators?' She opens the gate. 'We're here.' She steps out. I follow. She closes the gate and starts to a door. I follow.

'No, you're over there.' She points to a doorless opening while getting her keys out – still one handed. She does it every weekday morning – puts on something just respectable enough, just after she's shampooed – gotten her keys from the basket in the kitchen and gone to get her one coffee and whatever else was in the bag. But not on weekends. Weekends she stays in later? Doesn't go out at all? Brews her own? *'Why don't you just make your own?'* Claire would sometimes ask. I like to buy coffee in a shop that sells a good cup – just to check in, just to see if things aren't too far gone. Claire doesn't need that. Whether she likes them or not, Claire actually gets along with people. She's able to walk among them, even those she dislikes. Their presence doesn't vex her because she has the ability to make them feel good – when she smiles at them, gives them her approval with all that Anglican highness. *And she looked down with all her Anglican highness and deemed it was okay.* Not this one. She looks out in a secret way. She won't tell what she's thinking. Judgment isn't reserved, but it is withheld. And now she isn't even looking at me any longer. She's through her door, having opened it just enough to slide through.

And then as if on time delay the picture of her

appears in my head, not quite in memory, more like a flash at its gates, bidding them open. Her muscle, at least the mass in her calves, is beginning to change from fast to slow twitch – a light sagging beneath the skin that makes it ripple slightly. Older than Claire's but younger than that waitress at the Ramada: Janet. She had that fully baggy skin – baggy cheeks and jowls. Baggy triceps. She used to smile at me when we came in. She'd ask me how I was doing, point over at Charlie behind the bar, and ask him if he remembered me. He'd answer very quietly, *'Of course I do,'* in a singsong kind of way. Then she'd bring me things as though I was some nomadic prince whose arrival she'd foreseen: soda, beer nuts, pretzels, more soda, and sometimes a whole jar of cherries – which I hated but dared to eat anyway to see how sick I could make my stomach feel while I watched my father booboopbeedoo his way from the bar to the jukebox to a corner table and sit with someone in the afternoon's blind darkness. We'd have been outside playing catch and he'd have rubbed his shoulder or grabbed his elbow and walked to me, slowly exaggerating the throwing motion. And then later, me with the junk food and the sick gut and our two mitts and ball on the bar, I'd spin on the stool and he'd be gone. I'd feel a little panicky and scan the dark lounge for him. Baggy arms would've stopped talking to me, stopped giving me things, and Charlie would've moved himself to the other end of the bar – being busy. And I don't know why I think about it in this particular way, this particular tense, because it may have happened only once, or it may not have happened at all. And the subjunctive narrative I've created may only be myth culled from knowing the neon red sign of the motel, and years later, knowing what dim lights and strange perfume signified. Perhaps I'd only smelled it on him once – the stink of the lounge queen's sex on my father. Or heard it in my mother's hiss – muttering to herself, three scotches down, banging the skillet around the kitchen. I wish her hiss had remained inscrutable. Whatever the case, the memory, the myth, the vision rips through me awkwardly like a jagged blade. So it happens again and again. So it happened again and again – the lounge queen standing beside me – dye job, white-woman perm, blue mascara. *Don't make yourself sick, sweetie.* She'd rattle the bowl, the nuts or pretzels, smirk at me, and stare as though she had the power to hypnotize, not for my sake, not to help me forget, but for her own. Sometimes she would touch me – pat my head, caress my cheek with the same hand that had been pulling on my old man's cock. *What a cute little boy,* she'd say. And Charlie would still be ashamed at the other end of the bar. And Janet's eyes would signal that my father had returned. I could always smell him behind me, all the familiar smells, but also those that weren't his – soap and her. He'd have his hand on my shoulder and hers would be on my

277

face and it seemed as though I completed a circuit – him connected to the dark air of that skanky lounge, the air connected to her, then to me. I knew it should've made me jerk and wretch, but it didn't. I'd sit there on the stool and Charlie would continue to ignore and Janet would look at me, not like I was a prince, but some pitiful waif, and then to him, almost as if to say, *'I could take care of the boy if you'd fuck me like you fuck her.'* And now, like then, things go black, and I'm left only with the feeling: them having connected me to whatever it is they want, whatever it is they do to get it, and the price of the ticket, which they, in all their wanting, are unwilling to pay.

The elevator moves. I back into the space. I don't want to be here. There must be a stairway down. No. No escape. I have to work, but I don't have to stand in the hallway like a fool. I go inside.

The loft is L-shaped. One wall, almost fifty feet long with seven-foot-tall windows, runs south along the Greene Street side. The south wall has more, which overlook Broome. It's dark outside. The rain makes me remember that I'm wet. I look at the radiators. They're too small for the space. The ceilings are twelve feet high and broken up by sprinkler runs and ductwork. Even in the dim light I can tell most of the work here has been finished. In the corner are paint cans, a couple of ladders, tarps. The elevator doors open. I walk out of its sight line, around the L, into the kitchen. The cabinets are done.

'Motherfuckin' dark as shit.'

It's Chris. After all this time I can tell his voice – deep, but not truly resonant. Articulate with a bit of a Bed-Stuy edge. He turns on the lights. He's with other people. They walk heavily, slowly. It's eight now, but they don't seem to be in much of a rush to punch the clock. They all have paper bags full of deli breakfast. There's no one running this job. They're going to take their time. Breakfast is on Nancyboy, which of course gets passed on to the client.

'Jesus motherfucking Christ,' says Chris when he sees me – deadpan – to belie his surprise. 'What's up?' He throws a short wave and turns before I can respond. He goes to the corner sill and studies his breakfast from outside the bag. He reaches in, arranging the coffee and the buttered bun within. Then he takes the items out and arranges them on the sill. The other two, whom I don't recognize, follow suit on their own sills. They eat quietly. Young men slouched in preparation for becoming old.

'Well, well.'

KC's at the door. KC and Bing Bing. The others don't greet them, and they disappear behind a soffit and reappear again. By 8:30 everyone's ready to go.

'You're with us, professor.' KC beckons me to the paint supply. There's not much I hate more than painting – not so much the actual rolling, but the prep, the cleanup. He points at the Baker, sucks his teeth, then points vaguely at the first few windows.

'We have to set this thing up,' he says, more to himself than to anyone else. Because it's not a direct order, Bing Bing ignores it. He goes to the middle window and leans against it. He looks across at the other building – the apartments above the jeans store. Some of them are being renovated, as well, but they aren't nearly the size of this one. A squat white man with a thick mustache and a very young black man work on a countertop.

'What you doin', man?' KC barks. Bing Bing turns slowly and shrugs.

'Wa d'you won?'

'Set up the ting, mon!'

Bing Bing sucks his teeth, though not nearly as loud as KC, and waves me to him.

'C'mon, mon.' I go. We circle the broken-down scaffold and then stop. We both reach for the same side at the same time and both pull back. I let him pick it up. I'm not sure how he wants to go about putting it together – and a Baker isn't complicated at all. You can look at one and intuit how it should work: two vertical steel sides, like ladders, with slots in them; two horizontal lengths with ends that pocket into the slots; a metal-edged sheet of plywood to fit as the platform. It's the hesitation that gets us, the uneasy hierarchy that keeps us both staring at the section he's holding.

'Get dat a won.' So it's been decided. Bing Bing's lord of this particular fiefdom. And because we have a leader, things move smoothly. We put the Baker together and wheel it over to the first window by the front. Bing Bing starts back to the supply pile. I try to follow, but he raises his hand to me like he's a crossing guard. He doesn't pick up his feet, and his boots are only laced to the ankle. The tops fan out and his jeans are stuffed into them. They remind me of Eskimo boots, or what I've imagined Eskimo boots, if there are such things, to look like – hides and pelts wrapped tightly but seeming to be loose around feet and ankles. He shuffles back atop the sawdust and gypsum-coated floor with a box of sandpaper. KC meets us beneath the window.

'She likes these, you know. Yeah, she likes them like this.' He waves up at the window. 'Yeah, don't touch anything – she says.' He sucks his teeth again. The window frames are metal – old stainless or tin – it's hard to tell because they're so worn, gummed up and over with dirt and soot and grease and little chips of old lead paint.

'Yeah, mon, we burned that shit off,' says KC. I guess he caught me studying the paint. 'Three days with a torch – fuck.' He steps away from the sill as though the memory of the task is too hot itself.

'Yeah, she don't like no paint on no trim. Everything natural. Everything raw.' He smiles. 'But she likes this. She come up yesterday and she just smiled. She likes this.'

Bing Bing and I both nod our heads involuntarily.

281

'Okay,' says KC softly. 'Clean it up.'

Bing Bing aligns the Baker with the window.

'You bring a putty knife?' asks KC.

'Everything but.'

'There's some in the gang box. There's some WD-40, too. Boy,' teeth suck, 'I don't know how you g'wan clean dat.' He shakes his head. 'But that's the way she wants it – like it was when it was new. New, but still lookin' old.'

He takes the sandpaper from Bing Bing.

'Lemme see dat ting.'

He rubs it on the metal and cranes his neck back to get some distance. He shakes his head.'

'I don't know, boy.'

He takes one swipe at it, stops, turns to Bing Bing.

'G'wan get ma d'oil na.'

Bing Bing complies and KC continues to survey the frame, looking up the vertical then down the wall to the others. There are seven. My gaze drifts with him. Seven double-hung giant windows with nine lights each. Four hundred and sixty-eight linear feet of metal to buff. Bing Bing returns.

'Good. G'wan, gimme dat.' KC takes the oil and sprays a small patch, careful not to create too large a test area. He's always been careful. We used to call him the finisher or the fixer – the carpenter's buddy – with his twelve-inch blade and mud, patching holes, taping and plastering gaps, smoothing out everyone's fuckups, burying the mess and blunder of a bunch of half- and quarter-breed malcontents. I used to look at his work after he'd painted, touched up, and cleaned for the bulge, gap, or wiggle that I knew was there and at some point he'd slink up behind me and say, *'You don't see nothing, do ya?'*

KC buffs the oil blotch. He starts nodding. 'Yeah, that's the way – yes.' He studies it again, angling his torso away this time – moving his head slightly to the left, then to the right – studying. Finally, he straightens.

'Here.'

He holds the paper and the oil out for me. I take them.

'Okay,' he waves generally at the windows, then points at the patch he cleaned. 'Like that. She'll like that.'

He starts to walk off, then calls for Bing Bing.

'Come on, boy.'

There's really nothing to contemplate, but I move the Baker out of the way so that I can, at least, pretend to be formulating a plan – Top to bottom? Bottom to top? Frame first or stops? I look closer at KC's spot. There seems to be a pattern engraved in the metal. Now I see it every-where on the surface, but instead of the slightly whitish tint in the clean spot, the untouched flowers are outlined by the dark crud. I wonder if KC noticed this or if 'she' would want her old-new window frames so ornate – adorned by whimsical flora.

Someone turns on the table saw. Someone else

283

turns on a radio – the former comes alive with a snarl and metallic whirl, the latter with a walkie-talkie squawk, then a commercial in which someone is screaming, like an electronic barker trapped in the little box. The person on the saw begins to cut plywood – feeding it too fast. The blade slows and the motor sputters, then, no sound.

'What the fuck?'

'Hold up.'

I find myself waiting for the song to come on. There are so many sounds on a job site, some inter-mittent, some rigidly patterned, some constant, and the random ones – a dropped tool or material, a curse, or something from outside like a siren or a sudden burst of laughter – which let you know there's a world beyond your allotted space and task. It's always struck me as somewhat sad, not crushingly, but enough to make me drift to memo-ries, projections, remiss. I remember the job site, like a bar really, just without the stools and the liquor and the talk. The men are there – the men and the malaise and whatever sounds to which you attach yourself to keep from drifting inside too far, before the point of any real reflection, because in a bar, too far, and you're babbling your secrets (and how many secrets do you have left since you've already revealed that you're a drunk?) too far inside and – *Out! Out!* – there's your blood on the floor.

The saw's back on. I should tell him, whoever

it is, not to force the wood on the blade, but you can't tell a man on a job how to do that job – it would be like telling a man alone in a bar that he's drinking too much.

The radio stops barking. Now there is music, drums at least, then some bass. I don't know the song, of course. Drums, how strange: They wouldn't let us play our drums and now that we can, we won't. The not-drum accompanied by the not-bass. It's actually catching, certainly better than the shriek from ill-cut wood, KC's teeth sucking, or the idiot rasping of me endlessly sanding metal.

The crud doesn't come off easily, so I roll the paper around my finger and bear down. This method works better, but now I'm sanding a much smaller area. And the window frame seems to expand, rise through the ceiling, extend through the south wall, and out to Broome.

There are people walking the streets, some in coveralls, some in suits, different kinds of women – dressed down, dressed up – moving north and south. I wonder if they're natives or transplants. Why did they come – foolish question. Everyone comes to be a star, but the numbers don't bear out – winners versus losers. I suppose that one could say we were winning, Shake, Gavin, me, even Claire – having escaped our fates: artless concrete toil, drunken wife, and child-beating, brick-dry republican husbands. Death. Made so many dreadful mistakes and escaped many of them with impunity. And we were all still alive, relatively optimistic – trying to do something every day. But the *lucky to be alive* line doesn't mix well with the rasping, the banging, and all the people below moving with so much selfassurance. Yes, I made it through almost a year and a half – a free ride – in Cambridge, flamed out, came back in the city with the others. And we had some peace – writing, singing, staying sober, leaning on each other. Then I met Claire. Then Shake went insane, and soon after, Gavin fell off. Brian. Fucking Brian. Calling from across the world to wish me luck and say that *'a centipede bit me on the testicles.'* Where had he picked up that little English accent? – Ah, there but for the grace of God . . . It sounds hollow, even unuttered, a coward's mantra or some duplicitous line – like a malt liquor slogan on a ghetto billboard. It's the conspiracy of the haves – *How do you keep a good man with a wee problem down?* Keep him thanking his lucky fucking stars he's got what he's got.

I was supposed to have been somebody. I was full of promise.

'What happens to a dream deferred?' 'How can you mend a broken heart?' What if you don't keep your promise? But who made it for you? If not you, then why is it yours to keep? I was supposed to have been somebody – not anybody – somebody who mattered and to whom things mattered. I was born a poor black boy of above-average intelligence and without physical deformity. I was born

a poor Indian boy of above-average intelligence and without physical deformity. I was born a poor Irish boy of above-average intelligence and without physical deformity. I was born a poor black boy of above-average intelligence and without physical deformity, and therefore I should lead my people. It didn't work out that way. Even my father felt he could shake his head at me. *'When you were a little boy you were so full of light . . .'* People have spoken of the light: finding it, holding it, keeping it alive by torch or a memory of flame – the sun, a burned image on the mind-slate to be remembered until the next day, 'til rising. Or will memory eclipse it? What do we remember? What do we now see? I don't remember an exchange of vows. Who had passed that light to me? All that light he said he'd once seen? It hadn't come from him, Daddy Bing Cocktail, at least I thought not. It hadn't been passed down in backwash beer or hopeless baseball teams or hep and cool cats – the vacuum he'd left, nothing had rushed to fill it. Nothing displacing nothing – and so on.

Lila had told me there was a light. I've pieced it together over the years, why she left the South, why she drifted and wound up in Boston – some star she saw. We'd just moved out of the city to Newton. She was tired. She'd been lying to the school about our address, sneaking me across the border to the suburban public school. I suppose that I'd been kicked out of the private one I'd been attending. They'd revoked my scholarship – or that's how I put it together – for fighting perhaps. And I say perhaps because other boys fought, fought often, and were allowed to stay. I'd watch them fighting over things that seemed silly – cupcakes, candy, the rules for games – they'd tear and kick and curse and cry and have to be dragged apart, still crying and kicking. I didn't do that – at least, that's what I believe.

One boy had said to another that my mother was *'funny looking.'* Not so great a slight, but in another light, an enormous one. And they whispered it back and forth, giggling. *'Ugly freckle face,'* turning to look at me. Giggling, whispering for what seemed to be a long time. There seemed to be no one for me to appeal to – to make them stop. Our teacher, who was usually so quick to halt any disobedience, either hadn't heard them or hadn't cared. I don't think she cared much for me, the quiet boy who never spoke out of turn, who answered her questions, who looked up at her blankly – stoic little black boys must be unnerving to old white ladies – as though she was Bull Connor: not strident, nor with defiance, but without any discernible fear – the face of infinite cheek to turn once and again, again.

'You are the light of the world,' Lila had said. It wasn't fair when I hit the boy closest to me – the boy who'd started it. We'd lost the house the year before, moved to an apartment, been evicted from that, and had just moved into some dark little shit-hole. My mother, whose freckle face was odd, had

picked up her pace of drinking to perhaps counteract the burdens of money and parenting and whatever else failing people go through. So it wasn't fair. I had rage held in waiting, and I channeled it via my fist into that little pink face.

I think that, much as many Christians don't really know the beatitudes, most people don't really listen to or understand the blues. Most people don't understand, or have never experienced rage. It isn't singular, random, episodic. It's cumulative, with a narrative thrust like a black-iron locomotive. It's always there or on its way, started initially by some unseen engineer, some fireman wraith endlessly shoveling endless coal into the fire. Hot locomotive rage. Inexorable. And you can keep switching that train, switching it, keep it on the long runs of rail through your wastelands until one day when that rage is closing in, you don't switch. You let it run. And for an instant it feels so good – the smack-thunk of skinbone on skinbone, feeling yourself strike something and having it give. And what it looks like – brown fist on white face. It makes sense – to me at least. We've reached the end of the line, and for a moment it all makes sense. Even in the screaming, the chaos. Even when the station collapses. Even the casualties. The body count makes sense, until of course you realize that this isn't your stop – you're not supposed to be here. *'I wish I was a headlight, on a northbound train...'* But it's too late for that. Now your little classmate's on the floor, chair and desk toppled. Snot and tears and blood. The smeared, dislocated face huffing, gagging for air with an intermittent shriek each time he finds his breath. Then gasping to find some more. And Mrs Kline taking my wrist and leading me to the office. I remember waiting. It seemed like a train station. And when the balding white man (there always seemed to be one) opened his door and looked at me as though I should feel guilt and shame, I knew I was in the wrong place, the wrong time – that I should've died long long before or long to have yet been born. I didn't say much then. I just answered his questions, but I know what I'd have asked him if I knew then what I know now: 'Tell me how long the train's been gone.' The other one I was supposed to be driving. Although he probably wouldn't have known.

How had I missed it? I had been waiting right there. If it's not too far on down the line, then – *stop that train – my promise is leaving me now.* My promise. I was born a poor black boy of above-average intelligence, and therefore as the future leader of my people I was given the light for me to keep – not to let shine but to hold on to in the darkness like a star shrouded by night's sky cloak until I was ready to reveal it. But it's a strange thing to go through life as a social experiment: promethean metaphors; this school and that school; this test and that test; Moses and Jesus and Martin and Malcolm; Socrates to Baldwin; Shakespeare to Dylan; Jeremiah and community; community centers; marches, church basements, and city hall stairs; and the good white schools with the good white people – and I was like Daniel. I was supposed to have been someone. I was full of light – full of promise. I punched that white boy in his face, and all promises and contracts were cancelled. They ran me out, and then Lila beat me pretty good, or bad. She drew blood. O, the many uses of an extension cord. But I didn't cry. I looked at her as I had looked at the headmaster, like I did Mrs Kline – just as my mother had taught me – with the fish-eye, the deadeye, the mask of dignity; and it scared her. It stoked her rage. She went for me again, kicked over a box of plates. She hit harder. Then she stopped, dropped the whip, covered her eyes with her hands, and let out a high, long, broken whistle whine, shaking her head slowly. She cried for what seemed to be a very long time. And when she stopped, she peeked out from behind her hands as if to see if I had gone. I didn't show it, but I was scared to see what would be on her face when she saw me still standing there. She smiled. And the places on my body where she'd whipped buzzed and seemed to rise with heat. It didn't hurt. And I knew from her face, the crazy, random face gone soft and quiet that there was, shot through the both of us and through the air, love. There was light in that little room. It moved through me, warmer than my blood. It was in her. It was all around us – the sink, the table, the counter. Her face seemed to glow from a place I couldn't discern. Love. And it wasn't so particular as her love for me or mine for her; it seemed to have always been there, and through our rawness we both felt it – balm on wounds. Everything would be all right.

'You are the light of the world . . .' She shook her head, 'But you can't let anyone know – not yet.'

'Why not?' I asked. I flinched too – just a hair – but enough for her to see, because you didn't question Lila, especially when she was like that, all grave and steely, set to tell you true. But my flinch hurt her and she dropped her head in shame. 'I won't ever hit you anymore.' She sighed and looked at me as though asking my forgiveness. She started gathering the pieces of plate, trying to cobble together one out of the broken many.

'I'd been living in Richmond, but I came up and found your grandfather in Baltimore,' she said. 'He had a wife and a girl. And I got a little job, and I started spending some time with him. *He was my father.*' She looked at me as though she'd seen something of him flash in my face and then disappear – something she wanted to come back.

'After a little while, his wife didn't like it – told him to tell me to stop.' She pawed at the plated fragments. 'So I stopped. I came here.' She finished repiecing the plate, brushed away the dust and hopeless fragments.

'You're a good boy.'

Lila had said there was light, and therefore, love. And Claire had said she loved me – on street corners, in rental cars, on stairways. Claire didn't get it – perhaps still doesn't. Standing before me at the altar, in her vows she'd said she loved me, but she hadn't seen – the line of Ham, the line of Brown. I must have appeared to her to have been divorced from time and context – just a man, nothing but a man. Or, perhaps, a *formless creature*. I thought it was the wilderness that we were both about to step into – faithless, ruthless, perhaps even loveless. If love was the light and the light revealed all – how couldn't she see me? If she had, would she still say she loved – some postmodern Desdemona – in spite of the shroud that enveloped my alleged light, my love.

Edith doesn't love me. That's obvious. She's always thought that I was crazy – impractical. I've always made her nervous – talking about ridiculous things like art and freedom. But I'd done the bootstrap jig, bused tables, torn down walls, learned a trade, became – by some accounts – skilled at it. I'd sobered up and gone back to school, where some people believed I still had promise and made new promises to and for me. But Claire, her friends thought about sex – our sex – my biceps and balls. And after a while I came to think that that was where she was at. But she stuck around too long for that. I was too difficult for that. There was always some happy jigaboo she could've found for that. Sullen McBastard, Gavin had told her to call me, or Stoic Mombassa. But she wouldn't. She just blushed. He made her nervous in the same way I did Edith. No, Claire wanted to stay for the long haul. Silly girl.

I'm glad my mother is dead. She would be angry, with Claire, with me on the scaffold sanding scum off metal. *'You are the light of this world . . .'* I'm glad she never found out she was wrong.

The drums come back – the drums and KC.
 'That's looking good, man.'
 I nod a thanks, abbreviated somewhat because I really don't want to take credit for it. KC and I used to get along well – trade off buying coffee and such. I wonder if he still has the nail gun he borrowed. I don't care. It has been a while, which makes me think that there would be, even between two fairly stoic men, some nod to friendship. And true, we hadn't kept in touch since that time, but aren't friendships like that? KC seems to be feeling me out all over again, as though I'd hurt him before. Maybe he's high. I thought he wasn't into that – at least not on the job. *'Hey, man, what's up?'* as though I'd just seen him the day before. Maybe he had recognized the past – things were still cool and seeing me was no big deal. 'Take it

easy,' he says as he backs away, wiping at the frame. He looks down at his shoes and I think I catch it coming off him – shame. KC feels sorry for me. I turn back to the window, back to the rasping, the polyrhythm, with the drums. More screaming wood on the saw. I look beyond the stops – outside. They've got the countertop on. The white man runs his fingertips along the top. I follow the exterior wall down. Two women moving in the street catch my eye. They disappear into the jeans joint. Because of the double-height storefront, I can see over the first racks of pants and shirts, which bear the company logo. Beyond them are racks with belts and shelves with sweaters – all monochrome but rich hued. They look, on this gray day, juxtaposed to my still-damp clothes, to be warm and comfortable. Claire would like these things. I wonder what she'd say if I were to show up with a pair of Lucky Jeans and a monochrome sweater. *'How did you do that?'* But she wouldn't be angry. She wouldn't be suspicious. I think she would be happy. She needs new clothes – nice casual clothes. And a guy, even a broke one, needs to be able to buy his girl a nice little something every once in a while. It's good for the both of them. Young girls shouldn't get weary. Tenderness would be expressed in the fact that somehow, someway, you came up with the dough. You went through whatever it was you went through to get it, and in the end you were still thinking about her. I find it somewhat amazing, ridiculous, that I've never thought of a present as a symbol. Love manifested in the material, or better yet, the thought behind the material: *These jeans mean I'm thinking of you, baby.*

I have one small patch left to clean and I realize that I don't know what I'm being paid – if I'm being paid at all. How many passes over engraved dirty daisies equals one pair of designer jeans. Finally, the jackass on the saw stops ruining wood.

Everyone begins drifting – shifting around their stations.

'Break,' says KC, sneaking up from behind. He clangs his putty knife against one of the Baker's verticals. I drop my piece of sandpaper.

I climb down. Now everyone is mulling and going into their pockets for money. Chris waves me over. Now that the first stage of morning gruntiness is over, he seems a bit warmer. I join the gathering. Chris beckons me closer with a head nod.

'Yo, man, what's up?' He doesn't wait for an answer. 'Got a pencil?'

I produce one and he passes me a small piece of cardboard. I take it and try to decipher it. I'm puzzled – lost for a moment in its blankness.

'Regular coffee. Buttered roll. Thanks.' He says it all without looking at me, only at the cardboard, waiting for me to do something. I don't know what.

'You get that?' He gives me an eyeball – quick and lewd – like he's an impatient flasher and his eyelids are overcoats. I connect the blank slate with the pencil: *Write*. I write. I'm taking orders. I do it somehow: coffee, tea, biscuits, cigarettes. I do it. Somehow. Then I pretend to segregate the money they give me – discreet folds, mental notes. They each come in turn, Magi-like in their solemnity, as though each is making an offering. 'Banana, too . . . ,' sings the Dubliner. He's not a bad chap, I suppose, but now, of course, I despise him. He slips me his prefolded dollars. 'Thank you,' he says. Now Bing Bing. 'J'wan caffee – b'yan butta, na de toata – a'heet?' And there's apology in his voice, too, but what he should be sorry for is the brutality of the sameness and disparity between Kingston and Dublin. Shake's maternal grandfather was an Anglo-Irish missionary to Antigua. He found a wife there and then brought her to Jamaica. They had a daughter, who living on that island of *'rough people'* with all her island haughtiness married herself a rough Jamaican countryman. Shake was fucked from jump – split in two at least – but he tried to create some bastard language that pointed at where he'd been, where he liked to think he was going. These two bastards refused to even be American – to assimilate.

I go to the elevator and think about the elevator woman, elevator girl. What should I call her? I look at her door. What is she doing in there? Had she left for the day? Her elevator jerks up and then starts down – clanking. I sniff for her, but only for a second, then I'm ashamed – disgusted. I get out and go outside. It's stopped raining. The air doesn't feel like August. It's more like October – cool and sharp in the nostrils. A leaf falls from somewhere onto my shoulder. *Summer's gone.* It blew right through here, and I seem unable to recollect what happened. I don't remember heat. I don't remember long days or soft evenings. Soon the mornings will all be dark.

Across the street the jeans joint is jumping. People need pants, I suppose. I'd like to go in, but I don't. I have a job to do, and as I walk west on Broome, I wonder if it's more honorable to be a good lackey or a bad one. If anything can be claimed – any victory at all – in the fact that you've failed. Would a genius fail an errand for a fool? I have money. I have a list. But I have nowhere to go. I haven't spent time in this neighborhood in years. Something tells me to walk away from SoHo and the absurdly priced muffin shops. I'd like for the elevator lady to appear, but what would I ask her: *Excuse me, do you know where I could find an inexpensive muffin?* There's no reason it should, but the question sounds ridiculous in my head, and I push on. There must be a deli somewhere. It is after all New York City, where there seems to be one for every resident.

I turn south on West Broadway and stop at Canal. Nothing. I turn to face the east. The street is full of vendors and shoppers – carnival-like – the neon of the stereo stores, foam rubber stores,

298

barkers with counterfeit Gucci and Prada and Chanel. The sidewalks are thick with people and carts, and the street is full of honking and lurching vehicles in perpetual and eternal gridlock. Potholes, sinkholes, tar patches, steel plates, and a traffic cop who stands just off the sidewalk at the corner of Church – white gloved, futile, full of bad faith. Nothing good can be had down that way.

I keep heading west – outpacing the tunnel-bound traffic. Every car seems to be honking. Traffic jams have always made me nervous, whether I'm in a car or not. I'm troubled by the origin of the stoppage or slow down. There's a blockage somewhere, an accident perhaps, because of which, someone is dead or near death. And there are the obvious associations that come with blockage and death and the too close proximity of people and cars and carbon monoxide. My heart is about to explode. At the same time – and perhaps less reasonable – everything is too heavy. There's too much weight. You can see it – the potholes, the sinkholes. Manhole covers under which there are tunnels, tubes, grooves for pipe and wire, sewers, and of course, subways. You can hear it in the hollow boom of the steel plates covering the faults. And this isn't a strident judgment – not some puritanical metaphor. The city is, and I say it without humor, hollow at its core. There aren't any insides. I count the cars, the trucks, the squat and the tall stone and steel buildings; it's a wonder that it all doesn't implode.

Get coffee! I scan west. There can't be anything that way on Canal. I cross West Broadway and decide to look north up Hudson – nothing there, either. I stop and re-collect my thoughts – not that I've really been thinking about anything other than the tarmac folding in on itself and everyone and everything tumbling into the void. Not an apocalyptic vision, only an exercise in layman engineering.

A garbage truck bellows, and then I smell it – the stink – rotten chicken and ass. It goes right to my stomach and I gag, almost lose it right there. I hear a voice in my head say, *'Claire, oh, Claire.'* But she'd actually puked. She'd waded into traffic like she always did, and I, as always, had asked in the accusing and arrogant way appropriate for a rhetorical question, *'What are you doing?'* She'd stepped back onto the curb, made eye contact with the driver, and then retched into the gutter – shameless – like an old drunk. People watching had side-stepped her breakfast in disgust and the driver had looked down from his cab with the straight-faced Anglican disdain and horror reserved for use by her people. She apologized to me, but I was used to the puke of drunks and she was my wife. Within fifteen minutes we were home watching the dark blue line appear on the pregnancy test. She shrieked like someone who'd just seen a ghost or a rat and then realized that the haunt, the vermin would be back soon. And this was someone who'd believed she wanted children – an oddity, really, for her generation – her one ambition, becoming a comfortable housewife. And I don't think that it was in reaction to her mother, who was of course, ambitious. Who at the time of her husband's death, although already wealthy, started, then grew and sold her own business. She hadn't been a bad mother. Claire had never accused her mother of not loving her. But she wasn't, as Claire puts it, the nurturing kind.

So Claire in all her horror was pregnant with our first. And even though I couldn't show it, I was horrified, as well – another in the line of Ham, the line of Brown. For some obnoxious reason I wished that, and then was convinced that. C was a girl. I joked, or pretended to be joking when I said, *'I don't know what to do with a boy.'* Claire went along with that pretense, but of course we weren't ready for him or her. We were still in the netherworld of postadolescence. I was just happy to be alive, and she was still dreaming like a child. She had plans for herself, plans for me: some amorphous blend of art and love and sex and race where money needn't be discussed or considered; where the limitations of her inexperience would finally be realized, considered, felt; where the limitations of my experience . . . I'd already considered my experience and already understood on some basic level that things weren't going to work out, that I was, in every sense of the phrase, *born to lose*, that the day when people like me, whatever and whomever they may be, win wouldn't

301

be a good day for others. *'The Times They Are a-Changin'.'* Dinner parties, cocktails. *'What's he singing about mommy?'* I think it was the brown-like-poop kid who'd asked. His mother explained, quite well, I thought, what the song meant. But she couldn't explain that when the revolution did come, it was coming for her and hers and everything she thought she knew and loved.

And Claire. We watched her belly grow – snap-shots, narrated videos, sonograms, heartbeats, little feet kicking. I watched her change into a woman. I would spy on her talking to her baby. She'd wake me up every morning before dawn to put my hand on her tummy to feel him kick and stretch. And even in the dark I knew that on her long mouth was that crooked smile. *'She's perfect,'* she'd whisper.

In another time or place C and Claire would've died. Her blood pressure began to creep up in the last three weeks of her pregnancy – 140 over 85, 150 over 90. Then it jumped: 160 over 95, 165 over 100. Her womb began to calcify. C was slowly suffocating, slowly starving. Perfect to good to satisfactory to poor to the hospital – an emergency. Pitocin, blood pressure cuff, fetal heart monitor. The newly grave face of our midwife. The unfamiliar doctor. Every fifteen minutes the cuff would fill. There was the clicking, buzzing, the hiss of air and the velcro peel. Then the readout, always worsening. C's heart rate drop-ping, leveling, rising, dropping. And since there had been no explanation for this condition, there needn't be any explanation for anything else happening. She'd wanted to have him 'naturally,' but there wasn't anything natural about this: beeping, hissing machines; wires; strange technicians; institutional paint colors, the cold gurney rail; trying to hold her hand among the tubes and wires; trying to block her view of the monitors, which, had she been able to see would have read, *'You are dying.'* Our child was killing her; and my selfish indulgence – knowing what it meant to be born to lose.

They had to cut him out. I had to keep a straight face – a happy one, even – for her. I was all she had to look at. So at the same time, I saw her eyes and her ovaries, her restless, questioning lips, and her blood. Then my boy – his perfect, unsqueezed head. They handed him to me – balls first. I must have waited an instant too long to take the bloody, mucousy thing. *'It's okay. Hold him. He's yours.'* But I wasn't afraid of that. In fact, I felt that I should be the only one, in that room full of white people, to hold that dusky purple boy. And that made me of two minds: one was waiting for something to go horribly wrong; the other scanned time, scrolling forward to the future when everything would go wrong. I was premourning him and premourning his loss of me. And then, as best I could, I banished those thoughts from those minds and then banished those minds. They gave him to Claire. She got it.

It was simple. That was her boy. She loved him. He was beautiful. The only significance – the umbilical cord, which the doctor, scissors in hand, asked if I wanted to cut.

They tried to take him to the nursery to allegedly weigh and test and measure him all over again. I tried to insist that I go with them. Claire had muttered something like '. . . *no bottle. Nipple confusion* . . . ,' but I waited with her until they got her into a room and had the morphine pumping. Then I went up. The nurse was changing his diaper, handling him like a frying chicken. I pressed up to the glass. She put him down, almost naked, in the warming bin. His eyes were closed. I watched him startle, grabbing at imaginary things, spasming in fear. The nurse came in with a bottle and roughly jammed it into his mouth. I knocked on the glass. She came outside.

'Yes, daddy?' she said sharply with a lispy accent. I think she was Korean. She stood in front of me as though we were about to each take our roles in the bizarre deli wars between her people and mine.

'My wife doesn't want him to have a bottle, nipple confusion, you know.'

'He's startling.' She slowed her speech as though she was considering something. 'Sometimes a baby startles when the mother takes drugs.'

I walked past her, entered the nursery, and took my son. She protested and tried to block the exit, but when she saw that I wasn't going to stop, she moved. I walked briskly down the hall. I didn't know where I was going. They caught me waiting for the elevator.

'Daddy, you can't do that.' She'd recruited three black women to do her dirty work. This nurse, thick bodied and smiling, cooed calmly. The other two nodded and smiled along with her. One of them had a cart. She gestured for me to put the boy inside.

'Hospital rules. Babies have to ride. You can take him, but he has to ride. Okay, daddy?'

Claire was whacked-out on morphine when I found the room. Nurses from other departments peeked their heads in to get a glimpse of the renegade father, and that kind of got me through the day. They made fun, but they were kind. But when night fell, they stopped coming. I was exhausted, but I couldn't sleep. I was fixed on his breathing. Newborns, ugh, it seems to be such a struggle for them – sometimes panting shallowly, sometimes taking one short breath and then waiting, then one brief exhalation, then waiting. I couldn't stand it, so I spent the evening wheeling him around the hospital, skating under the fluorescents, atop the buffed bright floor. Skating the glowing, waxed hallways, the light so bright that it threatened to flash us into oblivion.

I got us out of there as soon as I could, got Gavin's harsh jalopy and loaded them in. Me, my bride, and our boy, going home in a borrowed car – bad shocks – over and into potholes. *Bang!*

Claire screaming again and again like she was being torn apart repeatedly. The three of us, some lost little tribe, descending, like it was the first time, into Brooklyn.

When the revolution comes, they might be coming for me, too. If they cut me open, they'd find that undigested prime steak in my stomach. I find a deli tucked in the middle of the block, Broome between Hudson and West Broadway. I go in and start grabbing things in a rush, then I remember the list, which of course I can't find. I replay each interaction: one black tea, four regular coffees, four buttered rolls, one toasted bagel. It all goes rather smoothly. I even get extra sugar and milk and such and get out without a hitch – back down Broome to Greene – when I realize I don't have a key or a phone number or a phone to call with. There's no buzzer, either. But of course, she's there, this time with a yoga mat and water bottle. She's also found her sunglasses.

'We meet again.' I don't know why, but I expect more from her. I know, for some reason, that she has more to say. Then I think that maybe she does – just not to me. I don't seem to make her nervous, and she probably figures she hasn't any reason to fear or respect me. Basic politeness is enough. *Any* acknowledgment should be enough.

When I don't answer, she wrinkles her brow and bends toward me slightly as though she's peering into my consciousness.

'Bad day?'

I shrug my shoulders.

'Break time?'

'Yes.'

My neutral accent betrays me – makes her straighten – reexamine me from a new point of view.

'How many breaks do you guys get?'

I pretend not to understand. She sees through this. I've equaled the stupidity of her opening line. We're even.

'Who's the general contractor?'

'John Leary.'

'Is he a smallish man who drives a fancy truck?'

'Yes.'

She feels better about my speech now, comfortable. The gopher bags and the voice – doesn't seem to bother her, as though the disconnect hadn't occurred to her at all.

'How is he? Is he good to work for?'

'I just started. I don't really know.'

I'm only able to spot the worst dye jobs, so I can't tell if her hair is natural. It's streaked – red and blonde in a majority of long, auburn curls – but some of it is wavy and it makes her appear to have an elegant mess of carefully coiffed snarls. There's a hint of sun on her head now, just one side. It makes the color of the darkened side rich, gives her hair a depth and volume that makes me want to touch it. Fortunately, she speaks.

'I don't care much for him.' She pauses. 'I'm sorry. I don't want to bias you.'

She changes her tone, brightening.

'Are you a carpenter?'

'I was.'

'Oh,' she nods – now she understands. Her eyes are dark brown, and, juxtaposed to her lighter hair, pale skin, and orange freckles, seem incredibly deep. There's the first hint of the pull of wrinkles at their corners. Knowing her age would dramatically alter her face, aging it or making it younger.

'Would it be insulting to ask if you'd like to do extra work – for me?'

I have no choice but pretend to be puzzled.

'I phrased that poorly. Were you a good carpenter?'

'Yes.'

'Would you be willing to help me with some things in my place? I was going to ask your boss, but . . . It isn't much and like I said – well, they've been working there for a long time and haven't gotten much done. I know Beth isn't very happy with the work – or lack thereof.'

She stops, as if she needs to check in.

'Have you met Beth?'

'No.'

'She's the owner. She's very sweet.'

There's a silence between us now. A bad one, as though neither of us can make sense of what she's just said. She points at the tray.

'You'd better get that stuff up. You don't want to mess up – being it's your first day and all.'

She opens the door for me.

'Thank you.'

I go in.

'So will you think about it?'

'Yes.'

'When can you come by – after work? Maybe six?'

'That's fine.'

She starts to go, then stops. 'But tomorrow – not tonight . . . I can't do it tonight.'

She's not quite so cool anymore. Perhaps her hair, her clothes are, in fact, accidents.

'You probably don't want to come straight over. You might want to make it seem to them that you're going home. I mean, I don't want to make it difficult for you.'

'Six is fine.'

She smiles sweetly, a bit girlish.

'By the way – Helena.'

'Good to meet you.'

She waits for a response.

'Ishmael.'

'Really?'

'Really.'

'Great.'

She lets the door close, looking at me, then turns away before it bangs shut.

When I get back upstairs, the lads are grumpy. I've been gone awhile. They do their best to hide it, the guys I don't know, because they figure that I'm stupid. The Dubliner holds up a hand of forgiveness for his forgotten banana. Chris shakes his head when he sips his tepid drink.

I sit on the other side of the loft from the rest, wondering when this steak will leave me, contemplating hunger as the flip side. KC wanders over.

'Get lost, man?'

'Long line.'

'Oh yeah?'

'Yeah.'

'You go to the one down the street?'

'Yeah.'

'Which one?'

'Down the street.'

He thumbs eastward. I point west.

'Broome, just before Canal.'

'Yes,' he says, too excited, as though he's a game show host. 'That's the one. They busy?'

'Incredibly.'

'Man, I'd like a spot like that.'

'I suppose they do okay.'

'Phhfft!' he blows spit. 'More than okay. More than okay. And you know the owner there?'

'No.'

'The big one, behind the counter, just watching. Sometimes he'll bag things when it's busy. Was he bagging today?'

'I didn't notice.'

'Yeah, sometimes he'll bag, but most times he's just watching. He's always watching, making sure nobody steals from him. If it was my place – pssst – I'd be gone.'

'You'd let people steal?'

'Mon, de wouldn't need to steal 'cause I'd be

fair with 'em. The motherfucking Mexicans he got back there – they got to steal. He don't pay 'em notin'.'

'You'd pay them?'

'Pssst!' He turns away as though I've insulted him. 'You know I do other jobs, mon?'

'I suppose.'

'You know what I pay him?' He points to Bing Bing, who has already fallen asleep on a windowsill. 'A whole lot more than he make here. You got to. You got to pay for it, man. Not be cheap like this guy.' He thumbs into the air at the unseen accused. No one else seems to be paying attention to his little rant. I don't know how it happened, but we're friends again, better friends than we ever were before. Perhaps the rest had already heard it all and I was merely a new ear. KC shakes his head and almost as abruptly as he started, ends his sermon. He feints a move away, then, as if to catch me off guard, stays.

'What happened, man?'

'What do you mean?'

'What happened to you, man? I thought you had big plans. Why you back with us?'

'I need a check, just like you.'

'Pssst! What you talkin' 'bout na?' He points. 'I thought you was a professor or something?'

'No. Nope.'

He looks at me with a canine suspicion.

'No, huh?' He nods his head. 'All right. All right.' His face closes up again, and I can't help but think that I've hurt his feelings. I offer up what I can.

'It didn't work out.' A mumble. More for me than for him. It's too quiet, and he's already moved to a more guarded place inside – not willing to hear my story now, even if I was fully committed to telling him. *I was born a poor black boy of above-average intelligence and without physical deformity and therefore I was chosen to lead my people, but some shit happened on my road to glory and I kind of lost my way. But I came back. They gave me another chance. But somehow it was different. And I don't know if it was because I'd sobered up or because my mother had died or because the world had changed – or because of all those reasons. Or because somewhere along the way I had become just too damaged to be of any use to anyone. And so I never finished. I never wrote that dissertation because what the fuck can you definitively say about anything unless you pretend? Act like some circus ape gesturing and mimicking for petting and treats. And so never was tenured and so became a career adjunct – an academic mercenary – drifting from class to class, school to school, and could scarcely do that until one day, you wake up and you're nothing and nowhere. Blah blah blah. Never finishing.*

KC looks at me as though he's witnessed me escape from a burning building – frightened, I suppose – morbidly and sympathetically curious.

'You okay, man?' he asks, giving me a bit more space. 'Because it looked like you were looking at something that wasn't there.'

312

'I'm fine.'

'Yo, you look high – not anymore – you looked high for a second. You had that faraway look in your eye.'

All of a sudden we go back to work. My lateness has actually done them a service – compressed the time between break and lunch. But for me it marks the amount of time left in this day – not so bad if I was building something, but the life of a paint scraper is tedious, hideous. The crud comes off but in no way is it archaeological. The strata, that past, is smudged and buffed into oblivion, and voilà: a brand-new skin. This is taking too long. I need toxic chemicals.

'What happened to you, man?' I see myself in the classroom slowly pacing in front of the students with a book held in the air asking, 'Whose cup trembles? Who will drink in the world's sorrows?' And them, looking back, some wide-eyed, some deadeyed. There was the odd white native slacker, but they were immigrants' children mostly – some, immigrants themselves, the blacks and Latinos, almost all of whom were first-generation college students, and mostly all of whom believed in the utility of knowledge. They'd made it through the city's abominable school system and were having to listen to me go on about the qualities of this one's syntax or that one's style, perplexed as to how this figured into possessing a marketable skill set. And me wondering what the hell it was that I thought I was doing to them – for them. Fixating.

Becoming vulnerable in public by immersing myself in the words. *'The bone's prayer to God is death.'* One day in some academic outpost, some student had broken the spell – raised his hand: *'. . . but my copy reads, "The bone's prayer to death its God."'* And I wanted to slap him, not out of embarrassment in the fact that I'd been reading it wrong for a decade, but because of the way he'd puckered his lips, as if he was now the secret master of that line. A little smug face quietly signifying that *he got it*.

'That's lunch!'

They've already prepared for their escape. Safety glasses and masks are off. Chris is already walking to his coat while drying his hands. I climb down off the Baker and wait in line for the sink. The steak has disappeared in form and benefit, and I feel as though I haven't eaten in days – light-headed, weak, jittery.

The sink is mine. A sandwich or whatever else I can scrounge up doesn't seem as though it will be enough. I need more. I figure I'll follow them to wherever they're going. I'm sure, having been working here awhile, they've sussed out the cheapest spot.

I get to the elevator just in time to see Chris look up and KC look down. The door closes and the elevator clanks down. *That's not very nice* is all that comes to mind at first, but each echoing metallic bang triggers a new qualification. The statement devolves to *fuck-chump bastards*. Then just to what I believe to be the sensation, the feel and sound of heat in the brain. *Fuckin' bastards.* I mouth it this time as though it will dispel the heat via tongue of flame, but it comes out as a mumble and a hiss. I remember to push the down button. I smack it. It doesn't light. I smack it again and try to remember if the light had come on before. I smack it again and then am contented to believe that the bulb is out.

The elevator clanks below and then the doors wrench open. I look out the window. They go into the street – south down Greene. None of them seem to be talking. They move like an errant shoal – not quite in unison, not quite apart. What is the secret communication between them that allows them to effect a pace and direction? Perhaps it's as simple as time and proximity – a tacit agreement, its only purpose being expedience. And they're gone.

They've left the radio on and I hear the horns – trumpet and sax – it's Sly. And the bass. *'I Want to Take You Higher.'* But no. It shifts. It cuts out. More synthetic drums. I try to continue with Sly's version in my head, but it's been corrupted, bent, and now I can't remember the first words, the tune. I think, but the monotone babble keeps me out of the song. *'I Want to Take You Higher.'* *'I'll take you there'* – fly away to Zion. *'What we call the beginning is often the end . . .'* I can still recall, quite clearly, holding my mother's urn while standing in a birch grove, wondering where my father was. The strange minister was waving his hand as though performing some hocus-pocus ritual to cleanse, or remember, or forget. Knowing that place then: knowing that place now; the street out there on a gray day. There aren't any trees down there, only lamp posts. Patterns on the street flicker in light's absence like leaf shadows in moonlight. Perspective and moonlight and memory shift, and you begin again and again. And what good is that? What good would it do to take a stand, to stop the cyclical occurrences? If the hero is the explorer, then the heroic act is to explore, to find origin, before the fragmenting effects of action, experience, memory, and meaning. Yes, I can smell the pear soap Claire uses for the children's bath, the residue on her hands, the whiff of it when she'd scratch my stubble and whisper, *'Shave,'* in front of the babes, pregnant with sex. The ridiculous twinning of sacred and profane, the innocent and the erotic. *'It's going to be a rough row to hoe.'* Whatever you said Gruntcakes, it was so true: No progress, Gruntcakes, in this twist of birth, fate, and fire.

Nothing has moved, so I push the button again. This time it lights and I can't help but laugh, but when it comes out, it sounds like a nasty little cackle – unfit for a prince of the world.

★   ★   ★

It's brighter outside than I thought it would be. Even in the gray I have to squint. I follow their trail, ignoring the fact that I can't actually track them across the slab. It's a shame, really, how dead my senses are. I want to be able to retrace their footsteps – moisture, scent, heat – like a pit viper perhaps, create an image in my brain with other sensory devices. Although I'm not sure what I would do when I found them – envenomate one, then swallow him whole.

I find them at the deli. Everybody's ordering the two-dollar chicken – half a scrawny bird from the old rotisserie with two sides. My crew stands by the case, single file, not talking to one another. KC is no longer my friend, I suppose. He doesn't acknowledge me when I get on the line. I look at the case, the processed meats with their claims of quality. The slicer on the back counter is gummed up with meat and cheese residue – mad cow prions on the blade. I follow their lead and get the special. I can't seem to convince the squat man behind the counter that I don't want the gray vegetables or any other side. He stuffs my container with gooey white rice.

They all pay and leave without me, still not talking to each other, and they stay a good twenty yards in front of me outside. When I get back to the building, they've already gone up, but someone's wedged a small piece of cardboard in the door to keep it open for me. When I get upstairs, they're all in their sills eating. I take my place behind the Baker and inspect my lunch.

When I open the Styrofoam container, I get hit with a moist blast of ancient fleshiness. I gag. That passes and then the odor turns somewhat pleasant and I'm suddenly very hungry. I poke at the breast with my plastic fork. The skin is dark and crispy with a slight oil sheen. The knife cuts through it all with surprising ease. My stomach says something rude and impatient. I take a bite. The skin is delicious, salt, olive oil, and garlic, but the rest is awful – overcooked to the point where the first bit of flesh has fused with the skin, transformed into an additional layer of dermis. It's hard and sharp like densely packed fingernail clippings. I swallow it anyway.

I try another tack. I cut the chicken up, discard the bones, and mix the meat in with the rice, which is close to pudding in consistency. It should ease the passage of the flesh shards down. The others have finished. Some recline in their sills. Chris is up, headphones on, but he's not nodding. He walks to each man, offering a cigarette. He makes it to me, offers, looks at my remaining food and apologizes with a shallow bow and step backward. I close the container and he offers again. I haven't smoked since C was born, but I want one. I go for one and then see the label on the pack. They're menthol.

'Why you boys gotta smoke on candy canes?' coos the Dubliner from two sills over. I lean out to see him. He holds out a pack of Marlboros.

'What you like?' asks Chris. I don't answer, but I try to bend my face into an expression of sheepish apology. He understands, takes another, deeper bow, and backs away again. 'Laddie, throw that back over this way.' He flips it to Chris with a slight grin, amused by his poor attempt at an accent. Chris takes one out, hands it over, and lights me. I drag and the smoke seems to fill my head instead of my lungs and I almost pass out. I exhale, and my senses return in time to see Chris zip the pack sidearm back to its owner.

I nod to Chris, 'Thank you.' He puts his hands together, bows again, and turns. I wave to the Dubliner, 'Cheers.' He waves back, shaking his head. He closes his eyes. I do, too. I take another drag and try to follow the smoke in, but all I see are hands passing chickens from a dingy walk-in, up a flight of stairs, to hands that skewer them, then hands that set the skewered birds in the oven; and I wonder how many times around does a raw bird spin before it transforms into a two-dollar special. I forgot how powerful and versatile a cigarette can be: as an appetite suppressant; a digestif; time bender, extender, or killer; a tool you can use to swap dull dinner conversation for a quick look at the moon and stars; and perhaps functioning best as something to focus on – an extension on which you can hang and let dry your rage and sorrow. I know I'm hooked already.

KC wanders over. He looks troubled. Everyone, through lidded eyes, watches him as though he's going to say something. He stops a few steps away from me and paws at the air in my direction.

'Hey, man?'

I don't respond quickly enough.

'Hey, man?'

'Yeah?'

He tries to keep a straight face, but he finds whatever he's about to say too amusing.

'I saw you outside this morning – you know?'

'Yeah?'

'I know what it was made ya took so long.' He rubs his hands together and sweeps the room to make sure everyone's getting this.

'You was rappin' to dat lady out there.'

'Oh yeah?'

'Yeah.' Pause.

'And notin', man. It's fine.' He checks the room again. 'She sure got some nice titties, though.'

They all fall out. For emphasis Chris rolls off his sill and onto the dusty floor. KC tries to talk over the yelps.

'Just kiddin', man – no, really, you g'wan see – she don't talk to none of us. You g'wan.'

Chris gets up and restores order by slowly walking back to his tool belt. He straps it on, and the rest of us follow. I catch myself smiling for no reason and gesturing at the window frames and unused sandpaper. This method will not do. I walk over to the paint supplies and find a new gallon tin of stripper, shop rags, a bag of cotton gloves, and a box of masks on which it's plainly stated that they are to be used only for filtering dust and pollen. I get a small bucket and an old brush and set up on the Baker.

The stripper is an amber translucent gel, which becomes more viscous as I whisk the brush around in it. The vapors penetrate the mask and shoot up my nose like cold fire and I'm instantly high and stupid. I lean away from the bucket until part of me returns – enough at least to begin.

By the time I've covered all the metal of this window, it's ready to come off. I wipe the tin down with the rags, and the crud comes off easily. What's left behind is gleaming tin and the clear image of etched daisies. It takes less than an hour to knock off one window.

I notice the radio again – horns and '. . . *ooo ooo oooo!'* Then static. I hear myself call out.

'Hey!'

Chris replies, 'What's up?'

'Turn that back.'

'Oh, shit. My bad.' He listens for a moment. He calls back, 'Who this?'

'Mayfield – The Impressions.'

'Sweet. This is sweet.'

'Yes.'

'All right.' He glides back to the kitchen area. Snaps twice on the beat and disappears. The saws stay off. Now there's only the intermittent drill-whine, hammer-bang, or KC's scraping from the bathroom. *'This is my country . . .'* We have our anthem for the day – community and soul. I've always found Curtis's voice enchanting. He could've sung just about anything in that falsetto, and I would've obeyed. The afternoon unwinds and the hits keep coming. Not all of the songs match the message, the elegance, but they all have the same effect – lulling this crew to joy. And this isn't the roughest bunch, but I know they've all seen and done questionable things between here and Dublin or Kingston or Miami or Brooklyn, but there's something tender even in the rogue at worship of his work and his song. Even up on the Baker with my stained toxic rags I rock internally to our collective groove. I make sure to keep the glass clean – work the rags into the joints. Progress. I'm well into the second window before I notice I'm being watched.

She's been in the middle of the room for some time. I can tell by how she stands, anchored, on her heels. She's wearing a large-brimmed hat that hides her face from me. Her long white and gray wavy hair tumbles out of it onto her back, mimicking the watermarks on her green overcoat. She looks from side to side and then heads for the kitchen. As soon as she disappears, Chris sings out over the music. He rushes to turn it down.

They speak in low tones – mostly him, but I can tell from his tone that he's answering her questions. They come back to the living area. Her heels sound odd – cutting through the dust, sounding out against the subfloor. Chris leads her to the middle of the loft and leaves her there. The two-dollar chicken repeats on me – comes up from the depths with such force I can't hold it back. It rushes out silently – not even a hiss – hits the mask and spreads in the air gap between it and my face, then reregisters itself as taste. Dog food is the first thing that comes to mind – salty chicken like dog food – but isn't dog food described on the commercials and on the can as being remarkably succulent? The makers never refer to it as gamey or raw, but only in terms a hungry dog probably couldn't care less about. Outside the window the red label from an Alpo can flashes for an instant and I know I've poisoned myself with the fumes and the food, and I wonder why this mask won't allow toxic vapors to pass out but only in.

She heads for the bathroom, where KC and Bing Bing are, and they call out to her much in the same way Chris had, excited, an octave higher than they should. They murmur in the same way, but their voices echo off the tiles, the pipes, and the porcelain. Then KC escorts her out, back to her original spot. She's looking up now, not at me but at the windows – studying them closely. She has a deep tan, like the one on Edith's supple leather face. Now she looks at me, not my face but my tool belt and the big framing hammer hanging uselessly at my side. She speaks.

'Those look lovely.'

I suppose that 'thank you' is the proper response, but I can't bring myself to say it, not to her, not for this. I'm dizzy. I feel the need to hold on to one of the vertical poles. And the moment seems to call for me to utter from this height a benediction, curse, or even a spell, but what comes to mind are the mutated greetings the men had cooed to her. She stays there, still looking up at me. Occasionally her eyes flit nervously away to the tin. KC finally saves the day for both of us.

'Yeah, Ms Crane, we've been working on those a bit. They all right?'

'Oh, yes,' she answers. She hesitates in turning to him, but manners compel her to finally do so. KC grins broadly. He wipes his knife with a clean rag. They look around the loft together. He follows her lead, as though he hadn't noticed some aspect of the job until she's discovered it.

'Oh, look, flowers – daisies.'

'Yeah, I just started noticin' them today. I was wondering if you was gonna like them.'

'Yes, I do.' And then – softer, 'Is he new?'

'Here, yes.'

Then up to me, 'I appreciate your thoroughness.'

I press the rag into the metal, focus hard on the task at hand. She gives up, says something pleasant to KC, and goes. KC stays where he is. He watches her leave, smiling at her back, then her absence. When he hears the elevator doors close, he loses his grin, puts his hands on his hips, and looks up at me.

'That was the client – Ms Crane.'

'Oh, yeah?'

He hisses through his teeth and shakes his head a few times. He gives up, too, and goes back to the bathroom. I start to go back to my work, but I just spin the rag like a propeller, looking for a clock. She crosses Greene, takes a quick look at the jeans store, and turns east up Broome. I whip the window with the rag, but there's no crack to it. I ball it up and let it drop down to the dust. I notice the fumes again. I taste them this time, all the way down in my belly. My shoulders and neck start tingling but not much more than skin deep, like some sympathetic reaction to the arid bird I ate, the bird's revenge, or both – the story in which the ghost fowl doesn't accept my apology. Then I see chicken tracks on the windowpanes – random chicken tracks – hopping the stops, disappearing into the frame, and reappearing on another sheet of glass.

I hang the bucket on the old gas nipple, sit down on the board, push off from the wall, and ride the Baker away from the window. Before I take the mask off I burp again: salty chicken like dog food. Breath like Grendel. Was it Grendel – the Midgaard? I don't remember – too many toxins to the brain – a taluine concussion. I remember forgetting many things. It feels as if I've forgotten entire languages, philosophical tracts, volumes of myth and story – 'Let me disclose the gifts reserved for age to set a crown upon your life-time's effort. First, the cold friction of expiring sense . . .' That is the conspiracy: to move a warrior to where he no longer remembers his rage, confused to the point of indecision, sword sheathed, wondering, *Am I the fiend?*

I stay away from the fumes until it's time to go. No one lingers. They move quickly, putting things away, going to wash in the slop sink. Chris points out a broom and gestures at the floor. The poison taste and the tingling are gone, but I'm still woozy, out of sync. The broom handle feels wrong and the floor farther away than it actually is. When I finish, I pack up and meet the others at the elevator. Chris frowns at my bag.

'I left the gang box open for you.'

I don't understand him.

'You comin' back tomorrow?'

I nod.

'Then put that shit away – lock it up!'

I nod again, cross the room to the box, but I don't put my bag in. I close the lid and try to lock it. My fingers feel dull and jointless. I fumble with the padlocks.

'You all right in there?'

I get it locked and walk back to the elevator, where the crew waits, Chris leaning in the doorway. I step in and he closes the gate. He looks at my bag again – shakes his head.

'Suit yourself.'

Outside everyone says good-bye with quick, silent waves. KC looks back one time to see what I'm doing, then Bing Bing turns to see why. They both turn again and accelerate north up the block.

I drift across the street and find myself at the doorway of Lucky Jeans. An angry-looking man in a suit comes out carrying two large shopping bags. Music trails him, *'Got My Mojo Workin'.'* He strides past me without a look. He smells like lavender. I try to picture myself in there buying jeans and a sweater, being predisposed to conceive of, pursue, and achieve one end: *If you're horny, buy her a present. If you're full of guilt and shame . . .* I used to be good at problem solving. Claire always admired how unflappable I was in a crisis. I don't know what makes me do it, but I jingle the change I pinched from Marco while staring at the door. Perhaps some unconscious aesthetic sensibility in me demands a particular tableau: I stand on the corner in the drizzle and put off going underground.

CHAPTER 9

More free coffee. The Sox are on a streak – so the newspaper says. It's silly, the *Times* doing a puff piece on the Olde Towne Team. The columnist has tried to spin it a few ways: detached interest, low-brow sarcasm masquerading as irony. He writes, without knowledge or history or context, the reasons this year's team is different. Gone are the days of twenty-five cabs for twenty-five players – which, of course, would indict a century of baseball with the characteristics of one group of players: New York trying to spin Boston via the story of a group of millionaire athletes as a folksy, blue-collar town.

They've cut the Yankee lead in half – three games with twenty-two left to play. They'll be in town this weekend to play four. Solid, fundamental baseball. No heroics. Good pitching and defense combined with timely hitting. It's insulting reading it, really, hurtful, like overhearing an acquaintance telling people at a party about the girl who broke your heart. Sally being watched by some bug-eyed teen jackass who thinks he knows her just because they share a locker row. It's ridiculous to be afflicted by some freckly moon-eyed girl still, but every good haunt must transcend its origin – grow and deform as time passes. Like addiction. Last time I checked, I had a drinking problem. Right now it seems worse than ever – having grown, deformed. I hear Sally married her college boyfriend and they've got one kid, living in L.A., rich off TV scripts and jingles. I knock back the end of my coffee and it just doesn't taste right. Not that it's tepid or bitter – it isn't a beer. I see the can I bought the junkie, empty by now but so what. I close my eyes and try to picture it: red and blue on white, the baroque lettering – the testament to quality. The pop-hiss when I pull the tab – '. . . *and the wilderness coalesced . . .*'

A girl of about sixteen walks by the window and I feel as though I might implode with grief. I don't know why. Over the speakers Miles bleeds through his horn, introducing the idea of an entirely different kind of judgment day – junk and funk, Big Muddy and Harlem. The gaps he leaves in the notes sound like distant wails – wailing souls from long ago. Perhaps it isn't that way. Perhaps it's the dead that allow room for the music to come through. Armageddon – sweet and cool and mellow. The girl, who is lovely, is joined by a black boy. They somehow manage to show their teeth through tight-lipped smiles. Their eyes close to slits. On most other people their expressions would seem hideous, sinister, but they're young and they don't know and they truly believe they care – for one another, for everyone else.

I know what day it is, but I look at the corner of the paper anyway: August twenty-second. One day after my birthday, six days before our anniversary and the march on Washington. We planned it that way. We asked everyone to hold hands – the bridal party, the congregation – a ridiculous mélange of the American gene pool. Together. Windswept. Marriage, for almost any couple, must be a rough road to hoe. And now, as well as then, I can name the reasons we shouldn't have tried. There hasn't been any progress made in closing the gap between black and white, rich and poor, insider and outsider, the damaged and the well. Claire still, up to at least the last time she saw me, looks at me in two ways: one that says she knows me and one that says she doesn't. And in the time we've been together I've never been able to span that gap – not with touch, not with words – for her or for me. That gap is a world unto itself in which there are battles over the validity of a cucumber and watercress sandwich, what box to check on some form you fill out for your children. Who is right? We both can't be. '. . . *when the fire and the rose are one.*' She believes, and I suppose most believe, her to be the rose. But I, to her, to them, am not the fire. I don't figure in.

It's a strange thing indeed to attempt to fit the forgotten social experiment into the equation. There are white models of morality, rich models of morality, and enfranchised models of it, as well. Nobody wants mine, this I am sure of – this one thing. What was it her aunt had said to me after the cellist had packed her things up, but I still heard her – Bach. Still saw Claire – my Claire behind her veil, which was pressed close to her face by the squalwind. Her cheeks, bright through the pale. My Claire. My love. My bride. She seemed to glide across the lawn to me like some ivory spirit, both angelic and terrible. Angelic, not because of the white, but because she was beautiful. And the August trimmed lawn and the periwinkle sky. Seabirds. But if there are angels, they are not innocent. They have seen too much: fallen brethren, fallen man. Terrible. Claire was gliding into awareness – into the wake of the slaughter. Coming to me. And the congregation said, 'Amen,' on the historic day. And they *'reckoned that she would sivilize me.'* She stood beside me in the span of the fieldstone wall as though she was whole, and now I would be, too, and *'all will be well and all manner of thing will be well.'* And we said, *'I do. I do.'* The red-haired girl played her cello and the rain came. And in the receiving line people blessed us. And her aunt, whoever she was, took her by the hand, smiling, but speaking with a gravity reserved for funerals, said, *'Beautiful, just beautiful. The day, the music.'* Then to me, *'Congratulations. Welcome to the family.'* Then back to Claire, *'We'll teach him about classical music now.'* And then she was gone. And Claire looked at me with two eyes: one as though I had an open head wound, the other as though I had just stepped onto the line. And that was the eye she chose, dispelling the first. The band set up under the big tent and, as I had instructed, played Miles – 'Yer Blues.' And as man and wife we walked into the chatter and cocktailing. And the people – both lines – clapped. But they didn't know. Outside came the rain's end – the double rainbow and the rosy sky. Champagne, cigarettes, and levity. Inside I heard the muted horn of judgment day.

The Cubs are on a winning streak, too, which is troubling because it's easy to drift to October: Game seven, Fenway Park, tie score, two outs, bottom of the ninth, full count. There's the pitch, then a flash of light and the world ends – without a bang or a whimper but without any satisfying resolution. *'And all manner of thing shall be well.'* The black boy and the white girl are waiting for their fancy coffee drinks. He has dared to hold her hand and she has dared to like it. And now she dares to press her hip into him. Miles bends a note, blue, and I scroll through twenty-odd years of white girls. The Black Studies units of history and English classes. The privileged children of the Bay Colony talking Jim Crow, learning about lynching. Learning and looking at me, as the white teacher lectured, with pity and sex on the brain. They, later, much later, away from home, away from Mommy and Daddy and peers, during their phase of social rebellion and sexual experimentation, in the privacy of a dorm room, or the relative squalor of an off-campus parent-paid apartment, could fuck and cry some poor nigger's blues away, or they, at least, could try, try and fail – *but at least they tried*. They could claim the effort, like some holy ticket to get them on the train, in the gates. Keep dreaming, blondie. And it occurs to me not to ask about the dream deferred, because almost everyone knows what it is, on some level, to fail. But what happens to a dream, and yes, a dream, not a desire or hankering or an impulse or a want, but a dream, realized? And yes, I say it again: It is a strange thing to go through life as a social experiment – to learn Latin and Greek and the assassination dates of the martyrs; to toggle between Christ and Keynes, King and Turner, Robinson, Robeson, Ali, Frazier, Foreman; to have a rumbling in the jungle of your black folk soul while a rough coon, its number come up at last, shuffles up from New Orleans to be free. *'And all shall be well'* when champagne sprays around the home clubhouse in the Olde Towne, character the only currency. Love won. Kingdom Come.

They leave and I fold the paper and go, too. I want to follow them. They do happen to be going my way, to the Heights, where the school office is. I don't know where it is exactly that I'm to go, and the idea of wandering the hallways seems stupid. I haven't called. I'm dirty. It's almost time to go home. The school office hours may not have anything to do with regular business hours. I remember being a student. Even worse, I remember teaching. There seemed to be, regardless of the institution, a casual regard for time. Perhaps not. Perhaps it was merely an environment in which I could indulge my casual regard for time.

I look up and the kids are gone. I remember nothing from school – *a nonrestrictive clause is . . . ?* Whatever the answer, it seems without application on this street under the elms and now a juniper. The carefully sculpted masonry: sidewalk, stoop, brick-point, lintel. It's too cold for August. I should send the boys to vocational school or have them apprentice with a topflight artisan. They can learn their sums and letters at home. Especially X, who just seems to be able to pick information out of the air – harvest it from the ether. He's three. He can read. He can write. He can add and subtract. Nobody taught him. It seemed as though the slate in his skull had already been written on when he arrived in this world and he recognized the symbols, understood and felt the weight of them. It scared Claire, and I must admit, it scared me, too. I would look at that man-boy face, the elfin imp eyes, and he would look back and somehow, smiling, wink without blinking.

X was named Michael until one of those Sunday mornings when there seemed to be nothing to do, nowhere to go – and that was good. Ella Fitzgerald was singing – 'Rockin' in Rhythm.' I had remembered to turn on the radio, tuned to one of those alternative stations at the top of the dial where the white boys play old black music, reciting play lists and band rosters in their quasi-cool voices – tidbits of this session with Miles or that one with Bird – but it's all right because they play the music they love and no one can say shit. They just play the music they love, which makes that music, by default, theirs.

I was on the couch thumbing through the *Times*. *'Ella singing a classic by Duke.'* Every once in a while I'd put down the paper and pick up the guitar. What a guitar that was – a cherry red Gibson 335. I got it used, flipped the bridge and nut around, restrung it. Usually, when you flip a guitar, the intonation gets thrown off and it won't stay in tune. It just sounds odd. Not this one. I kept it on a stand next to the couch, and both boys were good about not touching it – keeping the markers and the greasy, sticky paws away.

I was playing unplugged, and C was drawing a hallucination, some kind of dragon ritual, on a giant piece of vellum. X was lying on the floor. Strange child – naked, stretched out on his side, playing with his plastic dinosaurs. When he isn't stalking, smashing, or reciting facts about the ancient animal world, he's in a torpor – the only signs alerting us to his being awake, alive, the slight growls animating his toys.

Claire came through the door with bagels and

coffee. Maybe I sensed the hidden doughnuts. I was viscerally reminded of why I married her. She was pregnant and wore the new season on her. The October breeze had buffed her cheeks, long hair in a wind tangle, auburn, foreshadowing the leaves' turn. Green eyes like pale leaves. The boys hadn't looked up. I remember that made me happy. Selfish, yes, but it was a statement that said they were comfortable without their mother. She was being released. They were finally off her tit. The three of them had entangled in the sweet sorrow of psychological weaning. It could get hideous at times, her longing for them to grow up but then regressing; them longing for her to realize that they were both confident and scared. But sometimes, like that day, it was right, and we were all at peace.

'Michael, do you want some juice?'

He didn't look up. He just kept on growling softly – not ignoring his mother, just seemingly unaware of her presence.

'Michael?'

She lay down on the floor next to him and got in his face.

'Michael.'

He snapped up, wide-eyed, smiling, as though some mystery hand had flicked his power on.

'Michael,' she said, relieved. Then he yelled, not yet two years old, his most coherent statement to date.

'I'm not Michael. I'm Duke!'

Duke became X because Cecil became C and X was the only letter Duke could write – fist clenched around a Crayola. C rolling his eyes. Claire and I thrilled and worried – our boy, three years old, well over three feet tall, doing pull-ups, a vertical leap half his height – the crayon, a potential weapon. Blue eyes, just this side of scary.

Michael. I'd picked Moses first, then Miles, and Claire had winced at both. Troubled by their implications.

'They're so loaded. That's too much to put on a kid.'

'And Michael isn't?'

She didn't respond. But what is in a name? In between the two boys we lost a child. C had come too early. We were too young, too broke. X and the girl were *'accidents.'* But the one we lost had been planned. We were ready. It was May and it was windy and raining hard. A tree had fallen against the building and Claire called me. I was in the adjunct office grading papers. She said that she was scared. C was scared, too. I hadn't been very sympathetic because I was in the center office – windowless – and hadn't any sense of the weather. I teased her about lightning bolts and phone lines and she hung up, grumpy that I hadn't indulged her. Then she went to bed. I remember wondering if the student whose paper I was reading realized that I was the one who'd supplied him with the quote that he had plagiarized. The phone rang again. I sighed, shook my head, and answered.

'I'm bleeding.

I took too long to respond. She wailed.

'I'm bleeding!'

When I got home, Claire was in an almost unreachable panic bunker. There it was, on the bedsheets, small stains on the bathroom floor whose pattern made me think that something had dropped and shattered there. I had to lie to her. I told her everything was going to be all right. She had to believe it. What else could we do – accept that our baby was dead?

But it was dead. They vacuumed it from her the next day while I held C on my lap in the waiting room and lied to him. And looking out the taxi window on the way home we knew that New York City was too brutal for us. Edith was away, so I got a car, sped us north through rain, got to her house at night and broke in. C was asleep, but Claire wouldn't let me carry him in. He was almost too long for her to carry, but she wrapped his legs around her, pressed him to her chest, and buried her face in his crazy wave of hair.

She didn't say anything, just got in bed and closed her eyes. The room was dark, cold, and haunted. In the darkness her sorrow, which was darker still, hovered around her like a deep, vague shadow cut loose from its tether. Inside it she seemed safe. Outside it, in the other rooms, ghosts of all different attitudes spoke. So I went out. I turned on every light in the house to dispel them, send them out to the woods, to the beach, the ocean, or the lonely country road. It didn't work. I went back into the dark room, sat on the edge of the bed – C and his mother in a weepy, sleep embrace. And in the mess of sound, all the ghost voices, the clicking of forceps, the whoosh of the vacuum hose, and the footsteps of rain on the roof – I listened for my dead child's voice.

'Did you want this baby?' Edith had asked me in a private moment when she returned from her trip and found us there. I knew she was trying to be kind. But it was then that I gave myself full permission to hate her: because she was white; because she always had money; because she seemed incapable of mourning – becoming damaged or recognizing that there are some people who truly are and will always be *'out in the wind.'*

It was six months before Claire would undress in front of me and six more until I could look at her naked, and then, immediately, she was pregnant. And it happened again. She bled at night. She called me. We stayed up, this time, mourning. We went to the doctor, but everything was fine. X was the miracle baby, the fetus who had bled from her but somehow reconstituted himself in her. Instantaneous resurrection. So when he came out, blond-haired, blue-eyed, and oversized – two pounds heavier and two inches longer than any educated guess – we were both awed and terrified. Claire went into emergency surgery to repair her torn uterus, and they wanted to take him – put him under the lamps because they thought he looked a bit *'jaundiced.'* No one got the joke. I said no and kept my little ether baby with me.

As much as I fear for C, I believe that X will be all right. I don't drill him like C, don't obsess about his safety, his toughness, his manners. I haven't tried to teach him five different sports, read him dense poems or scrutinized the quality of his draftsmanship. Some say that it's because C is the firstborn, my parental training began with him. Claire thinks it's because X is almost unreachable – the boy does what he wants, hears what he wants, seems nearly immune to any threat of discipline or punishment, and none of it seems willful; he seems built that way. I think it's because he's white. There are the other factors, but I know that when I look at the boy who looks exactly like me, I don't know who or what it is I'm seeing. There's no history or experience within me to project onto him. He's a complete mystery to me. I can neither demand anything of him nor predict anything for him. This doesn't mean I don't love my boy. *He's my boy* – I know that. But just as he moves so strangely in my mind, he moves, will move in the world outside me – freely. I can extrapolate, I can theorize, cite examples – my best friend is white; I know what has happened to him, I know his story, and although in parks and train yards he has told me true – his story, bruises, tears, laughter – I still do not know his mind. All I have are reports, euphonic and cacophonic, from

340

the interior. My boy is only three. I can't see him as a man. His doctor swears he'll be at least six-foot-six. I can't see it. What does that mean? Somehow I helped produce an Aryan-looking giant – a testosterone-filled encyclopedia I will never understand. So what do you do? – Say he'll be just fine.

The school is being renovated – the main building, at least. They've had a scaffolding up for the last several years – since before we had kids, though no work seems to be getting done. I go inside and at once see one of C's old teachers. She smiles and waves by bending her fingers in unison. She scurries off. It'll supposedly be a new building for him – a big building. First grade – serious stuff. I wait for a while in the foyer and remember dropping him off and picking him up in the midst of the other parents and brown and black nannies. More eyeballing. If you're brown and in a place you're not expected to be, you'd better have public documented credentials regarding why you can be there.

'May I help you?'
'I'm here to see Jean Ray.'
'Do you have an appointment?'
'No, I'm sorry, I don't.'
She picks up her phone and dials the extension.
'What's this about?'
'Tuition.'
As soon as I say it, I become conscious of my

341

filth. It does matter, if not to her, then to me. She looks me over, trying and failing to be covert. Perhaps the rumpled, addled look is the one to sport here. Me in a suit, me in something clean and casual might not be believable. I'd look like a con or, worse still, a fool. Better to be a bum who's trying. I speak again.

'Tuition for my sons.'

'Your sons are enrolled for September?'

'Yes.'

'What grades?'

'First and preschool – threes.' She keeps holding the receiver, looking me over as though she needs more information. 'Am I in the right place?'

'Yes.' She answers as though it's a stupid question. I decide that I have enough evidence to dislike her. She's mean, and, worse, she's a bureaucrat, drunk with wee power. She dials. I straighten, almost regally.

'You can have a seat.'

'No, thanks.' I rise to my full height, rigid, as though prepared to address a mob or take a bullet. She speaks into the receiver. It's amazing that I can't discern what she's saying. Her lips barely move. Unable to eavesdrop, I look out the window behind her as though I'm surveying my empire.

'She'll see you now.'

'Thank you.'

I walk into her office – still regal. She doesn't stand, but she gestures for me to sit. I ignore it and choose a far-off point beyond the walls to stare at.

'How can I help you?'

Her voice is high and raspy, daemonic, as though the sweet-faced person has been possessed. Nevertheless, I stand my ground, staying fixed on that distant point.

'My boys' – I find myself calling on the Brahmin tone, but it's ridiculous, me aping Gavin, aping his old man, aping someone like Edith. She snaps her head up, startled by my voice.

'My boys, well, my eldest, has enjoyed his time here.'

I let it hang there. And then I have nothing to say, so my statement hangs some more and I listen to it bounce off the plaster, the windows, ricochet around the room until it sits on its own, disconnected from me. It would be easier for her to digest, I assume, not coming from raggedy black me. But after her initial start she seems unmoved, perhaps because she's waiting to hear from, needs to hear from, raggedy black me. I scroll through my voice bank, hoping to find the one that will, for her, match the man. Down in the quagmire of assumption and stereotype – to find a model of her mind. Nothing. It's been too long. I stick with my triple-adulterated Edith.

'My younger son will be starting at the preschool.'

'Michael. Michael and Cecil? They are your boys.' She's tightened her speech to match my cadence. 'Well, we're very happy to have them. Cecil is' – she checks her folder – 'a wonderful student. I'm sure Michael will flourish, too.'

She's too calm, too distant, and although I can understand why she doesn't share my urgency, I won't accept it. I exhale, audibly. And it seems to reach her. She folds her hands and leans forward. She exhales, too.

'Talk to me, please.' She gestures to the chair again, trying to recreate our meeting. I refuse again.

'When I was a boy, I went to a school like this. It was wonderful. On Wednesday and Friday afternoons Madame St Croix would send for me, and I'd make my way to her room, in the attic of a cottage in the corner of the campus. We'd have tea, and she'd do the best she could to keep our conversation in French.'

'That does sound wonderful.'

'I would like to have stayed. I couldn't. The Boston public school system, however, was crumbling. So my mother faked an address in a nearby suburb that had an excellent reputation for education. Every morning, until she felt I could do it on my own, she snuck me across the border.'

'How old were you?'

'Ten.'

She opens her hands and puts her face in them.

'That's what we did, until she found a place in the town.'

She keeps her hands on her face and I think that she doesn't want to hear anymore – wants to pretend that I'm gone. But when she reemerges, there's a newness to her, a burning in her eyes, more than curiosity or sympathy. It looks like anger. She traces a small circle on the desk with a finger, as though trying to focus her rage into the smallest spot possible.

'I have never understood' – she pauses, brings her finger to the bridge of her nose – 'how in a country where equality is said to be the rule, that access to something so fundamental as education is such an exclusive thing. Access – it is a thing, a tool, something you must possess.' She takes a deep breath, too big for her little body. 'Where, may I ask, is your mother from?'

'Virginia.'

She nods, answering for herself all the questions she could want to ask. 'And she placed a premium on education – your education.'

'Yes.'

'Quite a woman.'

'Quite.'

'Quite a boy.'

She restudies the documents, plumbing the teacher evaluations, Stanford-Benet scores. Finally, she looks back up. There's the flash of sadness again, then nothing.

'Your sons are a valuable part of our community. I want to help.'

She brushes imaginary dust off the corner of the desk, then reassumes her posture from when we first met. 'This is what I can do.'

I take the bait and turn my body to her.

'I can waive the late fees for both boys, and' – she

lets that hang for a moment to allow for my response.

'Thank you.'

'You're welcome.' She brightens, ready to reveal more. 'And I can extend you more time.' She starts nodding again. 'Friday.'

'This Friday?'

'Well, if you consider that you missed your final payment for last semester, as well as being quite late with this semester's . . . We have to determine who will be with us this year. There are several candidates for the spots.'

'But you have our deposit?'

'Yes.'

'Yes?'

'Your deposit, which we could have just as easily applied to your outstanding balance, which at this time is . . .'

'Eight thousand.'

'Eight thousand four hundred.'

'I thought you said you would waive the late fee.'

'That's true.'

'What about financial aid?'

'The application deadline was April first. The fund is spoken for. Next year, however . . .'

'You said they can't stay.'

'They could reapply. They would be strongly considered.'

'Could we pay off the balance over time?'

'We don't allow that.'

'What if we drafted something – if I signed a contract.'

'You already did.' She looks down. I wait for that flash, but it doesn't come. 'I can hold their places until the end of the day Friday.' She looks up again, squinting, waiting for an answer. And what can I do but scrape and nod?

CHAPTER 10

I have never really considered the shape, size, or location of my father's personal hell. I am ashamed of that. I haven't seen him since C was a toddler. Claire used to keep a picture out; the two of them hand in hand, walking through leaves beside a playground. She kept it out for our sake – mine and the boy's – as though we, or at least he, would honor the man. I know it made her burn with sorrow that her father – good man, father, and grandfather – unquestioningly so – was gone. C has no memory of my father. I haven't told him much about him, either. My father has never met his other grandchildren. I've offered to send him tickets, even rent a car to go get him, but he's always found a way out. Promises of meeting them stopped – no birthday cards, no holiday calls. He behaves much like a dead man: He haunts; he groans from the crypt of memory. He is a crumbled marker, a vague cautionary tale. Then word comes from up north through third and fourth parties that he's having a rough go, that he misses me, that he loves his unknown grandchildren, and that he is thinking of us, always – always thinking of his lineage, keeping them in the best of all worlds, the platonic. He's only held C's hand – no hugs, no scent, diapers, blood, tears. Ideal – best thought about in an armchair over a can of Miller High Life after a greasy sandwich, cigarette in the ashtray, television on too loud, but just the same, unheard, as one program becomes another and the voices become one. Then not even voices – only sound, then not-sound. It becomes solid, a fixed part of the environment: a wood-veneered end table with weeks of magazines; stacks of newspapers on the floor; a historical novel and the crippled spider plant on the sill; the juniper outside his front window: the distant whoosh and roar from the secondary highway that is hidden behind the young evergreens; wooden fence and dumpsters behind the strip mall where he walks slowly, bum-kneed, short-breathed, to get the pepper steaks and orangeade at the Greek pizzeria, the cigarettes and beer at the mini-mart while he waits. Sometimes they let him cash his government checks there and he upgrades the beer, gets a magazine. Maybe he thinks of us. Maybe he wanders over to the small toy section, stares at the miniatures hanging on the racks and thinks about sending the kids something plastic wrapped in plastic. He doesn't know what they like. He huffs and limps back home with a little cash and a greasy bag.

I think of his two little rooms, a grab bar and

stool in the shower. No visitors. There's dust in the air. You can see it floating. It rises from the armchair when he sits. You can see where it's settled – on the television, the windowsill, stuck to the pane. Dust and ash from cigarette ends absentmindedly dropped on his sleeve. He sits with his failures. The past ones echo and multiply in the now. They become solid iron, barring entry to the present, denying any future. And memory can be an affliction. I can feel it. He is sad. He is lonely. He has nothing – no wife, no teeth, no audience, and so, in a sense, no story, no language. He is old and he is not regarded well by his son, perhaps the only one who can free him from his flat bench in hell.

I miss my father. I remember liking him. I would like to go back there – to liking him, feeling safe with him. He exists across an ocean of memory. It is deep, almost frozen, and swimming with monsters. Beowulf, on a dare, once swam across an icy sea in his suit of mail. There were sea beasts – *fiend-corpses*' – that tried to pull him down into the dark, where they would rend the drowned king limb from limb. '*On a whim*,' he went. He made it, soaked, frozen, and spent. If he'd known what was waiting for him, would he have taken that dare? If he'd known what was waiting for him, would he have made it across, or would he have gone down?

My father was not a good father, but I'm not sure if that necessarily makes him a bad man.

I have been told by people that I am a good father, but I'm sure just as many have covertly called me an asshole. My father wasn't an asshole. And I know he wasn't a chump or a fool. There must have been dignity in him in some amount, at some time. What left him sucking ass for pennies and cheap, blonde sex? *What broke him?* I see him on a distant shore. To bring him back is to remember him well – good, kind, perhaps a hero at one time, strong before they got him. And I don't care about the details, who did it and how it was when he went down. I want him to have gone down fighting. But I haven't a myth of creation for him, nor one of his demise. The only chance I have in this life is for my children to remember me well. But I haven't any G-rated myth to spin or juggle, just a distant, malingering man, a gaunt-faced, odd-eyed phantasm, wraiths, demons, symbols, and signs. And there's no way to co-opt them, no way to co-opt hell – it has no voice, only soundless wails and cold fire. And if you speak of it, your escape and your triumph, you were never there. Nobody uses the prince of darkness. I wonder what it's like, sitting in a dust chair, knowing nobody will be coming. Watching yourself disappear.

It's late afternoon, but it's dark because I've cut across the shadow realm of Brooklyn. I had to get away from the suits who have emerged from the courthouses and subways of downtown. Their sheer numbers are offensive in that they look like a herd but on many levels don't behave like one. The mass cloaks the individual improprieties – a quick look at an ass or tit, a fleeting dream of sin, but they do nothing for the group, save add to its mass. Another dark suit, another dark pair of shoes, another professional – parasitic, dreaming that another paper pushed, another leer is an individual act. And of course, the subsuits, who believe themselves different because they held out for khakis.

I cut across the shadow realm because I cannot stand it right now. I walk in lightless Brooklyn, where the sun never seems to reach, between the jail and Fulton Mall, where strays run, miscreants, gypsy cabs, nannies released from bondage, fry joints, usury shops – they will never 'fix' this part of Brooklyn. And of course my response is dichotomized, but I'll take a petty criminal over a suck-ass any day.

I've seen too many apartments in New York City. Single or married with children, I've looked at too many, met too many brokers, tried to appease too many racist landlords, negotiate with too many slumlords while looking for that special something. They were all too small, too dark, too dangerous, and certainly, all too expensive. And our *friends,* or those people we were entering adulthood with, who may have become friends – good friends – were all gone to the North or West or back to their hometowns. We stayed, thinking

352

of ourselves as somewhat charmed until Marta showed up with that new lease. Her apartment hadn't spoken to us, either, but it had seemed relatively fair and she hadn't hesitated in shaking my hand.

The broker's waiting in front of the building of the apartment I know we can't afford. He's small, white, balding, dressed in an ill-fitting Banana Republic outfit. It makes him look like a child who's just emerged from the fitting room. I walk up beside him. He sizes me up and decides by way of my Gap clothes that I'm safe enough to acknowledge. He shoots his chin out at me.

'Hey, chief.' He checks his watch, reshoulders his bag, and steps to the curb. He clears his throat and spits into the gutter. He looks back at me, nods a few times, as though he's moving his head to a plodding rock song. I point to the building.

'Are you showing the apartment?'

He recognizes my voice from the phone. He tries to compose himself. 'Right on time' is all he can muster. He stares up at me, trying to reconcile the voice and the person before him now.

'Can we go in?'

'Absolutely, my friend.'

He unlocks the gate and gestures for me to go in. We walk up a narrow, wooden stair that seems ready to shear off the wall. We stop at the top landing, finished in peeling linoleum.

'No pets, right?'

'We have a fish.'

'Fish – hah. I think that'll be okay.'

He unlocks the door and swings it open for me. The entire apartment is almost immediately discernible from the doorway. You step into a large living area. To the right is a galley kitchen, narrower than the rest of the space to allow for the stairs and landing. To the left on opposite ends of the north wall are two doorways that lead to bedrooms.

'I thought this was a three-bedroom.'

'It's two plus a den.' He waves in the direction of the wall. 'There's another room off one of the bedrooms. It's perfect for a small kid.' He waits for my reaction. I don't have one. 'It's nice and quiet in the back. You can't see it now, but this front section gets a lot of morning light.' He steps into the middle of the room, does a half turn, taps the floor with his shoe. It's the old, plank subfloor, wood-filled and urethaned to look finished. He points to a door just inside the doorway of the east bedroom. 'Check out the bathroom.'

I walk to the back. The lumps of spackle and paint resemble cave wall sediments. The door jambs are twisted, and the hollow-core doors look flimsy under the deteriorating molding. Heavy applications of paint seem to be keeping it all together, like glue in places, like wood in others.

The bathroom has been refitted with a cheap pressboard vanity. One head butt from X would do it in. The floor is sheet linoleum. The new fixtures are ready to leak.

'Not bad. New, clean, right?'

I look back at him. The floor slopes down to the center of the room, making him a full two inches shorter.

'The school here, PS – I don't remember – it's supposed to be pretty good. It's just around the corner.' He starts walking to the kitchen and stops. 'Your kids go to public school?'

'No.'

'Oh, shit. I don't have kids, but I have friends. That's a big nut.' He pretends to consider the cost for a moment. 'Come see the kitchen.'

Outside on the avenue he changes, becomes more sedate but more direct at the same time. 'Listen.' he begins, looking at the traffic, 'we'll need your information.'

'I thought you had it.'

'Well, we ran your credit, and your – is it your wife?'

'Yes.'

'Yeah, your wife's credit. They're *okay*. Called your old landlady – that's cool. We need your financials. Did you bring a W-2 or something with you?'

'I didn't make a lot last year.'

'That's okay, okay. How are you doing for this year, you working?'

'Yes.'

'Can you get a pay stub, a letter to prove it? The owner is a good guy, much easier than most. I've worked with him for a while now and I've never given him a bad tenant, so he trusts me. As long as they check out with me, he's cool, you know?' He looks at me now for emphasis. 'I don't discriminate, with anyone. I think that's stupid. As long as you can pay the rent – you know, and don't wreck the place. But like I said, you check out fine.' He starts nodding as though he's agreeing for me. 'So the paperwork. And then we'll need a bank check – first, last, and three months security.' He keeps looking at me but mumbles the last of it. When I don't respond, he shuffles away from me, backward toward the building. He leans forward.

'Is that a problem?'

'How much is this?'

'Twenty-five. Twenty-five. So that's . . .'

'You want $12,500 up front?'

'Yeah, that's a big nut, huh?'

I don't answer.

'Yeah, that's big.' He steps closer to me and looks down at my feet. 'Listen, it's not a great market for landlords.' He reshoulders his bag. 'This unit has been sitting empty for a while now. I tell him. 'Let's just get it rented – get some money coming in.' He turns away from me and spits, but it's dry. 'Personally, professionally. I think it's overpriced.'

'Then why doesn't he lower it?'

'That's a good one – you're funny.' He inhales. 'But your mind-set is good. I think if you made him a reasonable offer, he would take it.' He turns back to the building. 'It's a really nice space, but like I said, it's a bit on the high side.'

'How much is a bit?'

'Like I said, make an offer. If you're serious, give me a call or come by – I'll get you in. Just don't wait too long – I mean, I'm always showing it, and it is a good deal.'

'I'll see what I can do.'

'Okay, pal,' he says, suddenly without interest, 'you see.'

I let him get far enough away, and then I follow. I walk west to Marta's on the north side of the avenue, the side I haven't walked since C was born – past the antique shops, the jail. I cross the multilaned Brooklyn Bridge Boulevard, where there never seems to be a walk signal, the dangerous parking garage. And finally reach safety in front of the Middle Eastern shops, the green grocer, and the market.

Marta's doorbells never worked. When people came to visit, they had to call from the street and we'd throw the gate keys down to them. Marta's not home, anyway; I can tell because the hallway light is on. She did this when she left, day or night. She never goes far – to the corner market or to the hardware store. I lean against the neighbor's wall, the Mexican restaurant, just starting to receive happy-hour customers, and take my list out for editing. The creases already have their own subcreases. The ink is starting to blur. I decide not to change the rent numbers. I refold it and put it away. This would be about the time we'd be returning home from a playground, the kids bubbling with the prospects of television, or lobbying for their dinner choices. Sometimes I would wait for them, just like this, looking west and east, wondering from which direction they'd be coming, trying to fight off the tiny pangs of dread, and then seeing C first usually. X trying to keep up, and then Claire with the girl, either in the stroller or toddling alongside it. Sometimes she'd be pushing it, hidden from my sight, and that tiny dread would flare into near panic until I'd see Claire's mouth move, encouraging her to walk a little faster.

I look east toward the river. They aren't there. The shipyard is full of crates – trailers – full of trade. I can't believe that in all my time on this block I only noticed the idle cranes and the sunset. I wonder what it's like to be a longshoreman, trudging up the slight incline from the yard with my hook over my shoulder. I've never seen anyone do that. I don't know why I remember this block, this view specifically, only as some kind of historical collective – thickly layered memories that, in the end, become one: that soft sunlight on the metal, on the water sweeping up toward me along the tarmac as imperceptibly as the sun drifts down in the sky. Memory, imagination, and crisis – surely a most unholy trio.

I wonder what others would do. Some would move away, but where is there to go? New York's no damn good. It seems that those born here become, ironically enough, provincial. Boston is too thick with history, yes, but now it's too small. This city has dwarfed it. Besides, Claire believes she loves it here; having grown up in the country, she never wants to go back to the homogeny, the boundless whiteness, in which she believes our children could not survive. But to escape that we've thrown them into another mess, the social experiment redux – an ahistorical one at that. Now, however, there is at least one brown kid per class instead of per grade. It's another disaster. Brown kids as cultural experiences for the white ones. The teachers, the administrators, seem to believe that they are all on equal ground, but if they'd stop and think for just a moment, they'd realize that there is no shortage in experiencing the glory of white people in this country – this world. I see him sometimes – C – when I've been early to pick him up, sitting alone, concentrating on a painting. And although I know it's a projection of my own consciousness, I cannot think anything other than that behind those beautiful and stoic copper eyes he is wracked by loneliness and pain. *Stand up straight*, I say. *Enunciate*, I say. *Dignity*, I say – the preparation for life is more daunting than the life itself. I'm too hard on my boy. I wish I could take it all back, but I fear already that my boy is too damaged. I've tried to cram what I've learned into his little body before he's experienced it himself. What else is a father to do? They tried to make me ready, but I was never ready. What am I supposed to do? Perhaps a brown father need only be a safe place for his brown boy, where he can come to be afraid, to fall apart and cry.

Marta appears out of the east, dragging a shopping cart behind her. She's never looked well. She's old and stooped, limping, and scowling perhaps from pain. She wears a black ski hat, an old navy blue windbreaker, and gray cotton sweatpants. She crosses Clinton Street with the light, but a car from Atlantic tries to turn past her. It doesn't make it and stops in the crosswalk, partially blocking her path. She looks at the car as though it's suddenly materialized in front of her. She freezes, not knowing whether to scold the driver or herself. Another car, trying to turn, honks at both of them. I go get her.

She doesn't seem to recognize me at first, but when we reach the sidewalk, the safety frees her to look at me closely. She gives me a cracked-lip, close-mouth smile.

'Oh, Sonny, how are you?'

'I'm well, and you?'

She finds her scowl again. 'Oh, Sonny, don't ask.'

'What's wrong?'

'You were so good. How are the babies?'

'They're great.'

'Beautiful babies.'

'Thank you.' It strikes me – knowing someone

for the better part of a decade and never having a conversation with them – pleasantries in the hallway. Silent car rides to her daughter's grave.

'Where you move to?' I point south. She points a finger at my face and then waves it. 'You should have never left. These people now – animals. Filthy animals. When you and your wife move here, you were young. I think they like you – *psst*. They complain – every little thing. I try to say, this is like family. They no want that.'

'What do they want?'

'They want to make trouble. They want to complain.' She starts walking to her door. I follow. She stops, fumbles with her large ring of keys, goes to unlock the gate, and stops again. 'You want tea or something?'

'Thank you, Marta, no. I have to get going.'

She looks to the river. Her face relaxes from anger to sorrow. She sneaks a look up at me.

'I got your message.'

'Great.'

'Listen, okay. I'm just going to tell you this.'

I can't look at her. I turn out to the street and pretend to watch the heavy traffic. She grunts and stutters behind me, then gives up. I hear her put the key in the lock. She opens the gate. She lets out a high, hurt dog whine.

'Don't be mad at me. I don't like it when you get mad at me.'

I can't turn, but I do my best to answer calmly. It comes out curtly. 'I'm not mad at you.'

'You just like when you moved out. I know you mad. Please don't be mad. You like my own son. You better son than my own son.'

I turn to her. She paws her keys and shifts painfully from side to side. She opens her mouth to speak but only manages a wheeze. I raise my hand to stop her, but she tries again.

'I'm in trouble, Sonny. He got me in trouble again.'

'Manny?'

'Si.'

I wave for her to continue.

'He was doing okay. He asks me for some money to go to school. He was doing okay, so I give him a little. He gets his grades and he shows me them. I don't ask, but he shows me them to prove he's doing good. He says he's going to summer school. I ask him if he needs help, but he tells me he has a job. He thinks he'll be okay. Okay, so it's his birthday. He's doing so good. He comes to me and asks – he needs credit card for books and things. He says he'll pay the bill but he needs me to cosign because he don't make enough money. I don't feel right. But he says he really needs it, so I say yes.'

She lowers her head and shakes it slowly. 'First the phone calls and the letters. And they keep calling me. They say they gonna put a lee, li—'

'Lien.'

'A lien on this building if I don't pay. They say they ruin my credit. They say I can lose my house.

362

Sonny, he charge five thousand dollars. They say I have to pay it all. He never make one payment. I don't have that kind of money.'

I wave for her to stop. She won't.

'I promise I pay you back. Every bit. It's a lot of money, I know, but I pay it – five dollars a month if I have to. I pay it all.'

'It's okay.'

She peeks up at me again. 'You not gonna sue me – no?'

'No, Marta. I'm not going to sue you.'

'I know it's hard times for you, too.'

'I'll be okay.'

She smiles again, this time with her mouth open. She has lipstick on her teeth.

'You should never have left.'

I shrug my shoulders and start to go.

'I'll call you . . . soon.'

I wave back to her without turning.

CHAPTER 11

Ichange my guitar's strings and play, but the new ones sound too bright, so I put the old ones back on. I play scales, moving up and down the neck. I've never been very good at them. My fingers aren't precise. I blame this partly on genetics; there's always seemed to be an interruption between hands and fingers, as though the nerve bundles were suddenly terminated at the calluses and then the builder used cheaper, less conductive wire. My hands are good for hammering, or crushing beer cans. I've always tried to be careful with my hands around Claire and the kids, especially their faces. They seem to disappear in them. Claire has always marveled at my hands, thought that they were beautiful – copper and ash – not hammy but far from fine. The boys have hands like mine, enormous, but they're children's hands, still soft, pink for X, russet for C, and they seem better integrated, more so than mine, which look like the contract between beast and man hadn't been agreed on.

I learned when I was able to buy my own guitar and cheap electric keyboard, that there was so much to do. I had to learn how to play – a song, songs I'd heard and loved as a boy. I wanted to play and I don't know if I sensed that my paw-hands would never move with the requisite dexterity, or if I was just lazy, but I skipped it – and then I wanted to sound the beautiful, individual note, but the older I got, the less my beast hands would learn. So I play strangely but with confidence, an odd strum-pluck, like an awkward athlete, a stumbling runner. It doesn't look good, but I get there. I make the song happen. And there are random notes, occasional buzzes and misses, but as a whole, it becomes its own thing, and I'm not sure if it's me, if it's my ear that's grown accustomed to what may be either music or discordant slop, but to me, in my private room, it sounds like something. It has a place.

I need to work out a play list. I should begin with something familiar, not obvious, but something a few in the audience will recognize, if not by name, then, at least, by tradition. Something that will situate, like an epigraph, what will follow, in a context. It has to be the blues. I want to make people sad, sad for me and sad for themselves, and then sadder still that they never realized that there are people so sad – that they have a connection to that sadness. I want to let them know what they've missed, to mourn it, then, in the booze-haze and their collective sorrow, have it be reborn. I want to make them happy, then have them see and feel the gap between the two emotions – have them see that the distance they assume is an illusion, a lie told to them, but not have them feel guilt or shame but celebrate the other half – the blues.

The blues – *'Baby, where were you last night?'* Thomas Strawberry has never had a woman fish, at least not one that I know of. He's bright today. His fins are high and proud. His good form makes me realize how ill he must have been. It'll be a shame to leave him. C only thinks of him in passing; X likes to empty containers of food and drop alien objects into his world. My girl is respectful, but her kisses won't sustain him. Claire will be overwhelmed, on her own with three kids. What if she remarries – a white man? Some high-wage earner, taciturn but gentle, raising my brood, feeding my fish. The blues. I strum a chord to dispel any image that may be forming of Claire rebuilding her life with someone else.

Thomas bloops to remind me that I owe him a song. *Pisci* – I play music *to the fish*. I hear words in my head, which I sing out – 'This little light of mine, I'm gonna let it shine . . .' It comes out of me strangely, with a hillbilly twang and cadence that I'm sure most purists would find ungainly. I like it. The country shuffle is a good beat for walking – plucking the bass notes to mark footsteps. *'Everywhere I go, I'm gonna let it shine . . .'* I invest a bit more into the words, let the last of each line hang out there, bright but warbling in the gravel.

When I finish, I see Marco in the doorway. He looks ashamed. I think he wanted to slip away unnoticed.

'You sound great, man.'

'Thank you.'

'No, really, you should so something with that. Let's take that out on the road. I'll quit my job. I'll be your manager.'

'I'd advise against that. Besides,' I gesture at the fish, 'that was a command performance.'

He laughs for a moment, genuinely. But when he stops, there's too much silence. He doesn't know what to do in the doorway, so he backs out. He looks uncertain of his place in his own house. His face falls, and I realize that I've never seen him sad – hurt. And I can't help but think that in an ice cream shop a quarter century ago, some wisp of a girl from another town whom he was sweet on came a breath away from calling him a wop to his face. Poor Marco – *Mahr-coh!* I still can't play him a song – can't make him forget through remembrance – not even for a friend.

'You going to coach this season?'

'I'm not sure.'

'Is Segundo going to play?'

'I don't know.' I look at one of the pictures of his boy on the bookcase. Handsome kid. Another half-breed, but he looks all his father. I wonder what he tells him in private moments. Marco looks at me as though he thinks I'm considering his question more deeply. I need to give him more. 'I don't know if he'll buy into the *team* concept.'

He snorts, shakes his head.

'Dinner?'

'No, thanks.'

'Oh, yes – messages: your wife and then some guy . . . *Kevin?*'

'Gavin?'

'Probably. It was hard to understand him. He had a thick accent.'

'Sounds like him.'

He waves good-bye and thumps down the steps. I wait to hear the front door close before I start again.

'Everybody is a star . . . ,' I fumble through the changes, trying to remember them, but while playing. I remember that there are four singers to account for – I can't get that out of my head. It would sound ridiculous – one fool, switching voices after every line. I need something else, perhaps an original, but I haven't played one of my old songs in years. I wasn't on very good terms with them back then, anyway. They seemed to miss the point.

Marco creeps back into the doorway. I startle. I'm surprised he could be so quiet. He tries to explain.

'I walked out without a dime.' He offers a smile as an apology. He can't seem to keep it from dropping to a frown. Then he brightens suddenly. 'I'd completely forgotten about that song. Who is that?'

'Sly.' I pack up my guitar and begin checking the case for things I'll need.

'That's a great one. I never thought you could do it acoustically.'

'You can't.'

If you've ever been broke – really broke – there are two things you know about being so: The universe is constantly conspiring to keep you that way: job interviews that require new ties; parking tickets on borrowed cars; late fees on just about everything; the need for legal representation to keep creditors at bay; the cosmic shame in your gut of showing your face in the light.

The second thing you learn is that the universe is plotting your redemption as well: when all fortunes are reversed. And so you get to split time in your mind between being vengeful and being good – doing things for those who stood you well, doing things to those who didn't. Making payback the rank and rabid *Über-hundin*. Lists have been made. Names have been taken. It's all been arranged.

And since it's all been arranged – my ascension – I find somewhere in the rising adrenaline that sometimes comes with a fantasy the guts to go out. I will go play in that bar, the one I've never entered, because I can't help but think there'll be somebody there. Who, I can't say specifically, but somebody who will listen. I will go play in that bar. Bars really don't bother me, and depending on what's going on, they actually feel quite comfortable to be in – as long as there's good light, good music, and enough people to blot you out. I used to write my college essays in bars. If Claire was a drinker, I'd probably spend more time in them. But I haven't really frequented any on a regular basis, which is why I forget that they can make me feel at home.

Al Green is on the box. *'I'm So Tired of Being Alone.'* There's smoke and low light and chatter, the clinking of glass and ice – cheer. It's a long, thin room, lots of dim wood and brass. On one side the long bar runs from front to back, and on the other an equally long banquette with small tables butted together in twos and threes. Opposite the bench are mismatched café and schoolhouse chairs. Everything stops about three quarters of the way back just before a low platform, a makeshift bandstand, on which is an electric keyboard, in profile. Center stage there are two stands, one high, one low, both equipped with microphones. Tall PA speakers flank either side of the stage. Two men, teenaged from their leather and denim garb, middle-aged from their gate and grayness, take the stage. One, very thick, tries to squeeze his thighs under the piano. Then he stretches his short arms and flexes and extends his fingers. The other man, much smaller, nuzzles up to the mike while strapping on an acoustic guitar. 'Check, check.' He turns to someone I can't see, gives him the thumbs-up. Al Green gets cut off, replaced by a wordless hum.

A gangly, pony-tailed man bounds up on the stage. When he turns to face out, I'm surprised by his youth. The small man makes way for him at the mike.

'Evening, everyone!' he offers in the fake country drawl that northern hippies tend to adopt. 'You all know me – Craig.'

'Yeah, Craig,' comes the response.

'Yeah,' he points in the general direction of the voice. 'Hey, dude.' He moves his hands as though he should be holding something – from his thighs to his chest, then down again. 'So most of you know what's going on – what we do here. First off, I wanna thank everyone for coming – making this night what it is. It's not easy getting folks out like this in the middle of the week.' A murmuring arises. He waits for it to end. He points to the ceiling. 'Now, remember, this isn't. I repeat, is not a competition. We're here to support artists – that's first of all.' He looks at his empty hands. 'Oh, shit, I forgot my clipboard.' He spins to look for it, then gives up. 'But we've got some great people here tonight, so they'll play and you'll vote in the end. And vote for the best – not just because it's your friend. You know, try to be objective. All right?' He extends a hand to the guitarist, who has been fidgeting up there the whole time. 'You all know Ed and Pete?' There's a whoop, a yell, and some applause. Craig claps, too. 'All right, let's get this thing started.' He flaps his arms, palms up. The crowd responds with anticipatory chatter. He turns to the men. 'You guys ready?' They both nod. The pianist grandly extends his arms out in front of him, raises them over his head and lets them part back to his sides. 'Then start us off right! Ed and Pete everyone – come on!' Craig gangles off the stage and makes his way behind the bar. The talk fades. The small man steps to the mike.

'Good evening. How are you?' There's a muted response. 'I'm Ed and this is Peter. We've been working on some new material.' Ed's voice is deadpan – almost lisping. 'The first song is an original, one we wrote ourselves.' He picks the individual strings, strums a few chords. Peter matches him on the piano, hammers out the opening of Beethoven's Fifth. He stops, lets the last chords ring out. Some of the audience force out laughter.

I make it over to the bar. The bartender's an enormous and hairy man, like someone you'd expect to find on a mountain – thick salt-and-pepper hair, tied back, and a full dark beard. He would seem completely wild save for his bifocals.

'What can I get you?'

'Oh, a Coke, please.' The order doesn't seem to bother him. He squirts out my drink and places it in front of me.

'Are you playing tonight?'

'If that's all right.'

'Fine with me. Did you sign up?'

'No, I'm sorry, I didn't.'

'No need to apologize.' He smacks Craig on the shoulder and gestures for the clipboard. Craig complies without looking.

'Put your name at the end.'

Ed finishes retuning, mouths a count-off to Peter, and cuts it off.

'I just want to tell you a little about this song.' Peter smiles and nods. 'I wrote it one night – Peter knows – it was when we started bombing Afghanistan.' There's a collective moan and sigh from the crowd. Craig nods his head, tries to catch the bartender's eye, doesn't; then someone at the bar to commiserate with, but everyone's either paying attention to the duo or their drinks. He finally looks to me, but I can't give him anything except the fish eye. He looks away.

'I had so many different emotions when I realized we were at war. The first, of course, was anger. I was outraged. I mean, *I wasn't asked*. There wasn't a vote.' He steps back and exhales. 'But part of me was . . . relieved. You know. I'll admit it. I was scared of terrorism and I wanted to act – because I was angry at them, too. So that's how it began. So I plugged in my electric and turned it up, started playing power chords because I wanted to make an angry song. And Peter will tell you, it just wasn't coming, and he said,' he turns to Peter as though he's going to let him speak. He doesn't. 'He said, 'I don't think you're really listening.' And I yelled at him, something, I don't

373

remember. He said, 'You need some space.' So I just sat there and didn't do anything. I just sat there and then I put down the electric and went to the piano and played a little. And what I heard was so sad. I needed to put words to it. I just grabbed some scraps and a pencil. And I wrote like a madman. And when Peter came back, I didn't say anything to him. I just showed him the – hah – scraps. And he told me to get up. He sat down at the piano, and we worked on it well into the next day until it was just perfect – you know.'

He backs up again, shoots a quick look back to Peter. Strums a chord, lets it ring out.

'It's a song about war, I guess – a war song. But it's about the sadness of it all, which is something people don't really see. People get so wrapped up in their anger, both sides, that's all they know how to express. But there's more. So here it goes.'

He starts his count again. Mute Peter stops him with a quickly raised finger.

'Oh, my god, the title. The song is called *'The Lonely Night'* – and two, three . . .' Peter hits a minor chord and holds it – lets it ring. Ed picks the arpeggio slowly, awkwardly, as though he's searching for the strings for the first time. They find each other's tempo, agree on a common pace – a slow, rolling egg waltz. 'Ooo . . .' They're both tenors. Ed's singing voice is lispless. They hold the harmony for two bars and stop for two beats. Ed closes his eyes and sings:

Why do they drop two-ton
Bombs on the heads of the old?
It makes me so lonely.
Why do they drop two-ton bombs
On the heads of the babes?
I hear them fall.

And the change:

I'm so far away
Why do I feel this way?

I leave – back out the door like I've left something burning on the stove. I slow up a block away
and then stop. Ed's voice comes up in my head –
the first line, 'Why do they drop two-ton
bombs . . .' I start walking again and it lets up.
The faster I go, the more it diminishes until, near
running, it's finally gone. I stop. It comes back
full tilt – the limp, high, cloaked exhortation. I try
to dispel it. Where was Al in his song before he
was so rudely interrupted? The overlapping
descending chorus of *ooos*. I've always wondered,
marveled, at how he, in that song, in that moment
where there should be some crescendo – some
answer, manages every time I hear it, to avoid
bathos in the anticlimax. *'Hmm hmm hmmm-
mm . . .'* The tone, so low and mellow. Maybe just
an organ hanging on, mirroring the backing vocals.
And then the blade-with-balm shriek, which
throws up image after image for me: Gavin and

375

his beer can litter; Shake's gently dancing shoulders; Brian's idiotic stoned grin; Lila's twist of the knob up to the end of the AM dial; my father's record stacks; the books he'd leave lying around the house, open. Sometimes when I was walking by, he'd stop me, *'I love this part – listen.'* Read what was to me an incomprehensible passage. It would knock me into a stupor. The words seemed to fly around the room with disparate half-formed images. I'd try to cling to something: 'Seawrack' blah blah blah. *'Seatangle.'* All I really took with me was how the words behaved – explosives stashed in everything – the sofa, the television, his face – condemned structures awaiting implosion. *'Seawrack'* and *'seatangle.'* Watching something else grow in the destroyed face. His eyes, darting from the page to my face, regarding both with equal, unguarded affection. Standing there he was – what little chest he had puffed out – powerful, as if he'd just unlocked the secrets of some ancient tome, an unknown benevolent incantation so potent that merely thinking it dispelled all impotent and childish notions of magic and power.

I go back. There's a young woman on the stage. She has crazy, long blonde ringlets that spill over her shoulders and onto her guitar. I don't recognize the song, although it does sound familiar – open tuning, droning unfretted strings. Her voice spirals up from a strained and wavering tenor to a light, easy soprano like a big bird searching for a thermal strong enough to lift it. I can't make out the words. They don't seem to matter to her except for giving her a reason to sing.

She finishes, bows her head slightly to applause and chatter. A whistle. She raises her head sharply, throws her hair back and catches it behind her head with both hands. There's something about her face – it's difficult to tell from this distance, over and between heads in the smoky dark – the shapes perhaps; eyes and nose don't match, maybe it's the nose and forehead. It's odd but not un-attractive – beautiful even. She drops her hands and her hair drops too. Craig hoots, and I snap around to face him. 'All right, Rosa!' He claps methodically. Rosa doesn't respond. She checks her tuning and leans into the microphone, 'This one's called "The Seagull."'

I wonder why she stopped her last one. This song sounds very much the same. It could've been, had she continued, a suite; slightly varied but linked songs, similar in melody, tone, and performance – or at least her hair. Perhaps none of us in the audience knows that it's the reason we're listening, because we could all just go home and put on a Joni Mitchell record rather than listen to Rosa fall short of the mark. Perhaps it's her odd face, covered by the cascade. From where I'm standing she looks small. Perhaps it's my distance. Maybe the guitar's too big or the stool too tall, her hair, or the sum of all these factors.

She finishes, stands, and bows. Craig is up there in the wings to congratulate her – an aborted lip kiss that morphs into a hug and a cheek-to-cheek rub.

'Give it up for Rosa, people. Great stuff. Thank you.' He checks his clipboard. 'Okay, next we have Polly. Get ready for something edgy, folks.'

Polly jumps up on the stage then pulls a medium-size amp up, then an electric guitar. Craig asks if she needs help, and she hands him the plug for the amp. He jumps off the stage, grabs an idle extension cord, plugs the amp in, and gives her the thumbs-up. She thanks him with a nearly imperceptible nod. She stands and pushes Rosa's stool aside. She's tall, perhaps even taller than Craig. She readjusts the high mike stand and lowers the short one to the level of her amp. She looks fully ready to rock – an all-black Fender Stratocaster, Marshall amp, an indigo tank top one size too small and indigo leather pants, the pattern on which, I realize as she stands up there knock-kneed, form the stars and bars of the Confederate flag. She hits a chord, loud and distorted, shakes the silver bangles on her wrists out of the way, down her forearms, and hits two chords this time. Someone lets out a whoop, then there's a whistle, finally a rebel yell, which is echoed by another.

'How y'all doin' out there?' She has bright red hair that even I in these conditions can tell is dyed. It's cut short and frozen stiff by some beauty aid. Her eyes are heavily penciled – black. She stomps a motorcycle boot on the hollow plywood platform, rips off a loud lick, another chord. 'How 'bout some Jimi?' The audience responds with an affirmative roar. She counts off to herself – '. . . two and . . .' Ascending notes – bom bom bomp – bom bom bomp. She sings. *'Manic Depression.'* Her voice is thin, but she tries to pretend that she can bark and snarl. I squeeze into the little space between the big window and the turn of the bar. Craig hasn't returned to his post. He's up front, sitting at the first table with Rosa. She watches Polly while he watches her, checking to see if she likes it or not – so that he can wear the appropriate face. Ed talks to Peter across the next table. I can't see either face, but Ed's head occasionally jumps forward. Peter nods and turns every so often to Polly, who's now into an extended, bombastic solo. The bartender taps next to my hand. I come up out of watching.

'Need anything, brother?'

'I'm good, thanks.' He winks at me, takes his drink from beneath the bar, and kills it. I grab a napkin and dab at it with my pen in hopes of coming up with a song list. *'Everybody Is a Star'* – I cross it out.

Polly breaks into *'What a Wonderful World.'* Playing it hard like the Ramones did, but she spit-snarls the lyrics, force-feeding us the irony of her performance. Perhaps she's only heard the punked-out version and never consulted Satchmo.

I go back to my doodling on the napkin. Nothing comes of it save for the growing apprehension that I'm about to make a complete ass of myself – standing up there without a damn thing to play.

Polly hits a last chord, yanks her guitar off, and, holding it by the neck, jams it into the amp. The sound feeds back, turning from rough and low to a high wail that makes people reach for their ears. She shakes the guitar, trying to coax more wailing, but the sound fades. Craig jumps up to keep her from continuing. He unplugs the amp and lowers it onto the floor for her. She shoulders her guitar and stands grinning at the crowd – triumphant. I don't, however, remember hearing any applause.

'You're up, brother,' says Mountain Man.

'Thank you.'

I begin to make my way to the front. Craig looks for then finds me in the crowd. He waves to me, causing people to look back. The nerves come – like I've swallowed several whole spastic moths washed down by too many cups of coffee. My guts are an ugly place, and I don't want to know what goes on in them. I feel myself disassociate, lose focus on my insides and then what exists out in the bar. I blur the faces until I find myself at the bandstand trying to figure out how not to trip.

Polly steps off the stage and gives me a pinched grin as we pass. I catch a whiff of her hair products and dense French cigarettes – maybe some

BO. 'Hey, darlings!' I hear them move the furniture to make way for her.

'You need anything, man?' asks Craig, pushing the stool at me.

I go to say, 'Yes, the stool,' but all I manage to do is point weakly at it. He sets it up in front of the mikes, takes another look at me, and readjusts their positions. I keep my back to the crowd, set my case down, and open it. I expect my guitar to be grounding, but it isn't. It looks plastic, beat, incapable of resonance. I pick it up, and it feels that way, too.

I strum a chord. It's out of tune.

'Here, dude.' Craig hands me a small device that I don't recognize. 'Clip it on to your headstock.' I do. It's a tuner. 'It's for tuning up in noisy places.' I tune up, strum a chord to check it. It sounds tinny, but in tune.

'Thank you.'

He beams at me like he's never heard the expression.

'Cool. Ready?'

I nod. He straightens up to the mike. 'Folks, we got some new blood here tonight. Please give a warm welcome to um – let's see. Teddy Ball-en-game.' He bends to me, whispers, 'I fucked up your name, huh?'

'Close enough.'

'Give 'em hell, dude.' He bounds off the stage, letting out another rebel yell as he does. A few in the crowd reply.

I hang my harmonica around my neck, stand up, and turn around. I don't have a strap. My legs start trembling, then my arms do, too. I remember the stool and try to drag it forward without dropping my guitar. I sit and the trembling stops, but the microphones are too low. Craig bounds back up, resets them. The crowd's quiet now, watching. Someone snuck a capo onto my guitar, fifth fret. I blur my eyes again to avoid seeing their faces – to make them one big whole. Craig leans out of the mass and nods for me to begin.

I start, a cappella, the words like a grace note – 'Lord I'm . . .' – B-flat – '. . . broke, I'm hungry, ragged and dirty too.' Slide up the neck for a fill – slide down. Repeat. Then, 'If I clean up sweet mama can I stay all night with you?' Fill. I look up the neck at the headstock while I play, but I don't really see anything – not the strings or my fingers, not the frets, where my hands go on the fills and changes. Even though they're a blur. I don't look at the audience. 'You shouldn't mistreat me baby, because I'm young and wild.'

When it's over they clap – loudly – there are even scattered whistles. No bar noise. Perhaps it's because I'm down here in the mix that it seems so much louder. Perhaps they actually like me. I still won't look at them. I go right into the second song – 'If You Want Me to Stay . . .' I drag it down, take whatever rhythm there was out, and drag it through the blues – my specific funk.

'Seawrack' and 'seatangle.' These are the blues:

coinage upon contact with the air. Traces of hope and joy from the fusion flash in my head. I like what I hear – the wordless neologisms created with voice, guitar, and air. I don't look up, I won't break the spell. A glance would sever the atmosphere – *'seawrack'* and *'seatangle.'* That isn't what comes out. Strummed chords. An inexorable internal rhythm. Not a train, but something coming down the track under its own unconscious locomotion. *'Seawrack'* and *'seatangle'* – I've always loved those words, never knew what they were, but they behaved in my mind like multi-faceted jewels – so many illuminations – so open and so bright. There is no sorrow in this room because it is filled with song – *and* – *'Hey, Mr Tambourine man . . .'*

When it's over, they clap. Craig jumps up on stage, motions for me to stand but stay there. He waves the others up. When he has us in a line, he calls out, 'Who's got the hat?'

It gets passed up to him, a Yankee hat. It's full of singles and change. He waves to the crowd to stop.

'Okay, y'all. You know what to do.' He moves behind Ed and Peter and waves his hands above their heads. 'What do you say?' The audience responds with loud enthusiasm. 'All right.' He moves behind Rosa and does the same. She gets polite but muted approval.

He jumps next to Polly, who, by the angry look on her face, has already predicted her defeat.

The crowd doesn't disappoint. He moves on to me.

'Give it up for Ted.' They yell back loudly, certainly louder than they did for the two women but around the same level of support the duo received. Craig knows. He hands me the hat. They yell and clap some more.

'Okay, people, let's hear it. Give it up for the artists.'

There is some more applause, the loudest by Ed and Peter, who have begun moving back to their table. Polly darts off the stage. Rosa lingers on the stage with Craig and me. She leans in to say hello. Craig stops her by speaking first.

'That was a really cool set, man.' I look at his face again. It's craggy. He's not so young, a few miles past and many tequila shots down.

'Thank you.'

'Although that Dylan at the end threw me a bit. I thought you were going in another direction.'

'I liked it,' she steps closer. 'You did it well. There's nothing worse than a bad Dylan cover.'

'Except a Dylan original,' mumbles Craig like a teen.

She slaps his arm. 'Oh stop.'

'I don't know.' He shakes his head. 'I just don't get it about that guy.'

'There's nothing to *get*,' she snaps. 'That's the whole point.'

'I've just heard he's a jerk. He seems like one.'

I pack up my guitar. She watches. He watches her.

384

I stand, ready to go.

'Are you going to stay for a drink?' She thumbs at Ed and Peter's table.

'Thank you, no. I have to be going.'

'Teddy?' she cranes her neck and points. I nod. She straightens quickly and throws that hair behind her. 'Are you gonna be around next week?'

'I don't think so. I'm not sure.'

'See you around.' She holds her hand up but doesn't wave.

'Good night.'

I'm drawn to the bookstore window, how the light falls on the covers. I can't make them out from across the street, but I know what titles they are. They've been there all summer. And while I can honestly say that I've never tried to picture my own book on display, I have imagined the window with these books gone, not *no books*, just not these books, although I can't picture the ones I'd want there. I've been inside, spent strange late morning and twilight hours when I should have been doing God knows what but something other than skimming through pages of nonfiction that read like the liner note text for cookbooks and fiction that read like lists – random and disparate images; loose, frayed metaphors used to stitch litanies of random, mundane events together written by brick-dry white people with polished syntax, sniping at dead poets, complaining that the dead folk had lived too much – tried to do too much.

And the ethnics, whoring out their otherness, pretending to be true to some alleged mother tongue or pretending that the language of the brick-dry will speak true – verisimilitude via assimilation. I get confused. They all seem to be exactly right. Their stories are so clean, so free of bafflement, stink, or cosmic funk – cosmic affliction. Their words shrink the world down, down, tapering to a point, as though they'd followed the line of a table leg down through the cellar floor to its subatomic origin, then claimed – *that's enough!*

And I've seen the larger in the microcosmic, but that has never been the end for me. When I find the pointed end of the tapered leg in the center of the earth, I get blown out the other side into space, yanked into orbit, and then slingshot out. The cosmic affliction faces me every day. And it may be hubris to believe your own trouble has enormous weight – your trouble is another's – but I think of the old Negro spirituals, their birth: Trouble is unavoidable, undeniable. It's in your face and seems to stretch for as far as eyes can see. The only end to it is a dream, a song. And so when I read about flaking skin, microscopic annoyances – whose panties to pull off – I am troubled enormously. It goes on and on, the complement to the rock of my alleged soul.

So now I prepare to enter the trance, out of which will come the incantation to dissolve this corner scene – the shrine to the *hard and dry*. And it's so predictable; the asphalt ripples like a lazy, black river. The night sky responds – *Amen*. The plate glass shatters noiselessly. The pieces vanish before they fall – *And the urbanness de-coalesced.* Now the reshaping: street and slab and stars to suit me. The cars are cat-eyed and quiet as leaves riding downstream. *Magic?* – or just some more blah-fuckity-blah, more yip-dipity-yip. There's a reason the sidewalk is cast in concrete.

I count the hat money – forty-three dollars, not even bus fare these days. I realize how nervous I was, playing in the bar, the cool air makes me feel my sweat on my shirt. I put the money away, scan across the glass, and catch my reflection in the dark part. I feel compelled to speak to it. *'Loser.'* It surprises me, the way it comes out: a sharp hiss. I shake my head, raise a finger to my lips, and shush myself. I step out of the picture but leave the finger there, flexing and extending it slowly – my soul finger.

I make a fist and wonder if I'm capable of vengeance – the payback of the spade. The dark fist could be useful to me, symbolically and concretely. But the wind blows through my thin coat and across my damp shirt. I shiver and my hand opens. I start to sing and shiver again, wondering if anyone I knew was in there listening. I hear my voice come back to me, not singing, not even exhorting, but whining. Me, up there on the makeshift stage, limp and slumped; big, brown, and whining, with the alms bowl going round. *I'll give you two bits if you shake your ass up there.* I go to close my fist again as if to squeeze out the image, it complies grudgingly. Who can blame it? It probably wants to belong to someone who'll swing it. I'm not up to speed – not fully evolved. There was a time when memory was an asset: which root to pick, which route to walk, where the lair of the death beast was, poisonous fruits and blossoms. Then over time, as memory became collective and things to eat were packaged, routes mapped and laminated, it became a vestige, an appendix waiting to burst and spread the horrors of the ancient world – the mammoth stomping and the saber tooth creeping through your guts. Death by spear or weapon of stone. But there weren't the millions to kill, or the technology to do so. Now, when there is time, when we neither follow the herds nor smear their images on our walls, when we have time for real intimacy, time and ability to listen and hear the voices of the lonely – panties, blood and semen, and a blank-faced woman-girl; twenty-thousand pink slips; clipper ships; Calcutta; barren potato fields; Geronimo; panzer tanks; napalm. We pay a price to have it all somehow neatly extracted, separated, named, reduced, and thinly rendered then served back to us with a pinch of wit and trope. It seems better to just forget.

Shake's reflection looks at me from the window. He can appear like this, on your doorstep after work, while you're going down into the subway, or packing the kids into a car – the wraith of transition.

'Why are you looking at that? There's nothing for you there.' He dismisses the books with a sweeping wave. 'Fucking trembling Anglicans, telling me about the nature of death and God.'

I wave, more like a gesture of benediction than a greeting, *'Between the idea and the reality. Between the emotion and the act falls the shadow – for life is very long.'*

He waves back. 'Between my foot and your head sits your ass – *for my boot is very big.'* He jab-steps at me. I jump back then gather myself, embarrassed that he startled me. He doesn't seem to have noticed any of it. We shake. He pulls his hand back, then steps away – right and forward and left then back – with an unrealized desperation, like a broken toy robot, forgotten, trapped in its last command.

'No seriously,' he nods, still moving. 'You look good, man. Real good.'

'Thanks, Shake.' He's wrapped his long dreads under a dirty turban. Through the graying beard, he's very handsome – strong-jawed. His eyes are slightly sunken. His dark skin, even though wet with sweat, is a bit ashy. His lips are thin, and his eyes look out like those of someone who hasn't completely woken up from a horrible dream. And although these aren't necessarily signs of age, they act in concert to connote miles, experience, hardship – a great weight hauled.

'Please don't call me that anymore.'

I watch him move. He's still well muscled and looks as if he could spring up and dunk a basketball or dribble past a defender with ease, but those muscles that used to move him in such an elegant way now seem to jerk him from corner to corner of his little box.

'Don't mind this. It's just the psychotropic waltz. It's nothing.' He looks at the books in the window, pushes his chin at one. 'Ain't that your boy?'

'Yeah.'

'Yeah. Who's that other fool? I never heard of him.'

'I suppose he's the heir apparent.'

'What the fuck is he inheriting, the right to talk bullshit?'

'I don't know, Shake.' He jab-steps at me again, glaring, as though a punch will follow. I go to slip it, but he slides back to his original motion, retaining the glare.

'What?'

'Nothing.'

'So that's your boy? So this fool is your replacement – that's funny.'

'Not really.'

'Hey man, take it easy. Why don't you give the man a call?'

'Why would I do that?'

'Why? His book's in every motherfucking store window, big and small, and it ain't even February. He's gotta have something for you, you know?'

'No.'

'No he doesn't?'

'No. I'm not going to.'

'Well why not?'

'It's complicated.'

'Fuck you then, be a fool. Walk these streets all hangdog dog-raggedy.'

'It's out of my hands now.'

'So put it in his. Make that call.'

'No.'

He shakes his head, stops, then pats his coat pocket like he's looking for a cigarette.

'You smoke now, Shake?'

'No. Don't call me that. Nobody out here knows me like that – Donovan, remember?'

'I'm sorry, Donovan.' It feels so strange to say it.

He nods, loses the glare. 'What's the matter with you anyway?'

I kick stupidly at the slab. 'I'm broke.'

'Broke,' he jumps back then starts waltzing again. 'Shame on you. And you used to call yourself a metaphysician.'

'I did?'

'Well, I called you one. I guess I still do.'

'Aren't you one?'

'Me, no. I'm insane.' He cackles. It's sharp. It seems that it would have cut him on the way up, but he stands there, unscathed. Right before he was committed he applied to the NEA for a grant to enslave three white people for thirty years and study the effects chattel slavery had on them. He was going to write a play based on the results.

I try not to, but I can't help but watch him be yanked back into the spastic steps. Now he adds a hand to the sequence – waist to nose and back again – and each pass seems to create and build nervous energy in him.

'Don't look at me like that,' he snaps, springing forward – still not punching.

I try to cover. 'Like what?'

'Like you're angry or you pity me – whatever – you don't know.'

'Covering all possibilities with that, huh?'

'Well, I have to.'

I look up into the night sky and wait for it to do something, it's crisp azure – autumnal – the stars are bright yellow. Shake grunts like he doesn't want the silence. I want him to go away. He resumes his dance.

'What's the matter, nothing to say?'

'You know what,' I kick at the sidewalk again. 'Forget it.'

'Forget what? You didn't say nothing.' He turns, walks in a tight circle and then is yanked back to the square. 'Damn, man. You're fucked up.' He starts shaking his head violently, raises his hand to speak, aborts the attempt, and drops it. Then, like the gesture was a feint, he mumbles, 'I didn't tell you to marry a white woman.'

I step back, shoot a hand up. 'Good night, Shake.'

He stops. 'Donovan,' he says quietly, with a tremble. It stops me. 'My name is Donovan.' He waits until he's sure I won't leave and then exhales fully. The pent-up energy seems to go out with his breath. He closes his eyes, either trying to see something inside or to focus on keeping his feet still. He starts swaying his shoulders, moving through the sequence, but slowly and on a smaller scale. He opens his eyes and looks down at his feet to make sure that his near stillness is real.

'I didn't tell you to marry her, but I never said it was wrong. It's not something I would do, but I'm not paying your bills, taking out your trash – whatever. Come on. I'm just saying that if you were with a black woman, she could tell you something. When you stand in the dark with that question on your face, she'd at least know there was something on your mind – right? And she knows, maybe not innately or anything, but it's something she saw in her daddy's face when he didn't know she was looking. It's on her brother's now, too. And she's not gonna hesitate, you know, she's going to, on her terms, know. She might be completely wrong – hell – she might be just a fool,' he slaps his cheek violently twice, 'but she won't be locked out by this. There are so many other barriers in place, but not this one, your color. Your wife doesn't have that. She probably looks at you and thinks, "I don't know that." But she thinks, everybody thinks, whether they admit it or not, that the skin is the thing. At least with a black woman you could hunker down together and start something – start hurling assumptions at the world. What happened to that painter you were with back home?'

'She's famous.'

'No, what happened to you two?'

'She stopped calling.'

'Why – you wouldn't fuck her, would you?'

I think about hitting him, but I hold back because there doesn't seem to be any malice in his voice. I exhale, too. My hand probably wouldn't close anyway. 'She didn't like my poems.'

He grins and then shakes his head violently to erase it. 'At least you would have someone you could talk about them with. Someone you could lie with. But with you, you look and all you can see is her white face – everything it stands for, all the ways it rejects you: *Your wife's white face.* And you're locked out. It can't tell you true, not a damn thing, except maybe how far out you really are. That's lonely. And then where do you go – for comfort – huh? Maybe you have that moment when you dare to say, "It doesn't matter," or "I'm beyond that." You may not say it in words, but you act it. But what does your boy say – '. . . redeemed from fire by fire.' You'll forgive him his abstract crimes against humanity . . . what about her? But I don't know why any brown person on this here earth in their right mind would pass through fire of any kind for someone white. I mean, why would you do that?' He shrugs his shoulders. 'Miles and miles of bad motherfuckin' road. No road, sometimes.

'I don't know, my friend, my brother. I don't know if I've said it or only thought it. You're either brilliant or you're a fool, out here in the night, unseasonably cold, all by your broke self. No allies to call on.' He points at the books in the window. 'What have you been doing, my brother, while everyone else was building networks, consensus, shared ideology?' He cackles again. It rips the night.

'No allies?'

'Well you can count me in, for whatever that's worth.'

'I will.'

'*I will.*' He mocks. 'G'wan claat! How goes the rest of the crew?'

'Gav's back in.'

He winces, as though the news physically hurts him.

'That boy never met a fight he didn't want. By the way, that was Gladys – yesterday.' He jerks his head back as though she's behind him. He shoots the imagined woman down with a sharp, quick stare. 'She ain't mine' – he leans in as though this is a secret he needs to keep from her. 'I'm just looking out for her, till she gets on her feet.' He cracks his knuckles. 'Where'd you get that suit you were wearing?'

'Had it awhile.'

'You a banker now, too?'

'No.'

He shakes his head again, closes his eyes, frustrated, as though he's trying to remember something he had to tell me. 'Looking at you helps me remember. Sometimes that's not so good, you know.' He springs forward, catching me with that old quickness, and hugs me. He rocks us back and forth. I smell sweat and pharmaceuticals – rubbing alcohol. He lets me go.

'What's up, man?' I sigh.

He smiles, gently puts a hand on my shoulder. 'Hey baby, gut me then haruspicate: Extrapolate from my viscera.' He bends, covers his mouth, and laughs to himself. He straightens but still smiles. 'I can tell you what's going to happen. I just can't tell you how. I don't know. Not a living ass can. Hell, the dead can't probably either. I've been outside a long time now – way outside – but when I see you, I think of things I saw when I was in. I think it might be worse, being in, looking for something, seeing all the faces, the places that you're locked out of, while they demand that you behave like they're going to let you in. But I praise my psychophar-macologist: I haven't spun completely out. I take my pills, try not to bust anyone in the head, and wait for my inheritance of the earth. Now that's a plan. Hope to see you there.'

'What about now?'

'What about now?'

'What are you going to do?'

'What, you got a plan? You want to raise an army and take the capital – shit – nothing but mercenaries out there anyway. And how you gonna trust them?' He looks at his wrist, but he doesn't have a watch. He lowers his arm, looks down, and goes back to the Thorazine shuffle. For a moment I wish I had the switch to shut him off. He looks up and jumps back, breaking the prescribed pattern. I can see the fight in him, trying to make his movements fluid, resisting being locked into a new box step.

He tries to shake his head, the effort to keep it slow requires him to turn his body in tandem as if it were all one piece. He whispers.

'I gotta go.'

I nod. We both exhale together. He spreads his arms, palms up, and waves them slowly, up and down.

'This collective consciousness ain't big enough for the two of us – remember?' He stops his arms in midair. 'That's your fight – so I'm off.' He turns, wades into the street, and starts across.

'Donovan?'

He cuts me off – a hand raised into the air. He doesn't turn, so I can't see his mouth move but it sounds like his voice.

'*Not fare well, but fare forward.*'

And he's off into the night.

Marco's asleep on the couch again – having tried again and failed to make it to the end of *Cool*

Hand Luke. He rouses at my presence and looks up blankly from the depths. I leave him alone, go upstairs, sit on the bed, and stare at a blank sheet of paper.

'Hey.' He's snuck up on me again.

'How are you?'

'Wiped. Hey, I have a question.' He lets it hang out there for a while, but not long enough for me to begin asking myself what it is. 'Are you around on Friday?'

'I'm not sure. Why?'

'Are those your clubs in the basement?'

'Yeah.'

'Feel like playing?'

'I can't.'

'Come on. Take a day off.'

'I can't.' I must have bent the last refusal – blue. He gets it. He loses the playfulness, puts on a face I haven't seen before.

'You're pretty good.'

I shrug.

'Listen, it might be worth taking a day off for this.' This time he lets it hang long enough for me to grab.

'I can't.'

'Friday morning. First thing. Think about it.'

Marco leaves. Thomas bloops, demanding a song I can't give him. It's quiet time in the house of Andolini, time for all good lawyers to sleep. Tomorrow I will scrape more paint and row that much closer to failure. Donovan once said that our action is our choice, our fate made by our own hands. *I choose not to be me.* I choose not to be afflicted, not to bear witness. Not to be wed to notions of transcendence – *as if they were real.* I choose not to be a postmodern loser – a fool. Real. I choose to be real, whole and solid – deaf to the wail of the haunt, mute for all future incantation. Dead to the wind. I call:

'Seawrack and seatangle.'

But I am not transformed.

CHAPTER 12

I seen the morning light
I seen the morning light
It's not because I'm an early riser
I didn't go to sleep last night

I am desperate for all the wrong reasons. It occurs to me now, sitting on the bed in the dim room with a legal pad on my lap, that this has always been so. Claire thinks I'm desperate to receive a six-figure book deal. Over the years she's woken up late at night and found me churning out pages and she's smiled. Even C has been afflicted by the notion that a finished manuscript means a contract and a contract means a new silver minivan. So my words, in a sense, are written to that automobile, calling for it to show itself to me.

I don't remember all of my desperations: desperate to publish before this author died; desperate to record before that singer passed – either to have them validate me or for me to tell them that they were wrong. I don't know when everything got so turned around. I once was desperate to have writing do things, to contain transformative powers, but writing has never done anything for me. It has never been cathartic or therapeutic. It names things, locates them, or at least when I'm writing, I can pretend to be involved in some kind of management of my netherworlds. I start with a feeling, perhaps even more substantial – an image attached to that feeling. I write something, even finish. Sometimes I think it is good. But the feeling is still there, unchanged, but now with a name and a reason for being, legitimized and calling for a permanent place in me. I can't do this. I am desperate because I know rage is still rage, sorrow still sorrow, and the only actions that can give them the voice each demands is to destroy and to wail. I am desperate because I write to the minivan and all that lies between it and me. I push a pen across a page, gesturing at symbol, metaphor – pasting a collage of willfully mute and deaf images beside each other within some self-conscious vehicle that masquerades as story. But I get sidetracked in the production, ambushed in my own head. I trick myself for a moment, believe the words arranged just so will metamorphose into a balm. Part of me doesn't believe. It tries to conceive the minds of unknown agents, faceless editors, and book review consumers. But part of me goes with it, chasing the words that follow the image as it moves up like braiding smoke offerings of ritualistic purification. It will never sell. I scribble a line across the page beneath the last jumble of words to signal I am done.

When I leave, I wear the grim face – the face of a man who wants to get this done, who'll brook no nonsense, not from conductors, commuters, or silly leaves that have fallen too early and lie drowning in gutter pools. It seems as though August is waging a war against the oncoming season. Since it can't be hot, it rains. Not the great neartropical cloudbursts. This is constant, cold, and unspectacular. I leave earlier this morning and take the A-train – the brown people's train – to Canal Street and walk north from there, but I wait around the corner from the entrance until someone from the crew shows up. I want a cigarette for the waiting. They are good for marking time. They are good when you are enraged; you can drag hard on them and throw them into the street – quickly light another.

Chris approaches from the west. He's wearing headphones, nodding to some private beat. He nears me, as though he doesn't see, then a few strides away, without breaking step he looks up.

'S'up, dude?'

He walks past me. I turn and follow. He unlocks the door, calls for the elevator. It clangs open. We get in. Chris is handsome, but he's lost his boyishness, as though since I saw him last he witnessed something that has aged him internally, some premonition – twenty years down the road and still banging nails. He'd fancied himself a poet, now it looks as though he won't ever write again – perhaps even forgot that he once had.

We get upstairs. He utters his obligatory curse to the darkness, heads for the circuit breaker. After he turns the lights on he goes to his sill and produces his breakfast.

The others straggle in, as distant with me as they were yesterday. I wait for the others to eat and drink and change before I start gathering my things. I roll the scaffold to where I left off. KC drifts by.

Chris reenters the room and issues a proclamation.

'Feeney and Johnny are gonna be here later so keep your shit together 'cause I don't want to hear none of their shit. All right?'

The crew collectively moans. Chris goes to his spot.

KC glides up to me quietly like he has a secret.

'Hey, mon, na more dat fuckin' stuff.'

'Excuse me?'

'The smell, man – the smell. There ain't enough air in here for that.' He points at the metal. 'Use the sandpaper like I showed you, the sandpaper and the oil. It's faster anyway.'

'Actually, KC, I think stripping is quicker.'

'Yeah, but it give me a headache. Dat shit rot yer brains, too. Don't you need your brains?'

'Apparently not.'

'You still funny, mon. Yer still funny.'

'I am?'

'Yeah, mon. Dat's why I was glad ta hear you comin' back. Not for you – 'cause when you gotta leave ya gotta leave and you probably didn't want ta come back. But it's good for me.'

'How's that?'

'Look at these motherfuckers here, mon. They don't know nothing.'

I get up on the Baker with sandpaper and oil, in part for KC, in part for me. I don't know what my next task will be – it could be worse, more tedious – the outside of the windows perhaps. This job isn't about productivity, it's about being here, gesturing at competence and effort. There really isn't any incentive to be good.

The pace of work seems to pick up just before break. Somehow the crew has sensed it. Nancyboy comes in with a big ex-marine-looking lug in tow. I suppose this is Feeney. They stop in the middle of the room and don't pay me any mind. I pretend to work and watch them from the scaffold. He's ruddy faced and sports a nose that looks like part of it might have gotten lopped off awhile back. His eyes are pleasant, though, and even though he only seems to grunt short answers back at Johnny, they twinkle each time.

Nancyboy waves at the entire space as though he's grandly concluding something. He's ready to go, but Feeney lingers around the Baker. He steps forward, picks at the clean metal, rubs his fingers, and seems satisfied. I suppose I should stop and wait for his approval, some sort of wink or nod, but anyone who's partnered with Johnny probably doesn't know what he's doing. I can tell that my continuing to sand annoys him, but he slaps Johnny on the arm and points to the back.

'Lemme see the kitchen.'

They walk off. I sneak a look at KC. He's been watching it all. He shoots me a quick grin and starts shaking his head to signify that he thinks I'm crazy.

The saw cuts out and frames Feeney's voice in the near darkness.

'Who's the big nig on the Baker?'

It's not anything he wanted anyone to hear, but now it's out there, for all of us, undeniable what he's asked and undeniable who he asks after. Johnny gestures to Chris, spinning his index fingers in the air. Chris bellows out, 'That's break!'

No one responds immediately. They drift around their stations as though in a time warp. Feeney begins to move away from everyone else, but then he thinks better of it and steps forward with energy. He twists his boots in the sawdust and gypsum and watches the little cloud form, rise, and dissipate. He lifts his head suddenly and brightly, smiling broadly as though he's just thought of something wonderfully funny. He shakes it, mumbles something to himself. Chris crosses in front of him on his way to the bath-room. The two other carpenters do, too, though without his directness. KC and Bing Bing wait by the doorway, alternating glares between Feeney, Johnny, and myself.

I climb down and walk toward the bathroom. KC and Bing Bing start on a course to intercept me before I get there like they're about to do a hit. Bing Bing takes me by the elbow. He doesn't say anything, but he squeezes it, imploring me to stop. I do and turn to him. He doesn't meet my face. He looks past me, over to where Feeney was standing. He sucks his teeth and shakes his head once violently.

'G'wan!'

He lets go my elbow and uses that hand to gesture to where he's looking. KC, grave faced, walks to us slowly. He looks down shaking his head but comes up smiling. Then it disappears. He goes rigid in his stance.

'You all right wit dat, mon?'

'With what?'

'Boy, don g'wan play dumb wit me. You g'wan let that go?'

'What would you have me do?'

'Mon, if I was a big boy like you. I wouldn't fear no man. No man couldn't say nothing to me.'

Both of their faces are dark and hot. KC leans into me.

'What you g'wan do – huh?'

I don't say anything. I turn from one to the other, but neither one cracks his expression. Feeney walks past us. KC and Bing Bing suck their teeth in unison. He stops and turns to KC, refusing to make eye contact with me.

'Problem, officer?'

'I ain't the one with a problem, man.'

'You don't have a problem.'

'Not me.' He slowly takes his toothpick out of his mouth and examines it. Feeney turns to Bing Bing and points at him from the hip. The bathroom-to-lunch exodus halts at the door. Chris watches Feeney from behind, nodding, either in some kind of agreement or to the beat in his headphones. Feeney turns to go, which draws another teeth suck, which makes him turn, shrug his shoulders, and open his arms to us. He finally looks at me, shrugs his shoulders again, and waits. KC and Bing Bing both lean away from me. His eyes follow them.

'You all seem upset. Something I said?'

They both look to me, as if no one else saw my cue to speak.

'What did you say?'

'I don't know. You guys are standing there like you want something – like you want to do something – I don't know. You tell me.'

'What did you call me?'

'What, you're here a day and you're getting in my face?'

'I'm not in your face. I'm standing here asking you a simple question.'

'Simple – oh fuck you. Get the fuck out of here. Go eat, drink – whatever. Think about it, pal.'

I take one step at Feeney and he holds his ground. He's conscious about not moving – not making himself any larger or smaller than he already is.

'Don't get stupid, brother.'

I feel my head cock to one side. My neck pops. It feels right to look at him slanted so I leave it there.

'I just asked you a question.'

'I don't care. Asshole.'

I hear KC suck his teeth again and I remember the scraper in my hand. I drop it at my feet and it lands with a muffled clang in the dust.

'That was your second mistake, fuck.' He curls his lip and slaps his thighs, then closes his hands into loose fists. Nancyboy grabs his shirt, but Feeney knocks his hand away with an exaggerated swipe. 'Come on!' He waves me in with both hands. I go.

I want to see if I can still take a punch, so I let him hit me. A right. He's surprised at the ease and so he stops his blow midway. It loses power, focus, and only grazes my cheekbone. Because he misses, he panics a bit, yanks his arm back crazily, and throws again, this time he lands squarely on my shoulder, forces me back, but I pivot on my right foot and square-up southpaw. A left goes past my ear. I counter right left. Nose and cheek. Blood and snot on him now and my knuckles. He throws a wild right off the top of my head, a weak left that bounces off my wrist to my ear. He doesn't bring it back. I slide inside him. Right hook flush on the jaw. He whinnies and his legs buckle.

Johnny wraps him up and walks him back. He's too small and they both almost go down. Feeney finds his legs and tries to break free. Chris gets him from behind, then Dewey – now Feeney can start yelling.

'Son of a bitch! Fuck you cocksuckin' bastard! I'll fuckin' kill you!'

He keeps screaming, his voice on the point of breaking, until they get him to the elevator. I don't know if it was there or if out of my sight he stops, but it's quiet in the loft. KC slides up in front of me, nodding his head in agreement with every one of his thoughts.

'You a crazy man, you know?' He offers me his hand. I take it. He slaps my shoulder with his other hand and then inspects my face for damage. 'I think you really fucked him up.' He stops his examination and turns to Bing Bing, who's grinning broadly and nodding, too. 'G'wan get de mon's tings na.' Bing Bing rubs his hands together, turns his shuffle into a bounce, and starts looking for my bag. I let go of KC's hand and get my bag myself, which prompts Bing Bing to skate over to the scaffold, get my loose tools and my belt, and rush them back to me.

KC's by the window looking down on Greene.

'I don't see 'em nowheres. I thought they'd take him to cool him out, maybe give you some room to get out, but they gone.' He presses his head against the glass. 'I don't even see that little fucker's truck.' He turns, leans back against the window, folds his arms across his chest, and rocks his body at the shoulder from side to side – gathering momentum. A quick blast of air escapes from past his lips. He rocks his head with his body. He looks pained – but it's a smile, trying to hold back laughter. 'You really fucked him up.' He lets it go, bends forward at the waist, and wheezes silently. He straightens, shakes his head once more as though to dispel the feeling, and weakly points a long finger at the doorway.

'You better get going, man.'

Bing Bing tightens the straps on my bag. I shoulder it and start walking. Bing Bing gives me a light slap on the back. KC stays by the window.

'You gotta number man? You in the book?'

'Yeah, sure.' I walk out, stop and turn at the elevator. I knock the button with my knife handle. The light goes on. KC calls from inside.

'Like I said, I get jobs of my own. I call you next one na.'

'Thanks, KC.'

He finally moves out of my view so he doesn't have to watch me wait.

Johnny is outside waiting for me with his hands in his pockets. He looks like a lost kid. He slouches when he sees me, drops his head, and then rolls his eyes up to look at me.

'Qué pasa, professor?'

'What's up, Johnny?'

410

He tries to smile but stops at kind of a half-grimace. He takes his hands out of his pockets, then stuffs them back.

'Nothing, man, nothing. It's cool. Here.' He pulls out a billfold.

'What's this?'

'Tuesday, yesterday, and today. I owe you. Take it.' I open my hand and he places the bills in them. I put them in my pocket without looking. 'I paid you for a full day today.' He looks down again. 'I paid you like a lead guy. I wasn't trying to be a dick. I was just trying to get you back into it, you know.'

'Thanks, man.'

'It's cool.'

'Where's your friend?'

He snaps up, spitting. 'That fucker ain't my friend.' He checks himself. 'Chris took him to St Vincent's.' He kicks at the curb. 'You gotta watch out. He's the type that'll sue you.' He looks at me, perhaps waiting for me to acknowledge his warning, or say something he can understand – an apology, but when I look past him at the people entering and leaving the jeans store, I know that I don't need to apologize for anything. And I feel a surge of adrenaline, greater than when Feeney's fist grazed my face – so large that I feel if Nancyboy looks at me with the slightest bit of malice, I'll backhand him into the street.

He flares his nostrils.

'I gotta go, man.' He points at my hand. 'Nice hook.'

411

He heads north and I take out the money – seven-fifty. I haven't had this much cash on me in years – maybe ever. My first feeling is that I'm rich. I start for the jeans store to get Claire a pair of pants.

The store isn't as posh as I thought it would be – not posh at all, actually. The shelves are painted wood, the jeans are just – jeans. There are tributes to America, splashes of red, white, and blue paint, and actual flags, too, both painted and cloth on the wall, hanging from the ceiling. There's dust, on the wide-plank floor, seemingly in the air. I don't seem out of place here. A slim, pale-faced brunette is leaning against the shelves, looking lost, but not in thought. Her face is blank until she sees me, then she crosses her arms behind her, and smiles. She put on a lot of lipstick today along with low-cut jeans and a short, tight pink T-shirt that's cut an inch above her navel. Her white skin looks a bit goosey.

'Hi, sir, can I help you?'

'I'd like to buy some pants – jeans.'

She tries to keep her smiley-faced sexy innocence going.

'Well, this is the place.'

'Perhaps a sweater as well.'

'We've got some great ones.' She puts her palms on her thighs and bends as though she's about to address a child. 'Would you like to see some things?'

'I'd love to.'

'Great, follow me.'

She leads me toward the back of the store, to the great racks of jeans – floor to ceiling – checking a couple of times to make sure I'm still with her.

'This is a gift for . . .'

'My wife. My wife.'

'Great. Do you know her size?'

'Four.'

We stop in the back corner. There are two blown-up photographs: one is of Dylan and the other Jim Morrison. Both are famous shots: Dylan with his Wayfarers and Minnesota afro, looking like he's about to let somebody know just how stupid they really are. The Lizard King arms spread, shirtless, leather pants, like he's auditioning at a cattle call for a bacchanal.

'We have five different styles.'

'I'm sorry?'

'What cut do you think she'd like?' She steps back and frames her jeans with her hands. 'These are the Urban Cut.'

'I don't think so.'

'Hmm.' She starts into one of the piles on a shelf. 'Classic?'

'Classic?'

She pulls a pair out and models them on an imaginary figure between us. 'These are the Classic Cuts. A lot of people like these because they're simple.'

'Perhaps too simple.'

She folds them quickly, in a way I've never been

able to master, and slips them back in the pile. 'She'll love these.' She reaches up to a higher shelf, pulling her shirt up her ribcage. She has a large birthmark on her spine. She finally gets the pants, turns and unfolds them simultaneously.

'Free and Easy.'

'That's great.'

'Aren't they?'

'Yes.'

'So what else can I help you with?'

'I'll take two.'

'Two pairs. Someone's lucky.'

'Absolutely.'

'Can I find anything else for you today?'

'No, thank you. That will do.'

The two pairs cost $150. I start north with my tool and shopping bag feeling about as good as I can remember feeling in a while. The sun seems to be gathering strength for one last push against the chill. And people of all types line the narrow streets of SoHo – some with tool bags, some with shopping bags, but none with both. Punching Feeney was the best thing I've done for myself in a while. I appreciate the transforming powers of violence. Awake. The air has a new snap to it. The light is sharper, as though some hand has made a small adjustment on my collective focus.

I get a triple espresso from the shop I've been avoiding. It's really not that expensive, after all. The pimply boy at the counter was eager to make it – perhaps even charged me too little, and seemed truly thankful when I dropped a dollar in the tip jar. Outside. North. Shopping bag, tool bag, no lavender spray but tingling knuckles, the notion that I can lick anyone and the anticipation of a solid caffeine high in the afternoon. The streets are crowded, but no one seems particularly busy or in a hurry. They stroll, chat, browse in the windows of the little shops – small inventories, bright paint, and thin women of varying ages and shades. I wonder if the mad Scot still has his little soccer shop up on Eleventh. I make for it, cutting east down Houston toward Second Avenue. This isn't the street I ran down the other night. That road is gone. *Why bother?* Whatever it has to offer has no place here. *Fuck it*, I say at the bottom of Second. *I'll get my boy a shirt if I want to.* I'll get a shirt for both my boys. *Ronaldo! Jogo Bonito!* X wouldn't want one, though. I'll get him a big T. rex model, or one of those fancy picture books – something like that. And my girl, what? I'm sure I'll know it when I see it. It will speak.

A couple of blocks south of the soccer store I see a narrow shop with a big window, white wainscoting and a few tables, a young woman with a ponytail holding a tray with a teapot. I know I've been in that space before when it was something else. I cross the street, cutting through the lines of stopped cars, and stop at the door to read the menu. I can't really focus on anything – the espresso's kicking in. The ponytail girl turns. Her face is striking: Eurasian, I think is the term that's supposed to describe her. I hesitate at the door. She pushes it open, one handed, and holds it ajar for me.

'Come in.' Her voice is squeaky but not unpleasant. She seems too innocent to be working in the New York City service industry. She couldn't have been here long. She certainly didn't grow up here.

'Come on, we're letting all the weather in.'

Squeaky, pretty – I feel like patting her on the head. I take the door instead. She smiles, wide. No braces for this girl: Her upper left incisor juts out. It must constantly poke her inner lip. I look at the tables to keep from staring at her mouth – one row of birch-ply squares screwed onto simple black tubes with four long feet. They're pushed against a long, tall, blue vinyl banquette. She starts for the counter. I follow.

'Sit,' she says, pointing at the first table. I obey. I stuff my bags under the table and sit on the bench. The tingling that started in my fingers is now more like the presence of a strong pulse, and in between beats they go numb, but not that heavy feeling of frozen or sleeping digits, more like fingers that don't exist. I hold my hands up and tell my fingers to move. They obey, but now they seem with each motion to wave in and out of exis-tence like reeds in a breeze under moonlight, defying sight each time they bend away.

She comes back.

'You look a little sleepy. Are you hungry, too?'

I try my best not to look at her tooth. 'I don't think so.'

'Really,' she squeaks. She slides a cream-colored card onto the table. It has indigo writing on it. 'You're a big guy,' she points at my tool bag. 'You need something to keep you going.'

'Oh, I don't think so.' I've disappointed her. It hurts – the way she closes her mouth, presses her lip against that snaggletooth. 'Perhaps in a bit,' I say, but it doesn't get her smiling again.

'I'll leave this here.' She pats the menu, whips her ponytail, and heads for the back.

I flex my hands. They seem to want to drift in and out of this realm. I crack my knuckles. The sound phases in and out, too.

Ponytail has left me alone out front. I look to where she disappeared, through a swinging door with no window behind a counter – more like a half-wall topped by butcher block – that has baskets and plates of baked goods. I am hungry. I hear my stomach complain from the place where my knuckle pop vanished. I wonder if there's a scone in one of those baskets, or a pie on one of those plates. I wonder if ponytail makes sandwiches. I want peanut butter and raspberry jam on wheat, and chocolate milk – no, ginger ale and very salty potato chips. I start to doubt the ponytail girl – her friendliness. She must be a jaded New Yorker – to be so two-faced. But she has left me alone, with the baked goods, with the cash box that I'm sure is hidden behind that little wall. I scan the room for a camera, but I don't find one. The café is a blend of old and new: white limestone tiles, white wainscoting, blue-and-white-striped wall linen, but the big window with its aluminum mullions points to something else. There's so much light in the little space – east facing, street level in the early afternoon. The brightness makes me rethink what it is to be old, to be of the old. There are simple pewter sconces – empty – and up in each corner, small speakers. Now I hear the music, a song fading out that had probably been quite loud – strings, falsetto – '. . . *Just my 'Magination . . .*' I don't know how I missed that one. I snap at myself, look out the window to Second Avenue, at the people walking by – students, *artists*, kids pretending to be homeless punks, a few suits in downtown casual disguise; they all seem underdressed for this chill. *Summer's gone. Don't ya know it?*

Someone picks out chords on a tinny harpsichord, bass kick drum and medium-ride cymbals. Pause. Bass grace note. *'I'll Be There.'*

I sit back on the banquette, watch the tireless stream of people and cars go by. I feel the espresso wearing off – so quick it was, so mild – and sleep. I close my eyes, lay my hands on the table and feel them pulse and fade. It spreads, up my arms, down – my back and legs pulse and fade and disappear. I hear Michael's voice coming from that vacant space.

I'm gone, too. Into that space where everything has been fading. I don't want to go. I snap my head up, open my eyes as wide as they'll go, but my vision seems to fade. Michael's baby-pitched voice, adolescent earnest and manish boy hurt that came too soon. Fuck – that song. I used to hear it in my head while I waited leaning on the windowsill three stories up on visitation Sundays. Lila's inscrutable hiss. I don't know if she was cursing him or mocking me, waiting for him to show. He wouldn't call, either. He wouldn't mention his absence unless I brought it up when I did see him. *'Car wouldn't cooperate. I got tied up in all sorts of things.'*

Something in that space, or the space itself, moves – peels itself away – the darkness of the void. Becomes a shape, slouching in the emptiness. The darkness keeps collecting around it, growing the form – a black blob nowhere.

'I knew you were sleepy.'

I snap up and bang the table, mumbling. 'I'm up.'

'Why don't you go home?'

'No. No.' I try to enunciate, but it comes out as a panicky mumble.

'Well, I'm sorry. I didn't mean to leave you for so long.'

'Quite all right.'

She lets that little tooth peek out, not a smile, but some relief for her lip. She catches me staring but doesn't seem to mind.

419

'Coffee?'

'Oh, yes. Thank you.'

'Are you hungry yet?'

I look down at the menu, but it doesn't register. 'Do you have a scone?'

'I think we might. Let me check. But I definitely have coffee.'

She spins away again. The older Jackson boys back up their brother's ad-libbing. '. . . *la la la, lala la la* . . .' I try my best to straighten, to be alert, and almost knock over the water glass she snuck onto the table.

She comes back with my coffee and scone, carrying them on a molded orange tray. She serves them formally, lip pulled tight over that tooth. She's taller than I thought. Her voice diminished her stature, but she is very thin, hardly a curve to her. I want to draw her, capture how that little bit of her lip is forced out, the struggle evident in the rest of her face – trying to hide, ignore, or bear the discomfort. The lights pulse once, inside and out – a collective surge. I'm awake again, with hardly a memory of sleep.

'Can I get you anything else?'

'I'm sorry, do you have paper?'

'Let me check.' She lowers the tray to her side and half skips to the counter. She comes back quickly, shaking her head.

'This is ridiculous,' she places a stack of napkins on the table. 'But it's paper.'

'Thank you,' I nod and pat the pile. She stays,

420

waiting for something I'm not sure of. I look up. 'Thank you.' She nods back and grins, though not enough to bare the tooth. She does her hair snap, spins, and disappears through the swinging door.

I take the Sharpie out of my bag and a napkin off the pile. I'm ready. I put the pen to the page and leave it. The point of black ink deepens and expands in the shape of a rough sphere. I lift the pen, circle the sphere, make a few dots out along the edges of the napkin. I get a new one but keep the pen away, creating similar shapes in the air just above it. I write:

> *Thursday is the cruelest day: scheming; needing; bleeding. You plan your weekend conquests – a shadow projection of the rest of your days – failures. Thursday afternoon we limp to bars after work. Happy – seemingly easy and free. Then Friday breath and bile from protracted happy hours; more drinking perhaps or perhaps sleep. And you know, in your own mind, the dreams of weekend empire are all lies.*

I ball up that napkin, stuff it in my bag, and go back to tracing shapes above the page until finally, something else comes:

> *Big Nig was schizophrenic, that's what he was told. So one day he stopped taking his medication. Nothing happened. So he went out, to be*

421

himself – walking streets that seemed familiar and strange at the same time. Familiar because they were the streets that he'd known as a boy, but now they were strange, too. They'd once been strange because they had been new – the names, where they led, how they would lead him back to where he'd begun. Now they were strange because he recognized them as layered. He'd seen, over the years, the men with the loud trucks and the heat and stink of tar. He'd walked them with both his mother and father and alone, fearing and fantasizing about the places they would take him. He'd run them, too, run away – being Big Nig, there was much to run away from. So Big Nig walks the multiply resurfaced streets of his now and then and they seem to move like giant black snakes, caterpillar-like, not serpentine in their locomotion, so it seems that they barely move – but they do – tendon and ligament and muscle under new skin set to emerge from the dull old. He does not know where he is going.

Big Nig was born in the summer of love, came into consciousness for Nixon, came of age in the age of Reagan. He was a late bloomer, so he didn't become truly sexually active until the age of AIDS and Bush I. When the time of Clintonian plenty came – premium cigars, specialty vodka and caviar, steak and small-batch whiskey, escalating stock and real estate prices – he went underground. He missed

hip-hop and grunge rock. He played his old
vinyl 33s bare.

I hear the back door open. Ponytail says something to someone, drops what sounds like a box
on the floor, and leaves again. On the bottom of
the napkin, I try a quick sketch of her standing
behind the counter, but the lines are too blurry.
I get a new one. I don't know where I'm going
with this so at the top of the new page I write
'Notes for a novella,' a disclaimer against charging
myself with nonsense later on. Notes, these are
only notes. I'll fill in the rest later.

Big Nig slides a note to the bank teller. He
feels guilty. Not because of what he's about to
do, but because of to whom he's about to do
it. For some reason, he based his plan solely
on memory and not up-to-date research.
He'd remembered when all the tellers were
white. Then they became machines. Now they
were all brown and for an instant he confuses
the teller with the institution – that they are
the same. He doesn't want to cause her any
trouble. He wonders if she can lose her job
over this. She isn't young – perhaps fifty. There
aren't many jobs for middle-aged women whose
first language isn't the King's English. Big Nig
pauses and then pauses within that pause,
wondering if his hesitation will cost him dearly
later. No matter, he needs the break. He has

to do this and it's too far gone now to stop. But her chubby face. Are those moles or freckles? The way her hand took the note. His hand on the white faux-Carrera.

'Are you trying to put us out of business?' a deep voice asks from above. A man who looks startlingly like me stands before the table, with a hand opened to the napkins. He leans, just a bit, pretending to read the blurry ink. He straightens again and produces from behind his back a small writing tablet. 'Joy,' he calls back to the counter in a high-end basso. 'Do you see what I'm doing?' She pretends to focus on him. 'I'm not wasting napkins.' He places the pad on the table, picks up the remaining napkins, and clears his throat. 'How are you?'

'I'm well, thank you.' I gesture at the used napkins. 'I'm sorry.'

'No need. I'm just asserting my right – one overly dramatic moment a day per person. I figured this could be mine.' He straightens, puts his hands behind his back. 'How is everything, okay?'

'Yes, thank you.'

'Anything else you'd like, or are you set for now?'

'For now, thank you.'

'We have lovely sandwiches.'

'Thank you.'

'You're welcome.' He turns to the back. 'Joy?'

'Yes.'

'There's no music. Will you put some on, please?'

'Sure. What do you want to hear?'

He leans toward the table. He really doesn't look like me at all, just the shape of his body, but his face is round, small, his skin tone has much more yellow, his eyes are almost black.

'Excuse me,' he croons. 'Do you like reggae?'

'Oh, yes.'

He straightens again. 'Joy, would you put that reggae mix on?'

'Sure.'

'And would you bring him some more coffee, please. I'm going outside to kill myself.'

'Oh, Ben,' she moans, hitting notes I would've thought to be too low for her. He puts a finger to his lips, silently shushes her, and leans into the door to open it. He gives me a warm smile just before he exits. I try to reciprocate, but I'm too slow.

Drum roll. Marley scats, introducing *'Ride Natty Ride.'* Joy appears beside the table with the tray and matching pitcher. She looks down into my full cup, to me, and then back to the cup. I lift it quickly, swallow half of it, and put it back down. She shows me that funky tooth, warms the cup, and spins, slower this time, away.

Ben is smoking a cigarette, watching people walk past. He goes to lean against the window and catches me looking at him. He gives me the same smile, warm, too warm to seem genuine, but what other reason would he have for flashing it? Behind the counter Joy tears into that box and begins

425

arranging things on the hidden shelves. Her thin leg and little foot stick out into view. She half hums, half sings along. She can't sing very well, but the fact that she is singing, discreetly, but without shame, makes me want to listen. I stack the used napkins, fold the pile in half, and put them in my pocket. I sit back with my coffee and watch Joy rotate her ankle back and forth in time.

I remember moving day in our old apartment. The boys were confused and moping among the stacked boxes. I put the stereo on – one of the few things left unpacked. The boys jump to their feet, ready to dance and sing. '. . . *the stone that the builder refused . . . ,*' sings Bob, '. . . *shall be the head cornerstone . . .*' They twist and dip and jump, moving so far out of time that any particular rhythm ceases to matter – it never mattered. My girl uses my leg to pull herself to standing. I bend down low. *'Fire!'* Bob and I cry. *'Fire!'* yell the boys in response. My girl, only a few months steady on her feet, rocking her head and body, smiling, watching her brothers: C, the silent brooder, the magician with his alchemical potions of toothpaste and juice and spit. X, the stomping tyrant lizard king, the warrior, little lord of the flying head butt. Everybody's dancing. *'Fire!'* Teaching my boys, right in front of their Brahmin mother, to hold the burning spear. Whipping them into righteous rage and indignation – the young lions. C, the griot enchanter. X, the Brahmin eater. The song ends. The boys are panting and sweaty.

My girl, still rocking, waits for our eyes to meet and blows me a kiss.

I stand up abruptly and almost upset the table. I catch it and step into the aisle, ready to do something, but I'm not sure what. I should go, but I don't know where. I think about the soccer store, the Ronaldo shirt, and admit that it's not in the budget – nothing's in the budget. Claire's pants will have to go back, too. The image of empty-handed me telling her, *'I got to go . . .'* I shake it off, get out the list, and still standing, copy it from the sandpaper to a clean sheet from the tablet. I start to write down what I have in my pocket, but it seems that such an act would concretize the amount – make it much more difficult to alter: Twenty-four hours to go, over twelve thousand dollars short, and I'm in a little café doing nothing. I've got to go. Ben has disappeared. Joy's foot is gone. I hear myself weakly call out to her like a half-doped patient asking for his nurse.

'Excuse me?'

'Yes,' she answers in that strangely low voice, peeking around the wall as she does.

'I need to step out for a moment. Is that okay?'

'Sure, honey,' she's squeaky again. 'You're not chewin' and screwin', are you?'

'Me, no. I just need to find a phone.'

'No cell phone?' she asks somewhat disbelieving.

'No, sorry.'

She thumbs at the counter. 'You can use this one. Ben wouldn't mind.'

'Thanks, but it's long distance.'

'Oh,' she exaggerates. 'I think there's a pay phone across the street.'

'Thank you.'

She looks at the scone, crinkles her face, and fakes a pout. 'You didn't like it?'

'Oh, no. I haven't started.' I look down at the little menu. 'I was thinking that I'd like a sandwich.'

'Really?' she perks up. 'So you're saving that for dessert?'

'Yes,' I lie. 'I'll have the grilled cheddar.'

'Great. Go make your call.'

I go outside to call Claire – the preemptive strike. I have to go up the avenue a ways to find a working pay phone. I dump a pound of Marco's change in.

'Hello?'

It's Edith. Tight-jawed Edith. I suppose it's good to know that she addresses everyone like this – formal and suspicious. Closed to anything moving or new.

'Hello?' she asks again, raising the tone, perhaps an eyebrow, as well. Someone, I think X, shrieks with pleasure or rage in the background. Edith's growing cross at both of us. I speak.

'Hello, Edith?'

'Oh, it's you. I didn't think anyone was there.'

'Sorry.'

'Quite all right.'

'Hey, is Claire handy?'

'No.'

I don't expect the negative response to a formality. I stumble.

'What's going on there? What's she doing?'

'She's out.' She says it with too much relish – especially for a woman like her: Edith the ghostless; Edith the sexless – no boyfriends – only vague peripheral suitors; Edith of the closed wallet, who, in spite of her only child's pleadings still maintained that public school – something she's never experienced – would be fine for grandchildren.

'Out?'

'Yes, out.' What had she said to her late husband as he prepared another miniature for a sculpture that wouldn't sell? Thank goodness they both had trust funds. He drained his to make art and put his daughter through school. She added the proceeds from his life insurance policy to hers.

'Where'd she go?'

I try to imagine her with faceless people at the Sizzler or Red Lobster out on Route Six.

'Boston.'

'Boston?'

'Yes, she's meeting some of her school friends.'

'When will she be back?'

'Tomorrow.'

'Tomorrow?'

'No sense in making the trip back late, is there?'

'No. No.' I try to regroup – to keep her from hearing my head winding up, preparing to spin. I don't want it to spin. Not in that way. Hotels. Mojitos – or whatever those murmuring, smarmy, preppy fuckers are into. 'We're having drinks with fun names, so that means we're having fun.' Claire would never fall for that shit.

'So she'll call you – when?'

'May I speak to the kids?'

'Which one?'

'Whoever is near.'

'Hold on. I'll see if they want to talk.' She lowers the phone to her hip, in part to keep from having to talk to me, but also to muffle whatever she's saying to the children – what they're saying back to her. *'No, I don't feel like talking.'* Getting kids to talk on the phone is second in difficulty to getting them to perform in public – it's mood based. Edith is censoring my children's response for me. She's not all bad – perhaps not bad at all. Second Avenue, the pale sun is like a yellow bruise, pain spreads dimly from the center. Light on the sky, on the six-story tenement walk-ups. The East Village has changed – Mercedes southbound on the avenue, jackets and ties. Upscale eateries. Strollers and well-groomed young mothers. Where are the squeegee men and the junkies? Where is the shopping cart brigade? The stolen-goods side-walk sales? Where are the flamboyantly gay boys walking alongside the old Ukrainian women pulling their pushcarts, the bag of rugalach on

430

top? Maybe it's just in this moment that I've chosen to look up that they are gone. The sky is like a fading contusion on white skin; the sun, the center of the blow.

'Daddy,' lisps X. His voice dispels the sky. His face fills the void.

'Hey, kid.'

'I'm not kid. My name is X!'

'Sorry, X.'

'Oh, it's okay, Dad.'

'What are you doing?'

'Playing.'

'Are you playing dinosaur?'

'No.'

'Why not?'

'I'm playing ancient sea creature.'

'Do you like sea creatures now?'

'*Ancient* sea creatures, Dad.'

'Oh yeah?'

'Oh yes!' I hear the jump in his voice and then the thump of his landing.

'Which ancient sea creatures?'

'Oh, I love Archelon.'

'Archelon, who's that?'

'He's a giant sea turtle.'

'Wow.'

'I also love Hybodeth.'

'Hybodus?'

'Yeah, Hybodeth.'

'Who's that?'

'He was one of the first sharks. I love sharks. Dad.'

'Oh yeah?'

'Oh yes. They're cartilaginous.'

'Really?'

'Oh yes. But Dad?'

'Yes.'

'Do you know who my favorite ancient sea creature is?'

'Who?'

'Megalodon!'

'That sounds dangerous.'

'Oh, yes, Dad. His name means giant toof.'

'Giant tooth?'

'Yes!'

'What is he?'

'He's a giant shark. He's like a giant great white shark – as big as a whale.'

'That's amazing.'

'Yeah.'

His focus drifts for a moment – Edith.

'Okay, may I have the phone back, please?'

'But I'm talking to my dad.'

'Yes, and you've talked to him for a long time.'

'But I need to tell him something.' His voice starts to bleed into a whine.

'What do you need to tell him?' she asks. The phone wants more money. I dump a dollar in. Edith tries to talk over the robot voice and X's protests.

'Hello, what's wrong with your phone?'

'Can he finish?' Edith goes silent but doesn't do anything. 'Can you put my son back on, please?'

'Oh, yes, sorry. Of course.' She fumbles, regroups, then holds the phone away, but I can still hear. 'Your father wants to say good-bye.'

'Bitch,' I mouth.

'Sorry?' She's still there.

'Nothing.'

'Oh, hold on.'

'Dad,' he's calm again. My first thought is to tell him not to yell at his grandmother, that he needs to be polite. Fuck it.

'Yeah, I'm here.'

'Dad, I'm worried.' My guts crash down into my bowels, explode, reform, and spring back up again, but not in their proper places. I fight off the urge to howl.

'What's wrong?'

'I'm worried about Megalodon.'

'Why, it sounds like he can take care of himself.'

'No, Dad – he's dead. All of them are extinct.' Even his breathing is lispy.

'What about the others?'

'They're extinct, too.' His breathing grows heavier, faster, the pitch rising. He's about to crack. 'Dad,' he whimpers, as though he's been punched in the gut. He waits, takes a deep breath, exhales. I know Edith's standing over him, looking down, puzzled, annoyed. Whatever it is, he somehow knows that he can't break in front of her. 'I wish they were back.' He squeaks the last word out, then comes the first breath of a sob. He bites down on it, holds it, refuses to let it go.

And I can see him – man-jaw clenched, squaring it even more, every muscle flexed, and those eyes, searching around and around for an answer to this rush of feeling.

I hate the telephone.

'I wish they were here, too.'

He exhales again – I didn't think he had any more breath in him. 'Do you love those guys, too?'

'Oh yes, of course. Megalodon must have been so big.'

'Oh yes – he was so big!'

'You're so big, too.'

'Oh yes, and I'm a good swimmer, too.' He chuckles. I can see him, ready to jump again.

'Okay, kid, I'll see you soon.'

'X!'

'Sorry.'

'It's okay, Dad.'

'I love you, X.'

'Thanks, Dad.'

'Bye.'

'Bye-eye, Daddy.' He hands the phone to Edith and goes thumping away.

'Hello?' she's ready to hang up.

'Hi. Where's everyone else?'

'Well, I sent Cecil to the beach with the Crumwells and their boys – they're nice boys. And Edith, little Edy, is taking a nap.'

'The Crumwells?'

'Yes. You know them.'

'Yeah.'

'They're having fun, I'm sure.'

'I thought you were away.'

'Well, I was supposed to be, but I'm not.'

'When are they bringing him back?'

'We're meeting them for supper at the farm.'

'Really?'

She ignores that. 'Now, I'm supposed to get information from you – your arrival.' For a moment I don't know what she's talking about. She takes the opportunity to be condescending with me, too. 'Tomorrow night, are you coming?'

'Yes.'

'When?'

I lie. 'Nine.'

'Nine p.m. sharp?'

'Nine . . .' I pretend to consult a schedule. 'Nine-fourteen.'

'Oh, nine-fourteen. That doesn't fit well with bedtime. Is there another?'

'No.'

'No more trains?'

'It's a bus.'

'Oh.'

'Providence. Smithfield Road. Nine-fourteen.'

'Well, we can arrange something with the kids . . . perhaps . . . Nick Weed's son is coming for the weekend from Brown . . . Perhaps . . .'

'Claire can come. She can bring the kids.'

'It's late for them.'

'They can sleep in the car.'

'Well, fine then,' she breathes coldly. 'Nine-fourteen.

Friday. The bus. Someone will be there.' She hangs up before I can counter.

Ben is back in front of the shop, cleaning the door with Windex and paper towels. I almost call out to him from across the street as if he's an old friend, but I stop myself and watch him work while I wait for the light to change.

Someone else is watching him, too, waiting at the bus stop leaning against the M15 sign. He's older, stout, light-skinned. He's so focused on Ben that he doesn't see another man, perhaps in his twenties, sneak up behind Ben and grab him. Ben doesn't seem surprised. He turns to face this new man, drops the towels and the sprayer, presses his palms firmly on his cheeks and kisses him lightly on the lips. The two of them laugh and then take each other by the hips and turn in profile to me. This new man is handsome in a romance-novel-cover sort of way – rugged, olive complexioned, short, straight dark hair. Ben mutters something, but his friend doesn't seem to notice. He's focused on the man waiting for the bus who stares at them, his face contorted in an ugly pucker. He coughs up phlegm, loud enough for me to hear, and spits into the gutter. Ben turns, finds the man, and stares back, never moving his hands from his companion's hips. And for a moment it looks as though he may say something. He doesn't. Still staring, he pulls the man to him – belly to belly and kisses him again, defiantly this time. The traffic stops, allowing the kiss to continue unin-terrupted. And then the M15 runs the light. Someone honks. The bus blocks the scene. When it pulls away, only Ben is left. He sees me. I can tell he's scrambling in his head for damage control – to explain. I want to tell him it's okay. I fumble for a sign. All I can offer is a short wave. He waves back, bends quickly to gather his things, and hustles to get inside before I reach him.

Inside there's a cold grilled cheese waiting for me, cold coffee, too, but Ben and Joy are gone. I sit down and look at the limp sandwich. The bread looks to have gone soft again and the cheese, hard – condensed vapor on the plate. No more Marley, just some strange, computerized dub playing.

I want to pay and go, wander downtown until it's time to go to the other job – *the other job*. I kind of shudder when I think about it, about her. At first I think I shouldn't, but then I sit down, lean into the cushion, and dare myself to re-create her – that little faux-English accent, the various hues in hair loops, and those strange brown eyes that didn't seem to belong to her. In my head, she's still not whole, only parts, long limbs, a little chuckle I imagine she has. Feeney's pug nose invades the frame for a moment. I wonder if I broke it.

Joy materializes beside the table and slips the check onto it. I look up at her, and she frowns.

'You didn't even try it,' she squeaks.

'Oh, I'm sorry. I just got back.'

'Well, it's ruined.' She slowly reaches for the plate, but I stop her attempt by softly pinning her hand against the table. It feels like the sandwich would. She pulls it away with a discreet revulsion, as if it was my touch that made her hand go clammy.

I hide my hand in my lap. 'I'm going to start on it right now. I promise.' I try to deliver it with gentle conviction, to her eyes, but she's looking out to the gray day, the passersby. Perhaps to the end of her shift – home – where she can hold her pained lip in any way she wants.

She leaves me without speaking and I look at the bill – two cups of coffee, a scone, and a cold old sandwich – sixteen dollars. I take out my fold and leave a twenty – then twenty-one. *What the fuck is Claire doing in Boston?* The question, along with the grilled cheese sitting in its sweat, twists my stomach. Then it straightens out again and I wonder why it did so quickly. I feel the pulse of my whole body – my hands atop my thighs, my legs against the seat, my back against the rest. I fight back a yawn, finish the coffee, and wait for my stomach to twist again. Nothing happens – just another yawn.

I wonder if this is what it feels like, falling out of love: feeling yourself fading out of existence – the gray sky, the coffee shop limbo – everything a way station of sorts. Making promises you know

438

you can't keep. Making promises – period. People in love shouldn't have to vow or demand, petition or exhort. Nothing. Not even question. No collisions with your surroundings or yourself – you move gently, unknowing, in time. *Wondering if you ever were in love:* false compassion; skinny girls with bad teeth; tall men and long kisses in diesel residue; kisses as political acts, which makes me wonder if there really is love. I wonder where Ben has gone and want to apologize to him for what happened outside, then for all the times I've said nancyboy without thinking. Why wouldn't anyone want another to love the one they fall in love with?

Can you even fall out of love? I remember mocking those who claimed they had. I certainly remember not wanting to love Claire – that little crooked laugh from that long crooked mouth – how it made me feel that I could make that face go rosy, make her forget her loneliness, the loss of her own specific garden; everything good now, flashing back to then. I'd been proud, so proud not to have been bullied or guilted out of it – the stares and snickers, the pure stupidity of people involving themselves in your own affairs, them knowing what's best. And it burns more, the understanding that I may have been wrong. Wrong to take that stand, mistaking her for the eternal face of the eternal heart I believed was beating somewhere. It burns me, but then it goes, the heat like waves of sleep. Then there's nothing.

I wonder if this is what it feels like to fall out

of love – mirthless, but too spent to rage or lament its passing; numb to old shames; alone, watching the sun bleed and not having the vision drop you to your knees. My bride across the summer lawn – not even a memory, one thin image – the empty gesture of a desperate man who knows it but won't feel himself going down.

CHAPTER 13

There's a surge of sun at the end of the day, one last push for heat and light. I can sense the moon. It will be low and orange in the east and then gradually rise and fade to yellow – high in the late summer sky. At Edith's the moon is just over the guery pond, not yet lit but bigger than anything else you can see, dwarfing even the sunset in the opposite sky, making you almost forget that night is coming.

She's waiting in the window of the hallway. She sticks her head out. Her hair rolls down. She waves and calls out to me like we're friends.

'Hey, you.'

She hangs her arm out and dangles a ring of keys.

'Catch.' She swings them, trying to give them a high arc, as though it will slow their descent. I catch them. 'It's the one with the blue.'

She's waiting in her doorway, still open just enough to slide her body through along with dim orange light and the murmur of music. She backs away from the door, still holding it, but blocking entry. I wait outside. We study each other. She's wearing flip-flops, painter's pants stained and cut off at the knees, a pink tank top, and a violet bra – the straps exposed. She's tied her hair up – piled it on her crown. A few loose tendrils snake down to her nape. I get caught up in it. It takes a moment to register her broad smile.

'How's it going?'

'Fine, I suppose.'

She takes it in for a second, cocks her head to the side, and mimics me, *'Fine, I suppose.'* I nod at her poor imitation. She steps to the side, pulling the door open with her, and waves me in, but I stay where I am and try to get a look in and see what I could possibly be doing in there – if there could be several thousand dollars' worth of work to be done tonight. She waves again, shrinking her smile, wrinkling her face almost to a pout. I give her the keys, taking care to not let our fingers touch. She gives me a wider berth. I go in.

I expected something else, but the orange light is only a colored, low-wattage, bare bulb, naked in a plain porcelain socket – mood lighting for a makeshift mudroom.

'Lucky, huh?' she asks, pointing at the bag. I nod. She points to the floor beside the door where she keeps her footwear and umbrella. 'You can drop that stuff there.' She turns her back and disappears around the wall.

It's a much smaller space than the other loft – a rectangle about twenty by twenty-five divided into three discrete areas. On the left is a living space – a dark velvet couch, ratty womb chair, and an old rocker surround a large painted wooden crate; dining – a large glass rectangle on sawhorses, no chairs; and the kitchen on the far right against an exposed brick wall. The appliances look old – not vintage, just old, but there's a new blue kettle on the stove. On the back wall are three closed doors.

'Yeah,' she says, half turning to me. 'It's totally illegal.' She points up. 'I put these in last year.' I look up to see three enormous skylights. 'No one would touch that job. I was up there on the roof cutting holes in it – totally messed it up. I had no idea what I was doing. When there were buckets of water pouring in, I made a promise – no more do-it-yourself jobs, no matter how easy.' She goes toward the kitchen, remembers something, stops and answers a question that she believes I should've asked. 'I had to find these guys, pay them cash – trust that they wouldn't screw me.'

She waves me over to the table and points. 'Are you hungry?' There's fruit, cheese, bread, a bottle of sparkling water, a bowl of ice, and some glasses. 'I didn't know what you like, so, I figured everyone likes fruit, right?' She waits a minute, then gestures at the fruit. 'Right?'

She waits for me to take something, but I don't. I don't even think I can speak. I hope, somewhere inside of me I'm appalled at my rudeness.

'Right.'

'Suit yourself,' she snaps, but then I suppose feels a bit guilty. She lightens. 'I can make you some coffee.' She points to the wall-less galley kitchen. 'That's the only thing that gets made in there.' She shakes her head. 'My mama didn't raise me right – no, not at all.' She starts to take a step to me but cranes her neck and squints. 'Do you eat, drink, talk – anything?'

'I'm sorry.' I shuffle in my spot, look over at the kettle. 'I'm just a bit tired.'

'Oh no, don't be, please. I'm sorry.' She straightens her neck but softens the rest of her body to curve backward into a *c*. 'You must be tired, shit, the double-shift.' She leans forward even more to show interest. It's convincing. 'How was your day?'

I decide to trust the question. I exhale and feel contradicting tensions I didn't know were there – caffeine and fatigue – release their grips, and I'm taken by the sudden levity. I hear the music now. I don't recognize it – a piano solo, no, an upright bass, too. Slow tempo – the high end melancholy and whimsical, the low, brooding. I find myself reaching for a pineapple slice. She follows me with her eyes, then quickly settles on my face. She looks worried.

'Work wasn't so good.'

'Why not?' She looks at my hands as if to check for missing fingers.

'I was let go.'

'What? Why?'

'I fought with the GC.'

'You had an argument?'

'No.'

She doesn't want to, but she gasps. 'A *fight* fight?'

'Yes.'

'With that little guy?'

'No, his partner.'

She scans my face. 'Well, you look fine.'

I shrug. She cranes her neck again. 'Oh, I see.' She narrows her eyes – almost whispers, 'May I ask why?'

'I think he called me a nigger.'

She looks over my face again, turns an ear to me as though she missed what I said, then seems to get it from some echo unheard by me. She shakes her head, slowly. 'No,' she stutters, 'I don't believe it.' She leans in again. 'What do you mean, you *think?*'

I look around the room again. Tall white walls, the same height as the other loft's, making this space seem vault-like. Everything's so simple, practical – the furniture, the painted plywood floors – there's nothing that encroaches upon me and nothing for me to encroach upon – a place to let your guard down. I almost close my eyes, but then I remember her – paint stained, disheveled, and beautiful – the faded pink cotton top, the soft loop of hair, and the warm glow of lights; that floor lamp by the sofa, the dying sun above.

'Are you okay?' She finally takes that step

445

forward, extends her hand. She gestures at my bags with her fingers. 'Give me those.' I give her the jeans bag, but she waits for my tools. I shake my head, but she demands it with her whole hand this time and grinds her foot against the floor. I give her the tool bag, holding most of the weight. She won't lower her arm. She thinks she can suspend it like this, her shoulder in such a vulnerable position. She rolls her eyes at me to let go. I do. The bag yanks her arm down so she has to grab it with the other hand and hop quickly to the side to keep it from crashing into her shin.

'Jesus, what do you have in here?' She stares at the bag as though she can see through the canvas. 'Shit – how do you carry this thing?' She drops it onto the floor; something inside clanks and rattles. 'Oops,' she knocks her knees and covers her mouth.

'It's okay,' I say. My voice sounds foreign – too deep and reassuring. We both look at the bag; then she does a little shuffle step and leans away, mouthing a strange benediction to it. It forces us both to smile. She is young, at least younger than I'd thought – the only wrinkles she has are at the corners of her mouth and eyes, and in this light there's no sag to her muscle at all. The duet ends abruptly: the piano on a lone bass note. The bassist slides way up the neck and stays there, high and tremulous, until both tones fade away. We wait for another song but nothing else comes.

She starts for the living area, and I almost grab

her arm. It stops her. She cocks her head to the side and studies my hand and raises an eyebrow.

'Yes?'

I pull my hand back, crack my knuckles rudely. 'What do you need for me to do?'

She nods as though considering a request, rubs her hands together, then pushes her palms at the kitchen.

'Okay, what I wanted to have you do was build the kitchen, but it didn't get here. They sent the bathroom instead.' She shortens her nod, puckers, and looks at me as if I know what she's talking about. 'So, can you do the bathroom tonight, and maybe the kitchen when it gets here?'

I confess. 'I don't understand.'

'Oh,' her eyes widen in realization. 'Of course you don't.' She turns and half shuffles, half skips to the door on the far right. 'Come on,' she waves when she realizes I'm not following. She opens the door, reaches around and turns on the light. She pokes her head in as though she was exploring something new and then turns back to me with a little, fake grin. 'Come on.' She goes inside. I stand in the doorway. It's a small, square bathroom with a large, claw-footed iron tub on the opposite wall, a cracked pedestal sink and no mirror to the right. Next to the sink is a worn laminate vanity with a small drop-in sink. Running up the tub wall to about eight feet are four-by-four-inch white institutional tiles. To my left is a blank wall with a doorless opening. The space beyond is dark.

'Okay, the plan.' Her voice rises, gains energy. I can't tell if it's out of nervousness or a growing mania. She does a few quick turns in the center of the room, gesturing at the walls and fixtures. She finally settles on the vanity. 'Okay, this – out. The new one goes in. But I want to keep the sink – the old one.'

'You want me to build a vanity?'

'Yeah.'

I look around the bathroom. 'Tonight?'

'Sure. If you can.'

'Out of what?'

'*Oh,*' she covers her mouth, turns, and walks into the dark space. 'Just a second.' The lights come on, orange and low. 'It's in here.'

I stand in the opening, the entrance to her bedroom.

'Come in.'

It's a fifteen-by-fifteen square. On the opposite wall are stacked milk crates filled with books, clothes, and random possessions – an old, medium-format camera. To the left is a couch covered by a light blue bedsheet. On the wall above the couch is a large corkboard; several photographs – too small to make out – are tacked onto it.

'Come in.'

She's to the right, next to her bed – a boxspring and mattress on the floor with a balled-up comforter in the middle. On the floor beside the bed are two large, flat boxes, with what looks to be warnings written across them in some Scandinavian tongue.

'Okay, here's the deal. I completely went against my better judgment and designed a kitchen online. I try to stay away from that whole world – technology – but it just seemed so easy.' She taps one of the boxes with her foot. 'So easy. I measure everything, I study all these kitchens in magazines. I go to all the expensive design shops around here – you know them? – And I chat up all the salespeople for hours, like I'm going to drop eighty thousand dollars on a kitchen. I get it all done, send it out, and they send me back a bathroom.'

She waits for me to comment, but I have nothing to say. She wraps her hands around her neck and sighs, exasperated. She releases her neck, stretches up toward the ceiling, exhales then quickly bends and stretches to the floor. She holds her pose for a moment, relaxes, and drops somewhat awkwardly onto the edge of the bed.

'So somehow I wind up with a bathroom and a kitchen. *For a substantial discount,* so they say. All I know is I spent more than I wanted to. They're supposed to be good, better than that Ikea stuff. But I've been too scared to open it. It's a vanity and a medicine cabinet. They look pretty good, pretty simple in the pictures, but I don't even know if they're going to fit in there.' She goes to run her fingers through her hair but remembers that it's tied up. She sighs. 'What should I do?'

'Send it back.'

449

'I can't,' she whines.

'Why not?'

'I'm not a good consumer. I can't complain.'

'Okay,' I point at the boxes. 'Let's see what's in there.'

'Wait,' she shoots a hand up. 'I don't want to see.'

'What do you mean?'

'I don't want to be here when they're opened. I think my presence will jinx it. My luck kind of runs that way. You know what I mean?'

'Yeah.'

'Okay, so take the old cabinet out, just leave it outside the door. We can sneak it down later.' I question her with a wrinkled brow. She leans forward. 'They have a trash pickup every Friday,' she almost whispers. 'Did you see the containers?'

'No.'

'They must have come after you left. They're just inside the door.' She looks through the bath-room opening. 'We can break it into pieces and kind of slip it in under their stuff. Beth won't mind.'

'Then why do we need to hide it?'

'Oh, come on. After what happened today – with you?'

'All right,' I nod. 'I guess I should get started.'

'Right,' she jumps up. 'Let me leave first.' She skips across the room looking for something she can't find. She stands for a moment by the door, then opens it and jogs out into the living area.

I follow her to the door. She senses that I'm there and calls out from behind the mudroom wall. 'I have to do a bunch of things I forgot to do, before everything closes.' She rustles through the coats and shoes. I hear her keys jangle. She pokes her head around. 'Help yourself to whatever you need. There isn't much in the fridge. I'm sorry.' She steps into full view. 'There's wine – somewhere – there,' she points at three bottles by the sink. 'But I don't think you should drink and use power tools.' She reaches behind her and puts on her transparent coat. Thinks better of it and drops it on the floor. 'I can pick up food for later – yes?' I don't answer, and it slows her, makes her listen to herself. She exhales, kicks at the floor, and twirls her keys around her fingers. 'I'm sorry. I'm crazed. I'll stop.'

'It's okay. I'm all set. I'll be fine.'

'So you're okay with being left alone. I won't lock you in – in case there's a fire or something.'

'Or something,' I mumble, but she hears it. It makes her laugh.

'Remember, help yourself to what you need – music,' she points in the direction of where the stereo is. 'Okay, I'm gone.'

'It's colder than that,' I gesture at her clothes.

'I'll be fine.'

All I need for the prefab units are pliers, a screwdriver, and a set of Allen wrenches – all of which she has laid out on the floor. The cabinets

451

simple – white laminate, predrilled holes for everything. The vanity has three slide-in glass shelves and a ready-to-hang mirror door. I ignore the rebuslike instructions and put them together by sight. It only takes about fifteen minutes each. I go back in the bathroom, eyeball the size of the vanity and find the studs in the wall above. I shut off the water, disconnect the supply and drain, and pull the cabinet away from the wall. There's a lot of water damage – mold, stains – on the exposed wall. It has to go. I cut it out.

I cross the hall and go to the job site, creep along the walls in the low light collecting supplies – cement board, screws, mesh tape, joint compound, plaster, and primer. I bring them back to her place and rebuild the wall, mixing a lot of plaster in with the compound so it will dry quickly. While I wait for it to dry, I salvage the sink bowl and fixtures, break the cabinet down, and stuff it, along with the other trash I've made, into the mix in Johnny's rolling dumpsters.

The place is too quiet without my moving about. The wind picks up outside, making the skylights creak; light rain, a soft tapping on the wire glass. I dust myself off and sit on her bedroom couch. Across the room, on either side of the bed, are two windows, the same size as the ones I'd sanded, but these frames are covered in thick coats of glossy gray paint. They seem to look out onto nothing – tunnels to the dark. There can't be

452

anything out there other than an airshaft or solid wall. The dim orange lamplight seems pulled to them as does everything else they've caught to reflect.

The couch is comfortable, soft, and smells faintly of lilac, but those windows make me get up, check the plaster that I know isn't dry, stir the primer once more, and decide if she really did mean for me to 'make myself at home.' I look through the crates; she has records and CDs – The Animals, Robert Johnson, Coltrane. I take them out, find the stereo around the corner in the big room, load them up, and wait for them to shuffle. I stand over the table and eat a pineapple slice and a strawberry, but they turn my stomach.

'Me and the Devil Blues' comes on. I go to the kitchen counter and fumble with the kettle as though I'm going to put it on. I see the wine she referred to – three bottles of red, two of which are open, one corkless. There's a partially drunk bottle of mezcal – dirty rocks glasses on the edge of the sink.

'Johnson claims he's going to beat his woman.'

I don't want to acknowledge the line so I get out a piece of paper and start to make an invoice – the specs for both jobs – but it's difficult to consider. She's got money, but that's not the point. How do you bill for this – hourly? By the scope of the job? I can't charge her ten grand, but I can't be here for a couple of hundred bucks either, and that notion makes me ball up the paper and job it into the trash. *It's not about the money.* It never has been, which, I suppose, is why I need so much, but that so much can't be gotten here – anywhere on this or any other night. *So why are you here?*

I look at the bag of Lucky Jeans. What will I say to Claire? *These jeans mean I'm leaving, baby.* How do you go? My father seemed to rehearse it – softly closing the door, the light click of the latch. To me it always sounded like he was just going out for a moment – taking out the trash or having a smoke in the cooler summer evening. He made it sound like he was coming right back. She must know it's coming – shaky breaths or silence on the telephone. We've got nowhere else to go, nowhere else but down. And I don't want it, another generation of inscrutable hisses and diametrically opposed truths. I was a husband and I'm not anymore. I was a father, now I'm not – *It is undone!* How will I watch those green eyes melt and that crooked mouth fall? But how on earth can a man just disappear? Gavin's ma used to plead with us not to be swallowed by the bottle. And Lila used to terrorize me with stories about uncles who'd vanished in the Virginia night. And I suppose that I've already disappeared from myself – that boy who was *so full of light.* That man who promised so much.

The wine. She said to 'help yourself.' That's not the way I want to go out, but it's better than some idiotic mumbling about the past and future and – *sorry*. Claire's never seen me drunk, never seen me trying to make myself uncrooked. Then she could go, vindicated, have some story to make sense of it all – *it was the wine, not him, not me. The wine.* A man could disappear into a bottle. I can't really remember what it feels like to be drunk. Only before – dread and dislocation – and after – dread and sorrow. I think I have enough of that, without having to add the insult of retching into some gutter. *Don't call for the wine because the wine might answer and then what do you do?*

The music shuffles in the player. I step back from the wine. The Animals' version of *'House of the Rising Sun'* begins. I'd forgotten I'd put them on. They always have seemed to me to be one of the mystery bands that only exist in the radio. The picked, trembling arpeggio on the electric guitar sounds both sinister and wounded, then Eric Burdon's husky baritone – funny fuckin' white boy – but he seems to feel it. It's so clear on her stereo. I'm only used to hearing it on the AM dial. He growls: *'There is a house in New Orleans, they call the risin' sun . . .'* I turn it up and go into the bedroom, half dancing, half stumbling, and I remember the photographs on the board. They're all four-by-six, black-and-white, arms and legs and necks seemingly disconnected from their bodies, but not violently. She's faded out the joints – elbows, knees, shoulders – so that they seem to float in space, nerveless, bloodless.

The demonic organ solo starts, and it sounds

like a plea either to deliver the player from evil or to speed him through it, and causes me to sway about the bedroom to the makeshift bookcase. She's sectioned it by genre – several art history books, photography, poetry: Neruda, Wordsworth, Hughes, Blake, Plath, Dickinson. Yes. Eliot. *Four Quartets*. I think the cover page of my dissertation is down in Marco's basement: *'Eliot, Modernism, and Metaphysics.'* I'd typed it proudly, looked at it from many different angles, and after leaving it on display for almost a week, filed it in the oblivion section. *'Oh dark dark dark. They all go into the dark.'* I look to the windows. *'The vacant, interstellar spaces. The vacant into the vacant.'* I know it by heart, but I take it out anyway and open it to the section. There's something about seeing the words that alternately concretizes them and explodes them off the page into abstraction. 'What do you think?' I'd paced slowly in front of my students, every once in a while peering over the top of the thin book and leaning toward them. I'd stand there, in the full force of their stupefied silence.

> *The captains, merchant bankers, eminent men*
>   *of letters,*
> *The generous patrons of art, the statesmen and*
>   *the rulers,*
> *Distinguished civil servants, chairmen of many*
>   *committees,*
> *Industrial lords and petty contractors, all go*
>   *into the dark,*

And dark the Sun and Moon, and the
Almanach de Gotha
And the Stock Exchange Gazette, the
Directory of Directors

A noble sentiment, old man, lovely even, but I don't think I'm one of those listed. Where do I go: Into the ground beside an all-but-forgotten skull, or perhaps I'm future clay for patching holes? They won't be burying me in Westminster Abbey for calling the cognoscenti out into the 'dark dark dark.' No. You can bury my body – by the highway too . . . *Mr Eliot . . . Mr Johnson. Well met. Well met.* Burdon starts screaming, '. . . *one foot on the platform. The other foot on the train . . .*' I drop the book on the couch and think to turn off the music, but it's too late: Delta morning, dark, bloody horizon, and you are, in every consideration, of two minds.

I go back into the bathroom, sand and prime the wall, then install the cabinets. I reconnect the fixtures and drop in the sink bowl. Her tiles need regrouting. I feel a drip from above – another skylight. The rain is getting heavier outside.

I try a bedroom window to see if it opens. It does. I close it quickly and think about finding some way to screw them shut – angle irons perhaps, screwed into the frame and sill. I shake that notion off, go sit on the couch and look back at them, try to see through – the imagined sway

457

of the outer wall in the wind. The airshaft is the space between the stars, seemingly nothing, but a place, space – darkness upon the deep. *No thing* – a mask upon the abyss. When I was a boy, I already knew of that double-dark, so I wondered what starlight was – an ancient message of good beamed from somewhere so far away it could only be measured in time. But stars burn out, explode, or collapse inward – everything near pulled into absence. Darkness on the deep: the temporary and ancient light – its death, the hole from its implosion, deeper than any interstellar shroud.

I put Eliot away and browse through the rest of her books. There's a compilation of early Superman comics. I start to take it out but then remember that I never liked him – the lost son of doomsday prophets, rocketed away as an infant just before his planet was destroyed. I always thought that he was too smug for that amount of grief.

Time passes. It's late. I don't know if I've been sleeping. I don't think so. When I sleep. I have nightmares and I wake up screaming. I don't think I ever convinced Claire that my inability to put myself in bed and then to sleep had anything to do with her. And when we had kids, each one spent a good amount of time in that bed. I'd roam from kitchen to couch, waiting to shut down – a small death – not sleep but a place before or beyond it where nothing happens, where you're safe from a cumulative history represented by some toothy demon calling for your blood. Even if I do sleep and don't remember the dream, I still can feel when I awake that I've been attacked.

The door clicks. There's a rustle of bags and keys jangle. I shoot to my feet, move quickly to the stereo, and turn it down.

She's soaked. Her stretched-out curls are matted to her long neck and face. She seems disoriented, looking down at the floor, holding a bag in either hand. Finally, she looks up with a start, sees me, and tries to smile. The little forced grin doesn't last for long. From across the room and because of the rain I can't tell, but it looks like she's been crying, as recently as the elevator ride up.

She puts both bags in one hand and drops her keys onto the floor. 'You were right,' she chirps, still trying to cover the sadness. She looks over at the spread on the table for some cheer, but I've disappointed her there. She exhales, lets her shoulders drop, then fills herself up again. Such a beautiful woman. The cold rain has washed all the red from her cheeks, and those strange brown freckles twinkle on her. For a moment I forget that she's studying me, too.

I gesture, dumbly, back through the doorway. She remembers the bags, bounces forward as though to jump-start a lighter mood in herself. She sets one bag on the table, stops, and seems to be locked there for a moment. She empties her pockets – some paper scraps, bills and change, then shakes her head like a child responding to a hurtful question.

'I hate myself when I do this' – she remembers me, looks up, and tries to spin it as a joke. 'I'm so unorganized.'

She walks to the counter in a way I didn't think she could – heavily, tired – takes the open bottle of wine and loops her fingers through two mug handles.

'You should dry off.'

'Thanks, I will.' She wrinkles her brow and nods as though my statement requires deeper consideration. And when her face goes soft again, I wonder when was the last time someone considered her at all. It makes me back up into the bedroom. She follows, sad-faced again. But as she comes nearer, she starts trying to regroup. 'In my new bathroom.' She sets the bag down and I smell garlic, roasted meat, maybe even french fries. She circles the bag then drops down cross-legged beside it. She starts taking things out, moving faster, regaining that earlier energy. She even starts to smile.

'I got this from my restaurant.' She spreads some napkins on the floor and dumps out a pile of shoe-strings. 'I love free food.'

'You own a restaurant?' I mumble, trying to sound interested – trying not to look too closely at her or what she's doing.

'I *bartend* at a restaurant.' She seems to have forgotten how sad and wet she is and snorts at my expense. 'You think *I* own something?'

'Sorry.'

'Oh,' she waves a fry at me but concentrates on pouring two cups of wine. 'It's okay, honey. I don't even know if I'd want to own one. There's something to be said about counting your cash and leaving,' she rolls her eyes up at me. 'Right?'

'Right.'

'Here's to living under the radar.' She raises a mug and drinks, then pats the floor beside the other cup. 'You have to eat some of this – so sit.' She keeps patting the floor until I do, with my back against the couch. She shrugs, eats the fry, hums something to herself, rolls her eyes back up to me, shaking her head with a widening grin. She stops suddenly.

'What's that smell?'

'Primer.' She pinches her face as though to question. I jerk my head at the bathroom and raise my pitch to help clarify. 'Primer.'

She frowns strangely, stands, and skates to the bathroom, wiping her hands. I stand, too. She enters. 'Oh, my god!' she sticks her head out, then moves her whole body to the opening. 'Where? How?'

'I stole it.'

She starts to turn in the doorway – looking at my work, looking at me – examining and re-examining as though I'd gutted and refurbished the whole room. 'Wow,' she mouths and then comes into the bedroom, toward me, more like a glide than a walk. She stops a few feet away.

'You're so bad – you're awesome. I would've

been so chickenshit to do that. Beth, she's great, but you know what, fuck her. I've dumped so much money into her place – making it better.'

'This is hers?'

'Yeah, I'm a renter. Even if I could afford it, I probably couldn't get a place – I'm on the lam. My ex, this was his studio, he wasn't supposed to live here, but he did. Beth hated him, but we got along. I think she inherited the building from her father. Everything he did was illegal – taxes, parking tickets. So when he left, Beth said I could stay. I've been here – shit – seven years.' She looks back into the bathroom. 'Oh, my god.' She shakes her head slowly. 'Thank you.' She reaches out, almost touches my arm. But she does stare at me, which forces me to look down, shuffle, and inch back to the couch. She looks down at my fingers – *for the umpteenth time*. 'I've turned you into a criminal.' She turns her voice down. 'Your wife won't like that much.'

'Well,' I stutter, speaking before any thought can intervene.

'Don't – it's okay. I didn't mean anything. You still together?'

'I don't know.'

'Kids?'

'Three.'

'Pictures?' she brightens.

'No.'

'I'll bet they're beautiful.'

I nod.

'It must be hard.'

'You should change.' I hit that note again, but this time it sounds off-key. It makes her neck bend awkwardly to the side. After it fades, she straightens and raises both palms to me.

'I'm sorry.' She thumbs into the bathroom. 'I'm going to change.' She glides over to the stacked crates, pulls out some things, balls them up, and glides back, with one last quick look to see if I've been watching.

How does a man disappear – *for a decade?* From others, from self – nomadic, hand to mouth, episodic in achievement. Never went to law school. No real estate license. What happened? You go to sleep young and somewhat stupid and wake up to new noises – the clock – new complaints, things that didn't hold any sway before. From the bathroom she lets out a semi-private *'Wow,'* turns on the tub, but stops it quickly. I can hear the sheets of ply creak under her as she shifts her weight – leaning, then sliding her feet along behind. She inspects the medicine cabinet, opens and closes it with a soft click and a dull thud. She looks in the mirror, scrutinizes her freckles, the beginnings of her age lines. The light is poor. She opens the door one more time and fills the cabinet with beauty products I hadn't noticed were there.

I feel naked, so I rub my pants to make sure they're really there. *Laura saw me naked*, I mouth.

And then I reconsider Marco – that stern look he gave me after I chased away his mistress. I hadn't connected the two – my nakedness and his near scowl. Laura had gotten into her car and dialed her husband on her cell phone while speeding away from my crime. What did she say? – *'I saw him naked.'* And each reading of the event, from the first onward is different – to her one thing, to him . . . what did he see in his head, some porno-pass by me at his wife. No words, just naked flesh, a blatant, literal gesture. In my case sex has been demystified. Sex as a by-product of love, or anything else – I just always thought the need to explain it folly. That first time I lay next to Claire, she thought I was nervous, shy, or sweet. Perhaps I had been all those things. I *was* all those things – *all the time*. I knew that what we were about to do would never bring me closer to her. I just hoped that it wouldn't push me farther away.

I've always thought that those who do mystify it, say that it is transformative in any way other than pregnancy or disease, were just horny, even a little cruel – masking want with imaginary emotions – and those who downplayed it, sad. But with her on the other side of the wall, I wonder if I'm damaged or just no damn good. Even so, damage is never an apt substitute for piety.

The music has almost gone through its complete rotation. I turn the stereo up a little, leave it playing Coltrane. I pick up Eliot, sit down on the bedroom couch, mouth the words, somehow trying to make them jibe with the melancholic sax and droning bass. *'I said to my soul, be still, and let the dark come upon you / Which shall be the darkness of God . . .'* I feel myself drifting off again, but I don't want to close my eyes. I stand up and I'm compelled to the quiet of the bathroom. What's she doing in there? *'Favorite Things'* comes up; Coltrane's flourishes seem to call for action rather than thought. I'd always assumed that he was giving license to drift, meander, or rant with him. No. Hearing it now, I realize he reveals his shape and size in song – whole, unique, solid. And the multifaceted images reflect not his fragmented self but, rather, mine. Why do things fall apart? Helena in the next room: ringlets and limbs, odd laughs, genuine joy and sorrow. She doesn't come to me whole. *'I said to my soul, be still . . .'* It doesn't seem to listen. It churns out image after image: Gavin's freckle-puss, Shake's shakes, Brian's charred bones, Daddy Bing's crooning gums, Lila's makeshift whips that crack when they elongate like a long, crooked mouth – rosy, rosy welts. I shake them off and concentrate on her – imagining sounds, even: the quiet stretch of wet cotton; pants dropped on the floor; the slip of thighs against each other – but I can't see her, nor can I judge the gap between us. Coltrane exhorts something I should understand – high and trilling.

Then it comes – *'snap'* – her bra strap slips off her finger onto her shoulder and snaps. It reverberates outward against the tiles, the porcelain, finds its way out and hits the side of my skull. The waves bounce back, and she takes form: her freckled shoulders, the way she can pull them back to make them broaden or roll them softly forward, deepening the wells behind her clavicles where scent collects – a citrus spray, the sharp metallic city rain, her breath; small breasts and the small points of her nipples; the soft line of her last ribs and its suggested circle, completed by the joining of her hips and belly. *'Snap.'* There was darkness on the deep and then she was there – pushing out against the void. The returning waves give her face shape and color. I see her, trembling in the darkness, like a string of clustered stars and the shape of things around her.

The floor creaks my way, and I back up quickly into the center of the bedroom. She comes back in, quietly, steers around me in a wide arc and sits on the edge of her bed. She's put on navy sweatpants and shirt, which makes her hair look like dark flame. She's pulled her hands into her sleeves. I've never cheated on anyone, not even Sally. Standing here in the center of this room, I can't believe that love has been the deterrent – perhaps damage has taken moments like these, diffused them into countless, useless metaphors, visions, and earnest words. Touch her. That is good. Really touch her – the word made flesh.

'How long have you been alone?' I ask.

She raises an eyebrow and cocks her head to one side. I point to the windows behind her.

'What?' She seems to ask it of herself.

I lower my arm. 'Is it safe?'

She stands quickly. 'There's nothing out there.' She hops forward into a jog and makes for the front. I follow. She stops at the table, leans against it, and pulls her shoulders back.

'Can you leave your number – so I can call you when the kitchen comes?'

Something in her tone makes me respond quickly. I nod, go back to the bedroom, pick up my tool bag, and count to five. I come back out. She's counting money.

'Do you have an invoice?'

'No, I don't.'

'Well, what do I owe you?'

I shrug, 'Whatever.'

She shakes her head. 'That's one hell of a nego- tiating ploy.' She picks up the bills from the table. 'Is this enough?'

'Sure.'

'You don't even know how much it is.'

'It's fine.'

'Did you leave your number?'

I nod and thumb at the bathroom.

'You left it on the bathroom wall?'

I force out a little smile, which I'm sure looks like a twisted grin. She pinches the fold of bills and holds it out to me, 'Cash is okay, I assume?'

Now she looks as she did when I first saw her, untroubled by my looming. And I don't know why I feel this way – like I already miss her. Her freckles, her now warm cheeks, the cascade of now cooling flame. I take the money, being careful not to touch her hand, and go.

CHAPTER 14

There was a stomach virus going around and both boys got it. Edith had come down, taken over the couch and allegedly the care of the boys – so I took them, both with bubbling stomachs, in her car on a bitterly cold February morning to the hospital. It was all the way up at the top of Manhattan, where there seems to be nothing but trestles, trains, and putty-colored stone buildings. The Harlem River bends there like a horseshoe – north from the Hudson, east behind the hospital and then south again, running with the tracks and the expressway.

It may have been the bug, but it also might have been the combination of that bright sun you can get on winter days – the sharp direct rays that seem to have had all the good parts in them frozen, and what remains is magnified through the glass. And the new car smell, the thick artificial heat. Just before we turned into the parking lot, both boys puked, covering the back with their breakfasts.

I didn't really have a choice: They needed

new clothes. Luckily their heavy coats were up front with me. I stripped them to the waist and wrapped them up. I put C on my shoulders, carried X in my arms and went out on Broadway. It's covered up there – a drawbridge I think – across the narrowest stretch of water. I headed uptown to one of those ninety-nine cent stores, bought long underwear shirts and sweatpants for them and cleaning products for the car. On the way back I stumbled and almost lost Cover the edge – down into the brown and white river. I took a step back from the rail and thought about how I'd rescue him: Leave the little one alone on the sidewalk and dive; carry X down with me – sprint to the end of the bridge, climb the fence and scramble down the dirt-weed hill and try to reach him from there. He'd just turned five and wasn't much of a swimmer. The river was fast that day – silver on top and white toward the edges – rushing to Hell's Gate.

He shivered up there and made me remember that I hadn't dropped him. He was still on my shoulders, groggy, sick, and cold, but alive. I skated over the sidewalk, to move quickly, but so as not to jar them too much. When we got back to the parking lot I put them in the front, cleaned and dressed them and scoured the back of the car. X wasn't quite two yet so I had to smuggle him into the hospital in a duffle bag. He loved the idea, and

470

even though he was still feeling a bit wretched, he giggled when I beeped his nose through the unzipped opening and shushed him.

He trembled in the bag on the way in, trying to suppress his laughter, but we made it in. I unpacked him in the bathroom and he jumped out of the bag as though the adventure had righted him – C, too. Neither boy could stop grinning or shuffle-dancing, bumping into each other, grasping at imaginary things in the air.

Maybe I only tricked myself, that they'd been magically restored to health because it wasn't such a great idea – bringing two infectious children to visit a convalescing mother and child, but it had been a hard week for everyone. The boys had never spent time away from their mom. And I'd been traveling back and forth from Brooklyn to Washington Heights. There'd been a lot of dragging hours filled with anxiety, even dread. A lot of pain and blood. And when you were finally born you were so small that I could hold you in one hand – dusky, bald, struggling for breath. They took you away immediately. I had to let them. I had to let you go.

I close the notebook. It's the best I can do. I put it back in my bag. Where is the moon? It should be high up in the eastern sky, way above the courthouse, but it's nowhere to be found – no stars

471

either, just overstretched clouds, purple-gray and static. They seem, at first, to be translucent, but I don't know – the glow – perhaps they're reflective instead, weakly returning the city's residual light. They look dry, but there must be moisture in them. It's not raining anymore but the air is thick and damp. Occasional drops randomly fall from above like tepid drips from sweaty cellar pipes. I don't know why I've stopped here – Foley Square. It smells like fish – old fish, dead fish, washed up, or floating, lost under the shadows of the bridges. The scent comes up on the wind from the south and seems to stop and swirl around the square. It's a strange little place. I've only driven or run past it. It's a narrow diamond – Worth Street to the north; Center and Federal Plaza run along the east and west and join at the southern tip. At the top, next to Worth, is Thomas Paine Park, an empty gesture at a fenced-in green space.

At my feet is a directional star – with thin strips of brass inlaid to accentuate the line – at the center of which is a large circle. The first clauses of the Constitution follow the arc along the inside. And inside that circle are strange engraved scenes of British persecuting Americans, as well as Americans persecuting Americans – early patriots, lynched slaves, burned witches – some vague apology of sorts, I don't know. This is an African burial ground – both free and enslaved – four hundred or more, under the tarmac, under the massive footings of the official buildings in which are engraved grave maxims: THE ADMINISTRATION OF JUSTICE IS THE FIRMEST PILLAR OF GOOD GOVERNMENT. It seems almost too sad to even attempt to offer commentary on the absurd conglomeration: Dead blacks honored in swamps claimed by Indian, then Dutch, then English, then Irish, all in the shadow of a soot-stained alabaster Greco-Roman monolith.

One of the points of the star is a path that leads to the center of the square. In fact, there are several paths that lead there – like a miniature of the Place d'Etoile. Perhaps that's too grand – or not even close. These paths are rose-colored granite, edged by gray, in the midst of lilacy-gray hexagonal pavers. The colors and patterns create the opposite of what I imagine to be the desired effect – they stop and push you out, make you focus on the garishness and want to leave. If you don't, if you hang on, you'll see the giant sculpture in the middle of the square. Two steps up – it begins with a polished black granite pool, rolled at the edges, making it look like an enormous ashtray. It's half filled with water. The spray and the caged lights are off for some reason. There's less change than you'd think – or perhaps more when you consider the easy access. But to me, the scale and the still water make it seem unreceptive to wishes.

An elongated, narrow trapezoid, like a heavy footbridge, spans the water from east to west. Atop it is an abstract sculpture. From far away you almost miss it – dwarfed by the official buildings. Up close, it dwarfs you. It's at least fifty feet tall and resembles, at first, a sword with an elaborate and asymmetric hilt, pointing skyward. If you step back and circle the pool, it looks more like a phallus, then a dead tongue of flame, or perhaps the marker the fire has left in space – black, solid, unlit – pointing up to the strange, double-layered purple sky, up to the faithless lights, defacto vacuums. A symbol, perhaps, of a debt either owed or paid or still disputed, like a lone protester, vigilant outside the courthouse.

I've read about it – three hundred tons of black granite – a memorial to the displaced dead. If you came this way, moving slowly, on foot, with time to spare, and followed the curve of the pool around the south side, you'd eventually see the large stone marker, which the heavy path across the pools abuts. There are words carved into it. *'Commissioned by the city . . .'* Then the words of the sculptor himself – a chiseled disclaimer yanking it from the abstract: *'The Chi Wara rests on a horizontal plane which symbolizes the canoes used by the Native Americans, the slave vessels that transported African men, women and children and the passenger ships that brought immigrants to this country. The part of the granite these words are inscribed in represents the land.'* Six years and three hundred tons of granite later he still wants to tell me exactly what it is. I give up.

If you come this way and leave the absolutely defined sign behind, resist the urge to look at the enormous structure that is One Centre Street, not consider the concrete barricades positioned on the sidewalk to discourage vans traveling toward the walls at ramming speed in an attempt to blow the whole thing down, you'll see that the rats use the gutter like an expressway, scampering to and from the grease spots left behind from the vending carts that line the sidewalk during the day. The way the cars dismounting the bridge seem to want you to stray off the curb and step into the end of their blind turn. The bush, the flower patch, the bench, and the plaque:

> *When the perfected bridge shall permanently and uninterruptedly connect the cities of New York and Brooklyn, the daily thousands who cross it will consider it a sort of natural and inevitable phenomenon, such as the rising and setting of the sun. When they will unconsciously over-look the difficulties surmounted before the structure spans the stream and will perhaps undervalue the indomitable courage, absolute faith, the consummate genius which assured the engineer's triumph.*
> —Thomas Kinsella, *Brooklyn Eagle*, 1872

Gaining the bridge is different from the Manhattan side. The incline is steeper and the traffic rises with you. I'm troubled by the flatness of things: the dull thud of my boots on the concrete; my uneven breaths; the couple – the girl who pretends

475

there's nothing odd about what she sees, the boy faking bravery. I thud past them, up the incline. The lights are electric, overhead and out of sight. To the left the projects rise up, framing quick views of the Manhattan Bridge beyond. To the right is the ancient swamp, built over by tanneries, then towers. There's the river – snatches of it between the still existing tenements and saloons. The wind picks up, snaps the flag, and seems to rock the cables. Swirling wind – it seems to blow simultaneously on each side. At first it drowns out all the sounds you might hear, but if you concentrate, you can feel that it blows only from the south. You know the tide is going out because you can hear the gusts pull against the surface of the river, twist it into superficial eddies, making the sound of water trickling down a drain.

I don't know why I'm running: I've got nothing. The sky up here is azure, slick, as though all the stars have coalesced to form an almost transparent yellow glow atop the blue. But it's just the electric lights below. I look north, up the river to the other bridges, the replicating strings with their own evenly spaced lights. I wonder where Claire is tonight – how those damned mojitos were, how the children fell asleep, if they're sleeping at all. There's no one there. Edith, but Edith doesn't count – never has. What will she do when they tell her they're afraid of the dark, especially there – the unfamiliar noises and the impenetrable dark of the moonless rural night? *Whip-poor-wills are whip-poor-wills; coyotes are coyotes* – cold comfort for a terrified child. What did she say to my girl – such a bad sleeper? What did she say to her namesake – *little Edy?* It's always made me gag when people have called her that – *but what's in a name?* Edith wasn't there when she was born: a month early and undersized for that. She came out with her umbilical in a tight knot. It seemed that we all just stood there staring – trying to understand who could've possibly tied it. The fact that she wasn't crying, wasn't doing much of anything, snapped me out of my shock. She was barely breathing. I had to let them take her. Claire was seizing from preeclampsia, bleeding from her torn uterus. Claire doesn't know how bad it was – for both the girl and her. And it wasn't because no one told her. I did. She switched between pain, blank-faced stoicism, and narcotic sleep. And I alternated between her and our girl. Claire had only the IV drip, but the girl, she was tangled in tubes, monitor wires, breathing apparatus. There in the incubator, naked except for the tiny diaper and the striped cotton knit cap – seemingly always with her eyes closed. I fit my hand through the twist of wires to rub her belly, hoping that she'd open her eyes, just once, for me. When she finally did wake, when I finally did get to lift her out of that antiseptic plastic cage, she opened only one eye at first – the coal-black pupil circled by the ring of earthen brown, circled again by an indigo halo. I thought I was looking into the eye of God.

I went to see Claire, who had awakened finally, too, and the two of us waited, it seemed through the night, for that other eye to open.

If you come this way, hear your heavy feet on the path, you'll see that the wood planks are weathered and thin and that there's nothing below – only the dark river. You run slowly up the ascent, watching the giant cables rise to meet the granite towers; the great blocks of soot-darkened stone, the line of the hundred-year-old mortar, and the strength they convey make sense. Their dual pointed arches – like the start of a great throat. The cable pairs rise up from the planks, like nerve bundles. The steel beams are close enough to touch – the giant, riveted girders, the cables holding the suspension line in place. The steel beams are disintegrating along with the putty-colored paint. It all seems to sway impossibly in the wind. The cross-hatched smaller lines are sheathed by the night and the artificial lights.

The benches invite you to sit and stare in either direction: north to watch the garbage scows, the bridges beyond; south – the docked clipper ship, the dinosaur cranes on the other shore. Most of Brooklyn is dark, save for the electric clock, high atop the watchtower. If it weren't so hazy, you'd see the islands, the statue, the narrows, and the promise of open sea.

I look down at the roadway and along the beams. Some are rigged with floodlights; others have side rails and function as catwalks, offering passage to the edge. I follow them out, watch the water twist northward.

I take the bait, sit, get out the notebook, and write:

Notes—
Big Nig climbs the cable. Saurian, simian. Bag full of money over his shoulder. It's a long way down to the water. He thinks about dropping the bag down, let the evidence disappear in the river – but they've seen him. They know who he is. So the way out or the way through is not to be taken alive. Courage, he thinks, would never lead a man to build a bridge. Courage would lead you in – unknowing as to whether you'd been buoyed or swallowed. Fuck you Thomas Kinsella.

I start running again. It's amazing how much the bridge shakes, even when a lone biker rides by. You can see it in the electrical wires that run along the sides of the walkway. It's not the wind. The moving wires match the motion of the bridge, not the blowing flags, so you know it's the bridge's rhythm.

You can hear them – their footsteps – lovers on the boardwalk, making vows, holding hands, sneaking kisses, or kissing unabashed. Their voices carry this way and that, beyond where they stand. You can hear them. Remember them, every evening, echoes of promises made.

I wonder if the children are sleeping, how the dark in their rooms collects and moves within itself, what flesh its given, what teeth and claws. Where is Claire sleeping? *Where is the moon?* Why do they have lights on the beams over the roadway – pointing up to bounce against that hazy damn sky? – illuminating some triumph of man's reason, the ability to cross the deep dark. *Look what we have done! We've spanned the sullen brown god* – with bone-steel, with sinew cable and stretched over it all a skin of light and shadow. And the bridge flexes and shimmers, not in the wind but with an internal motion of its own. It pulses, the motion complex, unharmonic, retching, shuddering sea beast. I am the howl of the sea belly, the echoing wail of its remains, the living memory of all the swallowed faces. Inside, now I'm out. But not for love or valor, not for the good fight – two dukes up for a fallen friend. What would Lila have said? *Into the toilet with you – out, get out.* A river *is* a good place for ghosts, but only because they are deep, dark, and old.

When I realize that I've left the lucky jeans behind, I have to stop and laugh. I take out the money she paid me and count it: one-fifty – a wash. The cosmos has no sense of humor, so it shouldn't play jokes on a soul, but I have to laugh again. I start to trot. When I hit the down slope, I break into a run. The paired suspension cables end, bury themselves under the planks. I'm off the water,

480

over the first knuckle of Brooklyn, descending into its topography. Cars speed by. Their headlights connect this bridge to the other. No more water. No more sky. One last elevated look over Brooklyn's grid – empty dark centers with points of light streaking around their edges. A new wave of fish rot drifts up mixed with exhaust fumes, just in time to make me remember that I should feel like shit – a strange, clammy sweat on me and inside, the burn of pure shame. *'You're so good in a crisis,'* Claire used to say. I have to laugh again. The crisis is over. I come off the heaving bridge, turn back once to the electric lights, then into Brooklyn, contemplating the life of an imploded star.

PART III

EVENING'S EMPIRE

You cannot face it steadily, but this thing is
  sure,
That time is no healer: the patient is no
  longer here.

— *T. S. Eliot, 'The Dry Salvages' III*

CHAPTER 15

Thomas Strawberry is dead. I know it before I enter the room. I had foreseen it on the stairs leading up, before that even – the early dark outside, the gloom of the bridge, empty windows and echoing bras. In Edith's voice. In Claire's absence. In all the days leading up to this: There is no light in this world. If there ever had been, it is out. He floats, head just beneath the surface. That elaborate tail folded. The bright scales are dim. The overhead light gathers and spins around the edge of his bowl. I wonder how long he's been floating here. I scoop him out with my hand. He's warmer than I thought he'd be, smaller. He fits in my cupped hand as though he was made to be there.

I stand in the kiddie room waiting to be informed, holding him as though he's sleeping, keeping the roughest parts of my palm away from his delicate scales. Waiting for resurrection. Waiting to be told what to do when he doesn't rise up. *What do you do with the dead?* No answer.

And so I go to flush him down the toilet, but as soon as I open the lid, I know it's wrong. I wrap him in a tissue and lay him on the counter. I stand back and wait – nothing. I hear Marco thump and start up the stairs. I pick up Thomas, skim quietly back to the bedroom, and shut off the light. Marco makes the landing, grunts, thumps over to the bathroom, pauses at the door, and then shuts off the light.

I don't know where to go so I head for the river, Thomas in my coat pocket, my bag over my shoulder, and my mother in her urn – some ashen, petrified gourd. Don't call her crazy even though I have before, more than once, to people I wish I never had. Lila never made excuses for herself, no matter how deep her sadness or her rage. No one knew that she'd died – early on a Friday evening, a warm stretch in December – so it took awhile before anyone looked for her. I'd just skipped Thanksgiving and was planning to do the same for Christmas. She was doing odd work – some cleaning here, some sewing there, even a bit of babysitting – but it was all irregular, so she had nowhere to report to on Monday, even Tuesday. And the phone went unanswered, the calls unreturned. She hadn't taken her coat off, but she'd poured a drink – started in on it even. 'I found her there,' the super had said to me, half looking to the spot on the floor where she'd lain, half examining me, somewhat in disbelief, wondering, waiting for some display of grief – anger even. I gave him nothing. I stayed unreadable until he left me alone in the strange apartment.

The housing authority had moved her into a smaller unit after I'd left, but there were the same linoleum floors throughout. No-name kitchen appliances and the electric baseboard heater pulling itself from the wall. The drink was on the table next to her chair and the record was still playing – Marvin, of course – fuzz and crackle in the speaker, the ghost voice, still echoing off the tiles and the blank dim walls. The man hadn't even thought to pour out the booze, rinse the glass, or turn the music off.

I used to dream of her as if she had already died, not wishing that she had, but hoping somehow I suppose, to transform her, make her whole, stop the hissing, the fear, erase the underlying hurt and terror that seemed to be twisting her apart – as though every waiting insult had formed an invisible hand, twisting her one way, and every insult past was twisting her the other, leaving her a constantly wrung-dry rag. She really didn't live that long. What I saw, I know now, was a vestige of her, a face from long ago, a voice exhorting from the gone past.

I tap the urn and rub it. I felt like this: a sudden weightlessness and quiet – not peace but a stillness that made me stop and listen. Her service was wrong – a strange pastor, a meaningless plot, and a generic, illegible stone, mumbling, distant cousins and neighbors. The few people who were there were at first respectful and then unsettled by my silence, but I had nothing for them other than: *Minette Brown left the reservation . . .*

We didn't sing 'Jerusalem' – 'Amazing Grace' – and it was fumbling, discordant, and without any of the revelation promised by the words, chanted emptily by those staring into darkness. And on the train back to New York I couldn't help but try to reconstruct her up-south odyssey. It only came in flashes though. *'My father's name was Murphy, but he changed it to Watson – either he or his father, I don't know. He worked in the Baltimore shipyards, like his father and his grandfather. It goes way back. His great great grandfather was one of those boys who taught Frederick Douglass to read.'* She hissed and snickered. 'And one of his cousins was who wound up jumping him later on. You can't beat that – Finbar Murphy to Joseph Watson and then – I don't know how he and my mother found each other, but they lost each other pretty quick.' I'd drawn the tree before, drew it then as the train hissed through the thin wild of south-eastern New England. The dates and the ages have never aligned: her attempts to make herself whole, always wanting.

Now she is ash and I carry her and the dead fish along the Brooklyn side of the river. Not on its actual shores, but on the deserted streets that try to mirror its wind. Beside the lots and the warehouses, some in use, some not. I keep passing abandoned things, cans, bottles, clothes; the coveralls, the baseball jacket, the sock, a child's sweater; resoaked heaps that look as though their wearers had suddenly been vaporized, or yanked down into darkness when they'd stopped for a moment. I feel the urge to stop and poke at each one – try to somehow discern their origins and therefore, by extension, recreate the moment when they lost their skin. *Keep moving.* Something seems to speak – perhaps the run of draining water, rooftop, street, and unseen eddies under the piers beyond the buildings. Maybe the trickle of the slowly draining river. *Keep moving.* Past sense and memory. Past shame to a place where there's quiet – the emptied river, the dead star, follow the inexorable pull of the void.

I need a drink.

There are plans in the works to make all of the waterfront a great park – an expanse of green wrapping along the shore from Red Hook a mile or more to the Manhattan Bridge. Things are looking up for the old borough: new money, new construction, new names for neighborhoods soon to be gentrified. I've always hated groundbreaking ceremonies: They date you; they point to your demise. Some public servant with symbolic hardhat and shovel, flanked by those who make plans for others.

But it's dark and empty now, and Water Street is nearly dry. And if you come this way, you'll see how low the cobbled streets have sunk, their original high mark etched into the twisted curbs.

The tarmac, peeled back from the stones like skin slowly shedding from some old, old lizard back. If you walked under the twist of road that connects the two bridges, you'd see that they are excavating the old city, readying it for destruction. There are gashes in earth and edifice left to be filled by the night. You can look back into time – the broken bricks, the bedrock, like fossil molars, useless, save for inaudible speech. They are digging toward the first order. The bridge hangs above – the underside of a ruined throat and belly. The missing scales are entries to its vacant core. Keep going. You'll see the rusted freighter ties, like heads squeezed to the point of cracking. Hypaethral warehouses with empty arches and mortarless bricks pinned back by black iron stars: now a slave fort; now a slaughterhouse; an armory. Empty. The lightless night fills them with the backward breath of the void. Then warehouses – rotten-roofed with rusted shutters keeping things out or in. Keep on pushing.

I'm leaving New York. I hate this place. This stink and grime – the husks of dreamers, bought out, strung out, or broke down. Maybe Philadelphia, Quaker traditions – no, they bomb their own; Chicago's lakes are far from oceans; and I don't like the West Coast – one-hundred-million-year-old scorpions, the sun is strange, and the buildings are too new. Boston. I'll start again in Boston, then, perhaps go backward, across the ocean – Eire. I wonder where Gavin is. Now that

I've lost, his debt is erased, and I can think about him without resentment – for a moment at least – until I consider that he realized a while ago that he was forgotten, bridged over during some unknown transition. He always knew he was a dead man. Maybe that's why he stayed unattached.

There's a light on at the corner. It's a bodega – strange, isolated, like some remote trading post in the wilderness – the first tenant in a remodeled sweatshop. I try to go in, but the door's locked. It rattles noisily. I try it again. Same thing. There aren't any hours posted. I hear, from around the corner, someone rapping from inside. I peer around. There's a man, perhaps my age, sitting at the counter. He's dark-skinned. Mustached. He stares at me – expressionless. I point at the door. He waves his finger at me and points to the window between us. I shrug and point at the door again. He slides the window open a couple of inches.

'Yes?' He has a thick, quasi-British accent.

'Are you open?'

'Yes.'

We stare at each other, he waiting for me to do something I'm unaware of. He looks down and points quickly at the window. I point at the door. He points at the window, sliding it open an inch more. He nods this time and cocks his ear toward me as if to listen.

I point at the rack of cigarettes, then realize he's not looking at me anymore.

'Pack of Luckies.'

He shoots a hand up and gropes for the pack without looking. He gets one, matches, too, and taps them on the counter.

'Yes?' he says, but looks down again – canid. At least, from behind his inch-thick acrylic, he could be polite enough to look at me. I look down at the cigarettes and all I can think of at the moment is the pleasure of smoking them in an open field somewhere away from the residue of halogen, neon, and fluorescent light. I know that I've made the right decision to leave this damned city. I hate the clipped, inelegant grunts that masquerade as speech. The rudeness and suspicion. I hate the eyeless stares, the look-aways, the pretense of service. I hate the absence of love.

I smack the glass hard with my knuckles. He startles but continues to look down.

'Yes?'

'Gimme a six of Bud.'

He spins off his chair and goes to the cooler. He gets the beer out. I smack the glass again. He looks up.

'Tall boys. Bottles.'

He waves, bending his head, and manages a shy little grin. He shuffles back to the counter, more puplike with each step. He sets the beer down carefully as though he were serving a table crystal glasses. He rolls his eyes up at me. I stare at him with a growing harshness. Perhaps it's a good thing that the glass is there.

'How much?'

'Twelve dollars, sir.'

'Fuck.'

I peel the money off my roll and toss it at the opening. He opens it just wide enough to sneak his hand through. He counts it, bags my beer and cigarettes – far too slowly and carefully – slides open the larger door, places it in, closes it, then signals for me to open my side.

I take my package and leave, think about turning and flipping him off, but I keep on pushing instead, back to the river again. The street runs downhill to the banks and then opens up into a small park in a shallow cove. The first thing you see is a small, fenced-in playground. Maybe it wasn't a good idea to come this way. I try to ignore it, keep my head down and wind around it along the path – more of those hexagonal pavers. I follow the path around the low iron fence, past the grassy knoll. It ends at the top of massive granite stairs that descend into the water. The bank upriver, to the right, is a steeply sloped pile of rocks. To the left the stairs end abruptly and give way to pebbles, bleached and crushed oyster shells, and odd pieces of plywood. The path continues, down-river, the land curving westward – a concrete pier and a finger of land on which sits one last darkened warehouse and then the base of the bridge.

There is wind down here on the water, more than I thought. It blows strong and constant, moaning low upriver with stronger gusts, which rise in pitch to a wail and then disappear. I sit on a bench and look out across the river at the buildings framed by the two bridges and then below to FDR drive. I don't know this city at all – hardly paused to look at anything, always fixed my eyes on something that wasn't there and missed everything that was. What a city – even down here across the river with this limited view you get a sense of its volume, much more so than when you're in it. This failure will go unnoticed, here, beyond the lights.

I light a cigarette, a pause before oblivion, and scan the scene again. The tide swirls here in the cove and you can hear it echo under the pier. There's a young gull on the small beach picking at the rubble – dark-winged, awkward. 'The sea is just around that corner,' I tell him, but he ignores me and keeps on with his search. Odd night bird. 'Go bird.' I stop myself from throwing my butt at him. Now he responds – a flutter of wings on the dark air. And I wonder if that bird can discern anything from the time it takes for the waves to return. I wonder if one can snap one's own string – test your own expansiveness and the void in which you live – a crooked soul finger plucking a busted instrument in a ghost jug band.

The gull warbles something unbirdlike. 'Shaddup,' I tell him, but he speaks again, this time a moan as he hops up onto one of the boards. 'This is not the ocean, you stupid bird.' He ignores me again and makes a sudden dash away from the tide. 'I'd watch it, bird. You're no plover.' He makes his way across the bank to me. 'I've got nothing for you, bird.' I point out at the water. *"'I don't know much about gods; but I think that the river is a strong brown god . . ."* Go to him.'

I don't know much about my mother or this fish, either – other than they are dead. And I finally realize why she never really liked me – she refused to believe in ghosts. *'You are the light of the world . . .'* She changed toward me – stopped her rages – as I grew older. I just thought that she was getting tired, but now, here, at the butt-end of the universe I realize that she just lost her faith, or, closer, that she never had one to begin with. She stopped believing that I was the one. Poor Lila. I stopped believing, too. And I know how much you hated when I would seem to turn my gaze inward to watch the dark reaches of inter-stellar space. What was it like, to watch the boy you let live be called to the *dark dark dark?* To you, a revoking of an inheritance of the earth. Conversely, that eased your mind. But you were wrong, Mama – and I know you'd hiss at me now if you caught me here, in the night, murmuring to ghosts – I am the one. And I don't know much about ghosts after all, what their purpose is, if they have any at all. I don't know much about sea birds, dead fish, what their moans, their silences signify. I don't know why the water always sounds like it's leaving. I don't know much about rivers, but I think that I am a strong brown god. I am forgotten – seasons, rages, past covenants – unrecognized ritual and symbol, effects skinned from their purpose, strangely practiced and then, of course, discarded. Fuck.

I open a beer. It makes sense: the rush of escaping gas, the smell of earth – wheat, hops, and barley. The scents hover around the opening as more come rushing out, making the gas cloud spin and expand. I look down into the bottle to see how much is left. Light spins around its mouth, but I don't know where from. There's nothing here, not even an ambient glow. I go to stick my finger through the cloud to test if it's really there – to test its density. I curse myself for caring. I go to take a sip. *Not yet.* I take a drag instead – exhale. The smoke mixes with the scent, folds and unfolds as it moves slowly up, a nebula of gas and matter: a galaxy in the making or one that's already been destroyed. Interstellar seeds or interstellar wreckage – inanimate dust that won't show me a sign, but only rises up, up . . . *It's the beer – the beer's calling* . . . and I listen, but nothing seems to be there.

I listen, now more trying to remember the vapor's initial rush. *What was that sound?* No sound. And its inverse – all sound, which is compressed into the wind across the water. A gust peels off from the main wind, swirls around the cove, builds in speed, works its voice up to a wail, then shatters against the pillars of the bridge.

It recollects and does it again – all sound and its multifaceted voice: birth's cry, death's rattle, and the awful wail of resurrection. Disparate, therefore discordant – *but listen* – there's a wholeness to that clamor, the hiss in memory of the vanished smoke and the river's applause, soft against itself, hard against the stone. And I still don't know much about rivers, but I think that I am a strong, brown god: *'sullen, untamed and intractable . . .'* no longer patient, as there is nothing left to wait for. A frontier, but only one in the distance, something forgotten when out of view, and when visible, suitable only to be projected upon, a future conquest, a longing, something to consider crossing, or a marker – reminder of all that remains undone. Utile and useless at once, so then something to co-opt with suspicion, as it threatens to twist its shape beyond meaning and recognition. And so misquoted, misappropriated, jailed, humiliated, rendered a cliché, an anachronism, and finally forgotten.

The gull finally behaves. He moans and I turn to watch him rising slowly above the shattered beach. And he's just a gull – hovering on dark wings. Calling out, seemingly to me, over and over. There's nothing behind that bird, nothing to the swirl of wind or water. And I don't know much about gods except that if the one or the many do exist, it must be a terrible thing to be prayed to – your perpetually multiplying charges calling out in their perpetually expanding voice to be heard and for you to make yourself known by infusing yourself in everything – but as a mystery, because the choice of a god revealing itself is to either perplex or overwhelm. So you come shrouded or in flashes – something moving quickly past the senses. But there is something – that dark twist in the water; the vanished river in the rubble shore; that bird, fixed in the air, betraying this planet's wobble – that I hold on to, something that enters me then transforms, like the way the smell of salt in the air flattens and extends the promontory, and I see from inside the river's mouth open. And once inside me it moves – that fusion of sense, memory, and promise – between the poles of doubt and faith, feeling and logic. And those poles suggest other ones that have gone unnamed, whose distances between remain unexplored. It must be awful to be a god – the voice of and the ear to all that wailing. Prayed to and rejected.

Another wailing gust, but this time inscrutable. This world is charged and then not. A rush of sudden meaning, then nothing, but the absence of meaning is meaning in itself. And so this land-scape is recharged, either by a revisitation or by my wondering where it all went, how long it's been gone, and if it ever was.

I hold the bottle under my nose. So this is how it ends – no *bang*, no *whimper* – just the hiss and scent of escaping gas. I blow more smoke into the scent cloud, but it's gone. The wind is voiceless, the river flat black. A perpetual nostalgia charges this world – nothing more – a memory of a collapsed dream. And its pull is inexorable.

I wonder how I'll say good-bye – call each child into a quiet room, or take them all out to the beach. I should do it at sunset, when, if you look west, the rich, muted light draws all the late summer's colors of the grass, the sand, and the water to their surfaces like blood to sunwarmed skin. And if you look east, the world is sheathed in a translucent skin of flint and azure. I shouldn't say a thing, just walk with them quietly and let them remember it as they will, if they remember it at all.

I raise the bottle of beer – one last chance. It is *brown, sullen, and intractable* – deceptively translucent – but there's no light for it to bend and not the slightest hint of a trembling.

I go to wordlessly toast the gull. He's gone, but I catch a line of headlights moving quickly, Manhattan-bound across the bridge. They span the dark water, connect to the roadway, more lights speeding northbound on the drive, to the Manhattan Bridge, east and up, then down and gone. But I know that beyond the vanishing point the circle is completed. I follow the loop around again and again – blur my vision to make the many seem to be one streak lashing around the edge of darkness. They're all there – faces, anthems, vows, frantic dreams glowing with super speed before they vanish into the dark dark dark. What is their last prayer – or plea? Can it be heard, or does it disappear as well – indistinguishable, lost in the clamor? I look and listen to the other systems: the wind between the bridges, the twisting water in the cove, the tide into the banks. I can see if you were a lost bird, how you could mistake this little cove for a beach, the river for the ocean, but maybe when you found only synthetic drift and meatless shells, you'd despair. And maybe, seeing me perched at the top of the granite steps, you'd call out. *What does the dark gull say?* Perhaps we are all in service to our own local god – each system with its own prayers or incantations. *Listen:* The wind's prayer to the bridges, the water's prayer to the cove, the speeding light's prayer to the dark says, *'Release me.'* That's why it sounds all a part when I listen: It's all one prayer – *'Let me go.'* My local gods are here: this fish, this woman, this bottle. I call: 'Let go.' I wait. Nothing. The water, the wind keep their futile twist. The light rips around the void – unentering. *'Let me go.'* Nothing is swallowed, but nothing is released.

I smell the beer again, and the image that follows is me, dead by the river. I don't want to die. I know there's no freedom there. *The bone's prayer to god is death – release me.* And I don't know what that release is, but I know it's more than fossilization, disintegration, or reanimation. It wants to disappear but also never to have been – carry no memory and leave none, either. But the bone isn't heard, or maybe it is, but perhaps there's no power that can do this. Maybe its god doesn't know it – doesn't see it. Does my maker remember me, and how do I move under that scrutiny? I watch the things I've charged, the residue of their movement, and then try to fill the empty wake. We are not moved by the epiphany but moved by the nostalgia. The movement gone, I get left with the vexing memory.

I have a beer in my hand and I know it will kill me, but I can't *not* drink now. I feel its pull. Perhaps I'll sit here through the night and speed around its emptiness. Maybe that's what I've been doing all along. I toast with two voices: *'To oblivion'* and *'Godspeed.'* I stand up and heave the bottle as hard as I can out to the river. It carries far and the sound it makes when it finally meets the water is more like a deep gulp than a splash.

I turn back to the bench and the five remaining beers. I don't want them. I pick up the urn instead and my bag, turn away, cross the path, and step down to the beach. I pull the largest section of ply away from the water's edge and set it at the top of the rise. I take the newspaper out of the bag, separate the pages, and spread it out on the board, adding layers until the dampness stops bleeding through. I get the notebook and tear the pages from the binding and lay them on the newspaper in four overlapping rows, five sheets long and three layers deep. I fold the edges of that rectangle into inch-high walls – repeating the fold until they're thick enough to stand on their own. I reinforce them around the outside with masking tape.

I open the urn and pour the ashes in. They almost fill up the vessel – charcoal flakes and tiny white pieces of bone, the inverse of the shell-and-gravel beach. I ball up the napkins and partially sink them in the ash so they don't blow away. I take Thomas out of my pocket, unwrap him, and lay him in the center on the tissue. It's hard to tell here in the dark, but he seems to have shrunken and gone dry – most of his orange is gone.

I drop the book of matches in, take off my coat and boots, and wade into. The pebbles and shells end quickly after the waterline and give way to silt, large stones, and broken things. I move slowly, trying to feel my way across the uneven muck-bottom – expecting any second to rip my foot open on a busted pipe or bottle. I stop when the water reaches my thighs and bend into it. Now it feels cold, viscous; it clings to my skin. I push the raft with one hand and half paddle, half scuttle across the bottom with the other until I reach the deeper water and can swim – sidestroke. The water and wind sound different here, more apiece – hypnagogic – now combined with the faint splash of my strokes. I upset the water, but the wave and wake I create will be erased. But what of the river – its memory? On the one hand each rip is irreversible; on the other, it never was. And so each stroke is just that, infinite and never, infinite and never, until I go beyond the cove, past the eddies, to the center of the river.

I stop and tread water. No big boats above. No great fish below. I steady myself, then bob high out of the water, take the matches with my free hand and hold them above my head. I try to light one – nothing. Then another – it flames but is blown out immediately. I lower the book, shelter it between my head and one of the paper walls, and try again. The match lights, but I don't move quickly enough and the others catch, too. The sudden flame burns my fingers, but I hold on, move it slowly to the pyre and light the wall, then one of the napkins, and drop the burning book in. I sink my burnt hand into the river; the oily water cools it. I tread water for a moment, and the current begins to pull the raft away. I catch it in two strokes and hold it still. And I almost ask something for forgiveness, but I bite down on that urge, drift a moment with the current, pull the raft back to me, feel the heat of the small rapid blaze, and call, *'Godspeed.'*

I send them away and they move with the water, quicker than I thought. The pyre burns quickly, too. And along with the increasing distance and the wind twisting the flame, it loses its form. Then it's out – just as it makes the bridge – a dark form with an orange glow and an imagined wisp of smoke. Then just the raft – *'darkness upon darkness.'* It passes from sight, under the bridge, into memory, through imagination, and back into sight – there – making the straits beyond the bridge and out the mouth of the river.

I look up at the bridge, then above to its cables, stretched and slack across the river – parallel strings, each with its own clusters of light and the darkness between them. These lights are still – fiery birds on wires. I reach out – a giant hand in the night: *Snap.* They rise, scatter, and then resettle. *Snap.*

I swim back to the cove but stay out in the water, turn onto my back and float, spinning slowly, just out of the pull of the current. The cables seem to sway, the lights flutter, rise, and settle and remember nothing. I see it in the air and I feel it in the water: The vision moves in time with the dark waves. The artificial lights are reflected in them, reflected and disfigured, until the heaving surface of the water is what the night sky should be – moving and wild, wavering reflections of buildings on both sides, dark and bright, like thin, shimmering clouds.

I right myself and look under the bridge for the raft. I know there would be, outside of this place, this moment, no way to track its progress across the gloom or for anything to hear my call, '*Godspeed.*' But this isn't a place of men and empire, this is my kingdom, where I belong, awake inside a dream.

There aren't any promises made on the dark side of the river, but if you catch the current right, it all goes out to sea. Four a.m.: All is well.

★　　★　　★

I wring out my shirt, put my boots and coat back on, shoulder my bag, and climb back to the path. I'm shivering. The wind seems to have picked up, blowing as hard now as the gusts were. I clench my teeth to keep them from chattering. Something moves near the bench.

'This your beer?' asks a coarse, disembodied voice. I don't answer. I turn to walk away along the path but keep my head turned to where the voice came from. Two figures step out of the darkness toward me. Cops.

'Excuse me. I asked you a question. *Sir*.'

'What?'

He steps forward. He's short and square. White. He already has his nightstick out and taps a bottle with it. 'Is this your beer?'

'No.'

The other cop steps forward now, a dark brown man, not as short as his partner, but equally thick. He fiddles with his radio antennae, looks past me to the river, and asks softly, 'You drunk?'

'No.'

'High?'

'No.'

'Need anything?'

'No.'

'Sure now?'

'I'm sure.'

His partner fidgets, taps his stick against his leg, and backs up into the darkness.

'You got someplace to go tonight?'

I point beyond the warehouse and nod.

'Maybe you should get there. This park is closed after dark.'

I nod again and start away. The white cop calls after me, 'Good night, *sir.*'

I go back to the bodega and knock on the partition. The man snaps awake, turns on the chair in a full circle, and shakes his head until he realizes who and where he is and what it is he's doing. He sees me and smiles weakly. He gets up and goes back to the cooler for more beer. I bang on the glass and he spins around, looking scared. I hold up my hands to calm him. I point at the beer and shake my head. He nods emphatically and puts it back. He points at the cigarette rack, and I shake again. He stops smiling and looks a bit lost. I tap the glass, lightly, and point at the coffeemaker. The pot is empty. He lifts it from the burner and shakes his head. He puts it down and clasps his hands together, still shaking his head. I put my hands together, too, and then wave while trying to give him the largest smile my face will allow. He nods again, then remembers something, shoots a finger into the air, then points it at the door, waving with his other hand.

I go to the door. He unlocks it, waves me in quickly, sticks his head out, looks up and down the street, then satisfied with what he's seen, pulls his head back in and locks the door.

'My friend, wait.'

I shiver visibly, and he frowns and shakes his head. He's a head shorter than me, small boned. He looks up over my shoulder, reaches out, almost pats it, but stops his hand and points to the ceiling instead.

He keeps the finger up, turns away, and heads for the back. He stops in the doorway and turns back, walking to me with a small silver coffee pot. He points happily at the stack of cups near the electric one. I take one, and he fills it with dark coffee. He puts a lid on it and bends the tab back in one motion, then hands it to me. He points for me to get another. He fills this one, too, and takes it from me. He goes to the cooler, takes out a half pint of cream, and gives his cup a long pour. He pushes it at me.

'No, thank you.'

He looks disappointed but shrugs it off. He goes to the coffee station, picks up the sugar, and offers it to me. Again I refuse, but with a short wave. He smiles this time, sets his cup down carefully, and then pour-spoons a good four teaspoons in. He inspects his coffee closely and then turns back to me. I go for my pocket, but he waves off payment with a finger.

'Thank you.'

He nods and guides me to the door. He opens it, and I turn back to him. He gestures to the night, gestures at my wet clothes.

'I'm sorry.'

I offer him a cigarette. He smiles, shakes his

head, and then slowly turns it into a nod. He takes one. I push the pack at him, but he waves a finger at it. I light him. He shrugs his shoulders then points at my cup.

'Spanish coffee.'

I nod.

'I'm from Bangladesh.'

I nod again.

'Where are you from?'

'Here.'

He nods. 'Good night.'

'Good night.' I back out, and he closes and locks the door. He raises his cup and sips from it. He gives one last wave, turns, and heads for the back.

I take a sip. It's hot and strong. I hold the cup against my cheek and start walking slowly, keeping it there until I feel my pulse under it. I stop and take a long pull, tilting my head back. The coffee going down seems to push away the encroaching chills. I lean back farther and finish it. There's the moon, hiding behind the thin clouds, threatening to stay there as though this was the last night of earth.

PART IV

EVERYBODY IS A STAR

And right action is freedom
From past and future also.
For most of us, this is the aim
Never here to be realized;
Who are only undefeated
Because we have gone on trying . . .

—*T. S. Eliot. 'The Dry Salvages' V*

CHAPTER 16

August has conceded. It's a cool morning. The sun is late. Marco and I wait on his stoop. We are silent and sip coffee from stainless-steel travel mugs. He got up extra early to brew a strong pot. He'd caught me, sitting on the edge of his son's bed in what looked to be some half-etherized state with my bag at my side. What could I have said?

Perhaps we're still friends and this gesture is a testament to that. Perhaps we're both hiding behind the mask of it being too early for talk – that we're both still too addled – the coffee has yet to take effect. He's put milk in mine, but I dismiss the possibility of a conspiracy. Friends, real friends don't conspire against each other.

A black SUV pulls up. It's one of those dark-continent conquest mobiles. This one, however, hasn't seen mud or sand. It's been buffed to a high metallic shine. It's a vehicle equipped for ghetto gentrification. The Mercedes Benz hood ornament looks like a rifle sight. All it needs is a gun turret for the roof.

'Let's go, man,' says Marco. He hops down the

stairs, shoulders his clubs, and makes for the gate. These four sleepless nights have shot my nerves. I have trouble with my mug, trying to figure out how to close it, then which hand to hold it in. The stairs are tricky, too – too steep and too narrow in the tread. I hop-stumble the last two, and coffee splashes up through the sip slot.

Marco has reached the car and talks to the driver through the passenger window. The other man sitting there looks past him and studies me openly. He's square headed, preppy, dark blond, sharp nosed. He reminds me of Buster Brown the shoe boy, but grown up. He tilts his head to get a good look at my clubs – unmatched no names and brand names in an old leather bag that may once have been nice. Marco has stuffed his old/new driver in, as well.

I remember that I don't have any balls. I need to play with new ones – Titleist. I don't know why, but I can't seem to hit anything else. And I want, like a child, to call out to Marco and tell him, but I know he'll say that he has balls and he'll hand me a half dozen of the ones he's found this summer in trees and tall grass, and when I hesitate, he'll tease – *'It's just a ball.'* I also don't want Buster to hear my voice – not yet. He's still curious but now waits for me to look at him overtly so he can nod his approval. I don't.

Marco calls, 'You ready?' and heads for the tailgate, extending an arm for my bag. I shake him off.

'Nice bag, man,' says Buster. I pretend not to hear him and put the clubs in the back.

The inside of the assault vehicle is as plush as Edith's sedan – perhaps more so juxtaposed to its rugged promise. I climb in. The driver turns to say hello, and I'm struck by his face; it's kind. He has a small nose like Buster, but it's rounded and soft. His eyes are hazel and twinkly, and he's smiling – almost meekly, more boyish than anything, I suppose. He's bald up top, probably has been losing hair since high school. He doesn't seem to care – no plugs, no comb-over, no base-ball hat. He reminds me of one of the likable coaches I had – polite, calm, rides home after practice in some oil-burning shitbox.

'Dan. Pleasure.'

'Good morning.'

He turns back. Puts the jeep in gear. Buster waves a backhand at me and doesn't turn.

'Hey. Bob.'

We pull out and I realize that I don't know where we're going – surely not to the little public course I'd been to. Jersey? Westchester? Long Island? We wind our way through the quiet Brooklyn streets to the BQE. Up front they speak in a strange and quiet code – some financial-legalese dialect. Marco looks out his window, across to Manhattan. Perhaps he's contemplating the fact that they're all derelict in their duties, and I wonder how to consider the three of them – the professionals playing hooky – whether their absence is arrogance

513

or defiance. Whether Marco gets fed up with the man – although, for most, he *is* the man. But I know there's the CEO, CFO, COO, the president, and each one possesses a deed on a section of his ass. And unless the other two were of that higher class, they were assed out, too. Marco and I both look out over the western edge of Queens, over the canal and the cranes – more warehouses and asphalt shingle-clad low row houses that line the anonymous streets below. He turns to me, gives a tight nod. It makes me feel a bit better, that all of us are doing something wrong, that we all may have some cosmic issue that has compelled us on this late summer morn to chance allowing our empires, both small and large, to expand or fall to ruin.

We hit the LIE eastbound. Still no talk. No music and the Benz is so quiet. It seems that we aren't moving save for Queens flashing by: brick apartment buildings, now Shea, now LaGuardia, and eastward, colonials and more anonymous streets.

'We're going to the club,' says Marco, turning from the window. 'Is that okay?' I take a sip of my milky coffee, which, even in the astronaut mug, has gone cold.

'I don't have a collared shirt.'

'Don't worry about it. We'll get you set up.'

I'm not sure who the *we* is or are. Driver Dan and Buster Bob are quiet, looking out the windshield. If the *we* is *they*, they aren't letting on.

Dan looks too honest, too kind to be involved in any kind of setup. *'Do you have anyone we can hunt at the club this weekend?'* I don't see it, not from him, but Buster, yes. I put the words in his mouth. *'Hey, Maracoh – got any sport?'* Marco watches Queens disappear. In purchasing his assimilation he's sold me out, but I won't give them the satisfaction of running, or even fighting. They can shoot me where I stand.

There's no outbound traffic so the trip is quick. We exit the highway. decelerate, turning. The trees thicken, and there are sudden breaks in them.

'You're an English professor, right?' asks Dan with a hint of reverence. I look at Marco, who refuses to turn from his window.

'Yes.' What else can I say?

'This place, the first time I came here reminded me of Gatsby. You know what I mean?'

'Oh, are we in one of the Eggs?' I reply, fumbling, which, I suppose, if one were to cut me a lot of rope, might sound interesting. Dan just nods – mouths a delayed and quiet *'Yep.'* I look out my window, but there's only trees. I look out Marco's. There's a great lawn – Gatsbyesque, I suppose. *Island Estates. Private way.* We pass more great lawns – driveways lined with pearly stones or crushed shells, which suggest that they retreat a great distance from the road and terminate at something grand, but most of them have multiple mailboxes at the gate. Hundred-acre estates have

515

been halved over the years, and then halved and halved again. If there is some postmodern Daisy up one of those drives, I'm sure she won't be coming down to the road to fetch her mail. I feel a quick twinge inside, like my stomach, for a second, has folded over and back, when I consider how dead she really is.

THE COUNTRY CLUB says the signpost. EST. 1921. We turn off the tiny road, disappear behind a line of junipers, down a gravel drive. We slow down. To the left is a green. Dan rolls down his window and waves to an elderly man who looks up from examining a putt. He recognizes Dan, waves back, and returns to his study. I've never seen a green like this one – two tiered, immaculate, almost arti- ficial. The man addresses his ball, and Dan speeds up. I turn to look out the back to watch him, but he's not ready. He steps away, reexamines his line, then is obscured by the first in a row of enormous oaks.

'Pretty nice?' asks Marco.

'Lovely,' I answer. Still looking back as though I possessed supernatural vision.

'Played here before?' asks Buster without turning. I'm offended by his lack of effort. I decide I don't like Buster – that it's all right for me not to, to make an aesthetics-based decision. Buster is bad: his smug nose and lips; the tiny cleft on his chin; his absurdly blue eyes – the kind that first his mother and later his wife bought shirts and ties to match. He takes care of his skin. It's well scrubbed, well oiled, but his close-cropped hair was done at a barbershop. He's not so far gone – maintains just enough old-world masculinity in his grooming ritual. He turns to me to check if I'm really there, not believing that I heard his question. How could he have been ignored? I get a better sense of him when he turns. He's much larger than Dan – more rectilinear; his shoulders, his head, his jaw – everything really, except for that smug little nose. In another time he'd be sporting a smug little mustache – lip cover. It fits too well here in Gatsby land. He's Tom, dreaming of future conquest and past athletic glory. But we all know that during Buster's playing days Ivy League football was already bush league and that the land grab is long over. I wonder what kind of car he has and how many Mexican workers he can hide in his trunk. I dislike Buster more than Tom. At least Tom had Polo as an outlet. This guy's violence is too contained. He speaks again, even more truncated.

'Play here?'

'Never.'

'Gonna like it.'

'Looking forward to it.'

They've all managed to shave – nickless. They're all wearing polo shirts – different colors, but the same nonetheless. Their assemblage – haircuts, smooth cheeks, collars, carriage – adds up to some sort of badge, a pinky ring for some sort of blue-blood mafia. I stop there because of Marco. I think he's my friend, but the evidence points away from that. Dan stops the car. And even though the analogy is offensive – makes no sense – I wait for Marco to put a bullet in my head.

Nobody shoots. They open their doors, and I follow suit. Someone has snuck around back and opened the hatch. Two teens, one black and one white, take our clubs out and stand them beside the walk. Dan whispers something to the white kid. The black kid does his best not to look at any of us. He fusses with the bags, tries to make them all stand up in the rack.

'Let's go,' says Dan. Buster and Marco follow him up the path to what I assume to be the club-house – obscured by more enormous oaks. I'm left in the netherworld between the house and the ride. I want to say something to the black kid, as though I possessed wisdom. some armored words for him for now and for later. But all I have in my head is the beginning of a disjointed autobi-ography. Now he looks up at me, queerly. He's a handsome kid – dark skinned and dark eyed: a question in them, asking me, perhaps, what I'm doing still standing there. He shoulders two bags and turns away.

My companions are gone, into the clubhouse. I walk up the cedar-chip path beyond the trees and up to a grand old Victorian. I stop at the door. An older couple walks up the path toward me – the man from the green, and another man, whom I thought to be a woman, I'm not sure why. They don't seem to notice me until, a pace away, they both look up. Not surprised. Almost calculated. The man from the green gives me an unreadable nod. The other ignores me and opens the door. He stops, says hello to someone coming out. It's Marco. He greets both men; neither cracks a smile and they go in.

Marco turns to me with a puzzled look.

'What happened?'

'I was talking to those kids,' I point back down the path, at the trees. 'I lost you.' He looks down, then at the big door, then sideways at me. 'Sorry. I thought I'd find you again if I stayed put.'

'We were in the pro shop,' he points at the wall as though it was cut away. 'You could've just come in. You're my guest.'

'It's all right.'

'However you want it, man.'

He seems hurt again but not like the night before – it's a hurt that, away from booze and maitre d's and young women, has room to grow, on his face, in his stance. Marco is my friend, and it becomes apparent that he needs me, and needs me to need him. I smack him on the arm, the best I can do right now.

He shows me the shirt.

'I hope it fits.'

'Thanks.'

'Use the locker room – it's at the end of the hall to the right.' He looks up almost cross-eyed, reassuring, 'It's cool – all right.'

'All right.'

'You need anything else?' He looks happy again – that innocent look he has – eager, can-do, optimistic.

'Yeah.' He perks up even more. 'I need balls. Pro shop?'

'No, not there,' he waves a finger at the house. 'They're criminals.' He points at his chest. 'I've got balls. I've got plenty of balls.' He gestures to the door with his head. 'Go get changed. Our tee time's soon.'

Marco is a good man. He's my friend, so I smile and give him another slap on the arm, which he seems to like. He opens the door for me, and I turn to go in. The clubhouse is like the inside of a hollowed-out oak tree – oak floors, walls, and long benches along them in the great room. The tarnished frames of the oil paintings have lost their luster, and they, too, seem to have been carved into their places. The charter members, like so many smears of berry juice on the wood cave walls.

'All the way across to that hallway,' says Marco, 'then the first door on the left.' He hands me the shirt.

There are people inside. Some sit and some move, but all are like bees in a torpor because of the early morning cool – safe for now. I'm backlit by the sun, still low over the first fairway. My shadow is long on the floor.

'Hurry up, man.'

Marco is my friend. He's given me food and

shelter all summer. He thinks I'm like him, and that because of this, he knows what I need. I can't tell him that he's trying to kill me.

I cross the great room without much ado – no one seems to look. The locker room is empty. The transom is open above the door that leads outside to the back, and I can smell the pool, hear the scrape of the pool man's pole along the concrete edge. I hate the smell of chlorine. It reminds me of day camp and shouting sadistic counselors – their barks echoing off the tile. Mildew in the showers. Naked boys in rows. Pot-bellied, squishy adolescents. The nastiness of their sharp laughs. The slap of their feet, running on those slippery floors, always made me think of gushing head wounds and broken teeth. After the afternoon free swim I'd watch the older boys play pool for quarters until it was time to go. I'm alone and this room is wood paneled, carpeted, and quiet. I check my roll in my pocket. I put it away and take a practice swing, then another, trying to check myself in the mirror. I take off my shirt, catch the reflection of my torso. I'm thinner than I thought I would be. I swing again – things seem to be moving in tandem.

There's a splash in the pool, but it doesn't sound heavy enough to be a body. I sit down on the padded bench and exhale. I could lie down here on the carpet, in a corner, and just close my eyes for a moment. There's another splash, and then someone curses sharply. This is the camp where

Marco's kid goes, the one C has come home talking about – *'They have things to do there . . .'* he chided his mother once, not being able to appreciate the time and space he had at the beach. We played bombardment in our camp – prison ball, some called it. The rules were simple: Whip a rough maroon rubber ball at someone else's bare arms and legs. Catch the ones thrown at you.

I stand and take out my new shirt. It's an extra large. It seems enormous, and when I put it on, it is huge – all except the arms, which are too tight. I check my proportions in the mirror, but I can't tell if it's me or the shirt that's wrong. It hangs off me like a dress, so I tuck it in, a good eight inches of shirt, uncomfortably into my shorts. I hope Marco knows what he's doing. *I need to hit the ball right.* A poor mantra, but one that will have to do, and it's done well already – gotten me to focus on the job at hand.

The door opens and a man with the same shirt walks in. He's whistling something – *'Ain't She Sweet,'* I think. He stops when he sees me or, rather, quietly holds the note until he passes. I cinch up my belt, bag my old shirt, and start out.

'You hit a long way?'

I mumble-grunt something at him. He straightens – somewhat surprised by my incoherence. I try to redeem myself.

'Going out or coming in?'

'Coming in. Played nine,' he says, not looking up.

Comforted or offended, I don't know. 'It's a bear. Really playing hard today.'

'It's always hard, for me.'

He doesn't laugh. He pulls off his polo, then straightens his undershirt.

'Best of luck.'

'Good day.'

Our clubs are waiting for us at the first tee. They've been scrubbed shiny – even mine. The boys are there, too, chatting with Dan and Buster, who gesture out toward the flag. They both have clubs and swing them slowly. They look like they know what they're doing. I can tell that they've had lessons – perhaps from the same pro. Marco stands on the path by the sign for the hole, a good five feet lower than the tee box – *345 yard par four*, it reads in script. Marco examines the sign closely, checks his scorecard, and then joins in the ritual of stretching, flexing, posing, and swinging. I'm still somewhat awed by how clean my clubs are and I don't know whether I should show my wonder or act like I've been to a place like this before, which, I'm sure, everyone knows I haven't. I pull out a club, a no-name five iron, and I think I hear the white kid snicker, but when I look up, he's looking down the fairway with Buster. They look almost like family in profile – perhaps involved in strategy or discussing club lore.

Marco calls out to me, 'How's the short game?'

I shake my head and they laugh, except for the

black kid, who looks as though he's checked into an alternate reality in his head.

'Gentlemen, 7:18 on the tee, please.'

I'm the farthest away, but they all turn to me. I shake my head and extend my hand back.

'Well,' says Dan. 'I'm here.' He places his ball and steps back. He has the same club as Marco. The shaft is too long for him, though. He takes two slow practice swings. His face goes blank – all that boyish goodwill erased. He takes a wide path around and behind the ball. He looks at it, then the flag, then back to the ball. He takes another slow swing and then one sharp step to address. One more look, then into his stance. He seems ready to swing, but inexplicably he opens up his stance to the point where he seems to be aiming at the row of oaks that line the fairway. His swing is quick and short – pinched. The ball heads straight for the trees, then slices back to the fairway, just short of the one-hundred-and-fifty-yard marker.

'Nice ball, Dan,' says Buster as Dan, still surveying his work, picks up his tee.

'Well,' he replies, 'it's in the fairway.' He walks off the mound. Both caddies nod their approval. He ignores them. 'I didn't get all of it,' he says back to Buster. He stops and fusses with a contact lens.

'No,' Marco calls out. 'It's fine, Dan. Nice one.'

I'm not sure if I envy Marco's ability to lie straight-faced like that, or disdain it. I do, however, want him to turn to me and wink – give me some sign that he is in fact, lying.

Buster is already over his ball. He's a large man – much taller than I'd thought earlier – like a pro-sized tight end. But he, unlike Tom Buchanan, isn't very athletic. He looks awkward in his stance, like he isn't quite sure what to do with all his height. His legs and arms are splayed horridly, like he's some arachnid partial amputee, his spider eyes looking in too many directions, seeing too many things for the humanoid brain to process. He swings jerkily. The ball goes up, disappears into the cloud bank above the fairway, then drops out of the sky about twenty yards ahead of Dan's, just to the right.

Dan claps. 'If you could just translate some of that height into length – man!'

'It'll do,' says Buster quietly and holds his club out for the black kid.

Marco looks at me, and I point to the tee. He pulls an iron out of his bag, then shoves it back and gets out his enormous driver.

'Oh, the big dog,' coos Dan.

Marco walks up the mound, places his ball, and stands behind it. I wonder what his fingerless father thinks of his son – if he would come to such a place. He must be proud of his boy. Marco looks the part in his beige pleatless slacks and his navy polo. He stretches his hamstrings and I think, while watching his head down there, that if Marco was the least bit vulnerable to perceiving the absurd, it would explode. He straightens, and at address, he looks tense. Perhaps I'm projecting, but I'm right. He rushes what would otherwise have been a good swing and hits a duck hook – two hundred yards straight and sixty yards left.

'Fuck!' he growls, and almost throws his club down, but he checks himself – keeps his back to us, cools off, and bends to pick up his tee, which, when he finds it split to pieces, he throws away into the thick grass in front of him. 'Quack,' he mutters, coming down the mound. No one laughs. 'You're up.'

I take the five iron I've been fondling and climb up to the tee. They try not to stare, but they do. It must look ridiculous – at least unusual. I place my ball – Marco's reject ball – and I know I can't hit it. I wonder if I'm the youngest or the first, the largest, Black Irish Indian to play at The Country Club. I wonder if they're considering it, as well – perhaps not. Perhaps they only see me in my wrinkled shorts, my hairless legs, and my shirt, identical to Marco's, only two sizes larger – sleeves like a muscle shirt, body like a muumuu. The shiny no-name club with the cracked vinyl grip.

'Playing it safe?' calls Buster, with just enough humor and politeness so as not to be considered an egregious breech of etiquette by anyone but me. And although Marco is my friend, I still haven't dismissed the notion that this is all a setup. And I haven't really swung a club in a year.

And I wonder if they can see my legs shaking. Even the black kid is watching, and I can't help but think that he has something invested in this moment, too – from a perverse claim to caddy shack bragging rights to the complete emancipation of himself and his people. And I know, as I look down the fairway one last time, that to them, if it is bad, my first swing will be my last – *the one* – no matter how well I play after. There can be no redemption, not for him, not for me, nor for those to whom – because of some treacherous failure or triumph of synapse or courage (whichever you believe in) the many thousands gone, here and yet to be – we are linked. And I hear them, be it by spirit, madness, or some ventriloquist's trick. I hear them pleading, exhorting me to hit the ball straight and long, just as I hear the founder rasping from his canvas on the great oak wall – *'Swing, nigger, swing!'* – and his brothers hissing in unison, *'Amen.'* It's too much. It's always been too much, even divested of all I love. I can't take it anymore. I just can't take it. I try my mantra – *I need to hit the ball right.* Head down. Go slow. I swing. Up then down. I hear nothing, but I'm standing erect at follow-through and the ball is like a supersonic missile, ripping the air. Silent, then the sounds: the whoosh of the club past my ear, the sharp click of metal on hard plastic, then the ball flying with a high turbine wail in its wake. It carries the ridge and drops out of sight.

527

'Goddamn,' snorts Dan – almost hushed. Buster says nothing. Both caddies grin stupidly. The black one snaps out of it and reaches for my club. I wave him off because I can tell I'm about to cry.

I stuff the five back in my bag and shoulder it. Marco steps to me and offers a high five. I shake his hand instead. He points to the bag and then to the boys.

'It's okay,' I squeak. I wish I had sunglasses. He looks at my eyes.

'Pollen,' I whisper. 'Something out here.' He nods his head – relieved.

'Great shot.'

'Thanks.'

I know it's rude, but I turn my back on him and start out on the fairway. My clubs rattle on my back like pans in a nation sack. He's right on my hip. The tears start to come. I wipe the first wave away.

'What was that you hit – a three? You don't have a two iron, do you?'

'Five.'

'A five – fuck!'

The next wave comes – harder. He reaches in his pocket and produces a pack of tissues.

'Thanks,' I snuffle. I take one and hand them back.

'Keep them.' He reexamines my eyes. 'You look miserable.' He slaps his pockets. 'Damn! Wait – no!' He turns back to the rest. 'I think I have Benadryl in my bag. Want one?'

528

'No, thanks.'

'Does it make you sleepy or jumpy?'

'Jumpy – anxious.'

'Me, too. Gave me palpitations once.'

'Is that yours?' I point to the next fairway, on the first cut. I don't really see his ball, but it must be in that area.

'It must be.' I don't know what he sees, but he starts for it. Then he stops. 'Hey, man,' he says, secretively.

'Yes.'

'These guys – you won't get anything out of them unless you back off a bit.'

I look at him for an instant because I don't understand. And when I do, I keep looking into his dark brown eyes, and I want to keep crying. I want to tell him why – *'My people were on that ball.'* He takes off his glasses, cleans them on his shirt.

'Capiche?'

I wipe my eyes again, take another tissue, and pretend to blow my nose.

'Capiche.'

'Bene.' He puts his glasses back on. He looks at me, then widens his eyes as if to refocus them. He looks out over the ridge and points. My ball is about ninety yards from the green. He shakes his head. 'Nice shot.' He turns and goes.

I stop crying so I can make my next shot – *Hit the ball right.* Or, as Marco has coached – don't. I try to fuck it up, but since I don't have any

529

semblance of a short game and am clueless as to what to do. I don't know what not to do. Golf, some people have told me, is unnatural. The movements are counterintuitive. But of course, many others have advised against thinking. All I know is that it's far easier to sandbag than it is to fake being good. I set up and take an awkward whack at the ball. It skips onto the green and settles about ten feet from the hole. Even Buster nods his approval.

'Not bad for first hole,' says Marco as we walk to the second. Dan, who I realize hasn't acknowledged Marco since the stoop, finally addresses him directly.

'What'll we play?' he asks. He stuffs his hands into his pockets, looking almost as innocent and stupid as the boys. 'Stroke? Match?'

'What about both?' asks Marco.

Dan nods slowly. 'Okay. Okay.' He keeps nodding but speeds up a bit – hands still pocketed. He keeps looking at Marco, but I sense that he's looking at me. He stops nodding, drags his hands out, and claps softly. He's made some evaluation. He's not worried about the other two, and now he's realized that because I have no short game, he can beat me. He's been taking stock – my bag, my clubs, my sneakers, my skin. He knows the only time I spent on a golf course as a kid was at night sitting with Gavin on some greenside hill, practicing at becoming a hobo.

'Match and stroke. Two a hole. No validation. How much for low score?'

Marco and Buster shrug. Dan looks to me. I don't respond. I pretend to be considering the yardage for this next hole. I don't want to admit to myself that I don't know what he's talking about.

'We all seem even,' says Buster. 'It always ends up as a wash anyway.'

'What do you think – five? Everyone kicks in one and a quarter for the pot?' He puts his hands back in his pockets and looks directly at me. 'Can you handle that?'

Instead of saying fuck you, I nod earnestly while trying to do the calculation. So the upside is a few grand. I can bow out if I lose my stake. We don't shake, just all nod vaguely.

'Anyone beat a par?' asks Dan rhetorically as he holds his hand out for a club. The white kid starts to hand him the driver, but Dan shakes it off and points to an iron.

It doesn't go well. At first the other three comment and question my poor swings as though they're aberrations. By the fifth hole, though, they seem to believe they're the norm. The white kid seems quietly amused by my plight, but I can't tell if he's smirking or squinting under his low visor. He doesn't talk to me – hardly looks my way. He's a little prick. A face you'd like to punch in, but not like Gavin's. There's nothing going on behind this kid's eyes.

Each hole the black kid gravitates toward my

bag, but I always pick it up first and walk away by myself up the fairway. Dan saw something in my long swing. So much can go wrong – some little hitch can throw it all to shit. There's too much room for error. And Dan keeps dink-slicing his way to the hole. By the turn – after the eighth hole – I've lost track of the numbers because I'm out so much. And no one, not even the black kid, seems to notice I'm there at all.

Dan rolls in a putt on the ninth and quietly applauds himself. It fills me with a sleepy, impotent rage. I would like to believe that there was once a time when there weren't any rules. When barbarians flooded endlessly over the embankments of the civilized. Dan sets up to sink another putt, to pocket more of my nonexistent capital, and I know that the image is all wrong. I retreat to the old boxing adage – *'A good big man always beats a good little man.'* And I assume that the queen's rules were made for the big man – but it doesn't make sense. I should, by decree of a much older rule, one people like Dan, like Marco, followed, be able to pick Dan up, spin him around, and shake him empty, take everything that drops from his pockets onto the green – cash, photos, memberships, the promissory notes to deep streams of capital – and call it my own. I should take everything, even the bald spot, the little paunch, which, because of his hatless head, his tightly tucked shirt, he seems proud of. I outweigh him by fifty pounds – so whose failing is it that

I'm tyrannized by his credit cards and his titles? And by extension, it doesn't seem like a crime to raise my ancient putter and drive it into the red patch of his skull. I'd take his fancy clubs, too. But somebody, some martyr wannabe, raised me right, or wrong, and I'm stuck with my gut and my own head rebelling, in chorus, the refrain: *Broke-ass chump*.

Buster asks if I want anything from the clubhouse. I'm hungry, but I figure I'm going to need everything I have to pay off my debt. He looks perplexed. 'You need to eat something,' he says – almost maternally – and stands waiting for a moment. I say no thanks again. Dan, comfortable with his lead, throws a soft salute my way – trying to convince me that he's the mild guy he was earlier.

'What's up, man?' asks Marco.

'What do you mean?' I say irritated by his concern. It seems phony. Either he doesn't get it or he doesn't care. His facade offends me – the sad eyes and the Roman nose are almost cruel in their mocking of both me and him.

'I don't know. You started off great, but you seem to be having a hard time controlling your shots.'

I stare at him, but he doesn't acknowledge. He's looking inside, trying to figure out my swing.

'It's not like you're doing one thing. One hole you're hooking it. One you're pushing it – like you're overcompensating for the last. I don't know.' He does a slow-motion backswing – holding at the top. 'You're good here.' He starts down. His swing looks nothing like mine. It's closer to his own. He brings it up again, swings half speed, and watches his imaginary ball's flight. I follow it, too – the sky, the trees, and then the promise of the bay. The marsh, the sea grass and seabirds. The beach. The swells and the beach break seem flat – without power – one roll of water and then another. And the colors are green, blue, gold, but without texture or heft, past or promise. They threaten nothing. They promise nothing and speak of no other time. And I, too, seem forgotten, a fleshy marker on the green. A scarred hand on the old club and the sunlight on it, then on my face as I turn away. And it's just warm. It stops there.

Marco takes another backswing. He's still trying to figure it out for me. I'm sorry I snapped at him – glad that I didn't say more. He's still talking, teaching me to salvation, but I don't really hear him. Dan and Buster come back, both chewing on something. Dan tees up and hits quickly. The rest follow suit. They almost walk off, but then remember me. I get out Marco's old driver, take a half swing, and dink the ball out in the fairway just beyond theirs.

The course opens up, becomes links play – rolling fairways, more wind. Even though Buster's keeping score, he doesn't say anything to me when I win the tenth. And I keep dinking the ball out there, punching out into the fairway, letting it roll onto the greens – ugly, near arcless shots with very little carry, but they go straight and they go far enough. No mantras, no internal instruction – two holes and then three. And because of my little streak, Dan seems to have regained his interest in me. It seems to rattle him a bit. He misses short putts on thirteen and fourteen, which would have won them both.

I win the fourteenth, but the black kid beats me to my bag and shoulders it. I wave for him to give it back. He offers me his hand instead.

'Houston.'

'Good to meet you,' I say in a paternal mumble. I point at the bag. 'I'll take that.'

'I've got it.'

Dan and I push the next two holes. White kid keeps his smirk and his distance from us, but Houston stays close to me, almost forgetting that he has another bag to carry. I can't help but be somewhat moved by his attention. And as we walk off the sixteenth green, I find myself striding toward the next tee. The kid keeps with me.

'This hole's made for you,' he says covertly.

'How so?'

'It's long. If you hit a full driver – swing like you did on the first hole, it's yours.'

I slow down and eye him warily from behind. He doesn't turn, but he feels it.

'Trust me.'

Dan takes an iron from White kid, points ahead, looks at the ground but addresses me. 'Number seventeen. Par five – five hundred sixty yards. Into the wind.' He looks over to me and then points to the tee box. Marco slides up to me.

'No one gets on in two. Especially on a day like this. Play irons – get on in three, but just make sure you get on.'

I look at Dan, then Houston. He sneers at Marco behind his back – his first open display of contempt.

'Tell you what,' says Dan. 'Five hundred if you carry the water.'

Houston studies the scorecard and speaks directly to me. 'Two-eighty to carry. Short you're in the water. Left you're in the water. Right you're in the marsh. Not much room to hit a monster drive in.' He looks out to the small landing area of fairway. 'Too long and you're in the woods.'

'He's never going to reach the woods,' snaps Dan, reminding the kid of his place. Houston ignores him. He shuts up, but it doesn't stop him from glaring at the trio of white men. They all look away.

'How much on this hole?' I ask. No one answers. They pretend not to hear, as though I'm pushing on some line of civility and they don't feel comfortable reprimanding me – or the silence is the reprimand.

I spread my arms. 'How much?'

'Twelve,' snaps Dan. Then grins. 'Twelve-five for you.'

I turn to Houston. 'May I have the driver, please?'

536

He beams. 'Yes, sir!' he answers like a Pullman porter. I wince at the association, but I have to shake it off.

At address I wait for the wind to stop. It's been blowing in gusts – both hard and soft. Dan won't look at me, only down the fairway and to whatever he sees beyond. I dismiss him. *That little fuckin' weasel's gonna owe me a ton of dough.* Buster and Marco stand together, Buster smiling, not malevolently, but with a kind of boyish wonder – like he's suddenly, beside the tee box, found some express route to his childhood. I can see it flicker in his face. He's happy, home. And Marco, mouth agape, is perplexed by the shapelessness of my plan – the recklessness. But Marco has never had nothing to lose, nor would he ever put himself in a position to lose everything. The sky is blue with creamy clouds, robin's egg at their soft edges. I put my head down and swing. The ball rips across the inlet and the rocks and marsh and the fairway and into the trees beyond. Nobody says a thing. I can't imagine that they know what to say.

'Too much,' mumbles Houston while staring at Dan, his face bright with wet light from sweat and sun.

Everyone else lays up. After they hit, I wander blankly down the slope to find my ball. When I make the fairway, I get rolled by an icy wave of sleep and I come out of it with a shudder – awake. The grass seems to buzz a brighter green, as though someone turned up a color dial. I look

537

back up the hill to the others. Buster cracks a joke, and everyone except for the black kid laughs. And then I realize that I just blew it, and I can't understand how or why. I look up and try to recreate my ball's flight, but that doesn't do it, neither does my jog to the edge of the wood, where I stop and ask myself, *'Why did you do that?'* Nothing comes, so I keep looking from the tee to the wood. Another wave hits, not sleep though, it's smaller, more like a swell than anything else, but it seems to suggest by the way it goes back out – the quiet left behind, that all the water has been sucked out of the bay and is gathering somewhere out of sight.

I scan the trees. I don't want to go in there. And they're not really woods, more like a long, narrow pine grove just before the rocky shore. It's fortified by thick, twisted lengths of honeysuckle and bittersweet. Inside are ferns, dead needles, moss, and the dappled light of the high sun broken up by the boughs. I hear the scurry of creatures through the soft underbrush, black flies, and the gentle slap of the hidden tide. I step in anyway. It's cooler inside the trees. I shudder in the middle of a yawn, and my jaw trembles and locks open. I hear something behind me and I startle but don't turn. A group of gnats gathers and twists in my face. I look through them. There's a big black wasp flying low, a dog tick waiting on a fem blade. I hear myself sigh but don't believe it's really me. I try to dispel the feeling that someone's behind me. The wind sweeps over the water with a hiss,

through the trees with a groan. I say it out loud –
'That's nothing' – but I start to panic a little
nonetheless. Then I tell myself that I'm hungry
and overtired, but that doesn't stop me from
crying again. Then I remember my lost ball and
almost turn my head to look for it, but I don't
think I should move at all. I say it out loud, 'You're
just tired.' I don't believe that. 'Not now,' I whine
and mouth a quick and empty prayer that even I
can't comprehend. Then it comes.

When I heard the door open, I thought nothing
of it – except *That must be somebody* – that silly
little thought. So I didn't turn – planting the seed
for questions later – *what if?* I always like to believe
that up to that day I had been a happy boy – *so
full of light* – but I know that's not true. Whether
I was already wounded, had already been bleeding
all that light slowly, I don't know. I had already
been questioning myself, my value, my capacity
to hold light, but in the way a small boy does –
feeling it in my guts – *What's wrong with me?* I
could trace some of it to my skin, to my parents,
and later to alcohol – the completeness it brought
me when I drank, which spoke to the fact, magnified when sober, that there was something missing.
Perhaps what I'd felt as a boy were the things that
would be coming – premonitions in the child guts,
mute but still calling – a silent wail of dread and
bile.

So when he smashed my head – one, two, three –
against the tile wall, it felt right. I remember seeing

my blood up there as he dragged me back – up there on the wall like a smear in a cave, the abandoned gesture of an ancient mind and hand. He punched me. He kicked. He was enormous, reassuring – a confirmation of evil. No more wondering about specters and boogeymen and the devil. I had proof – empirical. He stank like the old food on dental floss, the pop released with the decaying meat between molars. Like long-dried sweat. Like the grave – body, moss, and soil. I tore inside, so deep that I could taste it. And it was so strange, the things that flashed in my mind: why my father left; why my mother wanted me dead. And I wished that they had told me, but how could they have? *Everything you ever were will gush from you through a breach, and everything you would have been will be gone.* The tear in your anus a symbol denoting the eternal, fathomless gap. No one has ever reached that. I know no one ever will. The scarred brow, stigmata to remind you and them that you will never be whole. And I know it's so feeble, but I wish it would all go away – but it is me: the line of Ham, the line of Brown, the crooked soul finger, the jagged keloid scar that everyone eventually points to. I wish I would go away, but I shoot through everything – the tree, the dappling on the log, the voices that seem to rise up out of the bay. Everything begs for meaning, for origin, for redemption, and I can't do it. I know that I'm too damaged. I've seen signs and confirmations – evil, chaos.

Never good. Never a sign of pure, lasting, invulnerable good.

I don't startle when Houston crashes through the honeysuckle, looking up, as though he was following the trail of the ball to this spot. He sees me standing there, shoots a curious look over, then continues tracking his line. He points at the ground as though he's found some secret tunnel out of a place where we've been lost a long time.

'I've got it!'

I shuffle toward him like a zombie. He's straddling a log. What a handsome kid, especially since he's free with me here in the bush – all the tension needed to hold the mask in place is gone. His face has opened. He takes off his cap, revealing the loose naps that have been pressed into the first two layers of a ziggurat. He looks at me quizzically, wondering, perhaps, why I'm not rushing to him. Then he looks back down and shakes his head.

'Terrible lie.'

It's buried under twigs and leaves, with the log between it and the fairway. Only the top sticks out. There's no way to play it.

'What are you gonna do?'

I close my eyes, spread my arms weakly, and list back and forth. He looks at me harder, questioning again, but this time reversing the roles, as though he's asking if there's something I don't understand. He looks down at the ball, feels the balls in his apron pouch, then turns to the fairway, to the clearing he's come through.

'If this log wasn't here, you could punch right through that hole and have a chance at par, maybe birdie – *if this log wasn't here.*' He taps at it gently with his foot and stoops. He turns his eyes back up to meet mine, and he's a boy again, in the kitchen with the cookie box, waiting for the nod from me because his mother, in the next room, has already told him no.

'What do you think?' He turns, ducks to peer under the branches. He whispers, 'Are they down here yet?' He takes one more look at me and then walks away – mutters, 'It's cool.' He stands in the opening and gives me his back.

'Yo!' yells someone on the other side of the leaf wall. We both spin nervously to the voice. It's Buster, peering through the foliage. 'What are you guys doing in there – huh? Private party?'

'His ball's in there,' barks Houston, a bit too stridently for the both of them. Buster waits for him to lower his head, then turns to me and the log.

'That's not your ball.' He thumbs over his shoulder. 'Your ball's out here.'

I squat to examine it, and when I do, I feel something tear inside. I pick up the ball. It's not mine, but I can't get up. I think I'm bleeding.

'Come on, we've already hit.'

I don't stand. I dab at the back of my shorts, but I don't feel anything there. Houston has

542

already left the woods, marching almost, with my bag, in the direction Buster had pointed.

'You all right?'

I start crying again, so I cover my face, rub my temples with my thumbs. I stand slowly, trying to find a voice for him.

'I'm just a bit dizzy. It's gone.'

'You're hungry,' he states surely. 'You should have let me get you something back at the turn.'

With that point made, he leaves me in the woods. I sit down on the log and close my eyes. I feel sleep coming. I want to stay on the log, in the woods, in the dappling, slowly bleeding, and have the underbrush, the ferns, the buzzing, the moss and mushrooms cover me. These are good woods. They need a good haunt. And the golfers, the members, gambling, could tell their guests, their sons about the spook who disappeared. From the seventeenth tee, pointing down below – *When the wind is right, you can hear him – above the gulls, the yellowjackets, the sway and rustle of the branches. When the sun is right, you can see him sitting, waiting – there, that mushroom patch on the log. They say he had the hands of a giant, hands that could swallow you whole.*

Buster comes back. He looks angry. I wipe my eyes with my baggy shirt and square up, fists clenched at the hip. He sees them and stops two strides away. His face relaxes, then reforms into the expression he wore in the car this morning; he knows me.

'Here.' He holds out a candy bar. I stare at it. 'Allergic to nuts?'

'No.' I keep staring at his hand.

'Sorry, it's all I had in the bag.' He looks closer, into my face, like it's some curious symbol he doesn't understand.

'Your eyes are on fire, man.' I cover them with my hands, absentmindedly rub at them.

'You're making it worse.' He pushes the candy at me. 'Here.'

I have to take it. I open it and offer him some. He refuses. 'I just had one.' He nods for me to eat. I do. It's not candy. It tastes like dried mud. I try to swallow, but I'm spitless. He keeps watching me, some bizarre nursemaid with me in the forest primeval.

'That'll take care of one problem,' he says. 'Come on, everyone thinks you're lost.'

I pick up the ball and pocket it. Buster waves me out of the woods. Marco looks both worried and embarrassed when he sees me. They're gathered around my ball, and they look to Buster to explain it all with his face. He doesn't. He looks up the fairway at the flag.

'You got lucky,' says Marco nervously. 'You must have hit a tree or something.' I can't tell if he's nervous for me or himself.

Houston hands me a club. I don't check it. I can't feel the grip anyway because my hands have gone numb. The sport bar residue hangs in my throat. He whispers to me.

'Just straight.'

I walk up to the ball and swing. It starts out straight but begins hooking – short and left.

'That'll play,' mumbles Houston. He's regained his stance, uncaring about allegiance to me, but I can hear the disappointment in his voice. 'You can still make birdie from there and take this hole.' And his saying this, based on what he's seen so far, is a lie. He knows I can't chip or putt, and he knows Dan can. What he doesn't know is that nothing has changed since the woods. I still can hear the grunts and curses echoing off the bathroom tiles. I can still see the sign of blood. It's right there, on the wall, the smear and drip marks. Houston is further disappointed by my errant chip shot, my eyeless putt. And I would like to tell him that it's a difficult thing to do – concentrate on your short game while wondering when, if ever, you're finally going to bleed to death.

Marco blows his chance to halve the hole. Buster stands over his putt while I tally my losses – my possessions: the money in my pocket, guitar, books. I can work out a payment plan or I can plead ignorance – *'Thousand? I thought you meant hundred. I don't have that kind of money.'* We didn't shake. Or just *No. Fuck you. Foul. Just no. Setup. No. Try and take it. No.*

Buster sinks his putt and clenches his fist. He starts to pump it and then looks at Dan, who's staring at the hole in quiet disbelief, and stops. Dan turns to the eighteenth. Houston sighs, and the white kid loses his smirk and shakes his head ever so slightly. Marco looks lost. Houston sighs again and waves to me to follow him. I do. Buster comes up from behind and slaps my back.

'Pulled that one out of my ass.' He leaves his hand there. 'Trying to keep you going.' He moves his hand to my shoulder and squeezes. 'Next hole – what do you say? Beat that guy.'

I try to regain my hands – bending at the elbow and shaking them down. Wringing my forearms, massaging my wrists – covertly. But Dan is watching. He strides over – too cocky for such a shrimp. He reaches me just as the pulse returns to my fingers. I feel strong again, as though the instant nutrition has kicked in.

'You're not getting nervous now?'

He smiles wickedly. Houston shakes his head. The others pretend not to hear. Marco shuffles through his clubs, and Buster looks back down into the void. Houston gives me a club and stands behind me.

'Two hundred to the front. Two thirty-seven to the flag.' He looks at me sharply and mumbles, 'Stay out of the woods.'

I look at the club – a four iron.

'Can you hit a draw?'

'No.'

'Take extra club. Put your left foot a little closer to the ball.'

I do it.

'Okay, closed stance. Swing straight ahead. Just let the club head fly straight.'

'Little late for a lesson?'

'It's cool. You can do it.'

'No.' I step back and give him the club. 'Give me the six.'

He doesn't. He gives me an exasperated look, instead.

'What are you doing?'

'I need more loft.' I point at the woods. 'I'm going over the top.'

I know it's a good one as soon as I hit it. It gets high in a hurry and disappears over the trees.

'That's the shot,' says Buster calmly.

'Nice one,' says Dan coolly. Houston claps his hands together sharply and gives a little low whistle.

I get to the green well ahead of everyone, and I don't see my ball. My stomach drops and I feel the bloody leaking in my pants again. 'Stay out of the woods,' the boy said. I look up and try to recreate my ball's flight. It must be in the woods. I sway back and forth about four feet from the hole. I hear them now – just off the fringe.

'Hey, look at that.' It's Dan. I can feel his spectacles on me. I go down on one knee, back still to them, and let the ball drop out of my hand. I stand up, revealing it to them.

'Quite a shot,' says Dan. 'You land there?' He squints through his glasses, scanning the green for something. 'It didn't bounce at all?'

I raise my arm robotically, extend a finger, and

trace the ground. The green is immaculate, but I point to a spot anyway. Dan cranes his neck. I walk quickly to the imaginary point and start to work on it with Marco's green saver as though there's a divot that needs repairing. I'm tapping on it as Dan walks up to inspect.

'Quite a shot.' Everyone nods solemnly in approval, then slowly moves to his ball, lines up his shot. They miss their long putts. I sink my short one. Birdie. I win.

I tip the white kid fifty, and he introduces himself – *Chip*. He smiles, tips his cap, and shakes my hand. I give Houston a hundred. He won't take it. Now it's my turn to look at him quizzically.

'Nah, it was a pleasure.' He extends a hand. We shake. He looks like a boy now. He is – with his fuzzy mustache and delicate chin. No fat, but little muscle. Too much wonder in his deep brown eyes. I don't know what to say to this boy, so he repeats, 'A pleasure,' not letting go my hand.

After lunch at the club has been ruled out, we leave. Everyone in the car is silent. We turn the wrong way out of the drive, but I swallow the urge to ask where we're going. Dan turns on the radio – so low – AM murmur through the speakers.

We pass more broken estates, and then the lots begin shrinking. Finally, the road expands to a two-lane secondary highway. We turn into an office park. Dan pulls into a spot.

'Be out in a second,' he says, which, when they all open their doors, I realize was directed at me. He leaves the car running. I sink back in the leather, exhale, and close my eyes. I feel the first few tingles of fatigue-induced nausea in the back of my throat spread to my cheeks. I exhale again. If they're going to shoot me, now is the time – a bogus carjacking. If I want to live, I should steal the Benz myself. But I'm stuck in the comfort of my seat. The tingles move to my extremities. I'm hungry, too. I see the green. *I cheated.* I almost mouth the words, but I don't, as though that would make the words real, what I did real, judgeable. I open my eyes, but the image of the trimmed Bermuda grass and its odor linger. I open the window. The preautumn air drifts inside and is corrupted.

'Sorry to keep you.' They're back and somewhat upbeat. Dan closes his door and turns. 'Great morning, really.' He's pinching a fold of bills. He nods for me to take it.

I take the money. I take all of their money – thick folds of hundred dollar bills. They buckle up. They all seem to possess a new levity, or perhaps an old one. I stack the folds – keep it in my hand. The bills are so crisp and sharp that they seem fake.

'We're going into town to get lunch,' says Marco, as though it was any other day. 'Hungry?'

'No. Thanks,' I mumble.

'Come on,' says Dan, looking at me in the

mirror. 'Winner has to buy. It's tradition.' Then, softly, with that nasty little grin. 'Besides, you cleaned us out.' They laugh in unison. I wish I'd taken off my golf shirt.

'So, what,' Dan says, still pleased by his humor. 'Should I take you to the station now?'

I look at Marco, and he jumps like the seat just seared his ass.

'Shit! Shit!' He looks at me sheepishly. 'I'm sorry. I forgot.' He looks away. 'We're staying here. Vacation starts today. I'm sorry. I wasn't thinking.'

'Mar-cooh,' sings Dan. 'What's up?' He smirks again. Marco tries to nod and gesture a silent apology across the back seat. He goes to touch my arm and stops, then my leg. Then he does nothing.

'So, what'll it be, Tiger?' asks Dan. They giggle. They're goofy, as though they shared a big joint back at the office park.

'Lunch? Train?'

'The train, please.'

'Are you sure?' asks Marco – quietly, although they can still hear him.

'Yes, I have to get back.' I think about giving them a reason, but I stop.

'Train it is,' says Dan.

He steers the truck through the small town, which aside from a new peach stucco restaurant, could be the setting for a Rockwell study – low-slung, cedar-shingled shops and narrow streets with sandy shoulders. Parking meters that take nickels.

The station is a whitewashed hut on the inbound side. Its roof extends over the platform and twenty feet on either side. We pull into the lot and stop in front of the door. They say good-bye much the same as they said hello. 'A pleasure,' says Dan – convinced that he really feels it was. Buster looks into my face, nodding with knowledge. I give them all quick, firm handshakes. Marco paws at my shoulder as I get out but misses.

I buy my ticket for the twelve-twenty and a noxious Styrofoam cup of coffee, which I swallow in one gulp to keep from tasting it, and go out to the platform. Two teens, dressed like bikers and set for an evening of lying to their parents, join me outside. They take a look, snicker nervously, and whisper to each other. I walk down the platform toward them. It freezes their faces, shuts their mouths. I stop ten feet short of them at the pay phone and pick up the receiver. They try to hold their ground but can't help but inch away from me and out from under the cover of the roof.

I dump in more of Marco's change and call my father. When he finally answers, it sounds as though he's just woken up – gravel voiced and out of it.

'Hello.'
'Dad.'
'Hello?'
'Yeah, Dad.'
'Yes. Is that you?'
'Yes, it's me.'

'Well, to what do I owe this pleasure?'

'Just seeing how you were.'

'How I were, was, or am?'

'How are you?'

'What?'

'How are you doing?'

'Oh, I'm fine, thank you.' He pauses. 'And how are you – you keeping your chin up?'

'Yeah.'

'What's wrong? You sound down in the mouth.'

'Well, to tell you the truth, I'm kind of having a rough go at it.'

'How's that?'

'Well, you know, I can't seem to get much going – money, you know, money. It's kind of worn me down.'

He doesn't respond and for a while the silence is comforting, as though my father was considering what I just said. He clears his throat.

'Yeah, are you there?'

'I'm here.'

'How are the kids, good?'

'They're fine.'

'Good.' Nothing. 'Well, it's great to hear from you.'

'Yeah.'

'Good to hear your voice. It's been awhile.'

'Yeah.'

'I love you, son.'

'Yeah.' I hang up. The teens have moved away, beyond the span of the overhang, and are looking down the line for the train.

We board separate cars when it comes – the streamlined train with its silver and red engine. My car is empty, but I take a seat facing the rear anyway – sit sideways in it with my back against the window. We pull out. The chubby conductor slowly waddles down the aisle and seems to be oblivious of everything except for my ticket, which he takes and punches in a vacant way. He leaves, and I turn in my seat to face the rear. I take out the list and draw a bracket around the remaining items. I write down my liquid assets and then subtract the expenses. Then I create a sublist, which brings the dollar amount near zero – not even enough for a bus north. I see the fifty I gave Chip, who I realize didn't speak to me until I gave him money. I let it go in my head, but I grind my teeth and hiss to myself.

I split the cash into four equivalent folds and put them into four individual pockets. I fold the list and put it away, too. I try to sleep on the empty train, but it doesn't come – not yet. So I look out the window. We cross a strange body of water – an inlet at low tide. The exposed rocky bottom splits the remaining water like a cleft. We cut across a slight marshland, then a group of evergreens, and when we come out of the wood, I can see the bay – dark silver and green with pots of white-gold light wavering on it. The dark line of evergreens on the opposite shore gives the illusion of depth, density, but I know that the hidden land behind them was axed long ago – nothing's land, then ancient life, then beaver, fox, and deer; Shinnecock, or maybe some forgotten tribe, divided, cleared, and subdivided until the scope of the original claim was lost.

If I found Daisy up one of those drives, I wouldn't ask her to renounce Tom. I wouldn't make her say she loved me, either. I'd know, for her, the past is gone. Over there, east, across that bay, she has turned off her green light and she has run. With me, across the dark water, trying to dream away my newfound shame.

CHAPTER 17

When I come out of the train station at Atlantic and Flatbush, I see the unlit neon sign for a consignment shop. They take everything, so it says, repeated in the double plate-glass windows, and for the best prices in the city. I cross the street and look inside – guitars, amps, a drum set, and an electric piano are on display in one, a half-refrigerator, air conditioner, and stereo in the other. When I push the door open, an electronic chime sounds. The space is wide at the front but tapers sharply to the rear. A glass display case, topped by one-inch-thick plastic runs from the front door to the back of the store, where it becomes a steel door. It comes back to the front along the other side, leaving only a narrow aisle to stand in. On the walls behind the safety glass hang guitars, basses, woodwinds, and brass instruments. Standing at the back is the proprietor. He's short and slender, pale with neatly cropped gray hair and goatee. He's wearing a crisp white shirt and paisley bow tie. He smiles pleasantly at me.

'Good afternoon.' His voice is muffled by the shield.

'Good afternoon.' My voice, partially absorbed and reflected by the plastic, rolls back to me distorted.

'My friend,' he gestures at the golf bag. 'Is there something you'd like to show me?'

I take the bag off my shoulder and lean it against the counter.

'I can't do much for you with those.' He waves out to the busy avenue. 'Not too many people use those around here.'

'What about tools?'

'Well, that depends on the tools.'

'What about a guitar?'

'Acoustic or electric?'

'Acoustic.'

He wrinkles his face for a moment. 'I got guitars.' He half turns to the ones hanging up behind him. He turns back to me, shrugs his shoulders. 'I tell you what.' he starts nodding but without the original kindness. 'Bring what you got. I'll see what I can do.'

There's a man on the stoop. His head is down. He looks like he's asleep, but I see that he's deep in thought or concentrating on his cigarette. He's wearing a Sox hat from the seventies – red top, blue visor. It's Gavin.

He doesn't straighten when I open the gate, just cocks his head up – looks at me sideways, squinting.

'Gav?'

He has his coat, battered suede, wrapped about his shoulders like a shawl. He takes a hard drag, burning through a quarter of the cigarette. He exhales, but not enough smoke comes out. He clears his throat politely.

'Hey, pal,' he nods. Keeps his head bobbing for a minute, then slows it and stops. 'You're a hard man to find, brathir.' He eyeballs me again. 'Good men usually are.'

'Yeah.' I kick at something that isn't there. 'Sorry.'

'Don't apologize to me. You're a man with responsibilities.'

'How you feeling?' I push on it to let him know it's more than just a platitude.

'Ah, I'm still a little foggy – kind of lost track of where I was. Not sure if I knew from the start, though.' He chuckles. It sounds like he's starting to brighten, but he won't show me his face. He stubs his butt out on the step, flips it at the trash can, covers his face with his hands and starts rubbing. He speaks through them.

'What's your plan, pal?'

'I've gotta get cleaned up. Gotta change. Gotta go.'

'Go where?'

'Gotta see a man.'

'Oh, shit.'

'It's not like that – not that bad, I think.'

'You were at the links today.' He points at the bag without looking. 'How was your swing?'

'I got by.'

He thumbs back at the house. 'You went with this guy?'

'Yeah.'

'Club?'

'Yeah.'

'Fancy?'

'Pretty much.'

He exhales. 'Hanging with a select group. Shit, I can't keep up.' He presses his face into his hands. 'When's your big meeting?'

'I don't really have a time. I guess I was just going to show up.'

'Hah,' he breathes without energy.

'I guess I need to get cleaned up.'

'Yeah, yeah, clean's good.'

'Gav, you all right?'

'Yeah, yeah, I'm fine. I'm just trying to get my head straight, you know? They zapped me pretty good up there this time. I guess I zapped myself pretty good, too. So I'm just trying to get a little acclimated – you know. But I didn't think it was going to be this bright out. Shit. It looked so much warmer inside.'

'Summer's over.'

'Indeed.' He lights another cigarette and takes a deep drag. 'Look, I don't want to keep you from your appointments. I just stopped by. Haven't seen you in an age. Thought I'd see how you were doing. I called your wife to get the number, again, and the address, too. So I had what I thought was a legit reason for calling her. I wouldn't want to bother her. She sounded worried.'

'About what?'

He laughs. *'Me.'* He shakes his head. 'She kept asking me how I was. I must have sounded odd to her. You didn't tell her anything, right?'

'No.'

'Right. So I don't know. I like her, your wife. Always have. English stock or not.' He waits for me to say something – to validate the statement, but anything I could say about either of them, to me, would sound hollow. He nods. 'Mmm – hmmm. Well, I just wanted to maybe have a coffee, perhaps catch up, but I see you're busy.'

'I can do that. I just have to catch a five-fifteen bus.'

'Where you going?'

I kick at the slab again. 'Home.'

'What, to see your old man?'

'No.'

He spreads his fingers and peeks out through the gaps. 'A bus, huh? Oh, dear,' he closes his fingers again. 'Oh yeah, you were going to your party. You can't miss your own party, I suppose.' He rolls his shoulders, pauses, whispers, *'Why Boston?'* He shows me one eye, squinted, brow raised. He shudders involuntarily, making the thin coat wave as though there had been a tremor under sea. He turns his head, shakes it slowly a couple of times, and hides his face again. 'The five-fifteen to Beantown – well, you tell me when, where.'

'Bus station, Four-thirty.'

'How about the post office? People get bad ideas in their heads hanging around bus stations.'

'Okay.' I climb the stairs and turn back to Gavin. He's not looking, but I thumb at the door anyway. 'You want to come in?' He waves and shakes his head. He stands slowly and creaks to the gate.

'See ya, captain.' He cuts across the street, still keeping his face from me, still stooped, moving slowly. He disappears behind the trees and parked cars on the other side.

I shower, shave, put on the wool suit again, and pack my things. I start to write a letter to Marco about what has happened, what will happen, but it turns into a quick thank-you note – telling him obliquely that I will call him from wherever I land and straighten it all out.

I lay out all my money on the bed according to denominations and count it. It doesn't look like much spread out, so I put it in one stack. It's impressive, but when I count it again, it still comes up short – and gone – and I start to add up what they'll need next month, stop and redivide the pile, put it in separate pockets. I look around the room. Thomas's bowl is still there, cloudy water. I dump it out, take it with me downstairs to the basement, where I repack my tool box. I leave the bowl down there, put it in the box where Lila was. I haul the box up the stairs, scan the house for anything I may have left and anything that Marco may not miss – books, CDs – no, just change in the bowl. I take the quarters this time. Then I call a car and wait outside.

I go back to Flatbush and sell him everything. He gives me a ticket and four hundred dollars and swears to me through the Lexan that he 'holds everything for thirty days.' He slides the ticket to me under the shield, gravely nods, and pinches his mouth in a pucker for added assurance. I walk out into the harsh light and sound of Flatbush – cars and trucks crashing over steel plates, a traffic cop's shrill whistle, the bang and whirl of the never-ending construction. First they built an ill-planned mall, complete with ghetto-high prices. What are they building here now in Claire's and the kids' new neighborhood?

I walk west down Atlantic, cross the street just before the near-defunct jail to the other side, where the soon-to-be-defunct bail bonds-men are. He isn't there, but there's a note taped to the door – 'Back in fifteen minutes.' It's a crappy little place, jammed in between a closed bail bondsman and what looks to be a new boutique. There are two metal desks, one covered by manila folders and stacks of paper. The other is mostly filled by a computer approaching obsolescence.

A pack of kids storms down the avenue, trying to upset what little balance there is out here. There are about eight of them – preadolescent, black. They curse, either at each other or at everything else. Kids roaming the summer urban badlands. They're the kind of pack everyone despises – too old to discipline, too young to openly want to have shot or jailed. And I imagine my children watching them from the window above, wondering about the nature of freedom – the gang's, their own. I rarely saw kids like this. The cops broke them up. But these kids get a free pass past the jail – their brief reign of terror goes unnoticed by the cops. And I can't help but think that this is the new shit being pushed on the streets: rage – its instant gratification and momentary power. The latest trend in cost-effective policing – let the little niggers find another way to get themselves killed.

He turns the corner, pretends not to see me, so that he can act surprised when he gets to his door.

'So, I'm glad you came back.'

I don't answer him, but I get out a blank check to hasten the process.

'So, you're interested?'

'You said to make an offer.'

'Yes, I did.'

I write out the check for $6,300 and hand it to him.

'What's this?'

'It's to hold the apartment.'

'But this isn't the number we talked about before.'

'You invited me to make an offer.'

'How can you call this an offer?'

'It's what I'm offering you.'

He rolls his eyes and tries to hand the check back to me. 'It's not enough.'

'Yes, it is. It's first, last, and security.'

'But he wants three months.'

'Well, he can go fuck himself, and I can call the housing authority to tell them about his discriminatory practices. And then I can go after your license.'

'What are you trying to say?'

I point at the check. 'That's my offer.'

He looks it over again, looks at me, for a moment like he's thinking about screaming or throwing a punch. He thinks better of it, wipes his face, and tries another tact. 'I asked for the security because of your employment status.'

'I have a job.'

He holds out his hand. 'Pay stub? Letter?'

I scan the room quickly. 'I'll fax it to you.'

He nods skeptically. 'When?'

I look at the clock. 'By the end of the day.'

He takes a step back, nods once. 'Okay, get it to me and I'll run it by him.'

I go to a live teller to deposit the money because I want to see someone react when I hand them all that cash, but she gives me nothing, not even a good-bye, just a receipt. On the way out I take my bank card out again, pinch it from each end between my thumb and index finger, raise it over my head and bend it in half. Then I stare at the balance as I make my way through the Heights, trying to reconcile the account – but I'm not really sure what I'm doing other than adding and subtracting arbitrary amounts. I bend the card in half a few times, tear it at the new seam, and throw it into the sewer.

I reach the school and when I walk in on the assistant, she hardly looks up.

'Would you like to see her?'

'Yes, please.'

'I'll see if she's in.'

'Yes, thank you. She may have slipped by.'

She shoots me a look before she dials, and I meet her with a diffident stare. She quickly looks back down and dials.

'You can go right in,' she sings. Her attempt to look and sound pleasant is awful.

Jean Ray pushes a pile of papers away and stands when I enter her office. She tries to lean across the desk, realizes she's too short, and extends both hands instead – tiny, peach, freckled. I take one. She stares at the shake with a raised brow, perhaps wondering about her missing hand. I release her, and she relaxes her face when she sees it's still there.

'Good afternoon.'

Before she can say anything else I hand her the check. She pretends to be confused – wrinkles her wrinkled brow again. She takes it from me but leaves it folded, places it on her desk and frowns at it, as though commanding it to stay. Then as she looks back up, her face goes light.

She extends her hands again. 'How are you?'

'Fine, thanks. And you?'

'Me,' she touches her collarbones. 'Thank you. I'm quite well – just the rush of the late summer, preparing for everyone's return. I always forget how busy it is.'

She looks to me for agreement.

'Yes, well, you must be busy. Good afternoon.'

She lets a smile grow wide. 'I'm looking forward to seeing your children this year – really.' She extends one hand, palm down this time, as though I should kiss rather than shake it. I take it. Give it an awkward squeeze and wave. Her smile widens and she squints at me with approving eyes. Her face goes solemn. She closes her eyes and nods slowly. 'Your mother would've been proud.'

I drop her hand and go.

CHAPTER 18

Pincus was always there waiting, sometimes trolling the pages of a book or scrutinizing a student, sometimes staring down the hallway, fixed on an idea. And he's there when I come out of the elevator. He seems different than I remember – a bit lost and dreamy. His eyes look smaller. He's smaller, having entered since I last saw him that period in a man's life when things openly fall apart – once discreet failings now apparent. His lotion is accomplishing less. Gray hair and mustache – they're still immaculate. It takes a little too long for him to see me, but when he does, he opens his arms and smiles broadly.

'My boy. My boy.'

He takes me gently by the wrist while slowly shaking his head and leads me into his office. He pauses in front of his assistant, almost introduces me, but inhales deeply instead. He wraps what he can of his arm around me, gives a squeeze and a chuckle. The assistant looks up – just enough to make her believe that she can pick me out of a police lineup.

'Come in, son, come in. What brings you back?'

He sits down at his desk and, annoyed that I'm still standing, motions for me to sit. His office clutter is the same – perhaps not the exact components, but there are still stacks of books and photocopies of essays. The photograph of him and King is gone, however – replaced by a small bust of DuBois and a smaller picture of an older man I don't recognize.

He catches me looking for the missing photo.

'Stolen. Can you believe that? Well, I suppose it's easy enough to believe that people steal.' He goes to pound one of the bare spots on his desk, but slaps it lightly instead – checks his nails by rubbing the meat of his thumb across them. Then he sets both hands down, as though he was about to begin a piano concerto. 'I tell you, son, dark days have come down on us – dark days, indeed.' He points up at the drop ceiling. 'They came in through there. They took a panel out in the hallway, slinked above, and then dropped down in my office.' He points down. 'Just this past Christmas. There were footprints on my desk when I came in, footprints and that damned security force they keep around here – you know, the white shirts, the black shirts, the blue shirts. They even sent some suits up here, too. Here come I, with a poinsettia and a shoebox of cookies for everyone. Absurd. I thought of calling you for a moment there. I really did.' He gestures across the room with an opening then closing hand, as if to scoop a sample from the air. 'No number for you, though, no e-mail, either – nothing. I bet those cookies are still here somewhere.' He brings his hand down on the desk, really hitting it this time, exhales, closes and opens his small eyes, and fixes them on me.

'Still married, I hope. How's your wife?' He points at me. 'Claire, right?'

'Yes. She's well, thank you.'

'I heard you were expecting a child – a while ago, I suppose?'

'Yes, Cecil, he's six now.'

'Well, a belated congratulations to you. What are his interests?'

'He loves soccer and is beginning to like baseball. He's quite a painter.'

'Really, any visual artists in the line?'

'Yes, his maternal grandfather was.'

'Well, a real art pedigree. Where do you have him enrolled?'

'Saint George's.'

'Well, that's a trick. Quite a school. I read about it – dragon-slaying artists. Are they teaching him draftsmanship – how to *really* draw – or do they let them muck about abstractly?'

'Both. He has a good line.'

'Excellent.' He checks his mustache. 'Well, what else have you been doing for nigh a decade?'

'I have two other children – another son, three and a half, and a daughter who's eighteen months.'

'Well,' he sits upright. 'You *have* been busy. I never thought of that strategy – overrun the planet with your progeny.' He lets out a low chuckle and smoothes the sides of his hair this time. He folds his hands, puts them in his lap. 'But, what else, what else?' He unfolds his hands, puts his elbows on the desk, his chin in his hands, and leans in.

'I've been working.'

'Working on what?'

'Just working.'

He smiles softly – unexpectedly – and almost whispers, 'How's the writing? What are you working on?'

I feel a sudden jump of dull heat inside, as if someone tried to light a wet match in my throat. 'I've been *working*, Doctor Pincus. I've been trying to stay afloat.'

He loses his smile. 'I don't want to sound coarse, but – why are you here?'

'I need a letter, if it wouldn't be too much trouble.'

His eyes widen. 'A letter? No trouble, none at all.' He looks around the stacks on his desk as if one was already there. 'I'll do you one better. I'll make some calls. Are you planning on coming back here? I can certainly squeeze you in, but the funding . . .'

'No, sir.'

He stops searching. He seems a little hurt and tries to hide it. 'No, somewhere else.' He nods. Points. 'That makes sense.' He cocks his head and drops his voice. 'Ivy?'

'I need proof of employment. I'm sorry I have to ask.'

Now he looks confused. 'You need a job,' he says unsurely. Then he brightens. 'Did you finish your doctorate somewhere else and not tell me? I won't have you be an adjunct any longer.'

'No, sir, just the letter.'

His face turns, and he leans back in his chair like someone slowly realizing he's been insulted. He covers his mouth with his hand and looks away from me, out the window, down Lexington.

He speaks through his fingers. 'You know, since you left here. I've been keeping an eye and ear open for your name. Silly. I suppose, but I thought by now that I'd have seen you in print, or that you would come out of that elevator,' he gestures at the suit. 'And you would be well.'

'I am well.'

He nods, unconvinced. He rolls his eyes up to the ceiling. 'You know, after the break-in, I wracked my brain trying to understand why they chose to take what they took: the computer, the printer, a radio – I think I got it after you left; it was a good one – some other things, which strangely enough, I don't recall ever having here, ever owning. So I know it was, and forgive me for saying this, someone I know. And I'm no amateur sleuth. I've never found that world intriguing. But I can't help but think that whoever it was took all of the other things to get that picture. Every other item had value *out there*.' He points at the window, then waves at it. He covers his face, rubs his eyes, pushes away

570

from the desk, and then resumes his watch over the avenue.

'When I signed on to do what I was going to do, it was during a dark time. There existed in this country's dominant class a horrifying mix of paranoia, cynicism, ignorance, amnesia, sadism, and base desire, and it was wrapped in a synthetic cloak of privilege and entitlement. Forgive me – I'm mixing metaphors, I know – but that collective was like a seed, and things grew from it: the white American middle class, the immigrant middle class. And like thorny, dense hedgerows grew barriers between the classes, barriers between the races, and barriers between the people and their government – between the people and themselves. Strange times. We were kids then, so we didn't know, but we felt it. Well, I've lost my place – let me make it brief. I knew back then, *we* knew, that it was just a big lie – that it was all corrupt. From the military industrial complex to every untried lynching, *our* country had gone to shit – perhaps always had been shit since its inception.'

He clears his throat with a sharp bark, focuses on my tie, and then goes back to the window. 'I thought it could be, should be, *had to be* – different. So I tried, in my own way, to make it different.' He points at me but doesn't look. 'You were just a baby when we marched on Cicero. We thought every loud noise was a gunshot. *Cicero, hah* – an American town named Cicero, I never thought about it before. And *that* town – how rich.

571

'I wasn't in Memphis. I was here. I was ill with an extraordinary fever, so I remember it strangely. Bobby Kennedy told me, via the television, of course. I'm sure you've seen that footage. I thought I was going to die. I'd never been so scared in my life – not in Cicero, or anyplace else where they brought the guns and the gas and the dogs. Each time I exhaled I thought I'd never take another breath. I just lay there on the couch – *that room was dark, man.* And when I recovered and was up and about, I forgot all about my bout, until, of course, they killed Bobby. The same thing happened. I forgot, not the act, but that despair. I suppose that's the mind coping.

'But I'm older now, less prone to emotional swoons. Now I remember. I say it again, *dark days are here*, my boy. There's hardly any – *discrimination.* True, no one's getting their brains blown out – 'round these parts, at least, but I see the darkness in the possibility that there aren't any brains left to be splattered. Or perhaps I was wrong – perhaps we all were: black and white, right and wrong, good and evil, oppression and freedom. Did you know that I was the first black student to receive a doctorate in philosophy from my alma mater?'

'No, I didn't.'

'Ah, well, taking a dialectic approach to your potential and probable murderer. Synthesis during crisis – what would that look like? A man in the middle of a riot scratching his chin. At least, back then, only part of the world was mad. Nonetheless, someone's got to know right from wrong, son. Someone has to weigh in.'

He pushes a stack of papers to one side of his desk. 'In my advancing years I've been known to prattle on to my semicaptive audience. Forgive me.' He sucks his teeth and focuses on a point just above my head. He grins broadly, inhales sharply, gestures grandly a few times in the air and makes his voice loud and bright.

'Still the aesthete? Or have we dirtied our hands yet?'

'I'm sorry, sir.'

'You poets – practicing or not – you arbiters of taste, of morality, do you ever wonder who does the dirty work for you?' He brightens his tone even more, as though delivering a punch line. 'Now you come to me for assistance. Where were you when we needed your help?

'I'm sorry,' he taps the desk. 'But I had plans for you.' He looks at me with a toothy smile and turns his palms up to the air in mock bafflement.

'We all did.'

'They had plans for me, too.' He looks down Lexington like it was a tunnel of memory that he wished to go down, knew he could not – and it gave him great sorrow as well as great relief. 'There's still something in the works for me, I believe.' He sighs. His breath seems to gently expel the vision. 'Why do you need this letter? Wait – don't answer that.'

'It's for my kids.'

'Ah, a noble sentiment. *Righting your ship* at last, eh?'

It strikes me as being particularly mean. I jab back.

'Hegel missed the boat, you know.'

He seems unfazed. 'Didn't everyone – you, too?'

'Yeah, but no one's building shrines to my miscalculations, least of all me.'

'You sound embittered, my friend. What, did the aesthete take some real-world knocks?'

'I'm not an aesthete. I never was.'

'Really, what then?'

'Just a man.'

'Once again – how noble.'

'Someone's got to be.'

He wrinkles his brow thoughtfully and points at me. 'You know, when you came off the elevator, I thought that perhaps you'd struck gold – that we'd lost you to Wall Street or hip-hop. You know, sometimes when I walk through the mall down there and I hear the students and the music coming out of the idling cars . . . the clamor of and the clamor for lucre, I get so damn angry sometimes – sometimes just damn sad.' He shakes his head. 'I can't get through to them. 'The gospel of work and money' has taken hold of a new generation. A whole century later, they haven't read it, so they don't know it. And they think they're being militant. They're different from your generation. Then again, perhaps they're not.' He makes a fist

574

and taps the desk with it. 'So, tell me, although I know you don't want to, but there isn't anyone else but the two of us here, and this won't give you a leg up on another student. One, if I may, *black man* to another – tell me what you're thinking about all this.'

Now I lean back, exhale, and rub my face, too. I look up to the ceiling where the thieves dropped in and shudder with a wave of sleep.

'I've never found it useful to talk to anyone other than myself about where I'm from. And I think it's safe to say that most of the time, I don't understand. Sometimes I make it simple, say straight up that I'm Lila and Marshall's boy, that they were very different – wanted different things for themselves and for me and that really twisted me up, but that's too easy, and it's too late for simple rationalizations. I think I experienced most of what a black man – any man – can experience, late in America – the good and the bad, mostly the bad. And I think it's useless to blame. I have had, in my whole life, one black friend – he's now insane. They tried their best, all of them, whether they had the right or the power to do so, to make me assimilate, to *'sivilize'* me. It never worked. That is the heart of resistance – holding out for the good: That is what I always thought it was to be black, other, or any different title I can paste on myself.'

He looks sad. He puckers his lips and looks down as if to fight it off. 'So, tell me, please. And I

575

ask you this because I really am concerned, interested, and optimistic, and I do happen to have an excellent agent, what became of your dissertation – what was it called again?'

'Eliot, Modernism, and Metaphysics.'

He smiles and nods. 'Ah yes. Did you make progress? Did you finish it?'

'No.'

He slumps, showing his age. 'May I ask why?'

'Because it was "archaic and therefore frivolous and a man of my history, background, and talents should know better."'

'Oh.' His neck turns to rubber, and his head drops. 'My son. I am truly sorry.'

'It's okay.'

'All is well then?'

'Every little thing, yes.'

He slides his hand across the desk but stops when he has to lean.

'What about my book you borrowed?'

'I'm sorry. I don't know.'

He clears his throat, pushes away from the desk.

'To whom do I address this letter?'

CHAPTER 19

By the time I get to the post office, I've had it. I climb to the top of the stairs and sit down. My neck starts to tremble and I taste acid in my mouth. I close my eyes and start a letter to Claire in my head – nothing – just static mixed with the sounds of traffic moving uptown on Eighth Avenue. I try to see her; I can't – can't hear her, either – her face and voice are missing. A wave of sleep passes over me. I get lost in it – blind, breathless. It passes and I open my eyes.

I watch the city empty. They go north. They go east. The sun seems stronger – perhaps because of the late-afternoon redness it's acquired, the haze of pollution, exhalations from people and machines.

This used to be a station. I suppose it still is: once for trains, now for mail. Whatever the case, the whir and hum from the internal turbines, the trucks backing in and pulling out of the loading bays on the adjacent streets, and these warm stone stairs make the building feel alive. Perhaps all the people who've passed through – those who continue to pass and leave their marks – charge it.

Even now in this empty city they seem to materialize on the sidewalk below and, regardless of shape, size, or age, bound up the stairs in their own way to the revolving door. Some nod or even wave to me, mistaking me in their haste for the greeter. It's not what I want to do. This isn't a casino, anyway. They give those jobs to ex-fighters out in Vegas – the ones who went broke, were broken. Maybe it was a sort of punishment – watching the high-rollers who made money off the beatings you gave out and took, making more off a new generation of meat – your sentence for over-reaching. I get up and move away from the door.

Gavin had a special walk when he was unusually high, happy, or both. And crossing Eighth Avenue he has it now. It's different though. It has that boyish energy and lightness but coupled with a man's confidence – almost like a man riding a small unicycle with an oval wheel. He carries two coffees, holding them out in front of him like they're handlebars. He cuts through the stopped traffic. His brim's pulled down low – new shades. I start to wave when he reaches the sidewalk, but he looks up directly at me.

He mounts the stairs and when he reaches me, leans against the handrail, hands me a coffee, pulls off his shades and rests them on his visor. I expect to see a shiner or a hemorrhaged pupil, but his face and eyes are clear.

He points to the *B* on his hat.

'In town tonight. Pedro's pitching,' he mumbles.

He throws a slow-motion pitch, beans the imaginary batter, points, then waves him in, mouthing, 'Come on.' He puts his dukes up, sloshing the coffee out the sip hole, moves his head from side to side, then grins. He stops his mock bob and weave, checks his hand, wipes it on his new-looking jeans, and his face goes blank. Now he looks his age – older, even patrician. I see the gray poking out from under his cap, accentuated by the navy blue. Nicotine lips, the creases of time around his puckish nose. Darkening skin beginning to absorb his freckles. I can't help but think that if Gavin had a title, an address, a bank account – anything – people might actually listen to and respect him. Another wave comes. No, it's more like a clammy hand that passes through me into my guts and opens a compartment, secret to me, full of nausea.

He opens a new pack and offers me one. I refuse. He smokes.

'Nice suit.'

'Thanks.' My voice sounds low and robotic.

'Whose was it?'

'Claire's dad.'

He wrinkles his mouth, nods. 'Nice.' He takes a long drag and does one of those smokeless exhalations. 'You look beat.'

'Haven't been sleeping much.'

'Oh yeah?' He points at my coffee. 'Watch that stuff.'

I nod and leave my head down. I almost take a

sip, but I get a preliminary shot of what it will feel like to my heart and stomach. I breathe on the lid instead.

'Yeah.' He takes a deep pull. 'You look thin, too' – he yanks at the air around his whiskers – 'your face.'

I look up at him. He fills his cheeks with air. 'Oh no, not me. I've had three squares a day of institutional starch.' He grunts a laugh and pats his nonexistent belly. 'I just scarfed down two chocolate bars and a milkshake on my way here – should've brought you one. I'm sorry.'

The notion of sweets makes me gag and shiver at the same time. I check my hands to see if they're trembling. He checks them, too. He can't tell, but he sucks his teeth and shakes his head slowly, turning to look across the avenue to the Garden as he does. I follow his gaze to the marquee.

'Aerosmith?' He shakes his head, sings, *'Dream on . . .'* in a craggy falsetto. He finishes his smoke and jabs it out on the rail. 'You ever miss Boston?'

I shake my head.

'I used to, but walking here to meet you, it was odd. I used to get bummed out, walking around Manhattan, especially midtown – all that high-end shit that just yells out *'Chump!'* at a guy like me. But I walked all over today – Fifty-seventh and Fifth, all that, and I seemed to pick up on some internal rhythm – you know? Something felt right. So none of it got to me.' He studies my profile closely, covertly, and raises an eyebrow. 'So I decided that I'm taking over this city, but not in that typical revolutionary way.' He waits for me to respond, gets nothing, and continues. 'I'm not coming for blood or money. I want something more dear – I'm coming for answers.' He opens his arms to the city. 'But I need help – are you with me? Can't you see it? Oh my god, what a sight, what a notion, what a catastrophic, idiotic idea, Lorna Buffoon and Big Chief McBlackie running loose in the twenty-first century demanding answers!' He makes a fist, waves it in the air, and raises his voice an octave. '*Who's responsible, goddamnit! I demand transparency! I demand accountability! Throw the shrines to the founder and the cryptic and indulgent logos out of the boardroom, you sons of bitches! I want answers – one-to-one ratios, you slippery fuckers!* – Horrors! No. Don't let it happen. I mean, I just don't think that *I* could handle it.' He checks me again, waves the vision away. 'Sorry, man, I'm rusty. Haven't seen you in a while.' He bites his lip, puts his coffee down, and makes two fists.

'Wanna fight?'

I give him a dark, sideways look then turn to watch the people continue to mount the stair. I study each one, trying to pick out a specific trait to help me remember them, because no one seems to be coming back down.

Gavin watches me watch the climbers. He shoots a thumb at their path. 'What, am I causing a scene? Are you worried about them? Look, if it pleases you and them, I'm willing to be Billy Conn to your Joe Louis. You can knock me the fuck out – right here. Maybe we should go over to the Garden. Then they would love us, both.'

'Conn and Louis became friends.'

He slips his head and raises an eyebrow as if I'd jabbed at him.

'Schmeling, too – he was never a Nazi.'

He shrugs his shoulders, mumbles, 'Well, at least I got something.'

I nod vaguely.

'So what's that place you're staying at?'

'A friend's.'

'Nice digs. What kind of criminal is he?'

'He's a lawyer – for bankers.'

He goes for another cigarette, turns back to the street. 'You know, if I'd turned out like my old man wanted, I would've been an I-banker – after winning Olympic gold. Maybe I'd have been out there, been able to pin you down, give those guys the heads-up about poet-hustlers on the links. He elbows in my direction. 'Win anything?'

'Not enough.'

He sighs, studies my face again – openly – and shakes his head. 'Sorry.'

I straighten up, rub my face. 'I should've come to see you. I've just been – fuck – how are you?'

'Me – oh please – detox is detox. You know the drill, anesthetization and humiliation. It's just sanctioned.' He offers me another smoke. I shake my head and then have to hold my breath so I don't puke bile. Gavin leans down next to me, still offering the pack.

'Dude?'

'I'm a black hole.'

He straightens. 'Pardon?' He shakes his head, snorts, and pushes the cigarettes at me. He snorts again. I look up at him, but he's looking down at the sidewalk, grinning. He turns to me, widens his grin, buckles his knees, and winces with silent internal laughter. He shoots his head out toward the street, as if asking me to look. I do. Two young women make their way toward us and stop ten steps below. Gavin puts a cigarette in his mouth, thumbs at me, and mumbles to them, *'Don't sit too close ladies, lest ye be sucked in.'* I take the pack from him, and he continues mumbling, a little louder, to everyone now, 'Pretty sloppy, using an astrophysical metaphor to talk about being broke.' He turns to me and barks, *'Hey, Socrates, ever consider the B-side – you know, death star, dead star. What about calling yourself Super Nova?'*

The women are still standing. They both look up at Gavin and smile. One is brown skinned with a shaved head. The other is olive toned – lighter perhaps – with blonde hair, dark shades. She's holding a shopping bag. The brown one bends, picks through it, and takes out a small package. She points up at the revolving doors. The olive one nods and sits. Gavin sits next to me.

'A hundred bucks one of them bums a smoke.'

I light my cigarette, inhale, swoon, and almost

583

pitch forward down the stairs. I shoot my cuffs instead, and that seems to clear my head and settle my insides. The second drag feels good.

'You in?'

'Whatever.'

The brown woman starts up the stairs. She's wearing an indigo sarong and a charcoal tank. Her arms are well muscled, and she moves athletically. She makes sure our eyes meet and smiles broadly. She's big eyed, gap toothed. We both nod. She nods back and passes. We look down to her friend. She's lifted her glasses onto her head. Her bright green eyes, even from here, are striking.

'Shit, captain, some things never change.' I'm not sure what he's referring to, but I let it go and exhale smoke with a sigh. He elbows me. 'Come on, man. You're in your prime. I mean, you look a little sleepy, a bit thin, perhaps even emotionally devastated, but other than that, yer aces, kid – a fine poet-warrior like you. Go forth,' he waves out to the avenue. 'Do your thing.'

When I don't respond, he waves a few more times and gives up. Then he starts nodding.

'So I started writing my poetics last night, but it turned into a screed against consumerism, then an autobiography. Ugh – I detest memoir.'

I shift. The brown girl passes, does a half turn, smiles, turns back, reaches her friend. She sits, and then they both turn and smile. The olive one reaches into the bag and pulls out drinks and sandwiches.

584

Gavin covers his mouth with his fist and coughs. 'She looks like your ex.'

I perk up, look around, trying to find her. 'Who?'

'Sally.'

'No, I know that,' still searching for her. He points down the stairs.

'The bald one. Skirty.'

I sag again. 'I don't see it.'

Gavin waves slowly. 'It's her nose, but also the way she moves. I remember. She moved freely, she had a bounce when she didn't think anyone was watching.'

I put my head in my hands. 'Unless she was walking with me.'

'Fuck.' he hisses to himself. 'What do you want?' He squints, looks away to the south, shakes his head, and takes a long pull from his coffee. He turns back, softens his face, and looks for the right words somewhere above my head. 'You were a poor young poet and she was a poor shy girl. It was doomed.' He points down at the women. 'You know, don't get mad, but at first, I thought you were really stretching that Irish thing to get in her pants.' He starts to chuckle to himself. 'But then I realized that wasn't it. You wanna know why?' He seems too pleased with himself to stop.

'Why?' I grunt.

'Well, the last thing that bonnie lass wanted was some broke Irish poet. So, true or not, it was such an ill-conceived and misguided plan or confession or sharing that I found it moving.' He snorts and

585

spills some coffee. The women look back to see if he's laughing at them. The brown one raises an eyebrow at him and turns away.

He gestures down at her with his cup. 'Wee Sally has become emboldened over time.' He checks my face and my posture, then leans my way and whispers, 'Look, if you had some dough, would you be like this?'

'Like what?'

'Like what – slumped on the stairs on a beautiful afternoon with nothing but apocalyptic visions in your head. Give them up.' He sighs heavily as though conceding. 'We're a couple of horsemen light now anyway.'

'Sorry.'

He shakes his head, goes to pat my leg, but stops.

'No, I'm sorry about teasing. I shouldn't. You've got pressures I don't even know about.'

'It's all right.' I take a last drag, but it's gone out, and all of a sudden I don't have any wind.

'No. No. It isn't. It's just that I'm coming out of a strange place.'

I nod, though not convincingly.

'Hey, you got time for a story?'

I look across to the Garden. He looks, too. It's 4:50. I wonder if Gavin will want to walk me to the station to catch the nonexistent bus. I can't picture myself running or even walking fast for that matter – so ten minutes to Port Authority from here.

'Yeah.'

'Okay, but first, I have a confession. That night I called – I don't know how I got that number, probably from your wife, which is, now that I think about it, the reason she sounded worried when I called again. I did want to wish you happy birthday, but I also wanted to ask you if I was going crazy.'

He checks to see if I'm listening, seems satisfied, and continues.

'So there was Ricky and there was Mindy. Ricky was my roommate. The first morning I woke up to him standing in the middle of the room, eating a banana. They had me on a frightful amount of Librium, so I questioned what I was seeing: He finishes it, goes to his drawer, gets out an aerosol can of Raid, holds the peel out, sprays it, then puts them both away in the drawer.

'So then I'm in and out of time. The next thing I remember is finding a copy of *The Souls of Black Folk* in my bag. I must have clipped it from your place. I felt so stupid in that moment because I realized that I'd never read it. And you know, I've been to so many detoxes that I decide right there that I'm going to blow off the *"Keep it simple, stupid"* stuff and shove my head so far up my ass that they'll have to cut it off to get it out. I tear into DuBois. I'm really loving it. Then I start thinking about you at Harvard, and then me at Harvard, and a few days later I decide to talk about it during group. I look around while I'm telling everybody about you, and I can see that

587

they don't believe me. And I remember being in detox back when you were in school and telling people about you, and they couldn't believe that my best friend went to school there. And then later, my classmates wouldn't believe me when they asked why I was such an old undergrad, that I spent most of my early twenties institutional-ized.

'So I give up and say thank you. It's Mindy's turn. Ricky had a thing for her – this little blonde chick – heartbreaker. Fifteen. Drying out. Already a veteran trick. So she's sharing and I'm trying to pay attention, but I really don't want to: in part because I'm still a little sore, in part because I'm still a bit screwed in the head, but mostly because it's too awful to watch – a nearly ruined teenage girl. Everyone else is riveted to her, though. And she knows why – she says so: *"No one really loves me."* She's leering out at them like she's gonna tear their faces off. *"Girls hate me and I can't trust guys 'cause they're only after"* – oh my goodness, and I quote – *"my little pussy."* So Ricky stops leaning forward at her, snaps upright – and I've been living with this guy, listening to him talking in his sleep, his mad mumblings. Anyway, he stam-mers out, *"That's not true!"* And they let him cross talk for some reason. Mindy's like, *"You're full of shit, ya fuckin' screwhead."* Calmly – cold. So Ricky points at his heart and moans, *"No, fuck you. I'm not like that. I don't care about that stuff. I love you."* And she turns to him slowly, nodding, looking him right in the eye. She spreads her legs, puckers her butt cheeks and lips, points at her crotch, and hisses, *"You love this."* And they go back and forth until he jumps up screaming, *"I love you! I love you!"'*

Gavin makes a fist, holds it in front of his face, and stares at it – wide eyed. 'And Ricky balls up his fist, still screaming, *"I love you! I'll prove it! I'll prove it!"* And then bam! Smashes himself right in the face! Bam! Knocks himself back in his chair!' Gavin reenacts the scene, stopping his fist just short of his face but reeling with each pretend blow. 'Blam! He goes to stand, but he's wobbly – Bam! He's bloody!' Gavin knocks his hat off and his glasses go flying. 'Bam! *"I'll prove it!"'*

He lurches onto his back and pretends to reel. I shake my head, snort, and cover my face as though my nose just dropped off. Gavin stays on his back and snorts, too, which makes me grin and chuckle. He grabs his sides, wheezes, and shrieks. I bury my face in my hands, but I can't hold it off – the combination of his near hysterics and the recurring image of him knocking himself out play in my head.

'Hey, man,' he wheezes groovily, like he's stoned. I blindly slap at him, but he won't stop. 'Remember when I called you from that public joint in Waltham and I thought the doctors had turned me into a donkey?'

I let out a screeching laugh and wave for him to stop. I take my hands away from my eyes, and

589

wipe the few tears. He smacks my shoulder. 'Had to make an ass of myself to get you to quit your moaning – whatever it takes.'

I gesture blindly to him for a cigarette. He gives me one. I exhale to regain my composure, turn, and get a light. He points down at the women. They've packed up their picnic. The olive one shoots up a look that I assume to be withering. She nudges her friend with the bag, and they leave.

Gavin wheezes over a drag. 'Some things never change.' His face lights up as though he's just remembered something. 'Ricky, *oh Ricky*. They finally dragged him out of there.'

'What about Mindy?'

'Oh, she just sat there, lowered her butt, and slumped. I went back to my room. I couldn't help but try to tie this kid into DuBois. It worked for a while, you know – one body, two souls – and that kid punching himself out as a sign of his love and reconciliation.

'And then my head was a little clearer the next day. Ricky came in and started to pack his bag. He got the banana peel out – it was black, with white mold – and a little pipe. He stuffed a piece into the bowl and tried to smoke it. When he saw that it wasn't going to work, he ate the peel. He packed the rest of his things, said good-bye, and checked out.

'So I just sat there and it started coming back to me – picking up this last time. Your dinner party: Drinking that wine. It wasn't about the poems – not entirely at least. That woman liked me. I knew it. It wasn't just the poems. It was that quick calculation she did to see if she could be with me, regardless of whether or not there was love. It's funny, though, the few girls I've been with, they put up with a lot of shit. I know I'm not easy. So why would they split over the size of present and potential paychecks? Doesn't that strike you as kind of odd? I mean, I liked her, she liked me – *I could tell*. I know it sounds stupid, but if you love someone, would the fact that they might be a bit of a bum stop you from seeing it through? Ridiculous – after all that's happened – that what she did hurt me. Anyway, I started writing a play about it.'

'Yeah?'

'Yeah. I think I may turn out to be a half-decent playwright.'

'Oh yeah?'

'Yeah. It's a farce.'

I nod. A bell tolls from somewhere north. We both listen. Gavin claps, stands, and stretches his lower back by swaying side to side. 'Getting old,' he grumbles. 'You get all bound up so quickly.' He gets into his batting stance, watches the pitcher's windup. He doesn't offer at the first one, 'Uh-uh. Low. Outside.' He swings at the second in slow motion – watches the ball into the barrel of the bat, his hands roll over, then the flight of the ball uptown. He lowers the bat onto his shoulder and sighs heavily. He looks sad, like he used to, when he was a boy.

'So it made me think about picking up – drinking that wine . . .' He takes some slow practice swings. 'That wine – I was like, 'This'll show em' . . . you know – like . . . *"She'll weep when she finds me gone."*'

'Then what?'

'Fuck. What – then I was drunk. And I lost more time.'

He starts down the stairs, and I don't want him to go. He gets to the bottom and turns back to me. I lean back and chug the coffee. He watches me, holds his ground, and the people walking by have to pass behind or in front of him. I can still see his face – tall man. I think he nods. He waves for me to stand and descend the stair. I don't get up. He cocks his head to the side, squints, and starts back up. I put my head down in my lap. He sits down next to me, leans forward, and whispers low.

'What's up, captain?'

I feel tired again – sick and trembling.

'Gav.'

'Yeah, pal.'

'You ever feel *too* damaged?'

He exhales and straightens – trying to respect the question. And it's not respectable. So when I hear him gathering his breath to speak without mocking me, I almost cry. Then he leans back down.

'The day I was getting out I called Ma from detox. I wasn't going to. I wasn't even going to tell her that I'd slipped.' His voice cracks to a falsetto. 'You've done better than you think. And forgive me, please, for saying this, but your mother never saw you go down.'

He breaks. I find his wrist and hold it. He lets me for a moment and then softly pulls away. 'That may have been the most selfish thing I've ever said.' He exhales and tries to compose himself, but there's still a high tremor in his voice. 'So I call her and tell her that I've been out on a mission for the last few months, and she doesn't say much, just. *"Wow kid. I'm surprised you're not dead."* I don't know what to say to that. So we're silent on the line, and then she says. *"Remember when your father called you out?"*'

I turn my head to him. He looks at me and nods.

'Yeah, I don't think I told you this one. It was just before we met. My old man had sobered up, was on good behavior – he got me Ted's book that year. He was making some decent dough – trying to come back into our lives by spending. Anyway, he lost that job and went out on one of those jazz club benders – tears through his savings. He calls up Ma asking for money, and she tells him to go fuck himself or whatever – you know Ma. So he tells her to put me on the phone. I pick up, and he tells me that he's coming over to teach me a lesson. I hang up, and I decide that I'm going to kill him – and I wish I had a gun. And I'm looking at my bat. Anyway, he shows up and drives up on the sidewalk and starts calling me out – *"Come and get your beating, son!"* Just standing there, real calmly, with his hands behind his back like he was giving a lecture.'

He pauses, grins, and starts to nod.

'So I decide, you know – fuck that – I'm standing up to that fucker. So I open the window and yell out, "I ain't comin' out there, you drunk bastard!" So we go back and forth like that – me yelling and him being cool – *". . . come and get your beating, son . . ."* Ma's pleading for me not to go – he'll kill me. And a crowd gathers outside, but no one will do anything. So finally, he comes up to the window and he says, so just me and Ma can hear, *"I don't know if you'll win or lose, but I do know that I can't do anywhere near the damage to you that you'll do to yourself if you don't come out."*'

'So you went.'

'Yeah. Son of a bitch had a pandy-bat behind his back.' He shakes his head. *'So I tell Ma, "Yeah, I remember."* And there's more silence on the line. Then she asks me if I'm sober, and I say "Yes." And then she asks me if I'm going to stay sober, and I say, *"For today."* Then she says, *"You're a good boy, Gavin – you're a good man. I'm proud of you."* I fuckin' lost it.'

He forces out a chuckle, crushes his cup, and stands.

'Then she wired me some dough. I didn't even ask.' He looks down at me. 'How you doing?'

I nod and stand slowly. He slaps my back. We both look out over the avenue.

'You know,' he breathes. I try to find what it is he's looking at but can't pick it out. 'Maybe the only thing worse than believing everything has some kind of meaning is believing that everything doesn't.' He shrugs his shoulders. 'That don't make no sense.' He turns to me, studies my face, and then turns back to the street. 'I miss you, man, it's been too long.'

'Yeah.'

'We can't fall out of touch like that.'

'No.'

'How do we not?'

'Stop going out on missions.'

'Oh shit! Touché. All right – stop hanging out with assholes.'

'I'm not hanging out with anyone.'

'Dinner parties with the smart set. Golf with I-bankers at the club – fuck you.'

'Marco's okay.'

'Yeah?'

'Yeah.'

'Well then, maybe we'll all go out to the club when you get back.'

'I don't know if I'm coming back.'

'Finally getting the brood out – good for you – this is no place for a family. I'll bet you have to plan a whole day just to find a couple of blades of grass.'

I say it weakly, without thinking. 'I'm a dead man, Gavin.'

'Pfft,' he spits. 'Who isn't?'

He extends his arm to the sidewalk, and then we descend. We stand facing each other for a moment. The waves of walkers part around us. Gavin bends his arm and taps at his bare wrist.

'Your ride's here.'

I nod.

'So you're getting on a bus?'

I shrug.

'A rolling obstreperous ass? You know, when the seats on those things warm up, the smell of every butt that ever sat in them is awakened.'

He points in the direction of Penn Station. I shake my head. He nods with mock gravity. 'Ah yes – you *are* a true American. Nomadic. Romantic. Appearing out of nowhere to stake your claim on a place of dreams. Down the highway with you.'

I look at the clock. He doesn't. He points over my shoulder toward the Port Authority. 'You know I got here early and I got confused, so I went to the station to look for you. You're taking a Greyhound, right?'

I nod weakly.

'Right. Well, there isn't a 5:15. There's a 5:33 – express to Providence and Boston. Is that it?'

'Yeah.'

'Really?'

'Really.'

He taps his wrist again, then points north. 'Skedaddle.' He holds out his hand as if to shake, but he's pinching something in it – a folded bill. I hesitate. He pushes it at me.

'For your eczema.'

I look down, shuffle, reshoulder my bag.

'No, I owe you. Anyway, I'm set for a while. I'll try and get you more later.' I take the bill and put it in my pocket without looking at it. We shake. He slaps me on the shoulder. 'All right, captain. I'll be seeing ya.' He starts to turn away.

'Hey, Gav?' I mumble.

He cocks his head to one side, smiles, and croons in a baritone. *'Mmm-yess.'*

'What's the B-side of oblivion?'

'Pardon?'

'Its inverse.'

He smiles mischievously, squints. His eyes move slowly back and forth and upward behind the lids, as though watching something secretly ascend. He opens his eyes. They're bright. He leans in and whispers.

'Heaven.' And leans back.

'Is there beer in heaven?'

He rubs his whiskers. *'Mmmm-yess.'*

'Can we drink it?'

He smiles wider, clasps his hands together, and croons again.

'Why, mm-yesss.' He waves, points uptown, and whispers, 'God-speed, *brathir.*'

CHAPTER 20

Port Authority Bus Station is crowded and noisy, so I get on line without thinking. I don't feel sick or weak, just tired. That feeling grounds me, though – my limbs and eyeballs pulsing. It keeps me, oddly enough, awake on line – mindlessly though. I don't even think about Gavin's money until I'm given back change for a hundred.

I have a little time, so I go to the men's room to change. Strange: no junkies, no winos, just people going to the bathroom. I know it's filthy and it stinks, but my senses seem to get it only in part. I lock myself into a stall, knowing that I should feel a certain terror, but I don't. I don't even mind letting my bare feet touch the floor when I change my socks. I wash my face and look into the polished steel mirror. *Come and get your beating.* Out of the wool suit I feel the chilly air. This place is conditioned for summer's dog days, not its temperate ones. Now a shiver. I tell myself that it's the caffeine and hunger.

I go into a strange little store – part deli, part drugstore, part newsstand – a part of the strange fluorescent mall. I don't know what I'm getting, but then I taste my breath – *gum, water*. On the way to the counter I pass a bin of plastic dinosaurs. They look better than the cheap, squishy ones they usually sell in places like this – generic gestures at some sort of extinct monster type. These look to be near museum gift shop quality. I pick out a gray-green carnivore. It's hard, heavy. *ACRO-CANTHASAURUS* is written in embossed letters on its belly. I wonder if X has ever heard of this one.

I keep moving down the aisle. In another bin are some coloring books and a couple of stacks of random small notebooks. On the cover of one of them is a watercolor of a beach. It's actually quite skillfully done – simple quick strokes. The perspective seems like it's from a high dune, and out near the horizon line a great whale is breeching. I take that, too. I scan the rest of the aisle for C – nothing.

I look over the food, but all the meats in the deli-case look old and crispy, and the offerings on the steam table are gray. I take a small warm bottle of water, then go to the candy aisle and get two oversized Snickers, mint gum. I see the packs of baseball cards and next to them football and soccer. I take three packs of soccer cards and go to the front. I lay my things out on the counter, and the grim old man begins to silently ring them up. I give him a twenty. He swabs it with a marker, holds it in the air, and waits. I look over my offerings and get a sharp pang in my chest, which shoots down to my gut. Bringing these things is worse than coming empty handed. He gives me my change, reaches under the counter, but I wave him off. I stuff them in my bag and go.

The bus is strangely empty: Only one side is filled. I pick a seat in the beginning of the back third and drop into it heavily. I lean against the window and look across the aisle. There's a woman across; from the way she's settled in, looks like she's been riding this bus awhile – long overdue up south. She's older – maybe in her sixties, dark brown, a bit heavy, and her eyes are almost closed. She holds a summer hat in her lap. Her hands rest on her stomach – thick, long, ringless fingers interlocked. Her thumbs circle each other slowly. She turns, smiles, and nods. I nod back. We turn away.
    The bus is warm, but not so much as to release the trapped smells that Gavin had warned of. There's a rumble I can't place, then realize that it's the diesel engine echoing in the garage. The driver climbs aboard, looks down the aisle, sits and closes the door. And then we're out on Eighth Avenue. I look for Gavin on the sidewalk, but I know he's gone. I don't know where he will go and I think for a moment that I should've asked him to come with me. I close my eyes and see his face – what it is now – *'God bless Gavin,'* I mouth. I open my eyes and roll my head to the side. The woman across the aisle smiles as though she's

the recipient of my benediction. I fight back a yawn and nod back to her. She turns to the window, looks at the east side of the avenue rushing by – the remaining porn shops and troubled minds out in front, people in suits and people in coveralls. I've always liked New York City at times like this – the emptiness of late summer, the gestures of the absent population, the space and the silence, and the sun starting to fade and go down. All of it through a closed window. In motion. The city offered a perfect opening when we all rolled into it. I was anonymous, had my notebooks, and couldn't wait for my arm to heal so I could play guitar. Shake's now old used car, the Plymouth Duster – he called it the Feral Coupe, and he drove me down the West Side before cutting across Houston – sharp Indian-summer day. I'm not nostalgic. I'm out of that memory's orbit anyway, and now the closure is just right, as well – late-summer sunset with sleep coming on.

I take out the list once again and open the little table. I write, *'Get on the bus,'* and then cross it out. I reread the list and make dots next to each task, just to be sure. I fold it and put it away. I take out the little notebook and open it – more like a sketchbook, the pages unlined. I write on the inside cover, *'When you were born, you were so small I could hold you in the palm of my hand'* – I close it, and then question what I wrote – if I omitted, repeated, or misspelled any words and then what it even means. The book suddenly seems too private, even for me. I wonder if I should send it later – if there will be a later, or if it, like so many other plans and stories, will sit under a bed or in a closet, get lost or smudged and torn till it's illegible. I don't know how I'll give them these things: in private, each child alone, trying to understand the significance of my calling to them. And then later, much later, them finally understanding that it was the last time I was their father. The old woman groans. I put it away.

I get brief glimpses of scenery – the sun at the west end of 125th Street, the warehouses of the South Bronx, the thick stream of cars going past my window. We make the expressway, but the bus stops and starts like we're still on the city streets. I have a quick hunger pang and remember the candy bars. I take one out, start to open it, and feel the old woman watching me. I turn. Her eyes look sunken, and her breathing's rapid and shallow. She fidgets with her hat. I lean over to her.

'I'm sorry, are you okay?'

She nods weakly, not bothering to raise her head from the seat.

'Are you sure?'

She nods again and leans to me. 'It's okay, baby,' she says slowly with a thick drawl. 'I just have a touch of the sugars.'

I slide over to the aisle seat and offer her the Snickers. She looks at it, closes her eyes, and shakes her head slightly. I put it on the seat beside her.

'Sweetheart,' her voice brightens, but she keeps her head down. 'I can't take this.'

'It's okay,' I point at my bag. 'I have another.' Then I whisper, 'I'm not really hungry – just trying to pass the time.'

'Thank you,' she exhales but still doesn't move. I must look worried because she nods and says, 'Oh, I'll be fine now.'

I must doze off because when I look out the window again, there aren't any more buildings, only trees going by. We're moving quickly – no traffic, no city – now a break and a shore and the beginning of a bridge. We mount and I look west, up the twist of water. It must be a sharp bend up there, because even though we rise and cross, I can't see beyond the turn. So I forget about it and concentrate instead on the straight I can see – just beyond the obstructing bridge. I wonder what it was like one hundred, two hundred years ago. Who fished? Who drowned? What was it like to settle on these banks without the concrete and steel? Then, perhaps because of how the late light has cast the top of the dark water silver, I think of Pincus and his mustache – *the river as mustache.* I think the banks are moving inward, narrowing the water, but it's blackness on the border of my vision – a darkening, contracting scope. And I'm gone.

CHAPTER 21

In my end is my beginning.
—T. S. Eliot, 'East Coker' V

I think I was thirteen. I don't remember the
time of year, but it was mild – perhaps that's
why it's so hard to place, a quick shot of atyp-
ical warmth in a cold season. I was coming home
from some kind of practice, and my feet were wet
and puckered from the sodden field.

I came in to find both of my parents at the
kitchen table sitting over coffee. They weren't
talking, but they weren't ignoring each other. It
seemed almost peaceful, actually, the two of them
looking down at the table or into their cups with
quiet faces, like shy kids on a date. My mother
poured more coffee for herself. My father
gestured for me to come in and sit down as if it
was his house, too. I put my bags down, but I
stood.

'How are things?'

I looked to my mother for some kind of prompt.
She nodded slightly but kept her head down. It
had been three years since I'd seen him. I hadn't

considered, until that moment, that perhaps they'd been in contact – talking about me. Things had been going well for Lila and me – as well as they ever had or would. We didn't talk much, but I was bringing home good grades and staying out of trouble – fulfilling my promise, I suppose. Sometimes I'd catch her watching me strangely, as if she didn't believe she was seeing what she saw. Other than that, she left me alone. She had found a decent job, and I'd gotten money together mowing lawns and such. She wasn't drinking so much, and I'd yet to really start. The rent was current, and although she was three months behind on the electric, a debt she'd die with, we were well. I don't know why she let him in the door.

He sipped noisily at his coffee and tried again. 'How are things?'

I decided that being diffident would only make things drag, and I wanted him out of there.

'Fine.'

'How's schoolwork?'

'Fine.'

'So I've heard. So I've heard. What, were you at practice?'

'Yes.'

'How's that going?'

'Fine.'

He started nodding his head and smiling.

'Girls?'

'What about them?'

He wrinkled his brow and waved his hands in the air. 'Do you have a girlfriend?'

'No.'

'Too busy?'

'Perhaps.'

'Too young . . . you've thought about them?'

My mother got up and went to the sink. I watched her, trying to catch her eye, but she wouldn't look at me. I thought about knocking out the rest of his wobbly teeth, but I leaned against the wall instead.

'There aren't any girls.'

He leaned forward on his elbows and whispered with concern, 'Boys?'

'The girls at school are rich and white, Dad.'

'And?'

'I'm not.'

He frowned at this and shot a cruel glance at the back of my mother's head.

'That's unfortunate.'

'Is it?'

'You're angry.'

'Am I?'

He tried to show me something by slowly gesturing in front of his face with his hands: the size and shape of his idea. He looked into the space between them.

'I believe . . . in a wider society . . . not *whiter*, a *wider* one.'

He leaned back in the chair, looked over to the kitchenette, where my mother was pretending to be busy. I couldn't watch him watch her, with a tender kind of intensity, as though she was broken and he wished he could fix her. I almost told him to stop, but he turned away, tapped a quick rhythm on the table with his fingers, and stared into my face in the same way.

'My father was a very close-minded man. I suppose he can't be blamed too much. His people, they were a strange bunch – proud, almost arrogant – free North Carolinians who'd been swindled out of their land and wandered, strangely enough, farther south to the swamps of north Florida. The next wave claimed they were Seminole – but really a mix of landless blacks and Apaches trained east from the desert.'

He patted his chest, still staring at me, and found his cigarettes.

'Smoke yet?'

I shook my head.

'Good. Don't. Anyway, he finally made it north, first to New York, then to Boston. He did odd jobs, put himself through school. And sometime when I was a boy, disappeared back into the swamps.'

He dragged deeply and kept staring at me, through the smoke, as though he cared. My mother came back with a covered stew pot in one hand and three bowls in the other. She set them down on the table.

My father opened the lid a crack. Steam rushed out. He held his head away until it passed, then he peeked in, sniffing. He lowered the lid and sat back, clasped his hands together, and then spread them apart.

'A *wider* society.'

I wake up and feel so calm and quiet that I don't think that I exist, so I take a few short, shallow breaths, and when I realize I haven't disappeared, I slow them down and let them deepen. There's a bump, and I remember where I am. The bus has cooled, and the sounds are comforting: the rumbling diesel and the big tires on the asphalt, the big broad shape through the wind. I sit up and look out the window. I can see across to the southbound side and the landscape beyond. The trees have pulled back from the highway. It's a big road here – four lanes each way.

I wonder where Lila and Thomas Strawberry are, and I shiver because I realize I left her urn by the river. Maybe it got taken out with the tide, too, taken home, or just became part of the broken beach. *'It's all right,'* I kind of sing to myself and stretch out in my seat, remember my bag, and reach out for it: It's still there. The woman across the aisle's still there, too. There's the empty candy wrapper on the seat beside her. She's looking out her own window. There isn't much for her to see: the cars below, the dark wall of trees, the occasional building, and the lights, of course – street lights along the highway. We're almost there. She moves her mouth slowly – maybe singing – mouthing something. I watch, try to read her lips, even place her drawl and impose it on the silent song – '*I feel like going on . . .*' It's what she seems to be saying – perhaps unconsciously. I know that song, at least in part.

I take a sip of water and the lone interior light surges. And it seems to remind the user to turn it off. I taste my breath when I swallow – rank with ash and coffee. I quietly open my gum. She grunts and turns. Her eyes are closed. She wasn't singing, just moving her jaws slowly as though she was still working on the peanuts from the candy. I see things about her that I hadn't noticed before. Such a strange-looking woman – gray and violet hair, puffy eyes with growths on her lids and cheeks, blotchy skin, a great, round, solid body. She looks like she's been on a lot of buses, up and down this highway and others. And I want to look at her a little more, but she grimaces, as though whatever it was that she'd been dreaming about suddenly turned on her.

I look out my side at the rush of the opposite traffic. We must be speeding, either that or holding up traffic in the far left lane for a mile back. There are poles with doubled lights running between the roads, and they flash against my window like a slow, soft strobe. And after each flash, between the black landscape and the hazy, charcoal blue sky, I catch the last of the day – a softly bending narrowing pink band. It gets dark early so fast in late August. I lean against the window and sing,

'*I feel like going on* . . .' I barely know the song, so I just repeat that line a few times, changing the phrasing a little with each pass. Then I feel her watching me. I turn. She is. Even from across the dark aisle I can see that her eyes are jaundiced and rheumy. We just watch each other and the passing scenery behind. She exhales, long, and I can tell that she's had a taste of whiskey from a hidden nip. I expect the scent to jolt me toward either craving or revulsion, but there's only a brief hit of sweet, then it's gone.

'What's that you were singing?'

'I Feel Like Going On.'

'I don't know that one. What is it, gospel?'

'I think.'

'I don't know much about gospel, but I think I've always liked it when it's sang. It sneaks up on you, you know – sadness, joy, and what else?' She closes her eyes and shifts heavily to face the other way, turns to the front, but can't seem to get comfortable. She settles on a position not entirely to her liking and grimaces again.

We turn hard, almost banking, to the east, following the highway's twist north. I close my eyes: There are Lila and Thomas, the bridge and the harbor. They're still floating. I feel myself smile and feel the bus follow shallow arcs left and right. No sail, but I exhale anyway to give them a push. But then I shudder: The burnt pyre is actually returning – this way – into the mouth of the river. It passes under the bridge, and I lose them. I crane my neck to peer under, but it's too dark in there.

I gag, pant, snap forward, and open my eyes. I take some shallow breaths to make sure that I'm not drowning, then look across the aisle. Her eyes are still closed. We turn again, west this time. The lights flash, the highway winds, and we follow. And though nothing seems to change – the evenly spaced turns and flashes – I know we're moving forward. North. We track Polaris, roughly, adjusting east and west. And there aren't any visible stars, just more electric spill, which keeps the road navigable, uniform – a safe, glowing haze – but it obscures the first order. I press my face against the cool glass and try to see forward. I can't. Even on a clear night, turning east and west, it would be there out the window and then not. I sit back. It doesn't matter; I know where it is: here. I see its trail: outside; that woman still moving somewhere and in: the makeshift, upriver skiff. And then, both – like a small wave that has caught light while folding over into darkness. I am that star, its beginning, an expanding, deepening ball of fire in the dark, and its end – the dark itself. And in that end is a beginning, its last breath, bright dust – interstellar drift, waiting to be informed by a larger hope and love, waiting to be reborn. My maker remembers me, remembers me well, and I move to that place I'm called. *Listen*: the prayer to me – *Quick, I am here*. And I swear I hear Lila's voice folded into mine: *I am coming* – whole or broken – *I am coming*.

We keep moving, tracking residue – trace elements floating in the void. So real, assumed, or imagined, it is still there – the latter, perhaps, most important because it burns more brightly there – and that, I know, is real, consuming, sacred – wholly different from the burn of shame. And it leads me to other things I can really touch: my few friends, here and gone, my children, and my wife. It's what led her to me – she is that star, its end and its beginning. Its final breath, recollected, reformed. I can touch her face, trace its soft line, hold it in my hand and feel her pulse in her temples. And I don't care what it represents. *My Claire.* And unsung or not, I made a promise that *'I will be true...'* I love my wife. What else can I do? There's a break – no lights – then a bright flash from an overpass. Then it's dark again. And the bus stays dark, rolling through the dark, but it remains, a small feeling, not desperate, not bold, but present in a place I pray I never lose. And it hasn't anything to do with anyone other than me – here and now. I'm coming back, or closer, I'm coming. I'm coming because I'm in love. Now I see her: the dark horizon, like a long, crooked mouth and the last rosy glow from off in the west. There's a flash of the highway lights across the bus, then another. The road ascends as we enter Providence.

We pull off 95 and stop on the west side of the station. The old woman stays in her seat, gives me another hurting look, and closes her eyes. *'Not yet for me,*' she mumbles. I take my bag and limp and creak down the aisle and steps.

The air outside seems warmer and muggy – strange for these parts to have more heat than New York City. I turn south – no Claire. I stand there a moment while the other passengers take their bags from the storage compartments underneath. I realize that this area's only for buses, so I follow behind the others to the adjacent side, which faces the parking lot. Two get in waiting cabs, another in a car, and the last starts diagonally across the big lot. I think about him disappearing beyond the guardrail and cattails and the unlit road.

I don't see the Benz anywhere. It's not like Claire to be late. I get hit with a wave of panic as soon as I think that and then a streak of dread in the form of a bilious razor on my liver. I shake it off and try to focus on where she might be along the road – not why – just how the car moves down the highway, wide and squat with those white-blue halogen beams leading it on. But I don't get close enough to see inside or far enough away to be able to tell if it isn't just the same short stretch of road again and again.

Ten minutes pass, then more, with me standing there, watching the cars on the highway and access road, watching the headlights coming out of the black of the approach to the parking lot. Nothing. I put my bag down and feel my face with my my hand. There's strength in it. C sleep-talks something quietly, and X moves slightly as if to respond. There's all their breath in the quiet, my wife's hand on mine. I start to face forward, but I turn back, take one last look at my own: the boys, I hope, dreaming in their own hue and time and my girl in the fading light; the little, changing face of love.